The Third Generation Series
Book 11

The Serpent's Shadow

by

Margaret Gregory

Cover designed by msgdragon
Cover image: Pixabay/janrye

Also by Margaret Gregory
TYMORFAN TRUST SERIES:
Book 1 - Power Rising
Book 2 - Great Ones
Book 3 - The Return to Earth
Book 4 – Earth Mission
Book 5 – Alien Contact
Book 6 - Invasion

ATAPI SORCERESS SERIES:
Prequel – Korvu: The Beginning
Book 1- The Wild One
Book 2 – Atapi Sorceress

THE THIRD GENERATION SERIES:
Book 1 - Wanda: From Bad to Worse
Book 2 - Wanda: Choosing Crime
Wanda – Early Days (anthology) Book 1 and 2
Book 3 – Wanda: Risking Life to Live
Book 4 – Erin: The Forcing of Wisdom
Book 5 – Wanda: A New Life Part 1 – Hidden Secrets
Book 6 – Wanda: A New Life Part 2 – First Mission
Book 7 – Wanda: Full Circle
Book 8 and 9 – Erin: The Call

For permission requests, address the request to the author c/o
Permissions,
TAT Indie Publishing
PO Box 2728
Rowville, Victoria, 3178
www.tatindiepublishing.com.au

The Serpent's Shadow

The Serpent's Shadow

<u>Part 1 - Protecting a Prince</u>

The Serpent's Shadow

Part 1 - Protecting a Prince

Chapter 1 - Deported

Wanda Martin, clad like the local patrons, stepped into the café in the heart of Istanbul, a pace in front of her husband and partner, David. She glanced around, quickly scanning the faces or profiles of each of the dozen people within sight. She then headed for a woman, seated alone near the back.

The woman looked up, startled, as she sat down. Her quickly hidden reaction to seeing the US State Department ID flashed at her, was all Wanda needed.

"Janna Dupont, you are to accompany us. We are to see that you return to the United States."

"You are mistaking me for someone else," Janna protested. "I'm Nadia Shaston. I live here. I'll show you my ID."

"Janna, I don't know what game you are trying to play, but it's a dangerous one. Now, we can do this discreetly, or we can make it a public spectacle. It's your choice."

"How did you find me?"

A moment later her phone gave a very brief note from her ringtone. Wanda murmured, "It wasn't hard, though we really weren't expecting to find you."

"Huh?" Janna felt she'd been tricked. "What do you mean?"

"Well, David and I were asked to investigate the events leading to the death of an American tourist, two days ago."

"What's that to do with me?" Janna demanded.

"The young woman was identified from her personal papers as Janna Dupont. When next of kin were notified, her father wanted to know who did it and why. We've worked with him before."

"Who did it?" Janna's mind caught the innuendo, the killers had been after her. "How did she die?"

"An apparent back street mugging and robbery," Wanda said calmly. "She had personal papers, no passport, no phone and no money. We pinged your phone, not expecting a result, but hoping the thief was ignorant enough to still have it. Or, if someone had it, they could tell us who he or she got it from."

Janna went pale. "Nadia is dead?"

"Yes," Wanda confirmed. "I don't believe it was a random mugging. Could you identify her?"

A reluctant nod was the only answer.

"Come on then," Wanda directed.

Back in the dark coloured hire car, Wanda warned, "Don't try ducking out on us like you did on Pearson and Fox. We are State Department field agents, not soft-handed consular office types – who, I might add, received a severe reprimand for losing you. The Embassy people want to talk to you."

Janna closed her mouth on any further questions she had. She had remembered the name of her escort now. The ID had said Wanda Martin, her partner was David. Her father, a senior FBI agent, had mentioned these two, after some big case. They were frighteningly competent, he'd said. She should have been honoured, but the thought of what her father would say when she returned wasn't easy to contemplate. Still, he'd be glad she was okay. But there was her expulsion from Jakhabad, and her ducking out of custody. He wouldn't believe that she had been framed so that they could expel her. The deportation papers had been signed by King Rakhal. Her resentment about the whole episode returned, and began to spread to the two State Department agents. There was no way they would let her go back to Jakhabad. They would make sure she went home.

The bitterness increased when exiting the car on arrival inside the Embassy compound. David Martin handcuffed her.

"Protocol," Wanda told Janna. "It's only until we get inside."

"Am I under arrest?"

"That may depend on you," Wanda advised her. "How does it look? You were expelled from a country that is allied to the United States. You escaped from escorts sent to get you. You are impersonating a dead woman and whatever it was you did to get expelled, also caused the US Consul and his staff to be ordered out of the country."

"I didn't do anything," Janna exploded, but neither Wanda nor David showed any sign that they believed her. It probably wasn't their decision to make.

A marine sergeant escorted them to the senior Consul and then departed. Wanda stayed to listen to the questioning.

"Miss Dupont, you have caused the United States a great deal of embarrassment. Please sit down."

"Do I still need these?" Janna asked, referring to the handcuffs, and trying to sound polite.

The Consul glanced at Wanda and she obligingly removed them before stepping back again.

Then he lifted up a sheet of paper and said, "I am told that you were expelled from Jakhabad for gross disrespect for the country's rulers, customs and laws. Why don't you tell me about that?"

"I did nothing wrong! I was framed," Janna insisted.

"This document is signed by His Majesty King Rakhal. Are you saying he was lying?"

"No. What was presented to him, gave him no choice."

"Tell me what happened," the Consul invited.

"I'd rather not," Janna told him.

After a moment to see if see would change her mind, he asked, "Very well. Perhaps you would tell me why you escaped custody and were found with false identification on you. And why the true owner of that identity had yours and is now in the morgue of the city hospital."

Janna, white faced, didn't know what to say that wouldn't damn her. A slight reprieve came when her recent escort spoke up.

"Consul Jefferson, may I ask Miss Dupont a question?" Wanda asked.

She was waved at to go ahead.

"Why did you and Miss Shaston exchange identities and what did you intend?"

Janna took a deep breath. "There was a bunch of us that were travelling around together. Nadia joined us. Her father was American, so she could speak English. She was born in Turkey though, since her mother was a native here. She left us before we went on to Jakhabad. We all liked the country and decided we would take on any job we could find to stay there a bit longer. We all got taken on at the Royal Palace, since Crown Prince Ali and his sister, Famira, wanted to learn to speak American. I was made a tutor for Famira, and the others had various menial jobs."

"Why didn't you leave two months ago, with the others?" Wanda asked bluntly.

"Famira and her brother wanted me to stay." Janna blushed faintly. "I could see no reason why I had to go."

"We have spoken to a number of that group, and they all said they'd been receiving hate messages and warnings. Did you?"

"No, but that may have been because I was working with the royals, not the lesser servants. Any letters aimed at me were probably scrutinised."

"Did your friends say why they left?" Wanda persisted.

"They told me they had been given notice," Janna said.

"Did they give you any indication they were being targeted?"

"Some. Gary said it sounded like some people thought we had taken jobs away from the locals."

"Did you sense any of that? What about when you went out of the palace?" Wanda was looking for information on the political situation.

"I only ever went out with Famira."

"So things seemed calm and peaceful," Wanda suggested.

"As far as I could tell. The city seemed like any American one, really. Probably had good and bad areas."

Consul Jefferson took over asking questions and returned to the reason for her having the ID papers of a dead Turkish woman.

"She was fine two days ago," Janna said. "I didn't know anything had happened to her until today."

"That doesn't answer the question, Miss Dupont."

It didn't. Janna was avoiding answering.

Wanda spoke up again. "If you had some insane idea about returning to Jakhabad under a different name – think again. Now, we know Nadia Shaston applied for a visa to visit the US. Did you intend to have her pretend to be you? Take the flak for you?"

"No! She wanted to go there and I thought if I went back to

Jakhabad, not as an American, I could stay. They didn't know Nadia."

"And what if you were recognised by the people you claim framed you?" Wanda asked bluntly.

Janna said nothing, just looked down to the floor.

"You may well be lucky they simply deported you. They could arrange for a nasty fatal accident if you go back. Or, escalate the matter into an enormous diplomatic incident. They might also try you under their laws. If your friend Famira couldn't stand up for you before, you would be putting her in a very difficult position."

Jefferson demanded, "Miss Dupont, are you going to persist with your foolish idea?"

Janna shook her head. Wanda was right. "But why would they force us out?"

Wanda spoke again, still bluntly. "There have been rumours of a planned coup, coming from there. Nothing concrete, removing foreigners is often a first indication."

Janna's face lost what colour it had.

"What did you just think of?" Wanda asked, seeing the woman suddenly looking ill.

"I could believe the King's brother would be capable of that. The way he would regard me, gave me shivers. But what if he tries something? What would he do to Famira and her brother and father?"

Wanda shrugged. "Who can predict? Nothing has happened yet, and if something does, what could you do?"

That was the point, Janna realised. The United States could do nothing either. She might want to go back, and not just for Famira, but...

"You're right. I could do nothing but cause an incident." Janna slumped. "So, what now?"

"You will go home. You will be met. It's not up to me," Consul Jefferson explained.

Chapter 2 – Determined

Wanda Martin heard the car drive up to the front door, but didn't bother to go and see who it was. David would see to it, since it was likely more materials being delivered. She was up a ladder, giving the ceiling of her newly renovated farmhouse kitchen a coat of pale lemon paint. When the tentative knocking began, her attention moved from painting to wondering who it was. Their few friends still didn't know of their new home, so was it a neighbour?

After placing the paint roller carefully on the tray, she wiped her paint speckled hands on the old, cut-down overalls and went to the normally unused door. The knocking came again just as she got there. She checked through the recently installed spyhole, then opened the door.

Wanda and her visitor were equally surprised. How Janna Dupont had found her was a mystery, and in the visitor's mind was the contradiction between the 'painter' and the no nonsense State Department field agent.

"Janna. Come in. Pardon the mess. We've just begun renovating." Wanda kept her tone neutral.

"It's Janet Delaney now, don't you remember?"

"Why are you here?"

The farm was meant to be her, and David's, private retreat. Her tone put Janna's confidence into a dive.

"I want your help." She recalled the invitation to enter, and slipped in the gap between Wanda and the frame. When she turned, she saw Wanda was smiling.

"We usually use the back door, but I have a bit more painting to do before I quit. You can tell me about it."

"I wasn't sure you would remember me," Janna began.

"My mate doesn't forget anything," David startled Janna by speaking from right behind her. "How did you know to come here?"

"I...I remembered my father mentioning something about the

base near here," Janna admitted. "So, I asked around."

"You didn't say why you wanted us, did you?" David quizzed.

"No. Of course not. I just said we'd met overseas and now I was here. Why?"

"Never mind. It's just that we don't advertise that we are State Department," Wanda explained.

"What do people think you are?"

"A couple of young hobby farmers," Wanda grinned, moving back to the ladder. "And Dav's some kind of travelling rep."

Once back up the ladder, Wanda retrieved the paint roller and set to work on the last section of ceiling.

"How is your father doing?" David asked, to get the conversation started.

"I don't know. I haven't seen him for two years."

"Proper poisonous, was he?" Wanda suggested.

"You could say that. He must be easier to work with than live with."

"Unless you have done something downright stupid," David told her. "He doesn't tolerate fools."

Wanda gave a different version. "Or something so damn deviant that should have got you killed."

"You? Did he have a go at you?"

David chuckled wickedly. "Until someone explained to him why she knew it would work. Throwing in all the micro observations that led to her conclusions."

"So, what brought you here?" Wanda called down.

"I want your help."

Wanda finished with the roller and passed it down to David before descending the ladder.

"To negotiate with the dragon?" she asked their guest.

"I'm not going home!"

"Of course not," David murmured. "So...?"

"Is the State Department still checking up on me?"

"Not that I'm aware of," David became serious. "Where are you living now?"

"Albany, New York."

Wanda shrugged. "You've come a long way."

"Something spooked me," Janna admitted. "I saw someone I'd seen and disliked in Jakhabad."

"Where was this?" David asked sharply.

"I was in Washington. Attending a seminar for work."

"Come through to the other room. We have some chairs in there," David directed.

Once there, when they were all seated in various mismatched chairs, and David had grabbed his laptop and turned it on, he continued, "This person, do you have a name?"

"Quasim something. He'd hang around in the servants areas, but he wasn't one of them. I saw him with Prince Jabir, several times."

"Why didn't you report it?" Wanda asked.

"I did. To the Group."

"Janna, this is like pulling teeth! You still haven't got to the point."

David interrupted, "The sighting hasn't been confirmed." He had quickly logged onto a high-security site and begun scan reading. "What have you heard through your sources? You are still with that news distribution agency, aren't you?"

"Yes, and I've been in touch with the Group. They feel that something is going on in Jakhabad. The border security has been increased, more soldiers are in evidence there, and messages in and out have slowed. Rumours coming out - is really all they have."

"That King Rakhal has been put under house arrest by his brother Jabir? And all orders and decisions are coming from him?" David prompted, based on what he had just read.

"Yes. I'm worried about Famira and Ali. She has been seen in the palace, but he hasn't been seen for months."

David gave his wife a quick glance, that Janna couldn't interpret, and she nodded slightly. One puzzling piece of Janna's untold story fell into place. Possibly the reason she had wanted to return to Jakhabad two years before. She was more than 'just friends' with Prince Ali.

"This site was updated a week ago," David remarked. "What have you heard in the last few days to make you come here? If you want our help, you need to come clean and tell us exactly what you intend to do."

"I heard Ali was in the States. No, I don't know where, but the Group has contact with him. Just a mobile number to one of his guards – an ex-marine."

"Do you know the number?"

"No. But they also heard rumours of someone being after him."

"Here? Or in general?"

"Here, they think."

"Could it be that Quasim guy?" Wanda asked.

"I don't know."

"I will alert the relevant people about that one," David promised. "So what are you planning?"

"Well, the Group know of a number of Middle-easterners who have come to the states in recent months. They have a contact in the transportation industry. I want to be able to check these men out – without them recognising me, if they saw me."

David shook his head. The idea that Wanda had suggested to him, mentally, was being confirmed. "Well, not quite the same as jumping off the end of Fisherman's Wharf," David commented. "But you will be getting yourself in very deep water."

Wanda got his reference, even if Janna didn't. She had done that for David, back when he had another name. If Janna was that committed to Ali...

"By consorting with such men, any chance you still had of having your friendship with Ali acknowledged by his people, will be dust," Wanda warned. "And if you ever harboured dreams of matrimony..."

"I have no chance of that anyway. Not even if I had never been kicked out of Jakhabad."

"Are you prepared to be a woman of convenience?" Wanda phrased the question delicately.

"A what?"

"If you want to check the men out, you need to be close to them. In their blind spot," David said bluntly. "The women they let close to them have only one purpose – as a whore."

Janna blushed and shuddered, but said, "If that is how it must be. Can you help me?"

After a long, considering pause, Wanda said, "Yes. Have you a plan for what to do if you find out these men are endangering your friend or doing something adverse to US interests?"

"Only telling the Group."

"I will see what I can arrange," David promised. "Will you stay here with us for a bit?"

"Okay," Janna agreed, both relieved and apprehensive.

After a week of intensive instruction in more things than she had ever considered she'd need, Janna had come to agree with her Father's assessment of them – frighteningly competent. It didn't seem that either missed a single detail.

David taught her the basics of self-defence and how to always be aware of her immediate environment. He got her to quickly sum up defences, weapons, escape routes and potential hazards. Wanda taught her how to use the least amount of make-up to change her face. She went even further, and taught her how to change even her body language to switch from her current identity of Janet Delaney, to that of another. An identity that David was having prepared. There were so many details to remember.

The night before she left, David handed her a passport and other personal papers for her alternate identity. Her eyes widened in astonishment when she saw the same passport that she had once received from the now dead Nadia Shaston.

"How did you get this?"

"Well, we kept it," Wanda said. "Thinking it might be useful. Be aware though, the visa expired 18 months ago. So, if you are picked up by American authorities, it may be an issue."

David added, "We have infiltrated various US data bases. Nadia Shaston has been noted for a number of reasons – prostitution, theft, and so forth. In each case, questioned and let go – never charged. But nothing after the visa expired. If any of your targets can hack into records, they will find that you aren't clean and straight. It will imply, as you are still here, that you have been too clever for the police. At the same time, they can infer that you dare not be noticed and hence able to be manipulated by fear of being deported."

"I...really don't know how to thank you," Janna said sincerely.

"Stay alive, keep your friend safe and don't do anything stupid," Wanda advised.

"One other thing," David said, reaching into a pocket. "Use this phone. It has dual SIM cards – although you can only activate one at a time. This will allow you to have the same phone for both IDs. Just remember to switch from A to B when you change persona."

"You really do think of everything," Janna marvelled.

"We try," Wanda cautioned. "Our lives and those of others often depend on it. I just wish you had a personal back-up."

"It wouldn't work. It would have to be a woman and well..."

"Yeah," Wanda agreed sensing what she didn't say. It wasn't a role for the uncommitted.

David had his arm around Wanda as Janna drove away. "Worried?"

"Yes, but she picked up what we taught her, very quickly. I hope she practices all she can. We can't go rushing to her rescue."

"No, but I have flagged both her IDs – Delaney and Shaston – in the records with a 'talk to me' seal."

"I hope Prince Ali realises what a determined friend he has," Wanda murmured.

"She's another of your kind," David pointed out. "Come on – let's get back to fixing the family room while we can."

The phone call galvanised Janna into action. All the voice had said was, "The bastard must have him."

That possibility had distracted her all during her work shift. The fear had been so great, that she hadn't been reviewing the foreign news feeds, but contacting her local informants. None of them had noticed any unusual activity in the area of town where a lot of Middle-eastern immigrants lived. Perhaps that was good. Perhaps she had time.

Only one of her workmates noticed her abrupt departure. His glimpse of her face, sheet white, made him assume she was running to the ladies room to be sick. The whole shift thought she was pregnant, although she had denied it, time after time.

In fact, it was convenient that she had to go past the ladies toilets to get to the back stairs which let out onto the alley where she parked her old VW Beetle.

Within five minutes of the call, she was in her car, reversing it from the parking space. Only half her mind was on the motions of driving, the rest was considering the implications of the call. In another five minutes, she had pulled up outside a block of apartments and was out of the car, locking it.

Trying not to appear as anxious as she truly was, she merely trotted to her ground floor apartment. The detour there was an absolute necessity. Where she had to go, she couldn't go as Janet Delaney.

Inside and in moves that had become rapid and instinctive, she stripped off everything that made her "Janet" – the business clothes, the long sleeved shirt, trim skirt and sensible shoes. These were tucked away, along with her hand bag and work bag, in one room.

She went into another room and became a different woman. There, she pulled on a tight fitting, black leather vest, braided leather armlets. The lack of sleeves revealed a black rose tattoo on each shoulder. Extremely flexible leather leggings, and knee high studded vinyl boots completed the outfit. Both boots had a sheath for a thin flexible blade.

Then the makeup – not the delicate shades of pink, but darker shades that made her look like a Goth. Only her black dyed hair was common to her other self. Janet wore it plaited and coiled, now it was brushed out and roughly tied in a ponytail.

A quick mirror check was all she had time for, before grabbing the micro handbag already containing a roll of bills, her alternate ID as Nadia Shaston, and a few oddments that seemed like junk.

She left her apartment, and went through the covered walkway to the rear gate. The usual busy bodies watched her but dared not cause trouble. They were cautiously used to her comings and goings, and were satisfied if she didn't bother them.

To Janet, they expressed their concern, but 'Janet' was such a nice, kind person. They bided their time to say, "I told you so" when Nadia turned on her.

Not for the first time, she mentally thanked her teacher for showing her the brazen strut she now adopted. It was like a warning, "Don't piss me off."

Out the back, she had a second car – an even older VW Beetle. This one was dark blue – the other was white. Like night and day, or her two personas. This other car had been discreetly hotted up. It roared like a much larger car when she planted her foot.

Feeling the urgency to get to her next destination, she risked speeding along the back roads to the 'Ghetto' as the softer city folk referred to the district of immigrants from third world countries. The dividing line between 'respectable' and the 'ghetto' was the river – where many a body was dumped and much fewer ever surfaced.

As she neared her destination, she slowed and studied the activity. At this time of day, there was usually a lot of dirty children playing in the street, while their mothers were gossiping or shopping to see what their paltry housekeeping budget could get cheap.

Not so as she went past. It was the men who idled in the street.

Her car was known – some of them spat in her wake. She wasn't worried by that, it was the worst they dared.

In the Ghetto, not all the arrivals were illegal or otherwise wanted. However, those that were legitimate were tightly linked to those that weren't. Silence was an ingrained code and the melting pot of ethnics maintained an uneasy truce, and put up with the tyranny of the man who had decided to set himself up as kingpin.

Nadia Shaston moved around the dubious neighbourhood without fear of attack. Firstly, because she had proved to be able to defend herself against the occasional newcomer who considered her 'available' and secondly, because before the man could think of revenge against her, or try again, he had a message from the kingpin, known to all as Sam Tozer. A broken arm, or head, got the message through. "Don't mess with my woman."

Tozer didn't care if she slept with men outside the district – soft American men – because he knew she usually cleared out their wallets after putting them in a drugged sleep. He believed she was already a whore when he started with her and the money that he believed she earned that way, was useful. However, within the Ghetto, she was his property.

Just before she reached Tozer's squat, one of the better structures in the area, she caught sight of one of her informants. A quick flash of a hand sign from the weaver living two doors from Tozer, told her, "He's there. Not alone."

She kept one hand on the wheel and signed, "Prisoner?" The answer was a nod, and the woman spat and turned back into her doorway.

Her anxiety level rose several notches. How had the bastard managed to capture prisoners? She hoped that one wasn't Ali, but her source in the anonymous Group funded by the State Department had been sure. She parked her car and got out – not bothering to lock it.

Tozer seldom locked his door. In this neighbourhood, nobody robbed their neighbours, and Tozer was too feared to be approached except by Shaz and a few of his closest cronies.

If she wanted more confirmation of trouble, finding the door locked was enough. She scowled, swore loudly and kicked the door. Her boots had steel reinforced toes.

From inside, Tozer yelled, "Use your key, bitch!" It was followed by his gravelly cackling.

He had never entrusted her with a key, but the lock was easy to pick and she did that now, considering if she could leave it latched but not locked.

"Come here, bitch!" Tozer roared.

Shaz went to where the voice came from – a windowless, reinforced room within a room. The light inside was shining down on two prisoners, a slender dark haired male with an oozing head wound and a solid blond brute with a crew cut. That one had a number of bleeding slashes on his arms.

It was the younger man, unconscious on the floor, she recognised.

"Hurry, bitch!" Tozer urged.

"Not your usual style, Sam," Shaz remarked as if his amusements bored her. Her eyes studied the two men being covered by a high powered pistol. It wasn't Tozer's. He must have taken it from the brute. That man wasn't cowed, even now. She judged he was foxing helplessness, biding his time.

"Tie them up! Wet the leather first. Stuff's behind the chair."

Shaz grabbed a handful of the leather strips and went to wet them, but she kept several dry. On her return, she was told, "The blond one first. Nice and tight!"

Seeming to be obedient, she set to work, making the task seem fiddly. The brute moved, almost jabbing her in the face with his elbow. Tozer leant closer and put the gun in the guy's face.

"Move you bastard. Just move a fraction."

The threat was clear, the brute subsided. Tozer moved back once he'd made his point. Shaz heard someone else moving in the squat. One of Tozer's cronies who did have a key. If he had found the door unlocked, would he leave it that way?

Shaz had made sure to let Tozer see the wet leather before she began her task, but still managed to slip the dry ones into place first. She kept out of Tozer's line of fire, even though she judged he wouldn't fire – the gun wasn't silenced, and he would not want to draw attention to his place. Not by chance, she had her back to

Tozer – it was so he wouldn't see her lips move. While his lead footed crony was looking for him, he was mildly distracted.

Very faintly, so only the blond guy would hear, she said, "Make your muscles bulge at the wrist."

She felt the slight jerk as he took in the message. He obeyed, aware of the chance she was giving him. The man wasn't stupid, but he had misjudged somewhere to have been caught. Still, she knew he was sworn to protect his companion, who still seemed unconscious, and he would be looking to escape.

Shaz added the wet leather straps over the dry ones. They looked tight, but the dry ones could be eased out, loosening the overall effect.

Tozer glanced at her work, and said, "Now the other one."

Without being told, Shaz felt for a pulse in the younger man's neck. He hadn't moved and she wanted to be sure he was alive. She felt a pulse, then immediately went to his wrists and began to tie them, but didn't pull them tight, but Tozer didn't look. He was exchanging malevolent glares with the blond brute.

"You'll die for this, Hashim," the man promised.

"That's where you're wrong, Kane," Tozer countered. His crony hovered behind him. He spoke over his shoulder. "Got the stuff?"

A grunt in reply satisfied Tozer, who reached behind him for what the man took from his pocket – a syringe and a vial. "Shaz, here!"

Obediently, Shaz left Ali's side and reached for the things in Tozer's hand.

"Give Kane a dose of that."

"How much?"

"Fill the syringe!"

"Are you trying to kill him?" she protested after reading the instructions on the vial, "Says here 1ml for an adult."

"Make it two and shut your mouth. I'm not going to kill him. I have a better use for him."

Shaz filled the syringe carefully, and expelled the excess air and a drop of liquid before turning to the prisoner. She felt his arm – solid muscle – then she fiddled with his clothes.

"Hurry it up! If you want to be fucked, I will give you fucked."

"Nah! Just finding a tender spot," Shaz claimed as she pretended to jab and press. She didn't have the needle in the bodyguard's flesh, but she did have his genitals in a squeeze, so he had a reason to look like he was in pain. The she patted his groin with one hand while slipping a knife from her boot. She said, derisively, "What a stoic little man you are. Never mind, you won't feel it for long. That stuff acts fast. I'm sure you are noticing it already – there's a very rich blood supply down there."

Tozer grabbed Shaz by the arm and dragged her with him, away from the prisoner. She took it as an invitation and pressed close to him, moving her hand into the back of his black leather pants.

The newcomer, Shaz knew him as Ackbar, was told, "Keep an eye on them. I still think Kane should have got a full syringe. When's the truck due?"

"Soon as it's dark. Then we just have to get them to the boat."

Ackbar went back into the inner room, as Tozer dragged Shaz towards the room with his bed. He was either high on his victory, or some drug. He was going to use her to celebrate this victory – rarely a pleasant experience.

"I thought you had orders to kill the Prince," Shaz said, deliberately. "It's dangerous to have him here. Didn't you say he had eight guards?"

The hand that Tozer was using to fiddle with his belt flew up and slapped her face. Then he dragged her around to face him. The back of his hand slapped her then, causing his cobra ring to scratch her face.

"You don't speak of my business. Ever!" he said with a roar. "You don't try to tell me my business. Ever!"

Shaz knew she had angered him, but it was her intention to create a noisy diversion so Kane could get free. Tozer was already roused by his victory, and further by hitting her, and was pulling her further into his room.

She'd pressed a knife into Kane's hand and if he was any good, he'd get free and easily overcome one guard. Ackbar was probably already half listening for Tozer to take her.

"But what if someone saw them delivered?" Shaz went on. That was the ignition point. Tozer gripped her between her legs and lifted her to his bed while she struggled and roused him further. Shaz hoped the brute would get free quickly, before Tozer hurt her too badly. He threw her onto the bed, it smelt of sex and rancid sweat, and pinned her there with one powerful hand. The other was unzipping his trousers. For him, women did have one main use. Although she had made herself useful in other ways too.

He freed his maleness, huge and ready to come into her, then yanked at her clothes. It was always his arousal that mattered, never hers. She had accepted that fact before she had even made it to his attention. As with all the other times, she forced her body to relax so it wouldn't hurt so much. One whore's trick that had proved invaluable.

Instead of the jabbing force, Tozer gave the start of a roar of outrage. Shaz felt his body shift, the hand holding her down lost pressure, and she instinctively rolled aside as Tozer lifted from her. She heard grunting as she picked herself off the floor and pulled her pants back on. Kane and Tozer were wrestling. She would have bet on Kane being stronger, but Tozer was stopping him from throttling him with an arm and moving the fight towards where Shaz knew he kept an extra weapon or three. She didn't need to go that far. Tozer slept with a gun under his pillow. She reached under to feel for it. Tozer saw her and his eyes signalled for her to toss it. She gave a faint nod, and seemed to be watching for just the right moment. If Tozer somehow won this fight, she had to seem still loyal to him, but the gun wasn't intended for him. She met Kane's eyes, as if watching his moves.

Tozer managed to toss Kane off him. "Here!" he demanded. Shaz tossed it, aiming for his right side, even though she knew he was left handed. He missed the grab, and the gun went skittering towards Kane.

Both men went for it, Kane a fraction ahead, but Tozer had a knife in hand now – one taken from a leg sheath.

Movement in the corner of her eye, distracted her from the fight. Ali was staggering in the doorway. Glancing back to the fight, she edged herself around it. The prince was in no state to help Kane, and in danger of being hurt. At least he hadn't seen what Tozer had been about to do to her.

Kane roared as Tozer's knife dug into his thigh. The gun he'd grabbed dropped to the floor as Kane tugged at the knife.

"Get the gun, bitch!" Tozer roared. "Or I will fix you for good."

She seemed to make for it, but Kane's hand left the knife and got it first. His eyes met hers, then flicked to Ali, hinting to get him away.

Tozer gave her a look that should have killed her right then, but she backed away. "You deal with that brute. I'll deal with this one."

She doubted that Tozer had given Ackbar another thought, but she needed to know where he was if she was to get Ali away.

He was emerging from the prisoner's room, pressing a cloth to a bleeding scalp wound. "Where are you going, Bitch?"

"Sam's dealing with the brute. I'm in the way. This one won't be trouble. Where's the syringe I used on the brute?"

"Oh, no. I don't trust you. That brute should have been out cold if you gave him two ml."

"I did give it, you moron. Are you sure you weren't given water or something?"

Ackbar's face reddened. He pulled a bottle from his pocket. "Give him one of these. They worked before."

Shaz caught the bottle. "I'll need some water."

"Get it yourself!"

"Well, mind him then!" Shaz tried, just as a gunshot deafened them both.

"No. I'm off." Ackbar ran from the room.

"Ali!" Shaz shook the still dopey prince. "Lie down and pretend to be asleep, okay?"

"No!"

"Do as I say! I know Tozer. If I haven't done it, he'll make sure."

Kane, gripping the knife in his leg, stumbled from the bedroom. He had blood spatters all over him, and a large wet patch around the knife. "You! Get some of those leather ties, and do a tourniquet."

Startled, Shaz ran off immediately. She also brought a wad of cloth when she returned. Kane told her what to do, and then he removed the knife.

"Will you be all right?" Shaz asked, but only got a glare. "You can't stay here! The police will come."

"Get your stuff!" Kane ordered. They could both hear sirens.

"No! You get Ali away. If you can drive – use my car – it's the dark blue beetle. Key's under the seat. GO!"

"Come with us," Ali pleaded.

"No. I need to do things here – hide stuff. You are not out of danger yet, and if I leave with you, I'll have a death mark against me. Just go!"

Kane took her at her word. His face was contorted with pain, but he was a soldier and still had a duty to fulfill. He dragged Ali out the back door – Shaz stopped worrying about him. She went into Tozer's bedroom, saw him staring wide-eyed, with a hole blown through his neck. The sight made her stomach heave, but she had to be strong. What might Kane have touched?

The gun? It was on the floor, wiped of prints, judging by the blood streaks. Using a handkerchief, she moved it. Moved Tozer's hand to the blood at his neck, then put the gun in his hand.

It also looked like Kane had returned the stabbing favour. Her knife was in him. She removed it and put his prints on the handle, hopefully destroying any of Kane's, then dropped it.

The sirens were close. She took one tablet from the bottle Ackbar had thrown at her. The bottle went into Tozer's pocket. A quick check of the prisoner's room showed the cut bindings. These she shoved down the toilet and flushed. She took an old towel and wiped the door frames, hoping Kane and Ali had not touched anything else.

Doors slammed outside. She took a mouthful of water from the bathroom tap, swallowed the pill and ran for her sleeping pad. She knew the drug worked fast, and wanted to be out cold before the police found her.

They would take her in. She'd be safe. Ackbar, damn him, would probably run to whoever was pulling Tozer's strings. They'd kill her.

Within an hour of the moment the police stormed Tozer's squat, news of his death had spread throughout the neighbourhood. While his nearest neighbours stayed within their homes, peeking through blinds or curtains, a crowd still gathered. Those that were locals recognised faces previously only seen as a glimpse in a streetlight when they visited Tozer during the hours of dark. These did not dare talk to the police, because of the strangers, and claimed to know nothing when the officials came out asking questions. People who lived further away, who knew Tozer more by reputation, were less afraid, and willing to talk.

Shaz's contacts also stayed silent, but for everyone else, Sam Tozer's whore was fair game. They wanted her out of the neighbourhood too.

"Saw her car drive off after the shot," a man from well down the street claimed. "Going like the devil was after her."

"All sorts of odd people went in there. Foreigners, like him. Always at odd hours of the night."

"The woman, his whore, is as bad as he was. Stands by and watches him frighten people. Don't know why she'd stay with the vicious brute otherwise."

A picture of Tozer and his overt activities was quickly established. The police waited to question the woman found drugged in the squat. They had identified her as Tozer's woman.

Forensic investigators found traces that suggested Tozer kept prisoners in a small inner room, and that some may have been killed there. A stash of illegal weapons was removed from the squat, and sent for urgent examination. An hour later, one was identified as having been used in an out of state killing. The FBI sent representatives, plus the small amount of knowledge they had on Tozer.

Before the scientists finished, the place had been gone through with extreme thoroughness. Initial consideration of the scene, allowed for a number of conflicting scenarios – but that Tozer killed himself, deliberately, was ruled unlikely. A gun, blood covered and wiped, as well as a bloody knife, would be tested, these suggested a fight, but with who?

They believed the woman could be ruled out – she had no blood on her, and the fatal wounds had sent blood everywhere, but then they saw traces of blood on her shoes. At the hospital, security on the woman was tight.

The media tried to get close to the murder scene, but the best they could do was quiz the residents who were not too scared to be seen on TV or have photos in the papers. By then, the initial rumours had grown, through multiple retelling, until 'everyone knew' Tozer was a terrorist and the police had found enough weapons and explosives to start a war.

Late in the evening, Senior FBI Agent, Frank Dupont, arrived on scene. He did not interfere with the ongoing investigations, but heard reports from his junior colleagues, and added his own recently received information.

"Tozer's real name was Hashim. A hit man for a terrorist organisation known as the Cobra Sect. Some of those mysterious night visitors may well be other sect members. We need to identify every set of prints, or partials, that we can. If this was not an internal sect assassination, we might be looking at a retaliatory crime by one of his victims or their associates. In any case, we need to know what he was doing in this country."

"We will provide a report with all findings as soon as it is available," the senior on-site agent promised.

Dupont moved to the other 'victim' found at the scene. "The woman found here – what was her name?"

"Shaz, Sir. According to the locals. We found a bag in the victim's room – the ID gave her name as Nadia Shaston. The local police have nothing on her, not even priors for prostitution."

Dupont stiffened, trying to recall where he had heard that name before. "I will have the name checked out before we question her," he promised.

Frank Dupont returned to the office that had been provided for him in the police headquarters. Already, there were three urgent messages from his own superiors. This case had the potential to blow up into a nasty international incident. He would reply later. Everything needed was being done – except one. For this, he turned on his computer and streamed news articles, chosen because they had been flagged by a useful program. Most of the reports contained nothing he didn't already know, but there were some claims not mentioned by the local police that would be worth following up. He had noticed the phenomenon before – some people would talk to the media, and clam up for the police.

He would request further enquiries be made, and have the local police check the records of a number of people from other criminal events.

What he learnt from the media was that Tozer, had arrived four months before. He had fought with the local stand-over king pin and taken control. In the following month, others of the gang had been replaced by foreigners, and the original gang members found floating in the river. He had preyed on the local prostitutes, using them until he found his own place to stay. The few that came forward had horror tales of his treatment of them. None had stayed with him longer than a week. Shaz, had been with him three months. Surely, she must have learnt a lot about Hashim and his reason for being in the city.

Shaz woke in hospital, although it took a while for her drug fuddled mind to begin to function. Once it did, she maintained the drowsy attitude while she thought things through. The police woman seated beside the bed tried to ask some questions, but she gave only mumbled, incoherent answers. Having a father who worked for the FBI, had given her inside knowledge of how the police worked. She had done her best to muddle things at the squat, but she wasn't stupid enough to assume the police would not find some trace of Ali, or Kane. Both had been bleeding, but initially they would only know others had been there. She just hoped that they would not be identified, and confirm to those seeking Ali, that they'd had him. Although it was a vain hope, since Sam would surely have boasted of his prisoners to his controller.

The thing was, she wanted the police to be convinced that she had seen nothing and knew nothing of the latest visitors. That was why she had risked taking the drug. They would still grill her about Tozer, but she could be ignorant of his real background. If anyone in the Ghetto decided to accuse her of being an accessory to Tozer's tyrannical activities, she might be in trouble. What else? Her phone? Would they find the second SIM card? That would be a problem. When had she last cleared the call memory? She had no names stored in the phone book app.

Okay, she would claim to know nothing and demand to be released. She needed to disappear before Tozer's boss tried to stake his claim.

The police woman spoke quietly when Nadia Shaston stirred. The patient's eyes flew open. The sight of the police uniform, caused her to sit up – fast. Too fast, she realised as her head began to spin.

"Why are you here?" Shaz demanded with her usual rudeness. "I've done nothing you police types need to bother with."

"What happened at the house?"

"Huh? Did it fall on me?"

"No, but you were found unconscious there."

"Um..." Shaz focussed on a point on the wall across from her bed, as if trying to recall.

"I remember going there, I think. Yes, he was in a better mood than normal."

"This would be Sam Tozer?" the police woman confirmed.

"Yeah, of course!"

"Was anyone else there?"

"Not that I saw...but I heard someone come in. Probably one of his mates."

"Where were you then?"

"About to shag him."

"In his room?"

"Yeah, his shag palace. But he went out and when he didn't come back, I decided sod him and got dressed. I finished his beer, and was going to get a sandwich. Funny, that's the last I remember."

"What time was that, Miss Shaston."

Shaz did a mental calculation. "A bit after three, I think."

How long did those tablets work?

Now she was sitting up, Shaz could see that it was dark outside the window, and all the light was from the overhead fluoro tubes.

"How did you get the bruising on your back?"

She had actually stopped feeling the effects of Sam's latest beating. How could she use that?

"We was just getting started, he'd got me as horny as hell-"

The woman's face betrayed a slight grimace.

"What do you know about Tozer's business?"

"Me? Not my place to ask about that."

"People have seen you with him when he was standing over people."

"Yeah. He had me there for that. But that wasn't business. That's what he did for fun."

"What did you think of his fun?"

"Those people were all nasty little crooks," Shaz claimed, dismissing them. "Anyway, I know Sam was a bastard, but he kept some pretty nasty types away from me. But that's our business."

Then Shaz pretended to have a revelation. "What did you mean by asking what happened at the house?"

"Tozer was found shot dead!"

"What? Who did it?"

"That's what we hope you can tell us. Do you know if he had enemies?"

"You're joking! You already know what he did, you just brought it up. He probably had thousands of them, though none with the balls to face him."

"You don't seem sorry," the police woman challenged.

Shaz gave a laugh that sounded hysterical. She would have preferred to laugh because he was dead and Ali was alive, but she had a role to play. "Of course I'm damn sorry. I'm going to have to find another protector, but whoever that will be probably won't be so accommodating."

"What about one of Tozer's friends?"

The shiver she felt hearing that suggestion was real. "No. They never liked me, but didn't dare challenge Sam. What he wanted, he had. They will probably blame me for whatever happened."

"We could keep you in protective custody," the woman suggested.

"Yeah...no." In a flash, Shaz took that to mean they would want to milk her dry about Tozer, or they thought to trick her into staying around. "No damn thank you. I would be a sitting duck. When can I get out of here?"

"You will have to ask the doctor, but we will need you to answer more questions when you are."

"Yeah, yeah," Shaz muttered, in apparent agreement, but her earlier thoughts had been confirmed. She wasn't going to cooperate. She had other ideas, like making sure Ali was safe. She needed to call the Group, but she didn't dare do that from the ward extension, and she didn't even know if her own phone had come with her from the squat. The other fact was, Shaz aka Nadia Shaston, was going to have to disappear.

Shaz, collapsed back onto the bed, and curled into a comfortable resting position. The woman stopped with her questions. It gave her a chance to consider the recent events.

The Group had come through with the warning yet again, but the timing had been getting tighter. Well, she'd helped Ali and his guard get away, and hoped Kane had more ideas left in his bag of bodyguard tricks.

That day, it had been too damn close. The trouble now was, with Tozer dead, Ali's enemies would appoint someone else to take over. How would the Group find that person? How could she continue to run interference if Tozer's countrymen despised and distrusted her. She had to get away.

How, was the issue. There would be more police outside her room.

An idea occurred to her.

"Would you help me to the ensuite? I'm bursting, but I feel like I will fall over. Or I could call the nurse."

Even though the policewoman knew Shaz's reputation, nothing had been said about her hurting others, and her implication of not bothering the nurses, suggested a kinder nature under the outer persona. She was not expecting trouble.

Fifteen minutes later, Shaz used the room phone to call the Group and get a report. By the time the passage guards burst in, Shaz had moved out the window, onto a ledge and into the next room where she hid. From the almost closed door, she saw one guard sprint down towards the nurses' station. She stepped out and went the other way. She found the steps down and strode quickly towards the exit outside, unquestioned in the uniform stolen from the police officer. On the lowest level of the hospital, in the foyer, she looked around and noticed the arrival of more police. One group, who had been lounging on some of the chairs, rose and went to the exit. As an observer, she decided the timing was suspicious. The foreigners avoided the police who were taking up station by the lifts and stairs. Shaz moved into the passage leading to the emergency department. She saw more foreigners there, olive skinned and ethnically like Tozer. One from each group was watching her, but did not follow her.

Did they recognise her? Maybe not, they had washed her makeup off.

She was also in a police uniform. She ignored the men and strode past.

Before she had even gone five feet out from the entrance, two shadowy figures began to flank her. While she debated trying to elude them, one spoke to her.

"Nadia Shaston, there is no need to look around. Walk to the black car ahead."

The soft voice, accented as it was, identified the speaker as a compatriot of Sam Tozer. Probably an agent of whoever had given him orders. It told her that these people were more dangerous than the police. She would have to bluff them, particularly if Ackbar had run off to their leader with wild stories.

"Yeah, mate. If the damn car leaves here right away. I need out of here. The smell in my room was way too high." She hurried her pace, confirming her desire to leave, and not acting afraid. Now was not the time for that.

The door opened as she neared, sliding along the side of the luxury limo. A soft voice told her, "Get in," and she obeyed. The interior was dark, due to the deeply tinted windows, but now a dim light came on. Someone climbed in behind her and slid the door shut. The other went to the front and became a shadowy shape beyond a tinted glass screen.

A man dressed in traditional Arab style sat at one end of the wide seat. Shaz didn't need more than a glance to recognise him. One eye slightly squinted, and a scar alongside his nose, he was the last person she either wanted or expected to see on US soil.

"Well? Who are you? One of Sam's mates?"

The Arab was studying her, but even without her usual Shaz make-up, she was confident he wouldn't know her. Where her young, innocent, real identity had light brown hair, both her current ones had black, like the real Nadia Shaston. So too, was her skin tone darker, and her hair thicker, longer and roughly tied back. As Shaz, she wouldn't be expected to know him. She settled, not quite opposite the Arab. The other, her escort, sat beside the passenger door, effectively trapping her. Now she recognised him as a frequent visitor to Sam's place. He would of course know her as Shaz, and would expect her usual arrogance and aggressive body language. With room to stretch her legs a bit, Shaz did, crossing them like a man would, and crossing her arms as if waiting for the others to speak.

When they continued to watch her, she said, "Good of you to pick me up. You going to find out who killed Sam?"

A silky voice that she knew too well, said, "Indeed. Ackbar tells me you let the American, Kane, escape."

"No damn way! I injected him with the stuff Ackbar gave me. Right into the groin. Saw his face as I did it. Painful there. Before I did it, I tied him up with wet leather. Sam even checked it."

"So how did he get free?"

"Ask Ackbar. Sam and I were getting busy elsewhere."

"What of the other prisoner?"

"The scrawny one was loose too," Shaz admitted. "Was going to knock him out. Ackbar had some pills, but I didn't get a chance to use them. There was a shot, and that brute came out of Sam's room and came at me. Ackbar had already scarpered. I didn't have a chance. He knocked me out. Must have shoved one of the pills into me, because the next thing I know, I was back there in the odorous company of the people I religiously avoid."

"A nice story, Miss Shaston. I find it odd that Kane did not kill you as well."

"Kane? The blond brute?"

A faint head movement gave her confirmation.

"Can't say for sure, but I reckon American men are squeamish."

"And you're not?"

"Can't afford to be. Anyway, I'm not American."

"Do the authorities know you're here?"

Shaz recognised this as a power ploy, to warn her into silence. "They did...for a while." Shaz forced a faint smirk.

The Arab looked at her earlier escort, and he spoke in rapid Arabic. Shaz understood most of it. He was telling the Arab what the police had discovered so far. Too damned much.

"What have you told the police?" the Arab demanded. His eyes seemed to glow with their intensity.

"Implied Sam had slipped me something so I wouldn't see what he was up to. No way they can prove he didn't."

The eyes bored into her but she didn't look away. "And what will you do now?"

"I am going to find that blond bastard and fix him for killing Sam."

"No. Let us deal with Kane. There isn't much of you."

Shaz mentally translated that as, "Being a woman, you have no chance of success."

"Well, see that you do." Shaz glared as she spoke.

"Where will you be if we wish to find you?" That was her escort asking.

"Dunno yet. I'm scarpering. Don't want the cops looking twice at me. Certainly can't go back to Sam's. Gonna have to get a new ID. Can't ask the cops for it. Shit! I've got no money either."

The robed Arab spoke to the other, who reached into his jacket for a wallet and removed a slender sheaf of notes. These were passed across.

"My card is with that. Call me when you've found a place to stay. I am sure you'd like to know when Kane has been dealt with."

"Right! And ta."

The car stopped after some invisible signal. Her escort opened the door and stepped out, letting her out. As soon as she was, her escort went back in, closed the door and the car moved off.

Shaz let out a long, slow breath, and thanked the two who had trained her three months back. She doubted that Prince Jabir had concerned thoughts about her welfare, more likely he saw a use for her, perhaps as bait for Kane.

From what she had heard, back in his own country, he didn't even have the usual use for women that Tozer had. Obviously, she hadn't given him the feeling that she was a threat to them. That eminent bastard could be right poisonous to those he disliked.

Shaz looked around, recognising in the dim street lighting the border area between the Ghetto and the industrial zone. A nice, open area where someone could start watching her, and follow her. The Prince probably had people in place already. There was no way he would want her out of his control. The Cobra sect didn't trust anyone who was not one of them, and they didn't recruit women.

With a shrug, she headed off. The Ghetto probably wasn't a good place to go. She would be reported on sight now Sam wasn't protecting her. And she had given Kane her car, so wherever she went, would need to be close to her real place as Janet Delaney, and she would need to be careful getting there.

As she walked, she kept to the shadows. The stolen police uniform was both a threat and a challenge to people, depending on their nature. A lone woman, dressed as a cop, would also alert cruising police. She urgently needed a change of clothes.

Piles of stuff dumped outside of a charity shop solved that problem. The pile had already been spread around by the local homeless, so it was easier to see what to grab. With a well-worn pair of trousers, a shirt, hat and jumper, she found a dark alley to change. The uniform went into a nearby dumpster.

She hadn't heard anyone following her, but she waited at the entrance for a time, to scan for anyone in sight. There was no one moving in her line of sight. It didn't mean no one was there, if they knew the area, they'd have known that alley went nowhere, and wait well back for her to come out.

For that night, she went to the Nightingale Centre, with a story of being kicked out by her husband with only the clothes she had on. She gave a false name and personal details and became just another sleeper in a dormitory of homeless women. But sleep was the last thing she wanted right then. She had a lot of thinking to do. The first was what to do. Obviously, Nadia Shaston had to disappear, but both the police and Sam's mates had seen her without Nadia's usual make-up. That was half of her visual disguise. She would have to cut her hair. As Janet, she usually had her hair braided and coiled. Having it short would get a reaction, but it would enable her to distance herself further from Nadia Shaston. She'd have to make sure to lose any shadows first.

That decided, she went over everything she had heard. What Prince Jabir's gofer had reported of what the police knew. He had to have an excellent source, but if what he said was correct, they hadn't dug into Nadia's background yet or they would have found the data her mentors had planted. Nor it seemed, had they figured out about Tozer's prisoners. Ali did not want to advertise that he was in the country.

Well, now she had to tell the Group that Prince Jabir was. The game had changed. How best could she help Ali now?

The Group had targeted Tozer, they knew he was in the country illegally and belonged to the feared terrorist organization – the Cobra Sect. She had got close to Tozer to spy on him. She knew he was out to capture or assassinate Ali, the heir to the Principality of Jakhabad. Yet, between what she overheard or observed, what she learnt from news sources, and what the Group intercepted, Ali had escaped from Tozer five times. Yesterday, he almost hadn't.

The thought of Ali dying made her gut ache, though something else may have been making her feel sick too. She pushed aside the certainty that she was pregnant, but it was harder to push aside the memory of a drugged, Ali with a bleeding scalp.

Three years back, when her group of friends had been hitch hiking and working their way through exotic regions, they had entered Ali's country. Most of them were low on funds, and as they had done before, they hired themselves out to earn money. They guys had hired out as labourers, herself and the other girls as washerwomen or cleaners. Famira had met them first – the paler complexions of the Americans had fascinated her. The following day, they had been invited to the palace. Work was found for them so that Famira could learn about America, one of the allies of her country. As Janna Dupont, she and Famira had grown close, more so when Famira had made her tutor her in English.

In that role, she had met Ali. At first he had seemed arrogant, but he had also been keen to learn English. She had gone from thinking him shallow and a dilettante, when he proceeded to pick up English faster than his sister. Even then, she had put his overt interest in her down to mere fascination with the exotic. She told herself the same, for Ali was exotic to her, and fascinatingly graceful.

While it might have been acceptable for the King's son to be interested in her, the servant master made it clear that she should not show interest in him. He had insisted that her other friends, the men, be employed and be the ones he practiced English with. He charmed them as he had her.

Then once she had come across Ali when he was alone. She felt sure that Famira had contrived those precious moments, and they had ended up kissing. Something had happened to her in those moments. It had made it harder for her to be in the same room as him. Harder to ignore him, and she often caught his eyes on her.

They must have given themselves away to the ever watchful eyes of Prince Jabir. That must have been why he contrived her disgrace. Now Prince Jabir was in America, looking for Ali. Was he also looking for Janna Dupont?

On her return from overseas, after dealing with her father's anger, the legal red tape, the official reprimand and agreeing to help keep tabs on the situation in and around Ali's country – she had finally had enough and moved from home. Her friends from uni had arranged to meet her – they had already decided to try to help Ali and had started to grow contacts, and had gained help from the State Department. They wanted to know if she could help. As if she wouldn't, had been her thought. Already she'd received a new identity from her father's 'frighteningly efficient' State Department contacts. It seemed then, thinking back, that they had expected her to need it, perhaps only from the fear of retaliation from Prince Jabir.

Now, with Prince Jabir onto her Nadia persona, that same new identity was her only fall back. And she couldn't help Ali. He hoped he would keep away from her, not try to find her.

Three months ago, he hadn't. Somehow, he'd traced her, possibly through the Group. He and his bodyguard, not Kane, another one, had called late at night. It had stunned her, and proven that the connection between Ali and herself had not weakened. Away from his country, and the expectations on him as heir and Prince, he was free to express his feelings. Giddy with the knowledge, Janna had given herself to him and vowed to help keep him safe. She had convinced Ali, using logic, that they should not be together and he had been gone by morning.

He didn't know that she was carrying his child. He hadn't known what she'd been doing on his behalf - until the previous night. He had accepted her presence, not asked why she was there. He must have been drug addled still, surely...she hoped.

Chapter 6 – The FBI

During the communal breakfast at the Nightingale Centre, Shaz kept to herself. None of the other women there bothered her. She had been recognised by a few, and whispers had gone around. That was all.

Her looks out through the dorm windows and around the meal hall, gave her no indication that the place was being watched. She didn't assume it wasn't, but she had a plan in mind to enable her to leave unseen.

The two men in suits, who had entered the hall and spoken to the supervisor, were not in her plans. When they headed in her direction, she quickly decided that making a fuss, or trying to run, would not help her.

Instead, she turned an evil glare on two smirking women, former residents of the Ghetto, as she accompanied the FBI agents.

Her mind recalculated her plans. She had to assume they had found the information planted about Nadia Shaston. Probably thought she was more involved in Tozer's activities than she was. She rehearsed her story. She would have to be honest, and not incriminate herself, if she spoke of events other than Tozer's death.

Talking to the FBI would help Ali and Kane if she could implicate other Cobra Sect members she had seen. Yes...that would make them friendlier towards her.

Her compliance lasted only until she was within the building being used by the FBI. On the way to a room where they would question her, she saw a door labelled Frank Dupont.

What was he doing here? She tried not to panic. Last she knew, he was working from New York City. Then a quiet voice in her memory reminded her, "show no fear – maintain your persona".

Could she trick her father? The person who knew her best? She straightened, her walk became her usual strut, like she was a willing visitor.

Her arrival was ignored for a moment, so she waited opposite a table until the man seated here looked up. She had already recognised her father, and knew the long pause before acknowledging her arrival was a deliberate ploy. When he looked up, she was watching his eyes and her stomach dropped as an instant of recognition became a stony mask. She gave no sign of knowing him, just stared back, waiting for him to challenge her identity.

He didn't.

"Sit down, Miss Shaston," he directed. He was all business.

She could not judge if it was a good sign or not. Was he still livid with her? No, he was playing with her by making her confirm questions about herself. Some she answered, drawing the details from the background story she had memorised. Other answers she intended to be misleading. It was soon clear that it was her relationship with Tozer that interested them most. What she told them, was only what they'd probably already found for themselves from Tozer's neighbours.

"You were at the abode of Sam Tozer when he was killed. What happened?"

Any resolution to tell the truth went right out of her mind. Another man entered the room, a tanned man in a fashionable suit – and she recognised him.

He was the man who had escorted her from the hospital to the black car, had sat in the presence of Prince Jabir, and given her money.

Her mouth snapped shut and she eyed him.

"Miss Shaston, this is John King, our expert on terrorism. He has some questions for you."

If her muscles had not just gone taut with the adrenalin surge, she might have laughed. King must be very clever to have tricked her father. Telling him anything more than she'd told the police was out. Prince Jabir, had a mole in the FBI.

King spoke quietly, as he had when he'd accosted her. "Miss Shaston, did you know that the man you knew as Sam Tozer was in this country illegally?"

It was as Shaz, that she answered. "No. Why would I?"

"Were you aware that he was a member of a terrorist organisation

– the Cobra Sect?"

"Well, his ring had a cobra on it, but a terrorist? Yeah, he soon had the whole Ghetto terrorised."

"What work did Tozer do?"

"He reckoned he was a driver, but I think the protection racket was his main job."

Even without the Arab's presence, she doubted she would have admitted that she did know who Tozer really was and why he was in the country. If her father had recognized her, and she still had a few doubts, that was a minefield. He hadn't believed her when she'd been expelled from the Middle East, and now, if she admitted knowingly consorting with a terrorist, it would seal the rift between them. There would be no give from him.

However, with John King in both camps, anything she said here, Prince Jabir would hear about. So, for the next two hours, she answered simply as Tozer's whore, ignorant of his business, not interested in any case, and the little she admitted to noticing was vague and unhelpful.

The arrival of a messenger with two reports, gave Shaz a chance to pour herself a drink of water from a carafe on the desk. Moving to do so, gave her a glimpse of the folder now open in front of her father. It contained her Nadia identification.

In the back of her mind, she was relieved that her Janet Delaney passport was safe in her apartment. That name, even her father didn't know, and she believed that promise.

The next question, she should have expected. "Miss Shaston, were you born in this country?"

"No," Shaz lied, but it was still truth in that the real Nadia Shaston had been born in Turkey.

"How long have you been in this country?" King persisted.

"Twenty five years," Shaz said at once. The number just came into her head. She was on dangerous ground.

"Where were you born?"

"Turkey."

"Have you even been back to the Middle East?"

"I spent two years travelling around – went to Turkey – but my mother's people had moved from the city. Mostly I was in Europe."

She told them a quickly made up itinerary. By then, Shaz had a very good idea where the questions were leading, since the real Nadia Shaston had died, and for a time they had thought the dead woman had been her – Janna Dupont.

"We know your father was in the diplomatic service. Did he ever take out American citizenship for you?"

Shaz shrugged. "I assume so. I came here."

"Your father died overseas with your mother. Who looked after you?"

"An uncle. But he's dead now too."

"His name?"

For a moment, she debated what to say. "Abdul. I can't recall his other name. I never used it."

The subtle change in her father's expression warned her – she'd been caught in a lie. Probably multiple lies. But if so, why didn't he challenge her? Instead, he gave King a glance and said, "Have Thomas and Fletcher come in. Miss Shaston is going to be our guest for a while. Have them take her down to the holding cells."

"Hey! You have no reason to keep me here! I didn't kill Sam and I don't know who did!"

Her father cut off further protest. "While we may have more questions for you. It is your eligibility to remain in this country that is now the issue. A Nadia Shaston applied for a visa to enter America three years ago. It has now expired. While we investigate, you will remain here. If there has been some confusion, the matter should be clarified in a few hours."

Chapter 7 – Into Peril

For the first half hour, Shaz paced the cell in a vain attempt to ease her anxiety. Part of it was worry about Ali, but she had to believe Kane had gotten him away. Then there was the fact that she still hadn't contacted the Group about seeing Prince Jabir. The rest was the hanging threat of deportation. It was ludicrous, but she wasn't going to admit her real identity. Not with John King having a foot in both camps. Any hint that she was Janna Dupont would get back to Prince Jabir, and her success so far of getting him to think her of little importance and unlikely to betray him, would be gone. She would have no place to run to. She couldn't, or rather wouldn't, run to her father.

Then she tried to convince herself that yes, her father had recognized her. He wouldn't actually deport her, but this was punishment for their old argument, or for her telling blatant lies to him.

She knew other information had been seeded into the records by her mentors, what had they been thinking?

She finally collapsed onto the bed bench with her mind still in a turmoil – arguing with herself about the best course of action. Her mentors had promised not to tell her father what she was doing. They had warned her about the visa business, why hadn't they built a whole new identity for her? No, they probably couldn't, and would they have guessed that it would be her father who questioned her?

By the time two hours had passed, she was extremely tense. Her stomach was in knots and she had almost been sick a number of times. She was just taking a drink from the tiny washbasin, after the latest bout of nausea, when the door of the cell opened with an audible clunk.

She spun around to see John King enter on his own.

"What do you want?" she demanded rudely. "I can't tell you anything else."

"Yes you can. You can tell me who you really are."

Shaz saw his intent look and wondered what he knew. "The feds must be stupider than the cops. I'm Nadia Shaston, Shaz by preference."

He drew something from inside his jacket, a passport which he opened. "Nadia Shaston died more than two years ago in Istanbul."

"I'm no ghost! It's the only name I have."

"Or you will admit to," King said pointedly. "Where did you get her ID?"

"It's mine, you moron."

"I had Interpol check. A passport was indeed issued to a Nadia Shaston in Istanbul. There is a record of a visa application to come here. If you are indeed the Nadia Shaston that grew up in that city – why did you want to be thought dead?"

"Use your imagination."

"Tell me then, what school did you go to?"

"The lower city common school."

"What exists outside that school?"

"A load of factories."

"There is a statue near the front entrance, who is it of?"

Shaz thanked the long dead Nadia for sharing so much of her life. "The supposedly honourable bird shit recipient Bartholomew something. Meant to inspire us to greater things. Personally, anything would be better than being bird-shit Bart."

John King relaxed the intentness of his gaze, marginally. The answers were correct. He would not expect a mere tourist to know what the local kids said about that statue.

"Satisfied?" Shaz challenged.

"Yes, you have just admitted to being in this country illegally. The visa ran out two years ago. Most likely, you will be kept in custody until extradition arrangements are made."

"Bastard!" Shaz muttered, mentally kicking herself. "I will deny I said all that. You can't use it."

"You've become an American lawyer, have you?" he taunted.

"What's your effing game? You're mates with the FBI and with some of Sam's cronies. What do you really want?"

"I can get you out of here," King told her, and felt vindicated by her interest. "For a price."

"Huh! How can I bribe you? And if I could, how do you know I won't tell? And whose price is it? The FBI's price or your foreign mate's price?"

"We want the man Kane," King said without specifying.

"Kane?"

"Solid blond guy."

"I want him!" Shaz hissed, with feigned passion. Let King think he had distracted her. "Do you know where he is?"

"Not yet, but I think he will find you."

"Why?"

"You're a witness to him killing Tozer."

"I didn't see him kill anyone. And if my being there worried him, why didn't he finish me off then?"

"Like you said, Americans are squeamish."

"You're still a moron if you think he'll look for me. He'll be well away by now."

"Do you want to find out?"

"I want out! And if I am, I'll be gone. Won't wait to find out."

The slight smile on King's face suggested he knew things that she didn't. That irritated her, but she needed to get out and if she judged this conversation correctly, that was the offer.

"Fine! I hope you enjoy the accommodations." King abruptly turned and left, closing the cell door after him. She waited for the click of the lock, but didn't hear it. She moved to it, pushed on the frame of the observation window, it opened enough to get her finger around the door. She listened before opening it further.

All she heard was King's footsteps diminishing into silence. She risked a look. Coming there she had passed two guards –but now, the corridor was empty. She ran for it. All instincts screamed to her that it was too convenient, she was being set up – manoeuvred. It didn't stop her. She couldn't help Ali by being deported. She had become good at hiding, and she had her apartment and persona as Janet Delaney.

Her mind instinctively took in her surroundings, places where people could hide to follow her. There was no logic in the FBI letting her escape. Supposedly they were checking her out. King's words suggested they had found what they thought was the truth of her status. King had said they wanted Kane. Didn't specify which of his 'friends' he meant, but she had said nothing about him, or Ali to the police or her father. That narrowed the choices to one, and the Arab guy, she had already decided, would use her as bait. She still could not see any sense in Kane coming to her. Yes, he knew she had helped him, but his duty was to keep Ali safe. Was Ali going to insist Kane helped her? What if word got around that she was to be deported?

She was being followed, she soon realised, and she'd had enough of that. Now was the time to recall the tactics that her mentor, Wanda Martin, had told her for losing followers. She went into a random property, slipped down to the back, and jumped the fence. She then jumped two side fences, before edging to the street. A car came tearing along the street, a face peering from the window. It roared past her, the noise diminishing as it turned the corner at the end of the street. The road was clear, Shaz sprinted across, slipped through another property, jumped a fence, and seeing a pile of miscellaneous junk, decided to hide there until dark.

John King wasn't smiling when he entered Frank Dupont's office. "Well?"

"She did a runner," King said, sinking into a chair. "You've got watchers out?"

Dupont nodded. "Did you manage to get anything more out of her?"

"She still insists that she is Shaston. Did seem to know that she was supposedly dead. Wouldn't say why she pretended to be."

"What convinced you that she really is Shaston?" Dupont asked, interested.

"I contacted someone I know who is familiar with Istanbul, the part where Shaston grew up. He suggested some questions to ask that only a native would know."

"Well, if she is here as some kind of agent she would have those details down pat. But I know positively, that Nadia Shaston died."

"Which fits with official records. What did you mean implying she was some kind of agent?"

Dupont rested his head on one hand that was braced by the elbow on his desk.

"I ran the name and the details through the system. The file came back red-flagged. I'd have to have a level 8 or above security clearance to access it."

King leant forward in his chair. "State Department?"

"Could be CIA," Dupont suggested. "Let's hope we did the right thing and she doesn't lose the tails we put on her. If that woman is playing some deep game, what is it?"

The phone on Dupont's desk rang. His face tightened as he listened to the caller, and when he hung up, his face looked old. "Our watchers lost her. I can only hope she lost those put on her by your friends."

"What do you want me to do now?" King asked.

"Listen out for if your Arab friends find her."

After King had left, Dupont rested his head on both hands and said a silent prayer.

The woman they were calling Nadia Shaston was not the person who had grown up in Turkey. He hadn't let on how he knew, but it was fact. The flagged folder suggested the State Department knew about her – whoever it was. He was almost positive that he knew, and he dared not interfere with whatever she was doing. The folder, with its ridiculously high required clearance, had been sealed by someone he knew. Could he ask that person for information?

His right hand reached for the phone and he dialled a number from memory.

"Hello, Special Agent Dupont. Do you another job for us?" The cheery voice of Wanda Martin had no effect on his feeling of unease.

"No, I just need a word with your husband. Is he there?"

"Not at the moment, can I get him to call you back? Probably 5-10 minutes?"

"Yes, thanks."

He was trying to resist getting up and pacing, but the call came through at the promised time.

"David? Frank Dupont. I wondered if you might provide some information."

"If I can, Sir," David agreed.

"I was doing a routine identity check and came to a folder flagged by yourself."

"I see," David commented, waiting for more information.

"Nadia Shaston. I remember that woman as being dead. Now I find a woman using that name in my investigation. What can you tell me? I am assuming the woman is under cover."

"Yes," David confirmed the last statement. "I cannot provide information beyond that, and that much is for your ears only."

"I am in the position of having to report her to the Immigration department," Dupont suggested. He was hoping for a reaction and got one.

"That would be ... inadvisable," David told him.

"I have protocols to follow," Dupont persisted.

"If you look in the right place, you will find that her father, who was an American, did request American citizenship for her."

Dupont thought he could read between the lines. He could threaten deportation, but should that be pending, the information would be found in the records.

"Sir, could I ask for the bare details of your investigation?" David requested.

Dupont had his own expectations for not discussing cases too widely, but only wavered for a short time. David Martin had proven to be trustworthy and discreet.

"Have you heard the name Sam Tozer?"

"I don't believe so."

"It is not his real name, but the man was killed," Dupont began. "Shaston was found at the scene, though I don't believe she killed him. However, she won't talk to us and certain foreign elements are interested in her. I have the feeling I am seeing only the tip of a very nasty iceberg."

A silence on the line told Dupont that David was thinking. "Sir, I will check my sources and get back to you."

Across the country, in California, David Martin put the phone down.

"So," Wanda prompted.

"Dupont has needed to do an identity check on Nadia Shaston." He quickly told her the rest of what he had learnt. Then he reached the phone and dialled a number in Albany, NY.

"Hi there, bro," came a familiar voice. "How's things?"

The Group were always careful not to identify themselves, or their callers. Considering part of what they did was monitor calls, they didn't want anyone else learning anything if their own were being monitored.

"Thought you'd tell me," David countered. "Had any action worth my knowing about?"

"Some, some," the reply came.

"Shoot me the details, huh? Heard your man finally stopped playing the field. What's the girl like?"

His contact answered with a misleading chuckle. "Haven't had the honour mate. I'd sure like to meet her though."

"She a local?" David asked.

"Downtown," the voice told him. "Somewhere near the edge of the business zone."

David frowned, the casual conversation was actually a code. From it, he decided that Dupont probably had Nadia's phone. "Gotcha, I'll keep in touch."

"Think I should head there?" Wanda asked seriously.

"Let's see what the Group send through," David suggested. "We need more information."

He already had his computer out and booting it up. "I think Dupont has a good idea of who Nadia might be – but he may not be completely sure."

"Janna won't be admitting anything to him. I had no luck getting her to at least make contact."

"It's probably better at this point that she doesn't," David reminded her. "We don't want Janna on the foreigner's radar."

Within moments, the computer had received the data dump. Reports to a point, and then just raw data. David read the reports, using half the screen, Wanda scrolled through the raw data on the other. She was familiar with the format. He finished first.

"They haven't heard from Janna/Nadia for several days. The Tozer guy Frank mentioned was shot dead. Frank didn't mention any sign of prisoners, but he may not have had all the results back from the lab. However, Nadia went there. Tozer had captured prisoners. I would guess she helped them get free, and one of them killed him."

"They got the Prince," Wanda guessed.

"I would say so," David agreed. "So, both the FBI and the enemy are interested in Nadia."

"She has the fall back identity of Janet Delaney," Wanda thought aloud.

"Only if she can get back to her place and switch," David pointed out. "Let me think."

Chapter 8 – Bait

Nadia let her breath return to normal, and listened for people nearby. She felt sure she had lost the people who were following her, but she was cornered, and no nearer to getting back to her place. She was beginning to get hungry and realised she'd nothing to eat or drink, and no way to call for help. It would not be smart to move out until dark, since the area was probably crawling with watchers by now. Hours from now, when the sun set, maybe they would have lost interest. In the meantime, she considered what she needed to do. To get near her place, she would need better clothes than she had scrounged from the donations. She needed to call the Group. If she had money, she could use a public phone.

As much as she wanted to keep away from the Ghetto, where Sam had many contacts and she was despised, she did have some personal friends there. People who Sam had extorted money from, putting them and their families even closer to starvation, that she had later helped with money of her own.

Her visit would have to be short, or she would endanger them, but once it was dark, she should be able to sneak back across the river.

Darkness fell, and she quietly extricated herself from her hiding place. As she moved towards the river, and the ferry, the smells of people cooking their evening meal made her belly contract. She hadn't eaten since yesterday morning. Buying food from a street vendor was impossible, so she hurried onto the ferry due to leave to get to the commercial dock on the other side.

Some of the Ghetto denizens were on it, crossing back after finishing grunt jobs in the city, or thieving there. Shaz found an unobtrusive corner to stand, but it was where voices from nearby echoed. Remaining still and silent, she would be hard to see, and let snippets of conversation reach her. She heard her name mentioned – the speakers might have been within metres of her or on the deck below – she listened harder.

"Have you seen her?"

"There's a reward."

"Heard they'll deport her."

"Won't threaten us if she's gone."

Then a sharp voice that was right beside her. "What are you doing here? This part of the deck is off limits to passengers."

"Please let me stay. I'm hiding from my boyfriend, he's drunk and going to hurt me."

"Sorry, lady. You will have to go back behind the chain."

He didn't grab her, but it was clear he'd make more of a scene if she didn't.

The conversations had gone silent. Shaz shivered, feeling it was already too late. People knew someone had been hiding.

Klaxons warning the ferry was about to dock, gave her the impetus to join the crowd trying to be first off. She hoped no one would try anything in a crowd of witnesses. To try to make sure, she edged nearer the front until she felt her arm gripped, hard.

"Be a good little bitch." The warning came as a whisper into her ear. The distinct twang was familiar. One of Sam's closest cronies. "You are valuable merchandise."

"Really? Since when," Shaz retorted over her shoulder.

"Don't play dumb. Since that bastard who killed Sam let you live. There's word about that he wants you."

"Well, then." Shaz straightened up. "You give me a nice sharp knife to hide, and I'll let him find me. I have a score to settle with him."

The man chuckled unpleasantly. "So do we. So you leave him to us."

Another man she recognised came up on her other side as the small crowd surged forward. "You've been a bothersome problem," that man murmured. "Seems you weren't grateful for being let out."

"Maybe you could afford to walk around and wait for him, but I don't want to be deported."

Shaz had no idea where they were taking her, but her guess was to see Prince Jabir again.

First though, they came to an anonymous grey van, and she was shoved into the back. Before she even had a chance to look around, a chloroformed cloth was pressed over her nose and an arm held her down so she couldn't try to remove it. She felt herself blacking out.

Sunlight streamed through an uncurtained window. Dust particles floated in the air. Shaz groaned and pushed herself up. Her head felt like it had when she woke up from the knockout tablet. The room about her was devoid of furniture. All she saw was detritus that had blown in through the cracked window glass.

Was she a prisoner?

Sam's cronies had implied she was valuable, but why leave her where she was, alone?

Once on her feet, she moved unsteadily to the door, expecting it to be locked. It wasn't. That gave her qualms of a different kind. Still, she had needs of an urgent kind, and if she wasn't a prisoner...

No one had cleaned the toilet, but she used it anyway and tried to flush. Water filled the bowl to the top, but only seemed to trickle slowly away. She was thirsty, but didn't trust the quality of the water. What had flushed the toilet had been brownish.

The room had a dirt flecked mirror, and her face looked like it had been in the wars. Some of it was the remains of Sam's handiwork. Still, even without make-up, she looked more like Nadia than Janet. It was little comfort. Sam's friends didn't trust women. They had found her, put her into this house – why?

The thought alarmed her. She moved through the house, checking in each empty room, then stopped on the threshold of the kitchen.

A man slumped in an old metal framed chair, remaining on it only because he was strapped to it. Blood covered the front of his clothes, the cause still in plain view. A sharp knife, like the one Sam had often used to threaten people. The man's face angled downward, but he was blond, had a crew cut, and had been a solid man. Kane? She was about to move closer.

A hand on her neck made her jerk on surprise. She cursed herself for not hearing the man approach.

"You wanted revenge," a voice said. "Does this satisfy you?"

Shaz didn't know how to answer, her eyes were still on the gory sight, when she was shoved forward and an arm reached past her to flick the man's face up.

"No," she challenged. "That's not the right blond bastard."

"Smart, are you? No, it's not, even though he had a scrawny catamite with him when we caught him."

"I don't care if he had a whole herd of them," Shaz said, jerking herself free. She had to appear forceful, but her heart had stopped for a moment. Did they have Ali? Was he being shipped back to Jakhabad even now?

"So, you still want to kill Kane? A scrawny bitch like you?"

"Just give me a knife," Shaz challenged.

"Take that one. As you can see, it is wickedly sharp."

It was the last thing she wanted to touch, for countless reasons. They were setting her up.

"TAKE IT!"

The hand was back on her neck, forcing her closer. The suggestion of a squeeze, increasing to almost throttling, took away any choice.

"Now, practice using this meat. You need to be able to slip it between two ribs, quickly, deeply."

When she was allowed to stop, she was blood spattered, bloody handed and thoroughly sickened. She stayed erect by an extreme act of will.

"Now, you are ready," the voice told her.

Someone banged on the front door.

"That's Kane," the voice told her. "Take the knife. If you fail, I will take out Kane, and you. Go!"

She reached the entrance room as the door was kicked in. Two men, both armed, saw her. One held his gun on her, a stranger. The other was Kane. He took in her state, and the knife.

"Drop it!" he yelled.

The knife slipped from her hand.

"You alone?" he demanded.

Not daring to speak, she glanced behind her. Kane nodded to his partner, and the man moved in that direction.

"No!" Shaz managed to say, but in the next moment the other yelled, "Clear! Kane. In here!"

Kane grabbed her. His grip became vice-like when he recalled the blood on her, the knife, and now the dead man. He didn't have long to consider the sight.

"Kane! Out! Now!"

That was when Shaz heard the purposeful ticking that hadn't been present moments before.

Kane changed his grip, from her arm to her waist and lifted her off her feet as he raced for the door. The roar of the explosion blew out the back of the house, and them to the ground. It would draw the police and the smoke would pinpoint the location. Shaz had no time to get to her feet. She was lifted again, and shoved into the back of a dark car, parked a few metres away. Kane got in the front, while his mate went to the driver's seat. Once Kane was in, the car revved off at top speed.

"That was meant to get us," the driver said savagely. "Are you sure that bitch is worth it?"

"We have our orders," Kane countered.

"You saw Adam. I want answers before I take that bitch anywhere near...Peeuw! Is that bitch being sick?"

"Sorry," Shaz apologised quietly.

"Sorry? You sorry about killing Adam too?"

"I didn't...I mean...I think he was already dead."

Shaz felt the car slow as sirens grew louder. A fire truck rushed past, followed by police. Shaz kept down below window level, and covered her nose.

The driver resumed his rant as he increased speed again. "I thought when you took Tozer out, it was over. We could stop running."

"Have you ever heard of the Cobra Sect using women for assassins?" Kane asked.

"Bait," Shaz interrupted. "They wanted you."

"Why?" Kane demanded.

"I don't know, but you did kill one of them."

"They tried to kill you too," the driver told her savagely. "We should have left you there."

"No. She saved me and our charge. Gave me the chance to get free."

"What about Adam?"

"I didn't kill him," Shaz insisted, trying to believe it.

"You said you thought he was already dead. Is that why you have his blood all over you? Why should we believe you?"

Shaz's stomach heaved again. "Look, you need to let me out somewhere."

"No!" Kane stated. "The sect will kill you."

"If they find me, with you and your charge, we will all be killed," Shaz insisted, but it came out like a plea.

"Both the sect, and the FBI want me. You and your charge want to be low profile. You need to get back to him if the sect got another of your lot."

"Who are you?" the driver demanded abruptly.

"Now you ask," Shaz found the strength to retort. "I am someone who can better help you if I am on the street. Now Tozer is dead, they will have someone else hunting you. I might be able to find out who that is. Not that I want to go near that creepy Arab guy, Prince Jabir, again."

"Jabir? Here? Where did you meet him?"

"He met me at the hospital when I slipped out. Him and his FBI mole."

"Shit!" the driver exploded.

"Jabir knows me," Kane said with alarm.

"I am fortunate that he doesn't know me," Shaz muttered. "I said you overpowered me, but I half think he believes I helped you."

"I think you can safely say he doesn't trust you," the driver told her. "Have you considered that he has set you up as a suspect for Adam's murder?"

Shaz had. "Either way, I have to disappear. He will be sure I helped you if you persist in trying to save me."

"I could be intending to take you in," Kane suggested.

"No. If the FBI get me I will be a sitting duck waiting to be deported. Soon after, I will be a very dead duck. Free, Jabir has to halve his forces to look for you and for me."

"They will still kill you," Kane objected.

"Maybe not, though like I said, I have to disappear. If you toss me out, with a suitable insult like 'send a man next time', they may think you only wanted to question me."

"Ali wanted you!" Kane insisted. "What are you to him?"

"If he hasn't said, I can't. Now, if no one is following you, dump me out near Dimitri's. It's on the waterfront. Do you know it?"

"I do," the driver growled.

"I'll be okay. I have friends there."

Kane still didn't like it, but he was reluctantly seeing the sense in her plan. He reached into the glove box, tore a page from the supplied street directory, and scribbled on it with a marker pen from his pocket. He folded the page and gave it to her. The driver increased his speed again, keen to be rid of her.

Chapter 9 - Hiding

Kane's mate had slowed before Shaz dived from the car, rolled, and lay still. She sucked in a breath and hoped to never need to repeat that manoeuvre again. The sound of the car faded, and what little she could see through slitted eyes, was a deserted alley. The engine revving as the car took off, brought the curious out to investigate.

The first person to venture close shook her. She feigned unconsciousness. The hand clenched on her shoulder in a code gesture as she was rolled over onto her back. The murmuring of the other onlookers increased and she heard her name mentioned. Shuffling suggested some of the crowd were pushing to the edge, to go off and report seeing her. Most likely, they would be Jabir's agents, looking to earn the reward. Most people in this area wouldn't want to go to the police.

Shaz groaned, as if just waking.

Dimitri, bending over her said, distinctly, "You're a fool coming here, Shaz. I can't hide you. You clean up at back tap and get off. Don't want your friends or the police around here."

"Wasn't my choice," Shaz growled, weakly. "Have cops been looking?"

"Too right. Look here, look there, nose in everywhere. Say you killed someone."

"I didn't."

"Your boyfriend, good riddance, but can't help you. Get up, clean up, go!"

Shaz allowed his help. It looked rough but his grip was gentle.

Dimitri pointed, "Tap there!" He turned to the other people, "All you go! There was nothing to see here, okay?"

Dimitri herded his patrons back around to the side of the hotel, to the outside beer garden. He didn't look back.

Despite his heard and witnessed refusal to help, his hand grip had indicated to ignore what he said. As soon as the alley cleared, she found the hatch over the ramp where the kegs were delivered, lifted it and crept in. She slipped a bolt across the inside, to stop anyone following. She knew the way through to the hotel from there. She had to go through the kitchen, but no one was there, and into passages used by the servants and family. She came to an apparent dead end where shelving stacked with cleaning stuff blocked the way. By slipping a bolt, she moved the shelves just enough to slip behind. She pushed it back, and opened the door that was now in front of her. It led to a narrow stairway that went up to the residential floors of the hotel. She stopped at the first landing, and went through another door into a tiny room, with an adjoining en-suite. The room had a narrow cot, and a chair, and the only other visible objects were two cases. Both were hers. Here, she was safe. She could clean up and change between Nadia Shaston and Janet Delaney.

After getting a drink from the ensuite tap, she studied her face in the mirror and shuddered. Then she looked at her clothes. They would need to be burnt. She remembered the note, and took it from her pocket, leaving it on the edge of the basin. Dimitri could say he found it in the alley when she'd gone.

Only when she stripped off all the mismatched garments she had stolen, did she see the dried bloody patch on her arm. At first she thought the blood had come from the same source as that which was caked on her hands. She forced the horrid memory away, and began to scrub her hands and arms, only to realise some of the blood had soaked through a patch of plaster. She had no idea where it had come from. The area wasn't hurting her.

The desire for a hot shower was becoming hard to resist. She stopped washing her hands, and stripped off her underwear and stepped into the shower and made lavish use of soap and shampoo already there. When she felt she had scrubbed away a week's worth of grime and blood, she stopped the water and stepped out, knowing she would find towels in the cupboard under the sink. Not for the first time, Shaz wondered if Dimitri hid other people here at times.

The built up tension had eased, and now her mind could consider the recent events in sequence, and their consequences.

When she returned to the other room, clad only in a towel,

Dimitri's daughter, Felicia, was waiting for her. Shaz, knew her and they were friends, although casual ones.

"Is there anything you need?" Felicia asked.

"I think I need to cut my hair short, just above shoulder length. I still want to be able to put it up under a wig if I want to."

"Papa must have read your mind. He told me to suggest it." She drew out hair cutting tools from the deep pocket of the apron she wore over shirt and trousers. Why don't you bring your case over a bit so you can sit on it?"

Shaz chose to get dressed first, it gave her a greater sense of security. Usually, when she changed to Janet, she had long or mid length sleeves to cover the two very noticeable flower tattoos – one on each shoulder.

"What happened to your arm?" Felicia asked.

"Another tattoo," Shaz said with a shrug. She hadn't noticed it until the plaster had come off in the shower, and the rest of the blood there had washed away. The inch high poised cobra had given her shivers. She wasn't quite sure what it signified, but she doubted it was good.

Shaz let Felicia do her magic on her hair, and when the girl finally told her to go look at herself, she was impressed. The new look was nothing like Shaz's untidy pony tail, or Janet's neatly coiled style.

With the new hair style, and her Janet clothing style, no one should recognise her as Nadia Shaston.

"My deepest thanks," Shaz, now preparing to be Janet, expressed.

"You helped me that time, I'm glad I could help you," Felicia said quietly. "Oh, Papa said not to hurry out. A lot of the odd foreigners are about, and some guy he has pegged as official."

"Did he hear a name?"

"King, I think. Know him?"

Janet nodded. If he was there, summoned by the 'odd' foreigners who were not locals, confirmed in her mind that she couldn't trust him. She recalled the letter she'd had Kane write. And fetched it from the en-suite.

"Tell Dimitri this was found in the alley where the woman fell."

"Ok, and I will come back with food and a drink for you. Do you want to have a sleep before leaving?"

Janet shook her head. She wanted to get home, to get rid of the

Nadia stuff and contact the Group. Then she'd go back to work – let the FBI hunt ease off, and the covert one by Sam's friends. She would need a good excuse for the healing damage, unless her make up covered it.

While Felicia was gone, Janet finished her makeup. The effect of the tablets that caused her skin to take on a slightly olive tone had worn off, so she didn't need the extra layer of make up that negated it. That stuff, however, would help cover the bruising that was starting to come out. Then she used the girlie pink shades of makeup, with the subtle darker shade that helped change the apparent structure of her face.

She was contemplating the unwanted new tattoo – deep black – when her friend arrived with food.

"Papa has given me the rest of the day off. So later, we can leave as two girls going out together. I have a friend who runs a cab. He will drop you off and not talk."

"I can't thank you and your Papa enough."

"He said, the favour you did me, he can't thank you enough for."

She was warned as she went through the indoor bar, that King had not left. So her attention remained on watching where she was going and listening to Felicia's excited chatty plans for their girl's day out. In her side vision, she knew King had turned to watch them, but he remained sitting. She was certain he would have followed them if he had the slightest suspicion. On her part, she didn't even glance his way.

The taxi was waiting for them, Felicia greeted her friend and let him open the doors for them. The vehicle, however, already had a passenger. Someone Janet knew.

"Tim!" she greeted with relief. It was one of her friends who was part of the Group.

"Good to see you looking so well," he told her. "A few of us were right worried. The big fella told Johnno that he had dropped you here."

"Big fella?"

"You know – the blond soldier guy."

"Oh!" Janet berated herself for forgetting the Group kept in touch with Ali's guards. "Did he say anything else?"

The cab pulled away from the hotel and headed towards the city.

"Yeah, told us who you'd been rubbing shoulders with. You were damn lucky, girl."

"Yeah," Janet agreed.

"Oh. Had a special delivery for you." Tim pulled a package from within his jacket. "Only one SIM, new number, but it has your old number redirected to it."

He meant her Janet number, since she was in that persona. She would ask about the Shaz number later.

"Anything important going on?"

Tim shook his head, but he glanced at the package with the new phone. It meant she should call in later. He told the driver to let him out around the next corner.

Felicia was dropped off near her aunt's hair salon, and wished Janet well. The taxi driver stopped at the bus stop near her apartment and let her out there. She walked the rest of the way.

Janet approached her apartment as if she hadn't been away for some days. What an observer wouldn't know was that she was scrutinising everything. One of her neighbours greeted her and waved.

"Janet! A word!"

She stopped, and waited for Mrs Baker to put down her potting tools and come over.

"What's up?"

"Your boss came around, looking for you. Yesterday."

"My Boss? Mr Drysdale? Tall guy, balding?"

"Could be. Asked if you were in and when I'd last seen you."

"I'd better give him a call. Thanks. Nothing else?"

"What happened to you?"

"Minor accident. Twisted my ankle and fell over. Couldn't walk for a few days. Stayed with a friend."

The woman twitted sympathetically. Janet was relieved, though. This neighbour noticed everything that went on around the building. If strangers had been loitering, she would have said. It felt safe to go into her apartment.

"Anything?" Frank Dupont demanded when John King returned

to his office.

"No. I had word that she had been dumped at the back of Dimitri's, covered in blood. He said he told her to get going. Other patrons confirmed that."

"It was definitely Shaston?"

"I believe so. Dimitri said a note was found near where she had fallen when pushed from the car. Just a page torn from a road directory, with writing done with a thick marker pen."

"Any description of the car? Driver?"

"Just a dark car."

"Who was the note directed to?"

"The wording was, verbatim, 'Don't you have the balls to face me yourself? Hiding behind women now?' Odds on, it is intended for the people we are after."

"Well!" Dupont exclaimed. "Sit down, John. Did you pass the note on?"

King nodded. "The writer of that had better consider himself a dead man. Have you heard anything else?"

"More reports relating to the murder of Tozer/Hashim. That connection was confirmed by fingerprints. However, they have confirmed that a number of people – of interest to Interpol – have been in that house. Not a comforting piece of information. They had a partial set of prints for another man." Dupont passed a photo across his desk. "Ben Michaelson. American, former Marine major."

King studied the photo. "Tozer had Michaelson. Do you think he killed Tozer?"

"He's more likely than Shaston," Dupont said.

"She could be a witness," King proposed. "She told Jabir she was overcome by someone – a blond brute. She didn't have a name, and there was a scrawny guy as well."

"A fact she didn't mention to us," Dupont pointed out. "Has his Highness mentioned why he is in the country?"

"No. But I can think of only one person he would come after personally. Crown Prince Ali."

"Yes, that was my conclusion too. Here, this just came through from the city police."

King reached for the clipped sheets and read. He picked up on the important point, "A dead blond, marine type? Michaelson?"

"No this one was identified by his dog tags. He was Adam Ruskin. Nasty business."

"Where are your thoughts headed, Frank?"

"Could it be possible that Tozer had Michelson and the Prince and Shaston helped them get free?"

"I wouldn't say it was impossible," King admitted. "However nothing I have heard of Shaston suggests she would disobey Tozer."

"Keep reading that report."

King sank back in the chair, to keep reading, but suddenly jerked upright. "Shaston's prints on the blade that killed Ruskin? No."

"No what?" Dupont asked.

"Jabir would not trust a woman to kill, but I think we are supposed to think she did. Maybe Kane/Michaelson was meant to think that too. Or maybe, she was bait. Jabir, if he thought she'd helped free prisoners, might think Kane would try to help her."

"Her prints were on the knife," Dupont prompted.

"I know. She said she wanted to fix Kane for killing Tozer. If she had helped him instead, that claim was to mislead Jabir. He distrusts women, thinks them weak. He wouldn't send one to kill a man like Kane, or this Ruskin. It says here, he'd been tied to a chair. So someone else was involved. Jabir isn't one to tolerate those who cross him. I would have thought he'd have Shaz punished or killed. Having her prints on the knife – if she managed to escape that trap, as she did, the police will be after her for murder."

"How do you read that message, in that light?" Dupont queried.

"It is intended as an insult. If Kane thought Shaz was going to kill him, the woman wouldn't have had a chance. Maybe he won't kill a woman in cold blood, but if he took her from that house, it could be construed as him wanting answers from her, or information about Tozer's friends." King said immediately. He thought for a bit. "I would say, dumping her was a deliberate ploy. It looks like he doesn't care what happens to her now."

"I wonder if she told Kane more than she told us?" Dupont mused. "We need to find her, before your friend decides to finish her. We need to know what she knows. Do you get the feeling she was calling the shots? That she made them drop her where they did? What is special about Dimitri's?"

"Shaston went there quite often," King told him.

"Interesting. So, she disappears near there, and if she can't go back to the Ghetto, she must have other places. We need to find them. Surely her use to Prince Jabir is evaporating."

"What about Kane/Michaelson?"

"He should be able to look after himself," Dupont commented. "But there is a call out to have him brought in."

Chapter 10 – Observers

Wanda Martin found her husband staring intently at his laptop's dark screen, and drumming his fingers with impatience.

"What's up?" she asked, sensing his agitation.

"Had a call. One of the guys from the East Coast. Tozer is dead."

"Janna?"

"She went there. It's pretty certain that he had Ali and one of his guards there. They heard she was found on scene, drugged. Police took her to hospital."

Wanda released a sigh of relief.

"One of the guards, guy calling himself Kane, called the Group. He got away, but Janna insisted on staying. I am trying to trace what happened after she ducked out of the hospital. She told the group that she was going home – that would be to Janet's apartment."

"When did this all happen?" Wanda's concern ramped up again.

"Thursday afternoon is when Tozer died." That was almost three whole days ago.

David's screen brightened. He had just infiltrated the police net in New York State. His fingers played over the keys, opening files, scan reading, then moving on."

Wanda scan read over his shoulder, memorising whole screens of data in moments. "She doesn't have her phone," she noted, after reading a list of items taken from the Tozer murder scene. "Or money, or her bag."

David cross checked that detail and confirmed, "The police have them. They'll get experts to check the phone. Let me see..."

He found no report on it, and no mention of it being received in the tech lab. He took up his phone and hit redial. He waited for one of the group to answer.

"Hi bro, what's up?"

"It's that girl of mine," David put a tone of exasperation in his voice. "Dropped her damn phone somewhere. Think you can help find it?"

"Yeah, heard that. Not that it helps, but it was somewhere near the busy part of town."

David translated that as in the control of the police. "And now?"

"Let me check. Call ya."

David closed his phone.

"I take it they haven't heard from her since the call you mentioned."

"They are worried, yes." David confirmed.

David's phone rang again.

"You there bro?"

"Did you find it?"

"Your girl must have. It's moved back uptown. Was there for a while but now it's moving around."

Translated from the oblique speak the Group excelled at, David took that to mean the phone had been moved, and not to the tech lab. Uptown was also a warning that it was closer to Janet's apartment. Moving around suggested someone was searching...for Nadia? People she might stay with?

"I'll call you back, bro," David hung up abruptly.

He hadn't needed to tell Tim, the speaker, to send the data to him. It had come in as they were talking. The map with location and time data came up on his laptop screen. He enlarged it.

Wanda pointed to Tozer's house, police HQ, the tech lab location and Janet's apartment. "Well, she hasn't got it. It left the Ghetto, with the police because it was at the HQ for a bit. It didn't go to the tech lab, or to her at the hospital. I wonder if that location," she indicated a place where the unit had been for a while, "is where the top man is? And I wonder if he will find the second SIM?"

"We can't assume it won't be found," David cautioned.

"Should we cancel those numbers?" Wanda suggested.

"No...Janet's contacts will still need to be able to reach her. It's a risk, because if someone calls Nadia, the caller may have their number traced, and if the call was for Janet..."

"Let's hope they assume it's a wrong number," Wanda put in. "The real weak point is Janet's place. She has Nadia's stuff there. I am wondering if the reason that phone is moving around now is they are trying to find places where Nadia might be hiding."

"I can get the Group to organise a new phone," David proposed. "Have calls to Janet's number diverted to it, and those to Nadia's number diverted to one of my anonymous phones."

"Who is likely to call Nadia?"

"Personal contacts only, I expect."

An idea that had been skittering around Wanda's mind, finally surfaced. "If the wrong person does have her phone, and finds the two SIM cards, can they get Janet's number?"

"No. I disabled the 'own number' function."

"Okay, if someone uses it, will it default to going to Nadia's SIM?"

"Yes, until it is manually changed," David confirmed. "It is set up not to ask first."

"So, the caller will see Nadia's number?"

"What are you thinking?"

"Nothing specific. I am just uneasy."

"Do you think we need to pull her out?" David asked, watching then as his wife considered the suggestion.

"She's tricked everyone so far," Wanda said aloud. "There's been no reports of unidentified bodies," she glanced at David, who shook his head. "I think we need to trust her."

Wanda was silent for a while longer, then she blurted, "She'll turn up." It was one of her 'just know' moments.

David nodded. "Okay, I'll get Tim to get her a new phone. When she's able to get in touch, he'll be ready to get it to her."

"Maybe put a block on her Nadia and Janet phone records?"

"The police may need to look at them. But I think I need to provoke a request for an update on the phone so someone realises it is missing."

David put his decisions into action, and then set his computer to scan the news bulletins in NY State, and ding an alert when certain terms were mentioned.

The following afternoon, David received another call from the Group.

"Hi bro, you know that chick you were hung up on? She's some chick! I have her number. You can call her if you want."

David's face broke into a grin. "She's okay with that?"

"Looks like it."

"Okay, send it through."

"On its way. See ya, bro."

David trotted through to the room where Wanda was carefully placing new floor boards.

She saw him and said, "This was meant to be your job, you know. So what other reason do you have to grin like an idiot?"

"Janna's okay. Kane said he'd dropped her off. The place was near one of her safe holes. Tim has seen her, and given her the new phone."

Wanda stood up. She had taken on the task to keep her mind from worrying too much. When she spoke, it was on a seemingly unrelated matter. "Did you read that report about the explosion in Albany?"

"Yes, but it didn't seem related."

"There was an update. They found the remains of an ex-marine there. Part of him was still attached to a chair. They found his dog tags later. Until they released his name, I'd had the horrid feeling it might have been Kane. It wasn't."

"What had you been thinking?"

"Except for the fact that the enemy wouldn't have had his phone number, I had wondered if Nadia's phone might have been used somehow to lure the guy there."

"He was one of Ali's guards?"

Wanda nodded. "Or they caught and killed the guy, found and abducted Nadia, and got Kane hotfooting to help her. Or why blow the place up after killing the guy?"

David didn't have to say there could have been lots of reasons, but the enemy would want maximum shock factor to rattle Ali's remaining guards.

Wanda broke into David's thoughts. "Do you think it might pay if I head that way?"

"If that's what you feel is right. What will you do?"

"Stay low, unless I'm needed. I don't want to queer the play, but I think things are going to hot up."

"Go pack! I'll organise the flights," David directed.

Chapter 11 - Shocks

Janet went back to work after explaining her absence with the same tale she had told her neighbour. He'd been difficult, but she'd explained that she'd not had phone access during the time. He'd noticed one of the healing bruises on her cheek, where she had deliberately used less covering make up, and subsided.

To mollify him, she worked the full eight hour shift at the office, instead of her usual five. Sometimes she stayed longer, depending on when her street sources became available. Usually, she went to see them.

This job was now the only way she felt she was doing anything for Ali. Listening for clues from various news media sources, questioning them to see if they'd heard hints of various things – if she could get a hint of the location of Prince Jabir, she could call the authorities in.

Her friends who made up the Group had nothing to report either, and that was concerning. They were seeking other ways the foreigners might be communicating. Tim had suggested they had all changed to new untraceable phones and finding them would be difficult.

They hadn't had any further calls from Kane or the other guards, and their calls to them had not been answered.

Working longer hours at the office, kept her away from her apartment. She'd never been bothered before about staying there alone. Now she was spooked by the slightest sounds.

The lack of noticeable activity from the foreigners worried her. On one hand, it might suggest they had all left the country, but they would only do that if they had what they came for – Ali. There had been no reports of bodies, so unless Kane was dead and well hidden, he was still alive and protecting Ali.

Not knowing what scenarios might be correct, wore on her nerves, and exacerbated her morning nausea, making it impossible to eat breakfast, and sometimes lunch. By the end of a week, the search for Nadia Shaston had disappeared from the news, though she knew people would still be looking for her.

When she was away from her apartment, Janet took the self-preservation techniques she had been taught by her mentors, to a new level of awareness. Even when she was home, she maintained that state. Now was not the time to let her guard down. Paranoia suggested that the longer the apparent peace lasted, the worse the shock would be when the enemy struck.

The stress was impacting on her in other ways, complicated by the knowledge of being pregnant and the changes occurring within her. She'd not been to a doctor, or even confirmed the pregnancy, but the various aches and pains she was getting were worsening and she'd finally made an appointment for the following day. Part of her mind was distracted by that, even though she forced herself to concentrate on her surroundings. It would not do to be weak right now, she needed to keep the hardness of her Nadia persona as part of her new self.

She arrived at her address, gave the area a quick scan and saw no one. She stopped at the letter boxes that served the six detached ground floor apartments, and used her key to open hers. The faintest trace of a smell, amplified by her pregnancy it seemed, sent shivers up and down her back. It was the smell of Ali's preferred body spray. It had no place there, and her first instinct was that she imagined it. She glanced around again, as she reached into the letter box. Her hand touched something sticky, and she jerked it out. Blood tinged her fingers, and she fought the urge to throw up. She knelt down to look – there was enough light to see something with black hair or fur. If it wasn't that the smell of body spray had hit her nostrils, she would have thought it was some kind of small animal. Even if nothing like that could have got itself in her locked letter box. Instead, intense dread brought on a wave of dizziness, which threatened to make her faint.

Something within her said, "No!" and she drew on her Nadia persona to straighten, let the box cover drop down, and backed away from the horrifying object within it. Abruptly, she turned to walk quickly to her apartment, wanting to get safely inside, glad her neighbour, the nosey Mrs Baker, could not see her just then. The memory of the black hair, was nearly paralysing her mind.

With her hand shaking, she took her phone from her handbag, and pressed the key number. She thought it was the one for the Group, but a woman answered.

"Who are you?" Janet asked the voice, as her own sounded strained.

"Wanda. Jan, is that you?"

Janet suddenly couldn't speak, not wanting to verbalise her fears.

"Janet! What's wrong?"

"It's...it's...I think they have him. I found...hair, skin, blood...in my letter box."

"Janet! Walk away! Don't go into your place. Turn around now! Leave!"

"Where can I go?"

"Go to your father! Hang up now and call him."

"What if it's Ali inside, and I can help him?"

"Janet! Turn around, walk away! Call your father."

Finally the advice seeped in. "Okay."

Janet turned back to the street, as she started to dial a number she still knew by heart. She didn't finish. The need to be sure Ali was not there, and to remove Nadia's stuff which three weeks on she hadn't got rid of. Her slow walk became almost a run, as she reached her door and unlocked it. Caution made her open the door slowly, and she saw what looked like an untouched front room, but she smelt an odd smell, and tried to identify it. She took two steps in, and looked around. She had to swallow hard to control the bile that rose in her throat. Face away from her, on her couch, was a slender, dark haired figure, with a mass of blood where a patch of scalp was missing. Nearer, as if dragged in to be out of sight, was the still, plump body of Mrs Baker.

Only now did the advice of her mentor take control. She backed out, let the door auto lock. She tried to walk normally, but her body was shaking like she was cold. Her vision verged on gray. She forced herself to breathe, and walk towards the nearby bus-stop.

She collapsed onto the seat, as her phone rang. It took her some moments to realise what it was. She answered it.

"Yes?"

"Where are you?" Wanda's voice demanded.

"B-B-Bus-stop."

"Stay there! Help is coming."

"They're dead. In my apartment."

"You can't go back, Janet! Janet?"

"I'm here..."

"Listen! You have to stick to your Janet persona. You are not connected to Nadia Shaston's activities. You haven't seen her for over three weeks. That's not unusual."

"Yes."

"You let Nadia stay with you sometimes, because you felt sorry for her. She had enemies."

The initial shock began wearing off. Hearing her mentor's calm, decisive words, reminded her of the overall plan.

"I'll be okay now."

"Good, because David has just told your father where you are."

"No!"

"Yes, but stick to your guns. It's problematical, but if they keep you in custody, you will be safer than on the streets. They have no reason to think you are Nadia, but you don't want a hint of your real self to come out."

Janet felt the shivers returning. "How did they find me?"

"There could be multiple ways. If they discovered that Nadia stayed there, what you saw was probably aimed at framing her."

"Does my father know it's me he's picking up?"

"Not from us. David just said he traced some of Nadia's calls to that area – to your number. He just gave him your address and name."

Warned, Janna was able to hide her recognition of the man who emerged from the car that had stopped in front of her. Her relief was intense.

Frank Dupont saw the woman slumped at the bus-stop, just where he had been told. He didn't try to guess how his informant

- currently a continent away – had known. He guessed that this woman must also be a State Department operative. Probably Nadia Shaston's back up. The same red-flag had come up when he had the name checked. She looked bloodless.

His driver, and long-time partner, Jim Pearson, stopped the car to let him out.

"Janet Delaney?"

Janet focussed on the tall man with black hair showing noticeable streaks of gray. Her father had more lines on his face now than she remembered.

"Yes," she managed to say. "You were looking for me?"

"I'm Frank Dupont. FBI." He had his ID out as he asked, "Are you alright?"

"No. No I'm not." More shivers racked her. She wanted to throw herself at her father, and feel his arms around her. Like when she was much younger and woken from a nightmare. She couldn't. She dare not. The nightmare wasn't over.

"Here, put this around you." Dupont had taken off his jacket and now out it awkwardly around her. "Can you walk to the car?"

He opened the back door and helped her in, urging her to move over on the seat. He slipped in after her, and closed the door. Jim didn't need directions, he took off smoothly.

"What happened to you?"

Janet just shook her head, not wanting to recall what she had seen. Had it been Ali, she had seen, along with her neighbour? "You need...to get people to my apartment." She gave her address. She had to know if Ali was dead. If he was, nothing mattered. Her life didn't matter.

"Jim, get the local police to that address, then head for the hospital. This woman has fainted."

With practiced skill, Jim used the car radio to make the report, and still kept his attention on the road. At the hospital, he drove up to the emergency entrance. Dupont's identification got instant attention. A trolley was brought for the unconscious woman. He followed as the trolley was taken inside to a cubicle, and waited until the doctor came to examine her. When he was politely moved away, for the privacy curtain to be closed, his phone buzzed.

Jim Pearson passed on the report of what was found at the woman's apartment. It was little wonder she was in shock.

"Keep me informed," was his closing comment.

The doctor came out after he had been pacing for what felt like an hour.

"Are you a relative," the doctor asked.

He almost said, "Yes," for this Janet Delaney was so like his daughter. "No. She is a witness I need to keep safe. All I know is that she saw something pretty horrific when she stepped into her apartment."

"Do you know her next of kin, or any family member?"

"Sorry, no. We are making enquiries, I will take responsibility for any treatment needed. What concerns you?"

"We would like to keep her here, at least overnight," the doctor told him. "I have ordered a drip with glucose. I will know more when I get the results of blood tests. What concerns me most, is her child. I estimate she is about four months pregnant. Apart from shock, I don't think she has been eating or drinking enough."

"Where will you put her? I would like to arrange a police guard."

"Are you expecting trouble?"

"I have no reason to, it's more of a precaution until I understand where she fits into a rather ugly situation."

"I don't know that we have a private room, but I will see what can be arranged."

The woman was asleep, under warmed blankets, and had some colour back in her face. He could not get over how like his daughter she was, but his daughter had light brown hair, much finer than this woman had. He reached out a finger and moved the hair from off her neck. A pale brown patch of skin was revealed – lighter than the surrounding skin. A negative version of the patch of darker skin his daughter had from birth. His hand moved back and he had to sit down.

The truth jarred him. His daughter was mixed up in something nasty and vicious. How? Why? No! There was a reason. That damned business in the Middle East. His mind went in circles. The recent murders involving Middle-Easterners. His daughter was helping some State Department operative – now she was a target. Did she not care that they might kill her or torture her?

The two local officers arrived, but he really didn't want to leave. He had so many questions that he wanted to demand answers to. His daughter had put him in an impossible position. He had to admit she was his daughter. He couldn't stay on the case – he was biased. As he walked out the door, his phone vibrated.

"Frank? You need to come here."

It was Jim's voice, and he knew where 'here' was. His daughter's.... no, Janet Delaney's apartment. She hadn't shown that she knew him, obviously didn't want to. So be it. He wouldn't acknowledge her. She had chosen to do what she had.

Jim Pearson met him at the door. He could see in as the door opened, saw what his partner had described.

"Two victims, one an Arab, early forties. Knifed, and with a section of scalp removed. The other was one of the neighbours, Caucasian. The local busybody."

"What was the startling urgent reason for me to come?" Dupont asked.

"The fingerprint techs have been running all the prints they find through a portable data link. All the prints they have been found so far are from one person."

"The owner? Janet Delaney?" Frank said dismissively.

"Only if she is also Nadia Shaston," Jim said. "Frank? Are you alright?"

"Yes," Frank lied. "We just picked up Janet Delaney, not far from here, in a state of shock. She told us to get people here. There is no way she and Shaston can be the same person. Yes, they both have black hair, but Shaston is a hard piece of work by all accounts. Have you spoken to the neighbours?"

"The locals are doing that, but most have seen someone fitting Shaston's description coming and going at various times. Word is that Delaney was letting her stay there off and on. The descriptions though – Delaney and Shaston are totally different. They all like Janet, but will back off around Shaston."

"Okay, Jim. Keep on top of things here. I'll be back at the office."

He intended to go directly back to the city, but part way there he pulled over and used his phone to dial a memorised unlisted number.

When David Martin answered the call, he exploded, "What half-assed, brainless scheme have you had going, involving my daughter?"

He didn't think he was going to get a reply, until the infuriatingly calm voice asked, "What has happened?"

Dupont exploded again, venting his suppressed anger and fear. David let him finish before trying to pacify him.

"Frank, we did not appoint her to a task, and there is much that you are yet to see clearly."

"But you know what she's been doing, don't you?"

"In overview. The agent in question came to us with a well thought out and considered plan to achieve an important objective."

"Stuff your agent double talk! Do you know what that agent has been doing? Do you know she is pregnant? Probably with that terrorists bastard? Did she get told to commit all sorts of crimes for him?"

"Sir, I won't quote the maxim about the end justifying the means. The agent had training from both of us before getting started. She knew the risks. What you need to do is keep her safe."

"I shouldn't even still be on the case."

"That may be true, but has Janet Delaney acknowledged you?"

"No!"

"Then treat her as you would any other stranger. She has excellent instincts. Could you have fooled some highly suspicious foreign killers for four months or more?"

"I'm not a woman."

He heard David sigh, as if he was being dense. "Consider her heritage."

That put him in his place. He hadn't been able to stop his wife taking risky assignments – and one had finally killed her.

"Sir, I need to put you in touch with one of my local sources. Can you take down a number?"

"Yes. A moment." He took out the notebook he always carried. "Go ahead."

"Identify yourself to the person who answers. I will warn him to expect your call."

"And will your agent tell me what he knows?" Dupont demanded.

"When the time is right," David assured him calmly.

Dupont growled and hung up – distracted by the invitation to talk to one of that damn, uppity, young State Department agent's sources.

David Martin saw his wife smirking via the webcam, as he put down the phone.

"He went off at you, didn't he? What's up?"

"Something very nasty at Janet's apartment. I don't know more than Janet told you. He was still reticent about details. He found Janet where we sent him, he took her to hospital, found out she was pregnant and neglecting herself. He spotted the birthmark on her neck."

"I knew it was a risk, but he was the only person I would trust in the situation," Wanda admitted. "I hope he keeps that fingerprint info close to his chest."

"He has a reason to," David suggested.

"And reasons not to," Wanda argued. "However, that is the only evidence that Nadia and Janet are the same. It can be argued that Janet is a compulsive cleaner and any of Nadia's prints were cleaned away."

"The neighbours believe there are two people, Nadia and Janet. I don't propose to ask if any of the neighbours ever saw them together." David saw his wife grimace.

"I don't like how the bastards all just disappeared, or rather stopped being obvious about their activities. It reeks of them being up to something. It would be a lot simpler, if that damn young foreign prince would agree to go into safe custody."

"Well if Janna couldn't convince him, I doubt you will be able to."

"Who said anything about convincing him? I'd bloody well drag him there. He might go if he knew Janna was in danger."

David nodded, adding, "And pregnant. You were right about that, although it would have been really early."

Wanda just looked smug. "Can you find a map of the hospital where Janet is?"

"When do you want it?"

"Early morning, NY time. Say five hours from now."

"You'll have it. What are you planning?"

"Just a little talk with Janna."

Wanda was glad to have something active to do. Three weeks of sitting with the Group, putting up with their deliberately juvenile humour, had made her twitchy.

She prepared for her planned insertion into the hospital by studying the schematics David had sent her and memorising all the exits, as well as potential covert ways in.

All the skills learnt as a top thief, had been kept in practice, and so entering the hospital shortly before the end of visiting hours, dressed casually, was the first step. It was a simple next step to get into the relevant storeroom and find where spare scrubs were stored, and change to look the part. She moved on and found where trolleys had been prepared for the next round of blood taking, and appropriated one. No one questioned her, since she blended so well into what people expected.

She knocked on the door to the room where Janet Delaney was resting. "I'm here to do the bloods," she called through the door.

One of the police officers opened the door a crack and then wider. Wanda let them check the trolley and pushed it past them when they allowed her to enter. She went directly to the bed by the window and drew the curtain. For the benefit of the listening officers, she started a spiel relating to her apparent reason to be there, but interspersed it with low voiced whispers.

Seeing the wicked smile on the face of her mentor, gave Janet heart. She wasn't alone.

Wanda sensed the heartfelt relief and one of her low whispers was, "You still have the hardest job."

"What do I need to do?"

After a few more comments related to her apparent task, Wanda whispered, "At this point, you must adhere to your fall back identity as Janet Delaney. Say nothing to anybody about anything she wouldn't know."

"I think my father suspects. I think my birthmark was darker than the rest of me last night."

"He more than suspects. He rounded on David about us putting you in danger." Wanda switched back to more nurse patient talk for a while then told Janet, "I will be back later, to get you out of here."

"How?"

"Leave it to me. Where are your clothes?"

Janet pointed to a cupboard beside her bed. Wanda produced a bag and quietly bundled everything into it and slipped it onto the lower tray of the trolley.

"How much more do you need," Janet asked aloud, before whispering, "Does my father know you are here?"

"Not yet. Maybe not at all unless I have to run interference." She raised her voice. "This is the last."

"You were right though. I should have talked to him."

"Right now, I don't advise it – not unless you appear as yourself. Do you want to?"

Janna nodded. "Maybe now he will listen. And then arrest me."

"I don't think he will. So far, you have done excessively well keeping up two diametrically different identities. Even if he discovers that Nadia and Janet have identical fingerprints, trying to convince others will be hard."

Wanda dropped empty tubes into a metal kidney dish, covered them with a blue cloth, and a blank request form in a plastic bag, and gave the, "Keep pressure on that for a minute or two," spiel, then opened the curtains. She rolled the cart back past the policemen, and kept their attention by saying, "I've been told to come back later to get Miss Delaney for an ultrasound. I was told you would probably prefer a familiar person, so, just letting you know."

Janna leant back, energised. The shock of the previous night was distanced, but she still worried about Ali. Wanda had been able to tell her the male victim at her apartment had been too old to be him and that was the best news she could have had – it had really buoyed her spirits.

Just as well, for within five minutes of Wanda leaving, her father arrived. He strode in and greeted her.

"Janna?"

"Sorry? My name is Janet, not Janna. I'm glad you are here. Thank you for helping me last night, I was..." she met Dupont's eyes and gave no reaction except to shudder delicately at the memory. "I'm sorry, but if you said who you were last night, I really don't remember."

Dupont realised that it wasn't the time to confront his daughter. Not with the two police witnesses. So he introduced himself, showed his ID, just as if she was the stranger she obviously intended to be.

"I need to hear from you about last night. Are you up to it?"

"Yes. I'll be okay. What can I tell you?"

Dupont asked one of the officers to take notes, and asked the first of his prepared questions. He also had a recorder and asked, "Mind if I record this as well?"

Janet shrugged. "No, but my throat is really dry. I hope you don't mind if I suck a lozenge."

"No, go ahead." He waited until she'd taken one from a packet on her bedside table, and settled, before he began.

"Did you have any warning of what you would find?"

"Only a faint smell. Is that what you meant?"

"Partly. Had you noticed people hanging around? Following you?" Dupont prompted.

"No, and if there had been, Mrs Baker..." Janet had to stop for a moment. "Mrs Baker would have said something. She probably did see something. That's probably why they killed her too."

"Tell me about the smell." Dupont chose to move away from the mention of the dead woman.

"Well, I usually check for letters on my way in. That's when I had a whiff – of some kind of body spray. Thought I was imagining it. There was no one around. I unlocked the box, and reached in. I felt something and took my hand out. It had blood on it, and when I looked, I saw something. I thought it was a dead rat – something with fur. I left it there – wanting to get inside. I didn't think anyone would have been in my apartment. It never occurred to me if they could put something in the letter box..."

"Just hold it there a moment," Dupont requested. He used his phone to call his partner, requesting a check of the letter box. "Sorry, go on."

Janet closed her eyes. "When I opened the door, nothing seemed wrong. It was only when I stepped in that I saw..." she paused and took a steadying breath. "The man was on the couch..."

Dupont was impressed, 'Janet' had described the scene as well as the officer who had arrived first on the scene. However she had noticed little things at that time, which were different to when she had left that morning, all indicating that someone had snooped around.

He had some specific questions about what belonged in her flat before switching topics.

"You had Nadia Shaston staying with you?"

"Not all the time," Janet admitted. "She keeps stuff in my spare room and stays with me sometimes when her boyfriend was away."

"Why was that?"

"She said, even though her boyfriend was a bit of a brute, he protected her. But when he was away, his mates tried to come on to her."

"Where did you meet her?"

"At Dimitri's. A place I like."

"When did you meet her?"

"Two, maybe three months ago."

"Did she tell you much about her life? What she did?"

"Not really. I saw her eyeing off some of the big spenders that passed through Dimitri's. Had the feeling she was also a whore, and that's how she got her money. When I suggested she could stay with me, was after one of those types had got rough."

Dupont suddenly threw in, "Did Nadia have a passport?" He hoped Janet would answer without thinking, but she seemed to consider the question.

"If she did, she'd either have it in her bag, or with her stuff in my spare room."

His other trick questions gained him nothing. Finally, Janet dared a question. "Was the other person, the one on the couch, a friend of Nadia?"

"It is possible. Or be a friend of her boyfriend. He was Ackbar Ashwan."

Janet frowned. "Is that a Turkish name?"

"No. Arabic. You know Nadia was born in Turkey?"

"Yes."

"Did she say when she had come here?"

"I never asked."

"When was the last time you saw Nadia?"

"Three or four weeks ago, I think it was. Why are you asking about her?"

"We think the...business in your apartment was aimed at her."

"Whatever for?" Janet asked the question, but hearing who the male victim was, gave her too good of an idea.

"Someone killed her boyfriend. Perhaps his friends think she was involved."

If he had not been watching her so closely, he wouldn't have seen the faint shudder. She had caught his subtle warning.

"They can't think I'm involved."

"There's no way to know short of asking the killer."

"So they are looking for Nadia? Maybe think I'll call her or something."

"It's possible. Do you have somewhere else you can stay when you are allowed out?"

"I...I'll think on it."

Dupont retreated after requesting a copy of the officer's transcript. He wasn't completely satisfied with the outcome of his questions, but he could not fault the woman's eye for details that the police had missed, and she had provoked questions and ideas he wanted to check. But gods! The woman, if it was Janna, was perfect. Not once had she slipped in her performance.

Two hours later, Janet was in a van, being driven away from the hospital, amazed by how Wanda Martin had simply returned with a wheel chair, allowed the officers to follow them to the cubicle in the x-ray department and requested they wait outside the door. She cheerfully told them they would be about ten minutes, closed that door and continued out through the other door where they ditched the chair and found the back service ways out.

Frighteningly competent indeed.

Chapter 13 - Confrontation

They drove into the garage attached to a warehouse, then walked up to a mezzanine level and a large office. The Group were there to meet her, and they each had to hug her to show how glad they were she was okay.

Wanda shooed them back to work – they had laptops set up at intervals on a long table, and some other gear they used to monitor communications.

Tim remarked, "Frank D has been trying to get me since last night. Yon David said to talk freely, but wait for you to say when."

"Yes. Soon. Heard anything more?"

"Nope," one of the others, Glen, summarised. "We're scanning, but it looks as if they have vamoosed."

"They haven't," Wanda said flatly. "How many of your suspect immigrants and visitors have you scratched?"

"Three dead, four cleared. About six real suspects left," Glen summarised.

"How do you think HR Nastiness arrived here? As one of that six?" Wanda asked, intending to provoke ideas.

"Likely," Tim suggested and all the others there nodded agreement.

"Okay, what if you were to look into all kinds of travel bookings – between here and the mid-east? Although I suspect his Nastiness probably commands his own private jet. I don't suppose any of those pinged your radar when it came in?"

Head shakes.

"Never mind. Any outgoing flight plan from a private jet is likely to be last minute anyway. Okay. I think it is time that His Nastiness went home empty handed. David has got me up to date with events over in Jakhabad. The loyal forces there are ready to take on Jabir's forces – but – they would be in a stronger position if they knew Jabir was here. That is a piece of 'intelligence' I want the loyalists to hear. Can you insert it?"

"Done!" Tim agreed.

"Now...if there has been no movement indicating he has left here, it means his business here is not finished."

"He wants Ali," Janna said bleakly.

"Have you thought about why they staged that horror scene in your apartment?" Wanda asked.

Janna felt her jaw drop as the worst case scenario occurred to her.

"They think I might be me?"

Wanda laughed. "No, they think Janet might be – the name is suggestive. They will have their spies out to see what happens."

"King! My father's 'expert on terrorism'," Janna said. "He's chummy with Jabir, though my father swears he is loyal to US interests."

"David is looking into him. He has been very hard to get information on. Had you met him before? As yourself?"

"No."

"Right! Now, I don't know for sure if Jabir is after you as Janet Delaney. However, there is a number of reasons why he might. One is, he doesn't want Ali having outside, foreign, allies. He had you as Janna, deported back here. Now Ali is here, and he will be assuming Ali will try to contact you. You were wise to insist he keeps away. If Jabir is also looking for Janna, his forces are divided."

"If he suspects Ali likes Janna, he'd use me as bait – like he did Nadia."

"Yes, and proof of your performance, he didn't know who he really had."

The four guys snickered, hearing it put that way.

"Now we have Janet Delaney distracting him."

"So what now? My father will be livid that Janet walked out..."

"David advised him to treat Janet Delaney like he would any other witness or suspect. It will mean he will get rough with you – might even find charges to hold you on. Act like Janet would, but don't let it worry you. Janet can be bait for Ali as well. He needs to surface so we can offer him help."

"Yours personally? Or the State Department?" Janna asked.

"It depends," Wanda hedged. "First off, I think it is important to get from you a full observational report of conditions in Jakhabad when you were there, and your experiences." She glanced at the four young men and added, "That goes for all of you. Janna, what do you think of your father asking about that?"

"Depends. He wouldn't listen to me when I got home."

"He has had time to reconsider."

"Will you be here?" Janna asked Wanda.

"If you want me to be."

"Alright, I guess it will be okay. Will telling all that help you get help for Ali?"

"It might."

"Ok, when?"

"When I have got you looking like your proper self as Janna Dupont. So, half an hour?"

Janna nodded. Wanda glanced at the others.

"I'll call him when you give the word, Mam," Tim agreed, impressed by the ideas the woman had given him.

"It's Wanda! This is not the army."

Even though Janna knew the whole group was not present, she assumed they took shifts to monitor what they did. She had never come to where they had set up, so seeing the guys with their laptops set up, and the other odd bits of equipment, she just accepted it.

Wanda never even hinted that she was layering deceptions, although the Group probably thought she was being careful. They would bring Frank Dupont there, and when he left, the Group members would slip out the back way and return to their proper monitoring room with its more powerful equipment. Then, if anyone learnt of Dupont's meeting, and came to investigate, the passive security monitors would record them – and perhaps the FBI would catch some foreign illegals.

Janna envied how Wanda quickly made the subtle changes to her Janet look to bring it back to her once familiar visage. The light brown wig, already styled to match an old photo of her, finished the transformation. At first, Janet had wondered about her birthmark, but Wanda produced some very flexible 'plastiskin' to cover the area and make the mark almost invisible. She used more to cover the cobra tattoo on her wrist, and the two flower tattoos on her shoulders.

After taking a long, final look in the mirror, she told herself, "I am Janna Dupont."

The chime from the door at ground level came almost half an hour after Tim had called Dupont.

Tim challenged the caller, who they could see on CCTV. "Say who you are, man."

The officious introduction caused grins, and Tim to mutter, "Doesn't sound mellow," before releasing the door catch. "Up the stairs, man."

The heavy deliberate footsteps didn't auger well, either. Tim was ready to meet him, while Wanda and Janna were out of sight.

"Hi, Sir! I'm Tim. This is the Group."

"Are you lot a part of the State Department?" Dupont demanded.

"No, Sir. Not officially. We get a stipend, but we have our own reasons for doing this, and they make use of us."

"So what are your reasons?"

Gary spoke up from further into the room. "To piss off his nastiness, Prince Jabir of Jakhabad."

Dupont saw an unoccupied chair and moved to sit down. It gave him a moment to organise his thoughts.

"Who suggested you to do this monitoring? I am not sure it is legal," Dupont provoked.

"Oh, we have the required authorisation," Tim assured him. "As for your question, it was a group decision to help the friend of a friend."

"My daughter," Dupont stated. "Where is she?"

"All in good time, mate," Gary said, standing up to reveal his full 6' 8". "We were directed to give you info on what we are doing, and what we have found out. It's all on this." He held up a USB thumb drive, before tossing it over. He grinned when the visitor caught it easily.

Tim took over the conversation. "Yes, we are friends of Janna. We were all travelling together and ended up in Jakhabad."

Dupont's gaze intensified as he opened his mouth to voice a question.

Tim went on quickly. "Before you grill us about that, there are some points you need to hear. Firstly, we began this when Prince Ali Fazir came into the country, because he was followed by hitmen hired by his uncle Prince Jabir. He did not want his presence here to be known and we have been able, so far, to help him escape traps laid for him."

"And second?"

"His nastiness himself is here in secret."

"Yes, I was aware of that, but not completely sure of the reason why," Dupont admitted. "Thank you. Now, do you know where my..."

"I'm here!" Janna said, coming quietly up behind him. He rose and spun around, expecting to see the woman who had been in the hospital. He had sensed defiance in the announcement, but then they had quarrelled the last time they had spoken as father and daughter. He took in her appearance, she was leaner than she had been, but like...

"Well? No kiss and make up speech?" Janna provoked.

"Not unless you want it?" Dupont said tersely. "However, you and your friends have travelled overseas, and since then been keeping in touch with foreign events. I need to know what you know."

"I thought foreign affairs was more in the jurisdiction of the CIA or State Department," Janna commented.

"Not when murders happen that fall into my jurisdiction and have roots elsewhere." Dupont managed to control his tone, having the idea this Group were testing him.

Janna decided that she didn't want another argument, so she modified her tone. Tim went to fetch another chair, one instantly vacated by Andy, one of the four who had stayed silent so far. He gave no sign of seeing Wanda leaning by the now closed door.

"Ah, so that's it," Janna murmured.

"As if you didn't know." Dupont took a small device from his pocket, and pushed the on switch of a voice recorder.

Janna ignored that. "In case you are not aware, Special Agent Dupont, I did speak of this to the State Department. They didn't consider the matter of urgent importance, but agreed that the situation should be monitored. In recent days, their interest has intensified. I have heard that a coup has taken place in Jakhabad and all treaties with the US have been revoked. Any foreigners, still in the country, are likely to end up dead. That news, however, is at least two months out of date. I know that the King, and his daughter, my friend Famira, are under house arrest, and some kind of farcical trial is being arranged to vindicate the King's death. The only thing keeping the king away from the gallows, is that his son and heir fled the country. Prince Jabir, the leader of the coup, behind the general who is fronting for him, needs to neutralise Ali first, then by rights, he would be the next King after King Rakhal, as the only remaining male of the blood line."

"You were all better off out of that country," Dupont said in a modified tone.

"Are you saying I should be grateful for being deported?" Janna said, watching her father's expression.

"Did I say that?"

Janna shook her head, more in irritation than negation. "What else do you want to know?"

"Why was Nadia Shaston fornicating with a wanted terrorist and assassin?"

Janet felt the flush begin to suffuse her face, and turned towards Tim to hide the fact. In her true persona, she didn't have the answer, and she was not going to admit to her other identities, even if she was almost certain he already knew of them.

"I told you about her, Jan," Tim said, picking up on her intention. "She's dropped off the radar. I have a horrid feeling it's permanent."

Dupont countered that. "No, she was seen a week ago, at Dimitri's. Know it?"

"Yeah. They have great pizza's. Then what?" Tim asked.

"She ran off."

"Well, we've not heard anything from her since before that," Tim declared.

Dupont was getting the idea of how things were going. His daughter – as herself – would only tell him what she knew from information heard as Janna Dupont. So, if that was how it was going to be...

"Since all your activities should be in the report," Dupont patted the pocket where he had put the USB, "Give me a brief run down on what you know."

Tim obliged, concentrating on how they had managed to warn Prince Ali and his guards in time to escape the assassins, five times. He glossed over how many of the original number of guards had died. "We didn't know that Tozer had managed to capture the Prince and one of his guards until after it was done. We warned Shaz, and she went back. They got away."

"Tozer was murdered," Dupont pointed out.

"Eradicated," Gary muttered. "Bastard needed killing as a public service."

Tim was quick to say, "Shaz didn't do it. The Prince's guard was wrestling with Tozer, and Shaz was going to get the Prince away. There was one of Tozer's cronies there, Ackbar. Shaz said he took off when he heard the shot."

"Why didn't she leave too?" Dupont prodded.

"Mate, it would have been a flare lit tip off if she had," Tim told him. "She thought she could still help the Prince if she was thought to be anti-American. That was how she had worked to make herself useful to Tozer."

Dupont turned a snort into a cough. "Okay, tell me why you particularly care, and why you want to anger a powerful foreign national."

"Because he's a right bastard," Gary emphasised. "That country was peacefully prosperous before he started getting ideas. When we were told our visas were revoked, and we were sacked from the palace, we had already started hearing of people being taken for questioning, or accused of treason, or being a threat to the country."

"You may be missing important information," Dupont suggested.

Four heads shook in unison. In turn, they gave examples – even the so far silent Andy.

Tim finally summarised, "We probably don't know all the reasons, but many of those picked up were close friends of the King, had a lot of influence, or were extraordinarily wealthy."

"It seems the foreigners were evicted so no one would be able to reveal what was happening to people outside the country," Janna pointed out.

Glen, who had been listening as well as watching his computer screen, added, "We have been trying to figure out why his nastiness bothered, apart from being a power hungry bastard. We put our ideas on the USB. Some might be way out there, but the most reasonable relate to Jakhabad's geographic location. The country is in a strategic position for various scenarios."

"The one I like least," Gary took over the topic, "Is a rumour about him wanting some high tech stuff. We haven't any details of what. Whoever reported that conversation didn't understand all of it."

Still standing silently by the doorway, Wanda frowned. David hadn't mentioned that idea to her. She would have to ask Gary about it later.

"You asked us why we cared," Tim went back to the other part of the earlier question. "We made friends there! Prince Ali for one, but many others that lived outside the palace. Even the King was friendly towards us. What is happening is a nasty business, and we have a chance to make a difference."

Dupont really couldn't argue with that. It was much the same reasoning he'd had when he joined the FBI. He turned back to his daughter. "Do you know where Prince Ali Fazir is now?"

"No."

"He is still in danger," Dupont tried.

"Do you think I don't know that?" Janna insisted fiercely.

"Have any of you seen him since he has been in the States?"

The guys shook heads, but Janna stared for a moment. "Yes, briefly, because I was his sister's friend. I told him I couldn't help him. He was already fearful that people were after him."

"Was he the source of some of the information you have?"

Janna nodded.

"How did he find you?"

"His sister had my address, your address. Maybe he found where I had moved to. After he'd gone, I moved again."

Dupont had to admit to himself, she's smart, and quashed the rest – 'like her mother'. Somehow, she had found someone to help her do more. Found the best possible people.

"Why didn't you come to me?" Dupont asked her.

"Because you were a right jackass about things when she got home," Gary told him.

"You didn't trust her word, mate," Glen pointed out.

"And when she really needed an understanding parent," Tim went on, "she got the puritanical lecture from a jerk worried about his reputation."

It was Dupont's turn to flush. He accepted the rebuke, even though he'd had pressures on him at that time.

"I will accept that as a foreigner, you were a problem," Dupont began, trying to create a middle ground for discussing what he wanted to know. "That you were protected to a point by the royal family – unlike the others. So, what happened? How did you become so much of an anathema to the Royal family? Did you overhear things you shouldn't have?"

Janna looked away from him, seeming to glance at her hands, then somewhere behind him, then at her feet.

"We'll go out, Jan, if you want," Tim offered.

She looked at him. "No, you know a lot of it, you might as well hear the rest." Janna caught the calm gaze of Wanda Martin and seemed to gain strength.

"We were working our way around various exotic locations, and ended up in Jakhabad. Usually, Gabby, Moira and I hired out as washerwomen, animal tenders, whatever. Honest work, Father, never as whores."

Dupont flinched, he had accused her of that.

"The guys did other things, and one of them ended up meeting Prince Ali."

Tim inserted, "When we saw him first, from a distance, we thought him an arrogant prig. He was all dressed up and seeming like he expected adulation from every one. When we actually met him, we guys were all mingling with some of the local men. He didn't look like a prince then. He was pleasant, personable, told a few lewd jokes. The locals didn't seem to act any differently around him. He was just, well, fascinated by our American accents. The girls had already been given menial jobs at the palace, through Famira, by then."

"The guy told us that he thought all Americans had barbed tails, horns and lived in fires," Gary recalled.

"Next day, we were invited to work at the palace. The girls were already working as kitchen help, and we found out Famira had asked Jan to help her learn English. And Ali kept finding us to learn English from us," Tim said.

Janna found her fingers trying to pick at the plastiskin on her arm, and forced them into her pocket.

"We had been there for about two months, when the guys were told to leave, and that their visas had been revoked."

Tim broke in again. "We had started hearing some of the nasty rumours by then, of foreigners being blamed for people vanishing, and such. Someone was riling the locals up against foreigners. That was supposedly the reason our visas were revoked – to protect us."

"I was a different case," Janna explained. "I didn't get out of the palace, except with Famira, and naturally, I was dressed like her at those times. I only heard the rumours from the guys. I personally thought it was Prince Jabir being xenophobic. Anyway, I suggested to Famira that I should leave as well, but she begged me to stay. I don't think she had many friends, or anyone in the palace to confide in. When I said I didn't think it was a good idea, she told Ali, and he went to his father to speak about my staying. So I stayed, on after the guys left."

"We weren't real happy about that," Tim admitted. "But we thought that having the King's okay, Jan would be okay."

"I was, until the king went off to some kind of conclave with leaders from other Arabic states. That is when things began to happen," Janna revealed. "Things turned up missing – always just after I had been seen nearby. Little things at first, cheap trinkets from the servants' rooms, and then more expensive things from guests, or displays. Someone pointed out the coincidence of my being seen around, and my stuff was searched – and yes, the missing stuff was found. It was made to look like I was planning to run off with it.

The guards who found the stuff were taking me somewhere, I think they'd been given specific orders, but that time, the head servant saved me. He pointed out the holes in everyone's logic – like quite a few other servants had legitimate reasons to be in the same places too and I had never been near where one of the items had been taken from. Anyway, things got worse from there."

That was as much as she had previously told anyone. The rest was...too humiliating. Three years of putting it from her mind, had barely blunted the memory. She found it hard to go on, but this was the perfect time to tell all. Wanda was there, with her mind and memory for details. Her father was there, and he was quick to put ideas together. Some of the Group were there, ever supportive, and they might be able to add extra pieces to the retelling. And the little suggestion, she might have overheard something, had suddenly dragged her mind back to that awful time.

"I knew Prince Jabir was in residence, and he'd arrived just before the start of the conclave. I only saw him twice, and that at a distance. He may not have realised I was American right away. Once, I nearly walked into him, but I heard his voice, and ducked out of sight."

In fact, she had been sneaking off to see Ali at the time.

The events had begun about then, and Janna tried to keep the events in order, to show how they escalated. She found it easier to treat the memories as being those of someone else.

By the end of her recitation, Glen, Gary, Tim were furious and Andy, sheet white. Dupont was stunned, shocked, and angry. Wanda's expression was neutral, as if she had heard worse tales.

In every way possible, she was accused of wrong doing, and it always seemed that it was her own actions, not those caused by others. By the time her case was brought before the king for judgement, everyone, even the head servant, believed she was a thief, a deliberate vandal (defacing things as revenge for the accusations), a whore (over a dozen guards claimed to have been seduced by her), a user and seller of drugs, and a deliberate drinker of illicit alcohol.

The horrid part was, when they found her and a guard in a compromising position, she had only just woken to find herself there. Her protests were ignored, for testimony was received of other times when she had been challenged in places where she had no right to be, and where, later, things were missing, damaged or destroyed.

"It built up over a period of two weeks," Janna summarised. "Being found with the guard was the last straw. Jabir was called. He ordered me taken to where they held wrong doers – as I was – completely naked. I wasn't confined with others, but the cages for prisoners were only separated by bars, so I was ogled, had to endure lewd looks and indecent suggestions. If I went too close to the bars, the other prisoners, would try to grope me. One time, one of the guards came in and forced me against the bars, and let the men in the next cell...He was meant to be taking me to the City Justices. Ali and Famira had been forbidden to go near me, but Ali had ordered clothes for me.

"In the court, there were other charges – like I had been drunk and knocked over a lamp – usually a decorative piece, but this one had been kept ready for use in case of a power grid failure. They said it had caused a fire that may have endangered Ali and Famira."

Janna stopped, the anger and remembered humiliation returning. Then, somehow, a feeling of peace eased the memories away. A voice in her head said, 'It's over. It wasn't your fault. Finish the story, walk away from it stronger.'

Janna found the courage to continue. "The king returned. The whole sordid business was reported to him. He was given the official reports, the witness claims and testimony, the investigation logs. There was so much of it. Ali tried to tell him that it was all made up, but as they say, 'If you throw enough mud, some sticks.' In that light, I had just been taken in a mud slide."

"Surely you could speak out...?"Dupont blurted.

Janna looked directly at her father and explained, "The people of Jakhabad are considered to be progressive, but women are still subordinate to men. Women without a man – be it father, brother, son or some relative – are looked down on like they were spawned by the devil and cast out. Foreigners, by then, were considered the same. By that time, even the friends I had made amongst the servants wouldn't look at me. I had no one to speak for me, and no way to get or pay for someone. I was not allowed to speak for myself. The king had no choice, by the laws of the country, to pronounce me anything else but guilty. I hold no anger towards him – he was set up as well. The few times I had actually met him, while with Famira, he had complimented me on Famira's improved English, and wished me well. He had to pronounce the sentence on me, and he really made me feel that I had lost his respect. I didn't deserve the harsh words. The onlookers were calling for the traditional punishment, a beating or whipping, or stoning. They do that to adulterous women – "

"But not men," Tim interrupted.

"I didn't know all that until later. The guards escorting me to the plane explained in detail what I had avoided, because the king had been merciful and merely deported me."

From the doorway, Wanda decided to speak up – distracting Dupont from demanding to know why Janna had wanted to go back there. He spun around, and his expression as good as told Wanda, "I want to talk to you."

"Janna, can you go back in your memory to any time you saw Prince Jabir with people? You mentioned seeing that Quasim character. Did you overhear anything he and the Prince said?"

For a moment, Janna couldn't recall telling Wanda about Quasim, but she must have, in that first discussion. As she recalled that memory, she had the strangest feeling of a mind watching hers – watching the memory.

"Not when Jabir spoke to Quasim. I did ask who he was, and no one really wanted to say anything. One of the servants whispered to me, 'Keep away from that one, he is the Prince's something'. My Arabic was pretty basic back then. I asked Famira, saying what I thought the word was. All she could suggest was 'procurer' like he supplies unusual, rare or expensive things."

"Maybe technology?" Wanda suggested.

Janna froze, as if she'd been dunked in ice. Her mind went back to the time just before the troubles began. "Yes...maybe...though I am not sure. I mentioned I had ducked out of sight of Jabir, I was hearing him talking to someone – they were talking in Arabic, but I thought I heard him say 'skywatcher'."

That was all she could remember, and now she turned away from everyone, glad that Wanda was now quizzing the guys.

Dupont came and stood next to her.

"Don't touch me," Janna warned.

"Why don't you come home and we can talk about this?"

"No. There is nothing more to be said." If she went back to his place, he would keep her a virtual prisoner. She would have no freedom at all to try to keep helping Ali.

"What if they find you?"

"They are likely to do that a damn sight more easily if I am with you. You'd be a big bright flashing arrow."

She was thinking of John King, wanting to warn him against talking to the guy. However, as Janna, she didn't know the man, and couldn't.

"What happened to your arm?" Dupont asked, noticing that her fingers were worrying the area near her wrist.

"I hurt it at work. It's nothing. It's almost better and itching."

Frank Dupont didn't know what else to say to his daughter – she wasn't making it easy for him. His eyes went to her neck. Her birthmark was hardly visible. It stopped him in his mental tracks. The women calling herself Janet Delaney had a much darker mark. The coincidence, the placement...or had Wanda Martin helped create the mark on Janet Delaney and she was a decoy for his daughter?

"Why don't you take that USB back to your FBI buddies? The State Department already knows most of it. I'll be off."

Janna walked towards the other room, deaf to her father's quiet pleas to come back.

Thinking that the only way out from the other room was back through the one where the Group were working, Dupont gave the other door a final glance and went to listen to the conversation between the Group and Wanda Martin.

She stopped talking and told him, "Well. You have what you came for."

"What part are you playing in all this?" he demanded.

"Oversight. This has been a productive meeting."

"Can't you talk sense into my daughter?"

"Janna?" Wanda acted surprised. "I always talk sense to her. She is a very intelligent woman."

"Then why is she –" Dupont was about to blurt out that he knew she was playing three roles, then realised that the Group might not know that. It was sobering. His daughter might be being deliberately hostile – playing some dangerous game, but he didn't want to lose her or any possible chance of a reconciliation. What was the utter fool thinking?

As if Wanda read that thought, she said, "She's an adult. She doesn't need you to rule her life or tell her what is important. I'm finished here. Let me walk you to your car.”

Dupont fumed inwardly. “Did you encourage her with this damn foolishness?”

Wanda ignored that accusation. “I don’t suggest you try to come back here.”

He had been thinking of doing exactly that.

“And I would be very careful what you tell people.”

“Are you suggesting that I lie?”

“No, I am saying that Janna is not a part of this business.”

Wanda waited for the outburst that was about to erupt when her companion decided what aspect he could verbalise first.

“Could you drive me back downtown?”

The request distracted him. “Of course. How long are you staying?”

“Haven’t decided, but I need a secure phone to call David. I hoped you would let me use your office.”

“Right, that should be fine.”

Wanda decided, as Dupont drove away from the kerb, that whatever he came out with first would be a guide to what was most important to him.

“You know that she’s that Shaston woman, and the Delaney woman! Did you know she’s pregnant! She’s let that…terrorist… rape her over and over?”

“Perhaps she enjoyed it?” Wanda suggested, provokingly. “Or considered it worth enduring to help her friend.”

Dupont made a sound of disgust. “She’s already ruined her life. She will never be allowed a passport if she wants to go back there like she tried to. Whatever is it that she sees in that place? What can she and those young men think they can achieve by themselves? Why isn’t the State Department handling it? I can’t keep it secret that Delaney is also Shaston. That information will get out. I have to arrest her! There are a lot a charges pending against Shaston.”

“Frank! What you need to do is stop reacting. Stop thinking of Janna as your daughter. In other circumstances, what she does is her business. If she chooses to mate with Tozer’s ilk, it is no worse than when women were forced into marriages with men and had to endure rape and beatings.”

"But why? Couldn't someone else infiltrate that crowd? Why do it at all? I already have someone with them."

"Really?" Wanda pretended this was news to her. "How much intel does he bring you? Does he know where Prince Ali is? Do you know where Prince Jabir is? David has found no record of him entering the country legally. Why haven't you arrested him?"

"I didn't know Prince Ali was in the States until tonight."

"Tell me about your agent. How sure are you of his loyalty?"

"John? I've known him for several years. Met him about the time of that mess Janna was in because he was familiar with that country. He's an expert on terrorism, working with the Bureau. He got into that because of how his parents died."

"So, his speciality is not widely advertised?"

"No. And John is the American equivalent of his name. I learnt from him that Prince Jabir was in the country. John is the Prince's half-brother. Their mother was King Rakhal's father's second acknowledged consort. Then she fell out of favour and left the country to come here. She married an American. John was twelve when she died."

Wanda nodded to herself and then went back to the original topic. "I advise, that before you do anything rash, you sit down and think about all this – as an outsider."

"I am going to have to order the arrest of my own daughter."

"Frank, you aren't listening," Wanda stressed. "And I am not trying to tell you how to handle things. Forget Janna! She is a source, no more. Just keep on doing things as you would normally. What advantages might there be?"

Dupont subsided, and for a while he seemed to be concentrating on driving.

"If I pick up Janet Delaney, I can keep her in safe custody."

"And?"

"And no one will know she is Janna unless I say so."

"Which means, anyone looking for Janna is misled," Wanda finished the thought for him.

"I can see that point. I can protect her. But when all the rest comes out, she will have to go to jail."

"Frank, just do what you would, like I said, without mentioning Janna. Everything will work out for the best."

"Easy for you to say. Were you ever this contentions with your father?"

"Me? No, I was way, way worse."

Dupont gave a thoughtful grunt.

On arrival at the police building, Wanda followed Dupont to his office, or rather the outer office where up to eight other officers or agents could work, made her call, and then asked for directions to the ladies' room. She finished her business there, and returned quietly to the passage outside the borrowed office. At that late hour, not many people were around, so she slipped into Dupont's private office, and opened the connecting door, just enough to eavesdrop.

She had predicted that he would not heed her suggestion. He was on his phone, organising a raid on the building they had just returned from. She rolled her eyes, but then felt a shiver of disquiet. His team had better be prepared for trouble.

Her 'team' – Janna and the members of the Group – would be long gone. They had only been there for the meeting. It was not their usual operations centre. Janna was to go with them and change back to Janet Delaney.

She heard footsteps in the passage, and guessed where the person was headed. Wanda moved to the passage door and opened it enough to see the tall foreign looking man who had stopped outside the outer office door. He listened a moment, ear close to the wood, then tapped on the glass insert in the door. He obeyed Dupont's invitation to, "Come in."

Dupont had listened as Wanda had asked her husband to look into some vague references she had picked up on during the talk with the misguided group. He hadn't felt the need to go into his private office, for the larger area gave him more room to think. He had simply usurped the nearest desk and sat back. When he heard the knock, he'd had no hesitation calling for the visitor to come in. He wasn't surprised to see John King.

"What have you got?" Dupont asked in greeting.

As soon as Wanda left with Dupont, the Group were packing up their laptops and removing all signs of their presence. In the other room, Janna had already removed the borrowed wig, redone her make up to look like Janet Delaney and changed her clothes. Everything she had removed was stuffed in the backpack that had contained the change of clothes.

Tim was watching the street from the bigger room. He saw Dupont's car leave, and moments later a dark sedan pull up in its place.

"We've got company," he warned the others. "Jan? Come here. Do you know these guys?"

One glance was enough. "Shit! Yes. The guy just getting out is Quasim."

"Glen! Andy! Gary! We have to get out right now."

"I'll just double check we've got everything," Andy called. He was bending down, checking under the tables. Glen strode over and saw Andy was texting, and grabbed his phone.

"What are you doing? We don't have time."

"Nothing," Andy protested, grabbing his laptop. He quickly stood up and headed out.

Glen saw a piece of paper on the floor and grabbed it, shoving it into his pocket. He was racing down the second set of stairs that led out to the back. Their van had its engine running and the others were already in it. Tim slammed the door and Gary immediate sped off.

Andy fell into a seat when he saw Janet. "What? Where's Janna?"

"I'm the decoy," Janet said. "Janna's well away." Only Tim and Glen knew of Janet's three identities.

Tim spoke to Gary, "Check for followers."

Glen gave Tim Andy's phone. "The Group may have a problem."

Tim glanced from him to Andy, guessing the cause.

"Ask him what he was doing. I caught him texting when we had to hurry out."

Tim glanced at the number and the half completed message. The number was that of one of their target's contacts. His fist connected with Andy's cheek. "You little SOB. You are selling Janna out! You heard what they did to her before. They will kill her when they find her again."

Andy slumped further into the seat, nearly slipping off as he'd not put a seat belt on. "But she was already gone!"

"How did you know? Even I didn't know until I saw Janet in her place. In spite of everything, I thought she'd choose to go with her old man."

"You thought wrong," Janet told him. "You know how hung up she is on Ali. She can't help him if her father puts her in a cage."

"They only want Janna so they can lure Ali out," Andy babbled. "But he has all those guards."

"So you are willing to sell Ali out too, bro?" Tim demanded. "What had got into you? How much are they paying you?"

"Nothing, I swear, but they have my sister Felicity. She's only twelve."

That silenced Tim and Janet. Glen asked, "Why didn't you tell us?"

"I...couldn't. They said they would know if I did."

"How?" Tim demanded, wondering if another of their group was selling them out.

Andy couldn't answer. He didn't know.

"How long have they been controlling you," Janet asked.

"Since just after we last heard from Nadia."

"Hmm, that suggests they want her as well," Janet mused aloud, but she had expected that. They wouldn't want Nadia to talk.

"What else have you told them," Tim demanded.

"I said we each worked from our own place on this, but when they put the pressure on, I told them we were meeting up today and Janna would be there."

"Is there anything else we need to know? To be prepared for?"

"I think they have been looking for all of us who were in Jakhabad that time," Andy admitted. "They called me, out of the blue, and said they had Felicity..."

"Tim, you need to tell Wanda about this," Janet said.

Andy coughed. "There was one other thing. They found a way to reprogram the satellite link. I think that's why we stopped being able to pick up their calls anymore."

"More likely they sent a virus to one of our phones and it jumped to the computer," Tim suggested.

"I agree with Wanda, it's time that royal scumbag found an imperative reason to leave the country," Janet gave her opinion.

"How are we to do that?" Tim asked.

"I don't know yet, but I bet your Eastern bro has ideas, but first things first, you need to check your system for viruses or whatever, and reset the link to the satellite just in case."

Tim was already ringing Wanda's number, as Janet stared at Andy and thought things through. In her mind, Prince Jabir had sunk to new depths of depravity. Even if he didn't physically touch that poor little girl, the handling, the abduction, the incarceration, would emotionally scar her. Something had to be done, but was she the one to do it? She couldn't go to Jabir and announce herself, even as Nadia. Neither persona was meant to know about the girl and she was guarding a much more dangerous secret.

Another question was whether the Group's communications had been compromised?

"Tim, tell all the others to go offline."

Even though he was surprised, Tim quickly understood. His raised eyes glanced towards the back of the truck, and then at her again. Janet nodded faintly. Those of the group currently on duty, also needed to depart their real monitoring office.

"Why?" Andy ventured.

"If they found you, they might know of the place. We can set up again elsewhere, once the satellite is reset and the equipment cleared of malware. It would be easy for them to assume that we have been pulled off the job since losing contact with our targets. So, we'll spit up."

Janet went silent again. She was certain her mentors had an overarching plan. Even though Wanda had counselled making peace with her father, she hadn't condemned her for provoking him. Right now, her guess was that he would have her arrested on the spot, in whichever persona he found her, and lose the key to the dungeon. He would be feeling totally justified, but would he think of the fact that no one would expect him to arrest his own daughter? That her being in jail probably protected her better than he could?

She was in no rush to be found, for by now, they probably knew she was also Nadia Shaston. They would really hammer her to get an admission. She hoped she was ready for that – but what to do now?

Wanda felt her phone vibrate and moved from her listening position, back out into the passage.

"Yes?" she asked quietly. She listened, considered, and said, "Dupont sent a team to the warehouse. Let's hope they catch some of Jabir's agents. Hold Andy. Keep him with you. I will talk to him. Go somewhere neutral."

She ended that call and rang David, quickly filling him in, as she went up to the big office's door. She heard low voices from within, knocked and entered.

John King looked her up and down. He looked a lot older than he had in the picture David had found and sent to her.

"John, I don't think you have met State Department Agent Wanda Martin?"

Wanda smiled and accepted the hand he held out. "No, we haven't, though I have heard good things of you, Mr King."

"It's John, and it's mutual. What brings you here?"

"Rumours," she decided to say. "And I wanted to find out more." She had. Just gripping his hand. He was edgy and worried, and she wondered why. "Mind if I sit in?"

Dupont glowered for a moment, wondering if she was going to gag him, but then nodded.

"Not at all," he said. "Feel free to add any information that we have missed."

Wanda sat back as if ready to listen. John recapped for her benefit.

"I have informants close to Prince Jabir. I have known he was in the country for some time, and that he is trying to find Frank's daughter," John began.

"Janna, yes. Determined woman."

"I couldn't see a reason until Frank discovered that his nephew, Prince Ali, had also slipped into this country."

Wanda mused, "I wonder what made him think she would be of any use? I assume he thinks he can use her to find his nephew, though after what his country did to her... well, if it was me, I wouldn't want to have anything to do with any of them."

"Putting various hints together, I believe Jabir thinks that because Janna became friends with Ali's sister, she may have been sort of friends with Ali too, so if she were threatened, he would feel obliged to help her for his sister's sake."

"If that was so," Wanda argued, "why didn't Ali help her when she was in trouble in his country?"

John shrugged.

"Well, in my opinion, giving Jabir what he wants is out of the question. Do you know how many guards he has close around him?"

"My contact estimates twelve – mostly people from his country that slipped into this country. Tozer, the man who died, usually coordinated them."

"Okay, in your opinion, what would make him pack up and go home? Finding Ali? Killing him?"

John considered. "I think killing Ali is a very real possibility. Completely discrediting him would be another. He could use his coming here to find Janna that way."

"Frank mentioned that his country is under martial law, on his orders. Can he really afford to stay away? What if loyalist forces started a campaign to restore the previous order?"

"Yes, I think that would drive him back. The general is ambitious."

"Well, that's a thought," Wanda decided.

"The loyalist forces really don't have a hope of winning," King advised her.

"That depends on how motivated they are," Wanda suggested. "I was really thinking of ways to hack into is communications back home and make him think things. Does your contact know how he is getting info from Jakhabad? Does he have a sat phone?"

"I will ask to see if that can be discovered. But how will it help?"

"There are some pretty smart people around," Wanda said, not sure herself of the answer.

"We have been looking into Tozer's phone records," Dupont put in. "Most calls were to or from disposable phones. His was similar, but he didn't clear his call log and he had a phone book so he could call his allies. I will put more emphasis on checking the numbers."

They both waited for Wanda to say more, but she just waved them off. "Let me think for a bit."

"Have there been any sightings of the Shaston woman?" King asked. "I am sure she would know a lot."

"No. We found a place where she sometimes stayed. Someone left a very nasty message. One of Tozer's men, Ackbar, was found there – dead. It is possible that he thought the girl who owned the apartment was Janna. There was a second body there. One of the neighbours. She might have been killed because she saw something."

"I didn't hear anything about that in the media," King commented.

"We asked for a block on it," Dupont said.

"Tell me about the girl who owned the apartment," King asked.

"When I found her, she was in shock. I took her to hospital, had guards on her, but she slipped out when she'd been taken for some test."

"So, it wasn't your daughter?"

Dupont avoided the question. "Her name was Janet Delaney. There is a bulletin out about her. All I got from her was confirmation that Nadia stayed there on occasions."

King lifted a frame from Dupont's desk. "Is this Janna?"

"Yes, taken about five years ago."

"What was Delaney like?"

Dupont described her, but Wanda who was listening, noticed that he omitted a couple of distinguishing points. He reached for a folder and took out a copy of Delaney's driver's licence. King studied it and handed it back.

"You don't recognise her?" Dupont asked. "She does have a familial connection to the middle east."

"Might be why she let Shaston stay with her. Few would."

"Yes." Dupont seemed to be debating with himself. He glanced at Wanda who didn't seem to be paying him any attention. She had her hands steepled before her, as if deep in thought. He pushed a folder along his desk. "Preliminary reports from Delaney's place."

Wanda sensed the moment that King came to the fingerprint results. His whole body tensed. "Shaston and Delaney are one and the same?"

"I've told them to have their equipment checked. Seemed to me the unit was uploading an old file over and over."

"Most odd," King agreed. His mind was comparing his memory of Shaston and Delaney.

Dupont's phone rang. He answered, listened stony faced, thanked the caller and hung up. He looked at Wanda as he said, "After we left the warehouse, it seems that some of Prince Jabir's people went there. I sent a team there. We have captured four people. They are being brought here for questioning. However, there were no signs of anyone else being there."

"Who did you meet there?" King glanced from one to the other of the people in the office with him.

"I convinced Janna to talk to her father. To tell him what he refused to listen to a few years ago. I arranged the location. No one should have known about it."

"You saw your daughter?"

"Yes, and then she went off again, totally unrepentant. She has managed to totally screw up her life." Dupont snapped his mouth shut.

"So, do I take it that your daughter is in State Department custody?" King asked. "I was worried for her."

Wanda offered, "You can let your contact know that if you wish. I'd like for Prince Jabir to stop by. I've heard that, for a person of royal lineage, he has stooped to an all-time new low. Abducting a twelve year old girl, to force her brother to betray his friends."

King's face lost all colour.

Wanda went on, "And since he has arrested and imprisoned his own brother, and is trying to kill or discredit his nephew, it is obvious that kin ties inspire no loyalty in him."

Wanda stood, her intention fulfilled. King's inner wavering had hardened into loyalty to Dupont. She hoped it would hold.

"I'll be off. I'm staying at the Addison on Third, if you want me."

Dupont waved her out, feeling sure that was not where she would be, but that was not his business.

"I'm for home too. Do you want to drop by?"

"Not tonight, thanks. I still have a few people to catch up with."

Wanda went to where Tim had taken Andy. Janna, as Janet, was with the others in the secure building used by the group. Tim greeted her with relief. Andy, looking pasty white, pale and sweating, was pacing the room. He stopped when she came in and came over.

"Sit down!" Wanda told him. "Before you fall down, and then tell me everything the person who spoke to you said and did."

She listened to the verbal babbling, and inserted pointed questions to get additional details.

"Where was your sister when she went missing?"

"At the swimming pool."

"Where is it?" Wanda asked, then, "What places are nearby? How do you get to it?"

"What has this got to do with my problem? They want Janna and if they get her, we'll have Felicity back. My Mum is frantic. She keeps telling me to do as they say."

"I am sure she is, but I would rather get her back without sacrificing Janna. What were you trying to tell them when Glen stopped you?"

"That we were leaving. I didn't know that Janna had gone already."

"That was my doing," Wanda told him. "Okay, I'm going to get some people working on this. I want you to call whoever you spoke to. Don't let him rant at you. You had to end the call because someone came in. You are finally on your own now. Tell him Janna came in with some State Department person."

"How will that help?" Andy challenged.

"Because, that guy's boss has another agent that can confirm that statement. I will have someone tracing that call."

"Hell, Andy, you really should have told us," Tim insisted.

"You couldn't help. They hacked into the satellite so you couldn't get access and trace any calls."

"Try your laptop connection now, Tim," Wanda suggested.

Andy was intent, staring over Tim's shoulder.

"I'm in. How did you fix it?"

"Later! Get ready to trace Andy's call. And you, Andy, be forceful. Think – I have been doing what you wanted, but things went wrong. You haven't tried to do anything against them. Tell yourself to feel that conviction."

Wanda listened to the conversation – Andy had it on speaker, but the volume was low. His challenging attitude convinced the caller. Of his own volition, he added, "She wouldn't go with her old man. He's a real jerk. He was back then and still is now."

The man he called hung up first. "I didn't get to ask about Felicity," he said, turning to Wanda, but she had gone.

Janet Delaney finished work and headed for the nearest bus stop on the route to her destination. She wasn't heading for her apartment, as the police had not finished there yet. She was headed for the Addison Hotel. She was expecting trouble, because someone had rung her work and asked if she was in. Her boss had said it was the police, but as far as she was concerned, it was more likely one of Tozer's mates. However, the watchers she was sure were around, might be expecting to see Nadia, and not recognise her. Or they might know her by sight and want to know what she knew. They would be rougher than the police, or they might just watch her for a time before acting.

There was one place on her route where the rougher kind of people might jump out at her. At that time of day, later than her usual departure time, there were few people around.

Since talking to her father the previous day, she had expected him, or the police, to discover where Janet Delaney worked. Then, in her estimation, John King would hear of it and pass the word on to his other boss. She had thought it would take a few days.

In spite of her internal ruminations, the instant the hands grabbed her, she was fighting back. Three of them to one of her. It needed two to pin her against a brick wall, with her mouth covered to prevent her calling for help. She was in a narrow through way between two buildings and the only windows were small and of frosted glass.

"Is this the bitch? Don't look like Sam's broad to me."

Although the speaker didn't speak English, Janet understood what he said.

"We was told it was," another said.

The third said, "Look for the boss's mark."

One of her sleeves was pushed up. "Wrong arm, moron!"

The plastiskin was perfectly colour matched to her skin and not noticed. One edge was still hidden and another under her watchband.

Janet began to wriggle, and her mouth was freed for a moment. "What do you want?"

A knife appeared. "You'd better not scream, bitch. We want Shaz. Where is she?"

"I don't know! I figured one of her boyfriend's mates did something to her. I haven't seen her since I read about her boyfriend being dead."

"You been home?"

"Huh?"

"Left a message there for Shaz."

Janet struggled more, testing the strength of her captors. "You bastards killed a perfectly nice old lady."

"She got too nosey, see? And if you don't come quietly with us, you'll end up the same."

"Huh! You lot aren't the brains. You won't kill me because your puppet master wants answers that I don't know."

Janet glanced back at the road, saw a black and white car across the alley entrance. She glanced the other way, and saw two officers approaching purposefully. Her captors just shoved her harder against the wall. The shouted order, alerted the three to the police presence. One mouthed a foul curse, and all three forgot her and charged towards the road. She stayed leaning against the wall, trying not to laugh hysterically by itemising all the mistakes those three had made. Their boss, Jabir, had seen Nadia once, and knew Janna from three years before. She looked like neither, and that had confused these low down assailants. She had been about to exert herself to get free, but hadn't needed to betray her skill.

"Are you alright, Miss?" an officer asked.

"Yes, thank you. I think they thought I was someone else."

"Do you want to press charges?"

Seeing all three being hurried towards the police car gave her satisfaction. "Damn right I do! I think those guys know about two bodies found in my apartment."

"Excuse me?" the officer questioned.

"Sorry, assumed all you guys would know. I went home two days ago and..."

"Yes. Would you be Janet Delaney?"

"That's me."

"We've had instructions to look out for you."

"Oh, yeah. I suppose you would. I kind of left one of you holding nothing. I wanted to just forget everything I saw and I was scared as hell."

Janet did wonder what the police had been told, but had to admit this meeting was fortuitous. Having them help her, and pick up three more of Jabir's men was delightful. She could go to the police as a helpful witness, not arrested and handcuffed. She had no illusions that it would stay that way. Still, as Janet she didn't know much.

At the precinct house, an officer offered her coffee and she sipped that while giving her statement. She answered all their questions about the attack and what she understood of the assailants' comments, as if she had nothing to hide. They were taking their time having the statement typed up, waiting for the FBI to turn up, she guessed. Checking her prints from the cup, likely.

She had just finished reading the typed statement, and was about to sign it, when the two men in suits walked in. She recognised both. Jim Pearson, her father's long-time partner, and John King.

Janet signed the paper where indicated, and acted unaware. "So, I'm right to go?"

She turned, as if surprised when one of the suited men spoke.

"Miss Delaney, we would like you to come with us," Pearson told her, as he displayed his ID. He was always polite. King just loomed.

"What for?"

"The matter at your apartment," King stated, eyeing her as if for a specific reaction.

"Yes, right," Janet agreed. To the local police officer, she asked, "Can you send these gentlemen a copy of that statement and your officer's arrest report?"

"I will do that right away."

"What is important about that report?" King asked sharply.

"Some of Shaz's friends jumped out at me. They'd been told I was her. When I convinced them otherwise, they wanted to know where Shaz was. They told me they had left a message for her."

King's expression hardened, Pearson's eyes lit up.

"They will be in custody here?" he asked Janet.

"I expect so," Janet told him. "Will your business take long? I'm starving."

"Where are you staying now?" King asked.

"With a friend, until you guys finish with my apartment and I can get my things and move out."

King took the copy of her statement.

"At the Addison," she told King before he could read it there.

"Our car is out front," Pearson invited. He saw no need for handcuffs. He wasn't there to arrest the woman.

Janet fended off more questions, this time across town, back in the room in the building where her father was currently based. The session was being done by King and Pearson, but she was sure her father would be watching. However, she was sticking to her Janet persona, denying accusation based on what they thought Nadia had done, and any knowledge of Nadia's actions.

Her answer to the vital question of, "Why only her prints were at her apartment," was, "Well, I clean in there, so what? I don't know why you found no others."

King jumped in by asking, "Then how do you explain your fingerprints being in Sam Tozer's house?"

She let her face go blank for a moment, and said, slowly, "I can't." She kept eye contact with King as she answered, and that seemed to put him off.

Then he leant across the table and grabbed her wrists, which she'd had resting on the table, and deliberately examined them.

Then, while Janet tried to pull free, he moved around to where she was sitting. He released one hand and pulled up the short sleeve of her knitted top to reveal the flower tattoo there.

"Nadia Shaston has the same tattoos."

"I know! We got them at the same time. Let go! You're hurting me."

King didn't. He returned to examining her wrist, the one with the covered cobra tattoo. She resisted the urge to look there. He finally spotted the edge of the plastiskin. The texture and colour matched the surrounding skin, but he had seen the slightest difference when the real skin had paled. An involuntary 'ouch' escaped her when King ripped the plastiskin off.

"Perhaps you will explain where you got that!" he exclaimed triumphantly.

The actual truth was that she couldn't, so she kept her mouth closed, while King spoke for the recording, describing the mark and where it was.

Pearson's phone emitted a message ping. He checked his phone, and said formally, "Interview suspended at 8.17pm."

Janet didn't enjoy being charged with the murder of the blond man at the house where Kane had found her. They called her Nadia Shaston, aka Janet Delaney. She knew more charges would be added, and that protesting would be useless. So, all she said was, "I need a lawyer."

King, who with Pearson was escorting her to the remand prison, seemed to be enjoying her situation.

"What? Not going to use your one call to bring your State Department friends?"

She gave him one of her "Nadia" stares.

King went on, "Not that they could help you. Even they are not exempt from the law."

Janet knew the police still had to provide a better reason for Nadia to kill a man she'd never met than he looked like Kane. As far as she knew, the police had not spoken to Kane, or seen him.

When she was finally in a cell by herself, it was a relief. She should be safe from Jabir's men, for surely King would not dare do anything to her while she was in remand.

Her relief turned to depression. She hadn't seen her father at all. He had probably washed his hands of her – thrown her to the machinery of the law. And, in a cell, how would she know what was happening? If Ali was still safe? She hoped he would stay in hiding and not try to help her.

"Any trouble?" Dupont asked his partner.

"No. Just gave is glares. When John found that tattoo on her wrist, she just clammed up."

"I want to question her further," King stated.

"No," Dupont said immediately. "Let her stew. I doubt she can add anything to our knowledge base that you haven't got from your contact."

"What about Janna?" Pearson asked. "Is she somewhere safe?" He was reading subtle signs of stress in his partner's body language.

"Safe enough, I presume."

"What's irritating you, Frank?" John asked. "That State Department woman?"

Dupont sighed. "Only in part. I do prefer it when I am calling the shots."

"Has she come back at you for charging Shaston/Delaney?"

"Not yet," Frank said truthfully. "We have sufficient grounds to keep her in custody."

"Well, one good thing. Three more of Tozer's mates were caught. Delaney said they mentioned leaving a message at her place. So, what do you want us to do next?"

"I intend to talk to that woman again, later. I hope she will agree to testify against those three thugs."

"There are still more of them," John warned. "They will likely try to get at that woman."

"I will lay on extra security when she goes before the judge," Frank reassured them. "Before that, I am going to prepare a short press release – saying we have arrested Nadia Shaston, and imply the charges she will face, to see what that stirs up."

"Who are you after besides Prince Jabir?" John asked.

"His nephew. All this mess is because he came to this country – illegally. If he realises that Nadia, who has effectively saved his life a few times, is going to prison for murder, he might want to help."

"Even though she killed one of his guards?" John argued.

"Maybe...if he believes she didn't," Frank suggested. "I know how it looks. Another of his guards has reported that Nadia Shaston was there, covered in blood, knife in hand."

"Wasn't that where a bomb went off?" John asked.

"Yes. Kane dragged the woman out in time."

"Looks like someone was trying to kill all of them," Pearson suggested. "Stephens, who gave the report, wasn't happy about dumping the woman at Dimitri's. He said, though, that Kane/ Michaelson was convinced she was helping Ali."

"If she's State Department, she might well be," Dupont scowled.

"What's the latest on that mess in Delaney's apartment?"

"I'll follow that up," Pearson promised.

"And renew that call for Michaelson to be picked up."

Wanda waited with Tim and Andy in a room at the hotel where she had told Dupont she was staying. They were expecting a call from the man who had Andy's sister. On the table was equipment to try to trace the call if it came from a landline. Back at their operations centre, the rest of the Group were ready to pounce on a wireless call. Wanda knew that David was also monitoring calls to and from satellite phones. A SWAT team was on call, ready to move as soon as they had a location.

They were all tense, desperate to get Felicity to safety. Wanda expected action, knowing that Janet had been taken in, and three of Jabir's men arrested. On that subject, she had already left a carefully worded press release on Dupont's desk, and passed the information to the Group.

Tim's phone buzzed. "It's Dupont," he said before answering and giving his usual, "What's up, bro?"

As he listened, he scowled. Finally, he blurted, "She didn't do that." He handed the phone to Wanda, and listened to her side of the conversation.

"I hope you know what you are doing," he muttered when she had finished giving Dupont a hard time. "What makes you so sure Andy will get called?"

"To get confirmation. Dupont has just given a brief media conference saying they arrested Nadia Shaston. They must be confused as to whether she and Janet are the same person or not. They know you know Janet, so I think they will use their 'inside' man to find out what he knows."

Andy slumped further. They all continued to wait, and Wanda kept checking a five inch tablet. On the screen was a feed from a passive spycam set up in the room where she was supposedly staying. She had left things there that suggested that Janet was also staying there. Hints their targets had from Andy and King would bring someone there to check.

"Any time now," Wanda said quietly. "Send the signal to the others."

"What's happening?" Tim asked.

"Two uninvited types are checking out my room, and have found Janet's stuff. They are calling someone now...hmm, I don't think their report was well received."

A short while later, the man ended his call, spoke animatedly to his partner, then looked for a place to sit.

"Looks like they are planning to get comfortable. Good! Two less."

Even though he was told to expect a call, Andy visibly started when his phone pinged a message. He stared at it like it was a live scorpion, but after a glance at Wanda, recalled what he had been told to do. He waited, imagining himself sneaking off to a corner so he could talk without being overheard, and rang the number given in the text message. He listened and then spoke.

"Hey! I was right though! That's where she was. If her stuff is there, she must intend to go back there... Heck, how would I know? Perhaps Janna went out to a show or something."

"I can't ask her what she's doing. She usually only rings us! Look! I want to talk to my sister!" Andy's face betrayed annoyance. "Well tell her I am doing everything I can, okay?"

He held his breath then until he got an answer – it seemed a very long time. "Okay, I expect to hear her voice talking to me! Why then? Okay, okay, at five."

Wanda glanced at the time on her watch. It was only 3 pm. Andy voiced the question that had occurred to her.

"Why must we wait two hours?"

Wanda's facile mind could think of a number of reasons, but she only said, "The person you spoke to isn't with her. I think he had to contact the person giving orders."

She checked her equipment, it didn't surprise her that there had been no result. Calls from portable phones were harder to trace, but those callers had no conception of the other people she had working on the problem. She rang Glen, heard the Group's findings, and then rang David.

When she ended that call, she was smiling grimly.

"Well, we have located the area where that call came from. Not that far from here. We are now monitoring calls from that area, specifically from the phone just used, and from other numbers used previously. I am working on the idea that same person will arrange contact – not those who are minding your sister. Wait here. Text me if they get in contact earlier."

"Where will you be?" Andy asked, sounding as if he was on the verge of panicking.

"Doing something about my unexpected guests." Wanda drew out her phone, dialled a number and reported the intruders. Then, she left the room and went to a position where she could watch the door of her room. She left her tablet, still streaming the spy cam footage, with Tim and Andy.

It wasn't her intention to get noticed by overcoming the two men. The newly sworn in local SWAT unit, whose leader was an 'uncle' of her cousin – was ready to go in. They arrived within minutes, and efficiently removed two more of Jabir's help force.

Wanda slipped back to the other room.

"They won't be happy," Andy predicted. He was pacing the room.

"They can't blame you for that raid. It will be announced they were looking for a confederate of Nadia Shaston. Those two won't be allowed calls, and we might be able to make use of their phones."

Tim grinned, hearing that.

When the call came, Andy answered instantly. When he heard his sister's voice, he was quick to say his piece, and try to get her to answer some questions – innocuous ones, like was she okay? Had they hurt her? She was crying, and that made Andy edgier.

The voice was on speaker, so Tim and Wanda were listening as well. All heard, "She's fine still. You just keep on being useful."

The connection was cut. Wanda checked again with Glen and David, then quickly dialled another number.

To that person, she was asking questions about the background sounds.

"Well?" Tim asked when she ended the call.

"The call came from the same area as the first call, as it used the same relay tower. I think that guy is somewhere down near the river. I heard a ship horn, just as he cut off."

"I didn't hear that," Andy said. "And how would it help?"

Before she could answer, Wanda's phone rang. She grinned.

"Excellent. Thanks Dav. Send the file to my tablet."

She dialled out again, and quoted a string of numbers to the person on the other end.

Glen rang back, and Wanda put her phone on speaker. They heard a replay of the recent call, and had the three of them listening carefully to the background noises.

"There!" Andy shouted. "That harmonica music. There is a place about a block from the pool where some old guy plays. Flick and I like to stop and listen."

Tim added, "I heard what sounded like the fancy horn tones of the food truck guys."

Wanda used Tim's phone to call the information through to someone.

"Well?" Andy demanded.

"We have to wait," she said, as loathe as Andy was to do that. She wanted to go and get the girl, and do some damage to her guards.

Sometime later, Wanda had another call. She listened and asked, "Can someone pick me up?"

"What?" Andy demanded.

"I get a chance to do what I am good at...distracting. Wait here. I will stay in touch."

The police had blocked off an area, and started moving in and checking places where a prisoner might be held. They spoke to the old busker, and once they had managed to get the half deaf man to understand them, got lucky.

From him, they learnt the name of the food truck company that serviced the area, the timing of the trucks, and the names of the regular drivers. At the time the call was received, the truck was usually outside the local gym.

Wanda was asked to go in and look around. The likelihood of it being the place increased when she spotted two foreigners and recognized two faces from photos sent through by Interpol. She sneezed, and the signal went through the tiny microphone she wore. The next thing that happened was the eruption of the loud fire alarm klaxon. She spun around, as startled as any stranger would be.

"What's that?" she asked one of the foreigners.

"Fire," was the terse answer. The other added, "Get out. Likely only cook burning something." They began to walk towards the back of the building, Wanda scuttled past, "I don't smell smoke, but we'd best be sure."

They let her get well ahead, before continuing on. They did not see her duck into a store room, and watch were they went. When they went into the water pumping utility room, she spoke quietly, giving the location. She watched, mere minutes later, the deadly efficiency of the SWAT team, and emerged after two men were hustled away. The leader, Haroldsen, beckoned her in.

Wanda went to the girl who was lying unmoving on a narrow camp bed. She checked her eyes.

"Drugged," was her diagnosis. She checked heartbeat and pulse. "We'll need an ambulance. They have been keeping her quiet. From the needle tracks, I would say most of the time. Can I call her brother?"

Haroldsen nodded, and they both waited for the paramedics to come the short distance from the police boundary. He was watchfully on guard.

Wanda was keeping her hand on one of the girl's wrists, relieved that the pulse she felt - initially weak, was getting stronger. She kept up a whisper of talk. "You are safe now, Felicity. We will get you back to your family." She was also thinking the idea at the young girl, hoping her subconscious would hear.

Andy had arrived when his sister was brought out, and allowed to go to the hospital with her. A police officer was going to bring his mother to the hospital. Tim sidled up to Wanda.

"She was being drugged, but will be okay," Wanda told him first. "And we have two more of Jabir's men."

"He can't have too many left," Tim predicted.

"Let's hope."

"Think he will go home?"

"Not yet – he still thinks he's safe. We are closer to him though. Will you call your contact with the prince's guard crew, and mention about Nadia being caught and charged? Just in case they haven't heard the news release."

"Is Janna really in prison?"

"The remand centre. She'll be safe there and won't have to travel far when the three who jumped her face the judge. It should also help convince people she isn't Janna. And I don't want you mentioning Janna. Just say she went off from the warehouse."

"Do you think one of Ali's guards is a problem?"

"I don't think so. What I want is for Prince Ali to decide to allow himself official protection. Then we can help him."

Janna wondered who had come to talk to her. She had asked for a lawyer, but not even had a chance for a phone call. Seeing her father waiting in the small interview room, made her wary.

"Sit down!" he directed curtly, not greeting her by any name.

She noted that her guard escort had left and closed the door. That didn't mean their conversation would be private though.

"You wanted charges laid against the three men who attacked you," Dupont got to the point.

"Yes." Janna kept her tone impersonal.

"Why turn on your friends?"

"They were never my friends."

Dupont stared at his daughter, but she wasn't giving him any help.

"Very well, Miss Delaney, we have proof that you are also the person who was the whore to Sam Tozer. Why did you turn on the friends of your..."

"Don't say it!" Janet hissed, very quietly.

"...friend, Tozer?" Dupont felt petty, having seen the flush on the face of the woman in front of him. "Well?"

"They were not my friends. They mistook me for someone else and wanted information that I didn't have."

"And what was that?"

"Shaz. Someone said that was me. They thought they had a foolproof ID too."

This time, Dupont flushed. He said nothing for a long moment, until the urge to shout at the woman eased.

"Anyway, Agent Dupont, if you are here to question me, shouldn't you have arranged the lawyer I requested?"

Dupont tapped the table with the fingers of his right hand, as he wondered if he should have sent someone else. His mind said, 'No'. He tried a different tack.

"So, we have established that Tozer's friends mean nothing to you."

"Tozer's friends cared nothing for Shaz. And if those three are examples – they deserve what they get for being stupid."

"Then you will have no trouble coming to identify them as your assailants."

"None at all," Janet agreed. That was said loud enough for any listeners, but she added in a low voice, "By the names they called themselves." She didn't specify where, but saw her father's suddenly intent look.

He suggested, "They must have been watching you, from when you left work. Did you see any others like them? Any loiterers?"

"Well, I can't say really. No one I noticed looked about to attack me," she dropped her voice. "Maybe if you have pictures?"

Dupont spoke more quietly, "Maybe."

"If I identify any others, what's in it for me?"

"You will be kept safe until your court appearance."

Janet scowled at him.

In a low voice still, Dupont suggested, "You could of course come completely clean and help me find the full truth."

"No."

"And that dishonourable foreigner that hides behind a woman, and lets her dishonour herself. He will never acknowledge you."

"You are a rotten beast!" Janet hissed.

"And you are a bloody little fool."

Dupont stood up as the door to the room opened. King stepped in. The two men only exchanged glances, before Dupont stalked out and King sat where he had been.

"I'm not talking to you without a lawyer," Janet told him, loudly.

"Oh, I'm not here to ask questions," King said easily. "I just think you need some things to consider."

"Like what? How I have been set up by your buddies?"

Janet saw the rapid reaction. Anyone listening would assume she meant the FBI. She and he knew otherwise.

"Like the reaction if you identify a number of men now in custody."

Janet stared at him. "I wish you and your mate would get your stories straight. He wants me to, and you are suggesting I shouldn't?"

"Not at all," King said smoothly. "I just asked if you had thought about it."

In a low voice, Janet asked, "What if I tell everyone that you are best mates with a terrorist? Have you thought of that?"

In an equally low voice, he told her, "They know."

"Then why don't you consider it?" Janet wondered if he would get the implication that he should rat on Prince Jabir.

He did. "He's well protected." King's voice only carried to her.

"That's not what I heard."

"And what have you heard?"

"I reckon I know where the three murdering imbeciles came from."

"Yes?" King was wondering how he could get the woman on his side.

"Very well," King said in a normal voice, "Do you know what

your new tattoo is about?”

“Why don’t you tell me?”

“It means that anyone in the Cobra Sect that sees it, can do anything they like to you. Rape you, torture you, beat you.”

“But not kill me?” Janet sensed that distinction.

“I would not rule that out,” King warned.

“Okay, you’ve told me. Can I go now?”

“Not yet.”

“What then?”

“Listen! There is a person that now believes you were spying on Tozer and helped his quarry escape.”

“He has the wrong person. I have never set foot in the Ghetto.”

“Semantics will not help you. The person is very angry that you were brazen enough to get three of his agents charged with assault. He was not surprised that you didn’t get blown up. Now he is gloating because you are charged with murder, because it means that you will not be able to change your face and escape anytime soon. He has a very long memory.”

“So, has he rewarded you for proving Shaz took on a new identity?” Janet had a sour taste in her mouth.

“He heard about the woman who had the same fingerprints as Shaz. He does not want you helping his other quarry.”

“Other quarry? He’s had more than one?”

Janet felt herself go cold. Not that the news was really a surprise.

“Yes. Someone he believes you met in the Middle East some years ago. Who was deported from over there because of grave social, moral and ethical crimes.”

When Janet couldn’t answer, King went on, “He knows that Nadia Shaston died, and State Department agents collected the other woman. He believes they, or the woman kept the ID for their own use.”

Janet’s mind was racing, “He hasn’t made the connection yet. He hasn’t figured out that Janna is the woman Jabir truly wanted.”

“So, as things stand now, even your State Department controllers can’t get you off the murder charge, and he knows where to find you and silence you. Do you know where Janna Dupont is?”

“Safe! Obviously the FBI don’t trust you that much.”

“No matter,” King said, brushing her remark aside. He knew

better. "What matters is what you will do. Keep what else you know to yourself or tell us everything your handlers told you to do? Before you have no choice, no time, to get even. Think on it!"

At that, King stood, gestured for the guards to return, and watched a more subdued woman led back to her secure cell.

He went back into the observation room, not surprised to see both Dupont and Pearson there, but they both looked pale. "What's up?"

"Just the way you spoke to her," Pearson admitted.

"Is that an accurate summation of the woman's situation from Prince Jabir's point of view?" Dupont asked.

King nodded.

"It sounds like he now wants that woman as much as he wants his niece's English tutor – the woman who was deported," Jim summarised.

"I would say that was an accurate deduction," King agreed. "I hope that woman in there decides to tell you everything she knows. Do you think her State Department controllers know more?"

"Good question," Dupont remarked. "Though she obviously had no intention of telling you any more than she told me. She did agree to identify the three that assaulted her. How will that go down?"

"More marks against her," King said. "Can the State Department do anything for her? Do they know where Ali is, or that English tutor? Jabir believes his nephew was interested in her."

"I don't think the State Department knows where Prince Ali is, and he hasn't responded to the carefully worded press release I was given to send out. If I am right, and Shaston did help him escape, I would have thought he would be concerned because she is in so much trouble."

"Maybe his guards see the danger in that and are keeping him under wraps," Pearson suggested.

"If Jabir's people keep finding him, maybe they should come to the authorities to get help. Do we even know how they keep finding him?"

"Not yet, but we now have a good idea of how he is warned," Dupont shared. "Any idea of how many people Jabir still has to use? We've taken 11 now."

"When I last saw him, he was as arrogant as ever and as I said, angry. He thought it would be easy to find his nephew, and the woman he deported. He expected them to be together. He would have been able to have Ali disinherited, if he could prove that Ali came here to fornicate with a convicted adulteress and criminal. If he joined with a woman, so disgraced by the laws of that country, no one would follow him."

"Maybe Ali is too smart for him and that is why he is not coming forward," Jim counter-suggested.

"He is a fool then. I don't think Ali has many guards left. Jabir says he has taken out five or six of them now. The latest one was using Shaston."

Dupont didn't like that aspect of the case. "If she was truly on Prince Ali's side, and helping him, she might pretend to hate Michaelson, who she knew as Kane, but why would she kill a man she didn't know?"

John merely looked back at him for a long moment. "She won't talk to me for obvious reasons, and that is probably true for you too. Would she talk to that Martin woman from the State Department?"

"Perhaps she has already," Pearson suggested. "She didn't seem too worried by your warning."

"Maybe I can find out something from that maverick State Department agent," Dupont proposed, as he stood up. "Except that she has not been in touch for a while."

"Protecting your daughter, I hope," King proposed.

"She'd better be," Dupont growled. "Anyway, I have been advised that the three men who assaulted Shaston/Delaney will be fronting court tomorrow morning. Her own case is scheduled for later in the day. I have asked for extra security."

Chapter 17 – The Exile

The suburban rental property looked no fancier than its neighbours. Two men came and went from the house at all hours but were polite and made no trouble. The neighbours' interest waned when they admitted to being security consultants, on call to the local police precinct. Even the nosiest of them never saw the other three people who occupied the house.

Prince Ali Fazir resented the need for the 24 hour a day protection, but he also knew that if he was found by his uncle's people, he would be killed. Too many times, he and his guards had narrowly escaped Jabir's assassin – Hashim. Since coming to America, his team of eight guards had been reduced to four. In four months, he had moved locations a dozen times. This latest move, had been after the closest call yet.

He was beginning to think he should have remained in his country, even though his father had advocated leaving and seeking allies. Even now, he did not know what his father meant. All he could think of was to find the one person from outside his country that he trusted.

It had been harrowing and dangerous travelling from the palace to the border, but the troops still loyal to his father had distracted the General's men, even fought them, to ensure his safety. They had already created a line of communication, and once past the border, he was met by a group of eight ex-marine mercenaries, led by a man calling himself Kane.

One of the others, an IT expert, had traced the friends of his friend, Janna. Those Americans, that he had got to know well, had proved their loyalty to him. On reaching America, they had found Janna and brought her to him. Even now, that reunion was the most pleasant memory he had since leaving Jakhabad.

She hadn't stayed with him, as he had wanted. Here, on her home ground, she was stubborn. She insisted she couldn't help him, shouldn't be with him. Deep down, he knew she was right, but it made him feel like a coward. But he was sure, that the woman who had helped him and Kane escape from Hashim, had been her.

The American television news channels were his only direct way to learn what was going on. The other channels, once so fascinating, had lost all interest for him.

He heard one of the cell phones ringing – Kane's. Each had a distinctly different ringtone. He strained his ears to try to hear the conversation. The wireless phones continued to fascinate him. There was so much technology in America that would benefit his country.

Kane strode in. "That was Giovanni. He heard your uncle's federal spy talking to someone. He was saying that the FBI have Hashim's girlfriend in custody, charged with Adam's murder. He also heard that the tutor of your sister was in a State Department safe house."

"Did he say where?" Ali asked, considering.

"If he did, Giovanni didn't hear it, your Highness."

"Didn't you say that Hashim's girlfriend helped you get me away?"

"No doubt it was for her own reasons," Kane said, dismissively. "From what I have heard, we are well rid of her too."

"No! If she helped us, she is not our enemy. I want you to go see her, offer to be her lawyer."

Kane seemed to be silently counting to ten. "I am not a lawyer," he pointed out calmly.

"Just say you are. I want you to ask her a few questions."

"If you think she knows where your friend Janna is, I should remind you that Janna said she should keep away from you."

"It is not that," Ali said quickly, but Kane had more to say.

"And, your Highness, the more we go in and out, the more chance there is of being seen. We do not know how we were found before, and we have not got the next place organised yet."

"I am aware of that, Kane. But I think the woman in prison, is Janna."

Kane stared at the Prince, while his mind compared the image of Nadia Shaston with the one he had seen of Janna. He began to shake his head, thinking, 'Shaston was a whore!'

"The FBI and the police might be trying to draw out my uncle," Ali said patiently.

"They will want to draw you out too," Kane retorted.

"I need to know if that woman is Janna – the one in prison," Ali persisted. "Have you ever asked your contact where he got his information? How that woman arrived so fortuitously?"

"I can't tell you what to think, your Highness, but the woman in prison, is the same woman we found covered in Adam's blood, with the murder weapon in her hand."

"Do you think that woman also knew explosives?" Ali challenged. "You said she hadn't been alone."

"We found no one else!"

"Whoever else was there, used her to get away, and wanted to kill her too. They probably followed you away."

"We didn't see anyone following us," Kane stated positively. "And have you forgotten, Tozer's woman is a whore?"

Ali ignored that. "If you won't go, Kane, I will go myself." Ali stared at Kane until his chief guard capitulated.

"Okay, but the police are probably looking for me in relation to Tozer's death."

"There has been no mention of our being there," Ali told him.

"They don't always tell the public everything."

The recent narrow escape was still fresh in his mind. Therefore, before he went anywhere, he used his phone to call his unmet informants.

"Same, bro," he answered the usual greeting. Then he went on, "I heard the police have Tozer's whore in custody."

He listened to the reply and became confused. "Then if Shaston is either dead, or fled, who do they have?"

He listened again. "A State Department agent? What does she look like? So what's their game?"

Hearing his contact admitting the FBI wanted Ali to come to them, confirmed his theory. Then he heard they wanted Jabir to come after the agent – like the prince had suggested. "That agent had guts," Kane had to admit. "Was she Shaston's back up?"

When he ended the call, Kane was thoughtful. Maybe Shaston was more than just a whore that let Tozer shag her whenever he wanted. Maybe he should go see this Janet Delaney and hope she'd answer Ali's questions.

Dupont was advised when a man claiming to be a lawyer arrived to speak to Janet Delaney. He switched his computer to see the feed from the security camera at the remand centre.

"That's Michaelson," he confirmed, speaking to his partner. "The hair is lighter and longer, but that's all. Will you head over and invite him back here for a talk?"

Pearson nodded and departed.

Janet inwardly sighed as she was taken from the cell once more. After her father and his expert had taken a turn, she'd been questioned by the crime scene experts, an altogether harrowing experience. They'd been some agency that dealt with crimes against military or ex-military people. She hadn't expected that. She had no idea who wanted her now.

She was not expecting to see Kane, even though she had been told a lawyer had come to see her. She'd had some young man representing her when the forensic team had been there.

After her escort left the room, she waited for Kane to speak. After all, in her current persona, they had not met.

"Why did you help me the first time we met?" Kane started without preamble.

Janet shook her head, considering how to answer. Finally she said, "I wasn't helping you."

"My friend, then?" He saw the woman nod slightly.

"My foolish young friend asks if you know who Achmir Fazir is."

"His great grandfather. There is a picture of him in the passage outside his sister's suite in the royal palace."

Kane understood immediately that this woman who he had met as Nadia Shaston, now as Janet Delaney, was also Prince Ali's friend. "Why is your father saying nothing of who you are?" That question was not one Ali had thought to have him ask.

"He is probably still angry with me," Janet shrugged.

"You are probably safer here," Kane suggested.

"You shouldn't be that naïve! What else did your friend want to know?"

"What he can do to help you."

"Nothing. Like I told him when we met the after he arrived here."

"When was that?"

"Four months ago. You ought to know that."

"No, I joined up with him later, after a few of his original guards had been killed. I took over the name Kane. He said you were his sister's tutor for a time."

"So? If you matched that with the FBI guy in charge, you know that."

"Your father is making it seem like they have that girl being held somewhere else."

Janet stopped trying to needle Kane. "I would still trust my father with my life, to do the right thing. I know he hasn't opted to recognise me in his official capacity. He thinks I was co-opted into the State Department. However, while Ali is still in the US, all I can do is give his uncle multiple targets to chase."

"I guess that is what your father is doing," Kane agreed.

"Maybe, but the fact is, I don't dare tell him too much. My father has an expert on terrorism. His name is John King. He trusts him – I don't. I know he is chummy with Ali's uncle. I don't think my father has mentioned to him that I am his daughter, and I don't look like my normal self. I don't even think my father's long time partner has recognised me. Which is how I managed to fool Ali's uncle."

"That is all very well, but when I get back, Ali is still going to want to see you."

"Did he say that?"

"Not directly, but he wants to help you."

"Well, tell him he's a damned fool to have sent you here, and that we can help each other best by staying apart."

Kane tended to agree. "Why did he seek you out in the first place?"

"I was American, his sister's friend."

"There were other Americans that were with you."

"Yeah. They are helping too – working with the State Department. You probably speak to them."

That detail had not been mentioned to him. "But you - a woman –

what did he expect of you? Not what you have been doing, surely?"

Janet shrugged. "Ali, when I first met him, was a sweet, naïve young man. His people did not allow him to become interested in a foreign woman. Did he ever tell you how I left his country?"

Kane shook his head.

"What about your mates? Did they?"

"No."

"Well, to be brief, even here, if Ali were to be seen with me, and I was recognised, it would be enough to have him discredited as his father's heir. Then, since he has no acknowledged son, his uncle would be king if something happened to his father."

Janet looked down at the table, having just felt a solid jab from within her belly. Her baby had chosen that moment to make his or her presence felt. It was like an omen. She needed to let Ali know about...him. It had to be a boy!

Kane was talking again, but Janet wasn't listening until she heard, "...home soon."

"What?"

Kane repeated, "I think Ali is considering going home soon."

"Why now?"

"We have had word that the forces loyal to his father are preparing to head towards the capital to release him."

Even though it was the last thing she really wanted, she said, "He should. The loyal forces would have more reason to succeed. And if his uncle is still here, looking for him, they will have an advantage."

"He will want to know you are alright."

"I will be. I am not in this alone. I have two very clever State Department agents on my side."

"Okay."

"And tell him, that I know I can never be anything more than just a friend, and I wish him a long and happy life. I still have the gift he gave me when he first arrived, and that is enough."

"Let's hope he listens to reason, then," Kane said, standing up to leave.

"You'd better get back to him. His life is a hundred times more important than mine."

Kane gestured to be let out, while his mind was full of conflicting thoughts, foremost was of how women could make fools of men. Ali's friend, was no starry eyed wench. She knew the facts and accepted them. Even so, she had put herself in danger, and succeeded in making a fool of Tozer. Did the prince even realise what she'd been doing with him?

The man waiting outside in the passage broke into those thoughts. "Mr Kane? Special Agent Dupont would like a word with you," Jim Pearson told him.

The request was not particularly welcome, and he considered refusing it. If they had found trace evidence at Tozer's place, they might want to question him, or arrest him. If he didn't agree, they would be suspicious. He agreed, shelving his reservations. Janet Delaney, who he knew now to be Janna Dupont, trusted her father to do the right thing.

When led into Dupont's office, Kane took the initiative. "Good afternoon, Special Agent Dupont. I understand you wanted to speak to me." He reached out his hand and shook hands firmly.

"Kane, is it?" Dupont asked, gesturing him to a chair and then seating himself. He gave his partner a glance, and Kane was aware of his escort leaving. He added, "I don't want to be disturbed." He waited for the door to be fully closed before continuing.

"Firstly, Kane. I know your real name is Michaelson and you are currently a close contact of Prince Ali Fazir."

Kane gave no reaction, although his mind went into high gear.

"I also know you are a person of interest in a murder investigation. However, from various sources, I have come to understand that you were hired to protect the prince while he was on US soil. Is that correct?"

"Yes," Kane admitted cautiously.

"Well, then. I would like you to pass on a message for him. That if he chooses to come out of hiding, I will personally guarantee his safety."

"I will give him your message, but so far, he has not expressed a wish for official protection. However, if you don't mind my asking, why would you do as you have offered?"

Dupont was blunt. "Because I am tired of the fallout from the feud between him and his uncle. Now don't get me wrong, Kane. I am letting you go only because you can take that message. However, as I have hinted, I know you were in the house where Tozer was killed, and I intend to charge both you, and Nadia Shaston with his murder."

Kane rose from his chair, tempted to blurt out some unflattering remarks, but held his tongue and restrained his anger. "If that is all, I will be going."

"That is all. Here, take one of my cards."

Kane accepted it, and stalked out. He recognised that Dupont's threat was not an idle one. He knew how Ali would react. He would want to protest and that was likely one part of the reason Dupont had told of his intention. Another was the opportunity to follow him back to where Ali was staying. As far as that went, they could try. He had to consider the warning Ali's friend had given him, about the FBI man's terrorism expert. Would Jabir get to hear where Ali was, if he came out of hiding?"

Dupont, with his message passed on, watched Kane leave. He would be followed. His threat to have the man charged with murder was credible, but they didn't have enough evidence. He would have liked to question the man, to find out the truth. As for Nadia Shaston, and the threat to charge her with a second murder, that would never hold. He hoped it would scare his daughter into sense.

He doubted it though. She seemed hell bent on doing what she had set her mind to. Protecting that particular foreigner, even when she knew she could never be anything to him.

His phone rang, distracting him. The news was excellent. Four more Cobra Sect members were in custody, arrested at the safe house where his daughter had allegedly been. Two more had escaped, but the bait had identified them from photographs, as well as having taken down two of the captured ones by herself.

As much as Wanda Martin aggravated him, he had to admit she was extremely capable. He would question the four new captives, but they, like all the others, probably wouldn't talk. If they were also wanted by Interpol, they would be facing other charges elsewhere.

His daughter, wouldn't be safe until Prince Jabir was neutralised. Maybe his leaving the country would be enough, being captured would be better, but the man would claim diplomatic immunity. Still, he must be getting low in people he could trust after this latest failed attempt to get his daughter.

He wondered if Prince Ali would accept his offer. That young man was another he would like to see the back of. Him and whatever influence he had over his daughter. Maybe he should try to speak to her again.

Pearson came in with the report that their men had lost Kane's trail.

Dupont forced an ironic smile. "While I hoped otherwise, I am not surprised. I just hope our message gets a response."

"I heard that something happened at the house. Is Janna okay?"

"She's fine," Dupont assured his partner. "Mrs Martin disabled two of the men who got in. Can you see to it that the reports on that are complete and added to the rest? We identified all of them, plus the two that got away. They are all wanted by Interpol."

"Where is Janna now? Still at the house?"

"No. She was never there. Obviously the little fool has fooled you too."

"How's that?" Pearson was startled.

"You didn't find Janet Delaney somewhat familiar?"

Pearson's mouth widened in a soundless, "Oh!"

Aloud, he said, "No, I didn't. That means she is also..."

Dupont nodded, cutting off what he was about to say. Pearson collapsed into the spare chair.

"Why didn't you say something sooner?"

"Would it have changed anything?" Dupont countered. "She hasn't asked for my help, and she is deep in some State Department plan. She probably doesn't trust me."

"She spoke to you last week," Pearson reminded his partner.

"And went off right after. I didn't handle things very well. I have been asking myself why she is doing it. She can't possibly think he will acknowledge her, but that is no reason to ruin her life."

John King knew, the instant he arrived, that his half-brother was furiously angry. He would have heard of the capture of four more of his sect members, and would likely take the brunt of his anger out on his information source. King prepared himself to face it.

"Where is she? You told me she was at that house." Jabir's face was flushed, eyes glittering dangerously.

"That is what I was told. What happened?"

"It was a trap! The woman who was there was not the little whore my nephew is lusting after."

"What was the woman like?" King asked, as if he had nothing to fear of Jabir's rage, but inside, he was trembling.

One of the three other men present gave a terse description.

"That is the woman from the State Department. They must have stepped in. They have been putting pressure on Dupont."

"Do you know what I think, you craven piece of dung," Jabir hissed. "I don't think they trust you. Either that or you are a traitor. Do you know what I do to traitors?"

As soon as he felt both arms grabbed, King knew he was about to find out. His half-brother was not one to inflict such punishments himself, but he enjoyed watching and at a nod, Quasim began with a powerful punch to his stomach, another to his chest that forced the air from his lungs. The third powerful punch was to his groin, and he wanted to double up, but couldn't. He gritted his teeth.

"Now, what lies have you to tell me this time?"

The urgent need for breath was painful, and each new breathe equally so.

"I haven't lied," he managed to force out. That was the truth – it was just he hadn't told all he knew.

"Where will they take my agents?" Jabir demanded.

"The others are at the remand centre. Interpol wants them." King had to take another painful breath. "I expect the others will go there too."

"Will they have to appear in court?"

"I don't know, but I expect so."

"Those three simpletons, when will they be in court?"

"Day after tomorrow. The woman is supposed to testify then."

The look of pure malice on Jabir's face, make the hair on King's neck prickle. He came and put his face close. "You will ring your weak and ineffective agent friend and ask him when the ones he tricked today will be in court. Tell him you intend to be there to see if you can identify them, and tell him you will be there when the three simpletons appear too."

Having little choice, King did so as soon as his arms were released. His whole body wanted to collapse, but he forced himself to stay erect. His fingers though, shook as he pressed the buttons to bring up Frank Dupont's number. He wondered how he could put a warning in his words.

"Hello Frank. Oh, Jim. Where's Frank? Well, let him know I rang. Can you tell me when those four you caught today will be in court? I intend to be there to see if I can ID them, but I have a few things to do in the meantime. Is Shaston meant to be testifying at the same time as I heard? Good. I will be around for that too. Text me the other time, would you? Thanks."

Although he had tried to talk normally, breathing was still painful and his voice may have been uneven, He hoped Pearson would pick up on it.

Before he could pocket his phone, it was snatched from his hand.

"Lock him up," Jabir ordered. Once again, King felt his arms gripped tightly, but this time he was shoved roughly across the room and shoved into what he realised was a walk-in robe for the opulent suite. Inside was absolutely dark.

When he finally reached home, near midnight, Frank Dupont heard his home phone ringing as he unlocked his door. He let it ring out whilst he did his usual check of his security recorder. The outside rear sensors had been tripped, even though all the interior ones were green. The film, when played through, didn't show any figures moving around, but a drone had been caught in several frames. Someone was checking his house. It might be a prank, but he doubted it. He had to assume it was related to the case he was on.

He went to check his phone. The caller had not left a message, but he recognised the number. He pressed to dial the number shown.

"Hello, Jim. What is it?"

He listened to Jim passing on John King's message. Then he heard, "He sounded odd, like he was trying to speak normally, but speaking hurt."

"Did you try calling him back?"

"Yes. It just rang out. The next time, I got the device is switched off message. He wanted me to text the time when the four from today would be in court, I haven't yet."

"Don't. What you have said, doesn't sound good. Can we get a location from the last call?"

"I'll get someone on it," Pearson promised. "There was one other odd call. Person gave no name but left a number. Do you have a pen?"

"Go ahead..."

Kane drove around until he lost the police followers, then went to a supermarket to buy more groceries. When he reached the rental house, and went inside, he heard voices that he didn't recognise. One was a woman's voice. Immediately, his whole body went on alert. His neck hairs prickled him, and a surge of adrenaline had him reaching for the knife in his trouser sheath.

Ali's voice did not sound alarmed. On the contrary, it was animated. Kane avoided the lounge room and went directly along a passage to the kitchen. He was aware of Bryan entering after him.

"The prince's sister and her consort have arrived," Bryan O'Halloran, a former army mate of Kane's warned him.

"How did they know to come here?" Kane whispered back in alarm. O'Halloran shrugged.

"Maybe the group found out and let the prince know? Anyway, the prince wants you to go in as soon as you get back."

"Where's Evan?"

"Watching the back. Martinez is on the camera feeds from the front and the sides."

"What's the consort like?" Kane sensed O'Halloran was unsettled.

"Smarmy. Handsome enough, but I just can't come out and like him."

"Go back where you were. I will go in when I have done a few things."

O'Halloran nodded and went out. Kane noticed he had his weapons ready to grab. He decided to get his own back on. He had not dared to be armed where he had gone. He would do a perimeter check of his own before going in to Ali.

Trouble or no, if someone had told Ali's guests where to come, it was time to move again. He would have to push Stevens to work harder to find the next place, or get Ali to agree to State Department protection.

The warning prickling increased the moment he entered the

lounge room. He took a quick look around, saw the woman who must be Ali's sister. Her face was veiled, and she sat on the couch. The other stranger was perched on the arm of the couch next to her. That young man was slender, had the ethnic likeness of the people of Ali's country, and might well be considered handsome, even with the weak looking chin.

Ali, becoming aware of him, turned around, face full of eager anticipation.

"You saw her?" he asked, manner demanding an answer.

"I saw the woman being held by the FBI," Kane admitted, and decided to be careful of what he said.

"It wasn't my friend Janna?" Famira asked, turning her eyes his way.

Kane considered his answer, uneasy with the presence of the stranger.

"The woman admits to helping you, and says she can best continue to do so by keeping away from you. I understand that this woman, Janet Delaney, works with the American State Department."

Famira asked a question in her own language. Ali translated. "So this woman, Janet, is not Janna?"

"Your Highness, as the FBI agent in charge of the investigation is your friend's father, surely he would have recognised her if she was his daughter."

Ali caught Kane's swift glance to the stranger, who was now leaning over Famira as if comforting her. When Kane looked back at him. Ali nodded and changed the course of his questions. He had come to know Kane well enough to realise he was holding information back. He could wait to hear it.

"I wonder which of Janna's girl friends that was," Ali went on. "Did she tell you?"

Kane shook his head. "She assured me she would be fine as she was working with two highly competent State Department agents."

"What interest am I to your State Department?" Ali asked.

"I can think of a few reasons, your Highness. First, you are the heir to the throne of one of America's allies, a country that is now under martial law by an anti- American faction. Secondly, with your uncle looking for you, there have been a lot of illegal activities going on. Third. –"

"Fine! I understand," Ali stopped him. "Still she has helped me and I owe her my help."

"She told me, most emphatically, that she can help best by being an extra target, so your uncle has to split his forces. In custody, she is protected. Before you sound off again, Frank Dupont has urged me to tell you that should you decide to come out of hiding, he will help guarantee your safety. He also told me he intended to charge both myself and Tozer's girlfriend with Tozer's murder. He only let me go so I could deliver his message."

Ali's face hardened. "They did not follow you here?"

"No, your Highness. I made sure of that."

"I will think on Dupont's offer, but I do not think I will take it up," Ali decided. "So, he did not say where Janna was?"

"No, and all I can add to that is she wasn't at the safe house since they caught more of your uncle's men there."

"Will he be looking for me too?" Famira asked, her expression of concern only visible by frown lines around her eyes, above the veil.

Kane bowed in her direction. "Perhaps, if he knows you are in the States. I do not know if he views women as dangerous. Why did you decide to come here?"

Famira glanced at her brother, perhaps asking permission to give her reason. Ali answered for her. "She did not feel safe in the palace. General Ishkhan and his men were making her uncomfortable."

Kane had heard about when Ali had left and the dangers along that route, so he commented, "I am glad that you found a safe route out of your country."

"We followed the route Ali took and had little trouble. There was a plane waiting for us just across the border."

Kane had a lot of questions, but he didn't want to ask them in the presence of the newcomers.

"I will be fixing food soon. I expect your sister and...."

"Mohan," Ali supplied.

"...will be very tired and desire an early night."

Famira nodded, spoke to her consort, and he nodded too.

"Okay, I'll see to the food." Kane used that as his reason to leave. O'Halloran joined him, again. "We have Mohan in the front room, and Famira in the room at the back.”

“I would be happier if we could have her in with Ali. When you said consort, I thought you meant they were married.”

“Oh, no. Engaged.”

“How much English do you think he understands?” Kane asked his mate.

“Couldn’t say. I have only heard him speak in Arabic. He seems to be listening to conversations, but he asks Famira to tell him what was said.”

Kane mused. “I need to talk to Ali, but when I do, I would prefer him to be fast asleep.”

O’Halloran chuckled softly. “As good as done, mate.”

Kane went back to check in with Evans, Stephens and Martinez. All were men he’d known from his army days. Evans understood some Arabic, so Kane asked him about the arrival of the newcomers.

“They just turned up in a taxi,” Evans reported. “They had a letter from Kelly introducing them. That was legit – had all the right code words. I did get Ali to check before letting them in. He wasn’t expecting to see his sister.”

“Did Mohan, the boyfriend, say anything?”

“The girl introduced him to Ali, who asked about where he grew up and all that.”

“What did you hear?”

Evans told him. “He’s from the main city. A scholar in history and culture. Famira met him at a function prior to being put under house arrest. He apparently came to the palace to catalogue the books in the palace library.”

“Convenient,” Kane noted.

“That’s what we all thought,” Evans admitted. It tended to explain why he had been watching the back, instead of relying on the sensors. “You didn’t tell those young IT blokes where we were?”

Kane shook his head. “No. That was the deal. At best they wold know the general neighbourhood. I will be calling them to check, though. But what really has my hackles up is that the girl came out via the route Ali took – with very little trouble. And I know from you what that was like for Ali.”

"Huh! That was the safest route we came up with but it was still damn dangerous. If they had very little trouble, I reckon someone gave the General's men a wink to let them pass."

"I will pass a warning back, but it might be too late already." Kane took his phone out and was dialling the number of the Group. "I should whack you one, bro," he relied to Glen's greeting. "You didn't warn me about the bird and her beau."

"What?"

"Put Tim on," Kane insisted, and he waited while Glen went to get him.

"What's up bro?" Tim greeted.

"The princess and her boyfriend turned up at the house," Kane said. "Had a letter from Kelly."

"I haven't heard from him in over a month," Tim said, concerned.

"Did any of you know this address?"

"No, bro. Even I don't know where you are."

"I will call you back," Kane hung up abruptly. To Evans he said, "Slip into Ali's room and pack all his stuff. We may have to leave in a hurry."

"On it!"

Kane went to the room he shared with Evans and Martinez. He found an unused pre-paid phone and used that to ring Tim back.

"I'm sorry bro. I think we have a problem. I need you to get word back..." He explained his fears about the escape route. "It might already be too late. Or it might be under observation in case Ali comes back in that way."

"I'll get on it. Anything else?"

"Try to contact Kelly. For the rest, put Glen back on."

"Yo, what else is up, bro?" Glen returned.

"Pay particular attention to calls to the main target. Also, don't call on my old number, use this one. I don't know how the newcomers knew where to come. It is possible they have a trace on the other phone."

"Take the SIM card out," Glen said at once.

"Probably too late for that," Kane admitted. "We'll be leaving tonight. Did you have any inkling the girl was coming out?"

"None," Glen said definitely.

"Right. I'll keep in touch." Kane ended the call and sent a text to Martinez. "Can you do something quick for food?"

"Right, boss!" came the return text.

Kane went to where Stephens was watching the security. "I want you to get a small truck or van and bring it here. Back it up to the garage."

"We bugging out again?"

"Yes! Go!"

Kane wasn't going to bet that past instances would be a good guide, but he was hoping that it would be well after dark before any attack came. If Jabir had sent anyone to watch, he would report the van. And when it left, hopefully the watcher would assume they all left in it – like they had done other times.

He wasn't going to assume though. His best bet was to do things differently. Jabir had lost a lot of his followers, and whoever he sent this time might do things differently. Like those who had attacked Janet in daylight.

There was another, smaller van in the garage. This would leave after the other, if the watcher followed the first. This time though, they had two extras to worry about and one of them might be a spy.

Ali found him in the security room and when he entered, closed the door behind him.

"You don't trust Mohan. What else?" Ali asked, getting right to the point. Kane spoke, Ali listened.

"Yes, you are right to be concerned. My sister seems to trust Mohan and doesn't seem to dislike his attention. I have yet to feel I really know him. So far, he seems to be timid enough. Perhaps that is why my uncle didn't try to stop them being friends."

"Your uncle hasn't been in your country for several months. He might not know they are friends, or he might have encouraged it and be controlling Mohan."

Ali blanched. "That too is possible. Do you think their escape from my country was too easy?"

Kane nodded.

"I was thinking to return that way."

"It would be unwise," Kane warned.

"Yes. Now, what were you not saying earlier?"

"The girl I saw was Janna, and what she said is what I told you. Her father knows it is her, and has not officially identified her. Which is likely to get him fired if it is found out. But the State Department is involved, and he might be taking orders from them. By right, he probably shouldn't be on the case."

"Do you think I should speak to him? Ask for protection?"

"I do. It has occurred to me that allowing Famira to come here is a move to draw you out, since having Janna in her identity of Janet Delaney, set up for a murder charge has not."

"I will abide your warning. Are we leaving?"

"As soon as Stephens gets back. Evans is packing your stuff. How long has your sister been here?"

"She arrived half an hour before you came back."

"Then she probably hasn't unpacked. If you can, try to warn her, but leave Mohan in the dark for now."

"Will you be taking Mohan too?"

"Yes, but I expect he will be very tired and sleep through the move."

Ali nodded, understanding the innuendo. "What else haven't you told me?"

"My one concern with your going to Dupont is that Janna did not trust her father's expert on terrorism. She saw him in your uncle's company. His name is John King."

"That name is unfamiliar. Can you find out more about him? Perhaps get a photo?"

"I am not sure I want to go near Dupont to find anything out," Kane admitted.

"I understand," Ali said softly. "If I go to talk to him, I will want you there. If I need to I will claim diplomatic immunity, and include you under that."

"Very well," Kane agreed.

Ali went on, "I only had a short time to talk to my sister, but she tells me that people still think my uncle is in my country. Since I know better, I think it is more urgent that I return now and lead the loyalists."

"You should ask the State Department if they can help you," Kane suggested.

"I am not sure I want to take American troops there. My uncle has made it seem like Americans are horrid demons. Do you think Dupont will let me speak to Janna before I go?"

Kane sighed. "Your Highness, Janna also said that you were a fool to send me to see her. Don't make yourself a bigger fool. She said she would continue to help you when she could, and she is going to be testifying against three of your uncle's agents in court tomorrow. She appreciates that you want to help her, but you can't – not without risking yourself and making her efforts so far to be meaningless. I agree with her that she can help best by keeping away from you. She knows she can never be more than your friend, after the way she was set up and deported. She wishes you a long and happy life."

"Anything else?" Ali asked.

Kane thought of Janna's final words. "The last thing she said was that your life was a hundred times more important than hers, and that she still has the gift you gave her when you first arrived here, and that is enough."

Ali seemed to be thinking, then he paled and his olive skin turned a sickly shade. "I must speak to Janna's father tonight. I don't want anyone else to know I have gone."

"We have to leave here!" Kane reminded him, but Ali's intent stare reminded him who was paying him.

"Okay. We can do it, but it's risky. I will have most of the others go with Stephens in the other truck. I will leave O'Halloran here to close up and remove the cameras and gear and leave in our van. You and I can go off in my car. We will leave the VW here as cover. Warn your sister."

Kane went to brief his team so they would begin packing gear into the van. He kept Evans on watch and pulled Martinez from the kitchen, where he had made a pile of sandwiches, and gave him orders. He chose to take the sandwiches into the lounge room where Ali had retreated to watch the news. He heard a truck backing in along the drive and went out to meet Stephens.

"Where are we to go?" Stephens asked. "We haven't got the next place ready yet."

"Unless I tell you otherwise, park in the all night burger place near the police station."

"Where will you be?"

"I don't know yet. I need to make a call. Did you see any odd vehicles in the street?"

"No."

"Start putting stuff in the van. Whatever the visitors came with, Ali's stuff and half the gear."

Stephens went off and Kane pulled out the card Dupont had given him. He punched in the numbers, but the call didn't go direct to Dupont. He gave the agent that answered a terse message. "Tell Dupont to call..." he gave the new number, "It's about an earlier conversation we had."

Dupont didn't recognise the number, and was cautious about calling back. He hoped it was Kane.

He gave his name, when the call was answered with a terse, "Yes."

"Kane here. The young fool wants to talk to you. Tonight. Not at your work, or your house."

"At the safe house," Dupont decided on the spot.

"That the place that wasn't safe for some intruders?"

"Yes. A good omen," Dupont confirmed.

"Okay. Where?"

Dupont gave the address, then asked, "What will you be in?"

"Small dark car. You better live up to your word. We have to bug out from our current place."

"What happened?"

"Nothing yet. We had unexpected visitors. Do you have a second safe place?"

"Friends or enemies?" Dupont asked for clarification.

"Friends, in theory."

"One moment," Dupont pulled out his personal cell phone and called his partner. The call was brief, and he returned to Kane. "Yes." He gave a second address. "My partner, Jim Pearson will be expecting you. What names will your people be using?"

"Stephens and Martinez."

"And your visitors?"

"Not on the phone."

"Okay. I'm heading to the safe house."

Dupont checked his weapons and called his partner back to explain further.

"Two of the Prince's guards, Stephens and Martinez, plus two unexpected visitors. Kane wouldn't say who, he called them 'friends in theory'. Call for back-up. Kane said they had to bug out. My guess, he thinks the visitors may have been followed."

"What about Kane?"

"He and the Prince are going to the safe house. I'm heading there now. Has the Martin woman been in touch?"

"No. Want me to call her?"

"Yes. Bring her up to speed if she answers."

Wanda Martin was observing from the street as the SWAT team entered the exclusive hotel. Ordinary police had already swept the lobby clear of residents, and no one was being allowed to enter.

There was a risk that the quarry would be warned, but the police assured her that all possible exits were covered, if he tried to leave. She still had doubts, but had no authority to insist on being involved. All she could do was await the outcome and be watchful outside.

When she heard the sound of a jet powered helicopter warming up, she knew what the report would be. Somehow, the police had missed the helo on the roof. It soon took off, heading east towards the ocean.

Her phone rang. "Yes?" It wasn't the SWAT leader, but Dupont's partner, Pearson. She listened.

"I will get there as soon as I can," she promised.

The SWAT leader's call came as soon as she'd ended the other call. His scathing remarks echoed her own thoughts.

"It flew east," Wanda told the man. "Do a thorough search of the place, and let the obvious police presence leave. Some of his men may still go there." She gave an outline of what she had heard was happening elsewhere, and was about to end the call when she was told, "Hold the line!"

The voice came back. "We've found an unconscious man in a walk in cupboard. The ID says John King."

That caused Wanda to think. Had Jabir lost trust in his half-brother?

"Get him to hospital under guard. Advise FBI agent Frank Dupont. They are working together."

"Anything else?"

"If you find anything else, let me know, but my business here is done. Thanks, Lieutenant."

Wanda considered what Prince Jabir might do next, as she drove her car to the safe house. Had he another place to go, or would he need to find somewhere? Either way, even though he had eluded her, she hoped he had been seriously inconvenienced and less able to micro-manage a raid on the house where Prince Ali had been. Once again, Kane had managed to be a step ahead. He had understood the potential danger of the unexpected arrivals, not just that one was a virtual unknown, but the fact that somehow they had known where to go. At least, it had been the impetus to get the Prince to seek help. She would bet he had also seen the possibility that Famira's escape route was compromised. She'd ask him that, and offer help if the Prince decided to return home.

When she arrived at the house, she brought Dupont up to date, and did her own check of the security. It had been eased a bit, when she had been pretending to be Janna Dupont. Satisfied, and while waiting for Kane to arrive, she called her husband.

"Obviously, you have been having so much fun," David teased her when she'd apologised for not calling often.

"Almost had Jabir," she countered. "The police missed the camouflaged helo on the roof. It flew off to the east, but it might have headed anywhere." Then she told him all the recent events.

"I will give our friend a heads up," David told her. "So he can be ready if Ali accepts help to go back."

Dupont checked with agents placed in three local houses where they could watch the approaches to the safe house. He told them the description he had for Kane's car, and when it was spotted, the watcher sent through the registration number, and Dupont confirmed it was the car Kane had used earlier in the day. Dupont opened the garage for the car to drive in.

While it was possible that the occupants may not have been the people they were expecting, it was not a weak point in security. Until the occupants emerged, and were recognised, the garage with its roll door closed again, was as secure as a prison cell.

Kane emerged first, looked all around the otherwise empty garage, turned his face to the security camera, and then went around to open Ali's door. Inside, Wanda studied both men, then gave the okay to unlock the connecting door. She let the FBI man greet them, while making her own impressions, and only came forward when Dupont turned to introduce her. Both men nodded politely in her direction, but quickly returned their attention to Dupont, and followed his invitation to take a seat in the central lounge area. They would be unaware of the other four agents situated in various rooms.

"Can I get you anything? A drink, or something to eat?" Dupont asked, acting the host. He had placed four chairs around low table, but noticed Wanda had decided to perch on a tall stool, near the door to the kitchen, and Kane had positioned himself to watch her.

"You wished to talk to me?" Dupont asked, when the offer of refreshments was refused.

"I have long wanted to meet Janna's father," Prince Ali began. "She impressed me with her intelligence, and how well she adapted to the ways of my country. She also spoke highly of you."

Dupont watched him, waiting for him to get to the point. He seemed to be thinking of what he wanted to say.

"Sir, I have come to speak to you on behalf of Nadia Shaston, Janet Delaney and Janna. Perhaps you already know of some of the things I will speak of."

"Tell me what you wish," Dupont invited. "We can discuss things afterwards."

Ali nodded. "When I arrived in America, earlier this year, it was to escape a very real danger. My uncle, Prince Jabir, along with General Ishkhan came to arrest my father, King Rakhal. They expected him to be quite oblivious to their intention, which was to take over the rule in my country. I eluded both men by moments. My father's last words were for me to flee, and seek allies abroad. His personal secretary took me out of the palace via a secret way that I had not known. I was taken to the home of some people loyal to my father and given a false identity, funds for travelling and various items I would need. They took me on the first leg of the journey out of my country. Many times we were almost found, or shot at. When I crossed the border, I was met by a group of former American Marines, organised by those that helped me."

Dupont glanced at Kane who said, "I joined later, when four of the original eight were killed."

"I have the utmost respect for the memory of those men and the others that are protecting me," Ali admitted. "I have an equally great respect for your daughter and her friends – the ones I met in my country. Then, I was a naïve child, fascinated by a foreign culture and what I had heard of America. I thought to come here because of those friends I had made. Those people have proved, over and over, to be true friends. I believe you have met them?"

Dupont nodded. "Some of them, anyway. I know what they have been doing for you."

Ali nodded, preparing to continue.

"I purposefully kept my arrival secret, for to announce it would be to invite the attention of my uncle's assassins. I had not known of his connection to the terrorist Cobra Sect, until I was travelling away from my home. By the time I arrived here, one of my guards had located some of the friends I had met at home. Darryl, one of my early guards, knew these friends were all good using computers and finding information."

"Indeed," Dupont agreed into another pause. He refrained from calling them hackers. "And my daughter?"

Ali's face flushed. "I had wanted, very much, to meet her again. My sister had grown very fond of her, as both friend and confidante. She too wanted to help me, but I did not want her to risk herself. Women in my country are cherished and Janna was my sister's friend."

Dupont had heard a different version of that meeting. He decided to speak of his sentiments. "Janna finally told me what transpired in your country before she was deported. If I am to believe her, the way she was treated was a far cry from cherished. Seems to me that she had no moral, ethical, or personal reputation left."

Ali looked away before saying, "No. I fear I betrayed my respect for her. I have come to realise that my uncle did not wish me to have allies in foreign places. However, you must believe that Janna was never less than perfectly behaved, always kept to her role as a servant to my sister, and in no way disgraced herself. Nor did she tell my sister of the scandalous things she was being accused of. If she had, perhaps Famira and I could have done something. We did try..."

"And here, did you ask her to do anything?" Dupont demanded.

"I would have liked her to stay with me, but she told me she could help me more by us staying apart. Even then, she was putting my well-being before her own. After that meeting, she wished me well and walked away. I did not know she had not spoken to you for a long time. Truly, you have no reason to be ashamed of her."

"I am not so sure I agree with you," Dupont told him. "I am surprised that you still think so highly of her. Did you know that she has been whoring for that terrorist Tozer? It would have been smarter to turn him into the police and have him deported."

Ali looked away again, and Kane glanced at Dupont, wondering why he had spoken so bluntly. He still wasn't sure Ali knew what Janna had been doing.

Ali turned back, seemed to sit straighter, and said, "If we had done that, my uncle would have sent someone else. This way, we knew the enemy and had warning when our residence was found."

Kane inserted, "I didn't know where the warnings came from originally. I just knew that when that group of hackers said to move, we did. I knew where Tozer – "

"Hashim," Ali corrected.

"Where he was staying," Kane went on. "And I had asked around about his girlfriend. Everyone said she was a nasty piece of work. I wasn't aware that she was the source of the warnings, wouldn't have believed it, until she turned up and made it possible for us to escape. Nadia Shaston, as I knew her then, created a diversion. She allowed Tozer to rough her up so we could get free. Wouldn't leave with us either."

"I was still dopey from being drugged," Ali admitted. "So I didn't recognise her. It was only later that I realised who she must be. I owe her my life, for all the warnings she gave us. I am awed by her strength of will, and by the way she even fooled my uncle. I did not think that any woman could be so strong and dedicated in an unpleasant situation."

"I would phrase it as stubborn," Dupont admitted, "And had that trait honed by a very good mentor." He flashed a glance at Wanda, and tried to ignore the way his gut felt as he realised the dangers his daughter had faced alone.

"I do not know how you could even consider charging your daughter with murder!" Ali blurted.

Dupont heard the last traces of the young idealistic prince in that question. He modified his tone.

"It is very effectively giving us a reason to keep her in protective custody, and to draw people away from the idea that she is the Janna you once knew. Perhaps, while you are here, Kane, you would be kind enough to give me a statement about your part in Tozer's death."

"Not at this time," Ali said firmly.

"What about your view of events when Adam Ruskin was killed? Your mate, Stephens believes that Shaston killed him."

"Janna did not!" Ali protested.

This time, Kane spoke over him. "She had blood soaking her clothes, and a bloody knife in her hand. The conclusion was no doubt meant to be obvious. Except I did not believe she would have a reason to kill someone she had never met before. Maybe our enemy thought she wanted to kill me, and assumed that truth. In which case, we might think she killed Adam thinking it was me. I know that she had her chance at Tozer's place, but she helped us get free there. Besides, I did not believe that the Shaston wench would have any knowledge of explosives, or any reason to set an explosion likely to also kill her."

Dupont nodded. Apart from the blood, Shaston's clothes had tested negative for traces of explosives.

"So, your Highness, did you come here to demand I drop charges against Nadia/Janet?"

Once again, Ali looked away.

"I came because, whatever the woman known as Nadia did, it was to protect me, even if it damned her."

"Sounds like she already considered herself damned, and had nothing left to lose," Dupont remarked.

"Unfortunately, as things stand in my country, that is true. And I never expected the devotion that she has shown me here, when she had every right to hate me. I have come to realise that my life is a very precious thing. I have a great responsibility to my father and to the people of my country. They do not deserve to die because an evil general and a power hungry relative decided to control my country."

"When you came here, you should have sought official help," Dupont gave his opinion.

"I did not, because I pictured American troops trampling into our country to fight the rebels. I have been contacting people in other places that know my father, and seeking help in the form of supplies and weapons so we can fight our own battles. Janna, told me much of what you did. It seems she was already wiser than I."

"Which isn't saying very much," Dupont retorted, "Because she is still a damn fool. However, she is an adult, she chose her life, and her actions, and perhaps you will realise that she acted in a way that would preclude you having anything more to do with her?"

"I see it differently," Ali said, again seeming to straighten. "If she had truly wished that, she would simply have walked away from me at that meeting here, and done nothing."

Wanda chose then, to walk into a position at DuPont's side. "Janna harboured no ill will towards Prince Ali or his sister, even knowing she had become lower than a cockroach in everyone else's eyes in Jakhabad."

Everyone's eyes went to her. "There was more to her decision to help than merely friendship. In disgracing her so thoroughly, Prince Jabir showed his hatred for all Americans. She had heard rumours of the intended coup, and having evidence of that fact, realised that America was in danger from Prince Jabir's lust for world power. Before my husband and I agreed to teach her certain things, I made sure she knew what might befall her – in graphic detail. I too would have preferred his Highness had approached the State Department for help, and I say this now. The offer is still open for discussion."

"I do not wish for American soldiers to die in my country," Ali stated. "My uncle has painted Americans as demons. The General and his adherents would not be the only ones out to kill them."

"I did not mention that as an option," Wanda said. "Help can come in many forms."

Dupont decided to add his recommendation. "I have worked with Mrs Martin and her husband, on a number of occasions. I have never found them to be less than frighteningly competent. Earlier tonight, her information let to a raid on the hotel where your uncle has been staying."

Ali's eyes glittered until Wanda admitted. "Unfortunately, he had a well camouflaged helicopter on the roof, and something spooked him."

"Maybe that man King?" Kane suggested.

"No," Dupont denied. "He agreed to interact with his half- brother to try to find out why he was in the States."

"Half-brother!" Ali exclaimed.

Dupont explained the relationship and why he trusted King's word. He wasn't sure he had convinced them. Wanda added, "When your uncle fled, moments before the SWAT team went in, he left John King unconscious in a room there. He is in a bad way. That does not suggest a close trusted relationship existed between them."

Silence fell, and all eyes went to Ali as being the one calling the shots. He was fully aware of the scrutiny.

"I know I am young, inexperienced. I am trying to do as my father would wish. I already know that my uncle is not the sort of role model I wish to follow. In other ways, my father is not either. In my country, a woman cannot speak for herself. A woman who has no man to speak for her is the lowest of the low. I do not agree with that. While I do not criticize my father for ruling against Janna as our long tradition demands, based on the evidence presented to him, it is something I intend to change.

"Being here, I have learnt so much. Here, people are innocent until proven guilty. In my country, it is the opposite – no one gave Janna the chance to prove her innocence. No man would speak for her. My father relied on those presenting the case to be telling the truth."

"Your Highness, why don't you get to the point?" Wanda suggested quietly.

Ali jerked a little, and nodded. "Like I said before, Janna never disgraced herself, or betrayed contempt for the culture of my country. She was my sister's friend, more than a servant, and I came to think of her as a friend too. If she had been a woman of my country, no one would have questioned me if I chose to take things further, even if I had no intention of marrying her. Since I have been here, she has done so much for me, without expecting any reward. Yet I fear, I have put her in grave danger."

Even Kane stayed silent, wondering what was coming.

"At that meeting, when I had just arrived and Janna was about to walk out in me, I feared I would never see her again. I wanted her to know what I felt for her. It was a moment of weakness on my part. I fear I have made her pregnant."

Dupont rose from his chair. "You! Can you be sure the child she is carrying is yours? As Nadia, she flouted her relationship with Tozer."

"I am sure. Janna said so."

"Huh?" Kane exclaimed. "She only said she was carrying the gift you gave her."

"The only gift I gave her was myself," Ali said with quiet dignity. Dupont settled back in his chair, needing to re-evaluate many things about his daughter.

"What do you intend to do, your Highness," he asked after a while.

Kane blurted, "You cannot possibly intend to marry her and take back to Jakhabad with you! They will never accept her, and you might just as well stayed there and let your uncle kill you."

"I know the charges against her are unfounded," Ali insisted with calm dignity.

"What about here?" Kane demanded. "Maybe she isn't the murderer certain people believe she is, but she was still Tozer's whore."

"No! She selflessly put herself in danger for my sake. I cannot do other than honour her above all others."

"What of my five mates who died protecting you?" Kane went on.

"I regret that, very deeply. However, as paid mercenaries, you all knew the risks. They all had training to minimise the risks. What did Janna have? She did not expect payment."

Kane opened his mouth to argue further, but Ali said, "Enough, Kane!" The steel in his tone was a new thing and Kane closed his mouth.

Wanda spoke again. "It has not been a complete waste of time. Over a dozen of the Cobra Sect members or associates have been arrested and will be deported to face more serious charges than for crimes they performed here. I think you should let his Highness finish what he is trying to say."

Ali looked at her, wondering if she had guessed his intention.

"Mr Dupont, it is a custom in my country for a man to seek the blessing of the father of the woman he wishes to marry. Sir, do I have your blessing to marry Janna?"

Kane just shook his head. Wanda was holding her breath.

Dupont remained mute for a long moment. Finally, he said, "I wish I could advise my daughter to have nothing more to do with you. However, she is an adult who has already made it plain to me that I do not rule her life. She has continued to want to associate with you, in spite of the dangers, ignoring every advice I gave her. No doubt she will continue to do so. I want her to be happy and safe. Perhaps happy for a time will be enough. So yes, you have my blessing, but it is not I that you must convince. I will abide her choice."

Ali had been tense as a bow string while waiting for the answer. Now he asked, "How may I arrange to meet her?"

"Your Highness, it is very late. I doubt anything can be arranged before morning," Kane interrupted. "And have you forgotten your unexpected guests?"

"No. You are right, Kane. My sister will also wish to meet Janna. Can I have them come here?"

Before Dupont could reply, Kane asserted, "Until I am certain of your sister's fiancé, I advise against that."

"Perhaps you might share what has happened," Dupont suggested. "Are these the ones you referred to and would not name?"

Kane nodded, and gave a terse recitation of the facts and reasons for his decision. Dupont phoned his partner.

"How are your guests?"

"Sleeping. I have the local police on site. There have been no alarms."

"Keep alert. This isn't over. I have a lot to think on."

Ali was still watching Dupont.

"There is another consideration," Dupont pointed out. "Nadia Shaston is still expected to appear in court..." he checked the time. "Later today. To testify against three of your uncles agents."

"Perhaps the session could be deferred to the following day?" Wanda suggested.

"Do you have that kind of pull, Mrs Martin? They would need a damn good reason to consider it."

"We will discuss it. After you have your guests settled."

"We brought very little with us," Kane told them.

"Not a problem," Wanda told him. "I happen to know that they keep a lot of basic needs here."

"We do," Dupont confirmed. "I will show you where you can rest. Neither of you need to be concerned. There are four other men on duty here to watch for trouble."

Chapter 19 – The Start of the Fight

Dupont returned to the lounge when he had finished seeing to his guests. He found Wanda ensconced in one of the comfortable chairs, in the process of bringing her husband up to date. When she finished, he challenged her.

"Do you really think it a good idea to delay the hearing?" Dupont asked from the depths of another comfortable chair.

"My thought was, that if Prince Jabir has plans to disrupt it, he probably already knows it is currently scheduled for today. He is undoubtedly quite aggravated right now, and may make an unwise decision."

"Do you think he would try to free his people?"

"Or kill them for being idiots," Wanda proposed. "He won't be impressed that Nadia/Janet outwitted them."

"Might your forcing him to find a new hole to crawl into, distract him?"

"I don't really know," Wanda admitted. "My other thought was, that if Ali does intend to return home – the sooner the better. So if we can keep him thinking that Ali is still here, he stays out of the picture in Jakhabad for longer. So, I think it is probably a good idea to let him speak to Janna – to clear the air – and so he is not so distracted."

"What do you think my little fool will decide?"

"I think you already know."

"I think you are right." Dupont sighed.

"Frank, she's in love with him, and it's not the dewy eyed marry and happy ever after kind. It is the in danger and peril kind. Plus, she is carrying his child."

"You are sure." Dupont stared intently at Wanda.

"Yes. She had a kind of glow about her that I have seen about other mother's to be. And that was before she even met Tozer."

Dupont pushed himself up. "It is going to be a long night. If I want to petition the judge for an adjournment, I have a lot to do.

You'll be staying here?"

Wanda nodded. "I'll nap in a chair."

Looking like he had just showered, Ali wandered into the lounge in borrowed pyjamas and robe.

"We weren't formally introduced," he said, reaching down to shake Wanda's hand. "I am Prince Ali Fazir of Jakhabad."

Wanda stood and gave him a brief bow. "Wanda Martin, US State Department field agent." She drew out her ID and let Ali examine it.

"Are you the one who helped Janna?"

"Yes. My partner and I. She sought us out."

"Then I feel I must thank you. I did not think her strong enough to do and endure all she has."

"She is highly intelligent and a very fast learner. And she was highly motivated."

"Do you think she will be able to endure all the denunciation, should she return to my country?"

"Could you?" Wanda provoked. "You will be judged too if you bring her back and show your preference. You have thought about that, surely."

"Yes. I know the charges were all false, or she was set up. I don't know how I might prove it."

"Time might do that," Wanda counselled. "You don't intend to take her with you when you leave?"

"I...No, I have thought that she should have her child here, but then she would have a child to consider and the way in may not be safe."

Wanda let the younger man think things through. He was still growing into manhood. Finally she said, "While the situation in your country is so volatile, it will be dangerous if she is there."

"It is just that by tradition, a royal heir should be born in our country."

"I understand," Wanda said gently. "However, there are still a lot of loose ends to tie up here."

"Surely the charges against Janna are just for convenience."

"Not all. But don't worry. I do not think there is enough evidence to convict Nadia Shaston."

"I really should return home, but I want to marry Janna first, so our child is legitimate. I really shouldn't risk her, and going back will be dangerous. It is possible that the route I took to come out is compromised, and Kane thinks Famira was allowed to escape to draw me out."

"If you wish, I know of people who can help you return. I know you don't want soldiers. I am talking stealth. Then when Janna is free to do so, if she wishes to, they can help her too. My friends excel at this sort of thing."

"I will consider your offer. Can I meet your friends?"

"My partner, David, is on his way here. He'll arrive in the morning. He has already started to plan things – just in case. Why don't you talk to him?"

Chapter 20 – The Judge

Frank Dupont had dealt with Judge Galloway before and the two men respected each other, even if their relationship was formal.

"Don, this is Wanda Martin, State Department representative," Dupont introduced, and Wanda handed the judge her ID across his desk. He studied it and passed it back.

"How can I assist you, Mrs Martin?"

"Your Honour, I need to provide you with some privileged information relating to the case against Nadia Shaston."

"Oh? Are you trying to have the charges dropped?"

"Not at this time, Your Honour," Wanda spoke formally. "However, what I have to tell you needs to be considered in addition to evidence presented."

As Wanda explained how the person known as Nadia Shaston was working to uncover Tozer's purpose in the US, the judge studied her intently. When she finished her initial speech, he asked, "You have documentation?"

"Yes, Your Honour." She handed over a folder containing several pages, and noticed the slight twitch in his brows as he read them, and noticed the signature.

"And has this target been located?" the judge referred to something mentioned in the pages he'd read.

"Yes, Sir. He has been identified, but as of last night, that man, Tozer's controller, escaped a raid on his hideout."

"So what exactly are you asking of me, Mrs Martin?"

"Only that you listen to all the evidence, critically."

"And are you authorised to tell me the real identity of the person being tried as Nadia Shaston?"

"I have been granted discretion to do that, but if I do, you must first sign a specific amendment to the official secrets act."

The judge stared for a moment and then smiled. "Why don't you tell me why you don't want to and forget the made up spook speak? Frank, do you know who this person is?"

"Yes, your Honour."

The judge waited for Wanda to speak. "Her name is Janna Dupont."

"I see, and I recall certain things about her." The judge didn't look at Dupont.

"Your Honour, I have a sworn and witnessed statement from Janna, that the charges in Jakhabad were completely false. If that is not enough for you, I can ask Prince Ali Fazir, of Jakhabad to make a statement as well. The reason I wish Nadia Shaston's true identity to be suppressed, is the same as the reason I am not advocating the charges be dropped at this time. Prince Ali's uncle, Prince Jabir, is the man who was controlling Tozer. He is also the leader of the terrorist Cobra Sect. He was the one who organised Janna's disgrace so his brother's children would not have foreign friends. She is the first person Ali sought upon arriving here. As Nadia Shaston, she has already earned the antipathy of Prince Jabir, but should he learn that she is also Janna, I am quite sure she will be targeted for death."

"It seems she has played a masterful role," the Judge had to admit. He moved his gaze to the poker-faced Dupont. "I authorised the arrest warrant for her part in the death of ex-marine Adam Ruskin. The case was very strong."

"As I heard it, I would agree. Except that I could not find a suitable motive for her to kill a man who was part of the protection on Prince Ali Fazir. I can find a reason for the opposing faction to do so – to frame her, have her punished by the law. I also know that she had no knowledge of explosives or any reason to blow up herself and the others."

"I am willing to consider a deal, if the evidence continues to damn her. What can the young woman offer the United States of America?"

"She has already been responsible for helping the authorities to find and arrest over a dozen members of a foreign terrorist sect. She can offer to identify as many of them as she knows from those who visited Sam Tozer. She is also willing to cross the boundaries of her two assumed personas, as well as her own, to give a wider view of her activities. It may throw extra light on current investigations."

"When can you arrange a meeting of all the investigating bodies," the judge barked at Dupont.

"I can try for this morning, Your Honour."

"Okay. I will have the two cases scheduled for today deferred to tomorrow. Have the appearance of the four terrorists brought forward to today. Shaston wasn't going to appear for that was she?"

"No, your Honour," Dupont confirmed. "However, we will be showing her photographs before the hearing."

"I will set aside from 10 am to noon. Confirm when you have everyone organised."

"Thank you, your Honour," Wanda stated.

On the way out, Dupont asked, "How much more is Janna hiding from me?"

"Nadia Shaston and Janet Delaney have only ever told what they knew in each persona," Wanda specified, obliquely reminding him that Janna's name had never been mentioned. "I don't believe that there is much that has been left unsaid. However, some things, such as motives, will become clear when the personas are combined. Also, understanding the personal motives of each might give the forensic guys from the military investigation team, a new vision."

"In simple words, do you think the charges will stick?"

"No."

"How am I to explain taking Nadia Shaston out of the remand centre and not returning her?"

Wanda reopened her document folder and passed him a piece of paper. It was authorisation, from a level higher than the judge, to place Nadia Shaston into protective custody. "You have to take her out for the meeting. You just don't take her back. They will be advised not to expect her. Tomorrow, you will bring her to the hearing, and at the end of the day, I will spirit her back to the house."

"You seem to have thought of everything."

"I hope so. Have you thought of getting more security at the court building?"

"Yes. Do you expect trouble?"

"I wouldn't rule it out. How is your friend, King?"

"Do you still not trust him?"

"I'm being careful."

"He is still unconscious. The drug they used on him affects people differently. He is still alive, which is promising, but until he wakes the doctors won't know how he will be."

Chapter 21 – Secret wedding

Janna Dupont did not let on that she knew the uniformed guard who led her into the meeting room. She caught Wanda winking at her, and that encouraged her. She knew both Wanda and David were on the alert for trouble.

Frank Dupont merely nodded briefly, and continued to organise the various representatives of the FBI, local police, NCIS and Shaston's lawyers. He had been introduced to the senior lawyer when he had arrived, and assumed the State Department had appointed him.

The judge listened to all the questions, and to Janna's answers and his impression of the woman rose sharply. The session, lasting almost the length of the time he had set aside, was gruelling, but he noticed that the initial hostility lessened as the combined story came out.

Judge Galloway was inwardly relieved when David presented the witness protection order. Although, he had come to decide that all charges were likely to be dropped before Shaston went to trial, though not before her initial hearing.

David was again the escorting officer, as Janna left the meeting room. Most of those who had attended would naturally assume she was heading back to the remand centre. They had no way of knowing that the van backed up to the loading dock for the small cafeteria, was to take her to the safe house to meet Prince Ali Fazir. Janna herself had not been told.

In the short time between the meeting room and the van, David had removed the handcuffs and picked up a long coat to cover the bright orange remand uniform. Since he was to speak to the Prince anyway, he had the job of driving her there.

Frank Dupont had said nothing to Janna about Ali's surprising announcement. Wanda was sure that Ali's sister had no inkling either. However, she would want to see her friend too, and Wanda planned to arrange it. For a start, she would go and introduce herself, and take the opportunity to make her own impression of the unexpected fiancé. She had asked Dupont to warn his partner that she was coming.

At Pearson's house, Wanda was immediately aware of the scrutiny of the extra police guards. Most were not visible from the street, but those close to the house met her before she got to the door, and scrutinised her ID. When they allowed her to go inside, two more officers scrutinised her and quickly checked her for weapons. She smiled wryly when it was over, but didn't betray the reason.

Pearson told her, "They are through there." He gestured for her to precede him.

The television was on in the room, with the volume low. A man was sprawled inelegantly on a couch, but his attention was on her as soon as she came in. Famira was seated in a chair, reading a book. Her hopeful glance turned to one of disappointment as Wanda approached to sit in another chair beside her.

"I'm Wanda Martin. I'm with the US State Department," she introduced quietly.

"Have you seen my brother? I thought he would come here too," Famira asked.

"Your brother is fine. I have arranged for him to talk to my partner," Wanda noticed the young man sit up from the couch. He sauntered over to take up a possessive position behind Famira's chair. She nodded to him.

"This is my betrothed, Mohan," Famira introduced quickly.

Wanda echoed the name, nodded again, and told him her name. She decided to begin with small talk.

"Do you have everything you need?" Wanda began. "I can arrange for any special woman's needs if you have them."

"No. I am fine. I have my case."

"Did you have a chance to see much of America on your way here?" Wanda asked next.

During the chat, Wanda noticed Mohan's attention straying back to the football game on the TV. However, when Famira asked about seeing her friend Janna, his attention switched back, making Wanda almost certain he did understand English.

"I will see if that can be arranged," Wanda said, careful to sound neutral. "Have you heard much from your brother since he has been here?"

"No, but we were told the address to go to. I assume he provided it. I don't understand why we had to leave that other place."

"Ah, well, that is because people have been trying to find your brother."

Famira frowned in concern. "Has Janna been with him?"

"No. She told him she would only endanger him," Wanda told her.

"I would still like to see her."

Mohan leant down and asked what was being said. Famira told him briefly in Arabic. Wanda gave no indication of how much she understood. She wasn't fluent in that language yet.

Her phone beeped. She took it out to read David's terse message. "Soppy reunion, hitching agreed, priest coming, bring F not M."

Wanda stood up and spoke to Famira. "Janna has agreed to see you. We can go now."

She was on her feet quickly, and Mohan moved to stand expectantly by her side.

"I'm sorry, I'm only to bring Famira," Wanda explained.

She saw Mohan tense before asking for a translation. "It is not my decision. I have to obey orders."

Mohan voiced a spate of irritated or angry Arabic, but Famira spoke firmly.

"Janna is my friend. She does not know you. I will introduce you later, if I am allowed. I am sure she will want to meet you. For this trip, Wanda Martin will be a suitable chaperone."

On the way out, Wanda gave Pearson a quick warning. "Watch that one. See if he makes any calls or texts."

Janna entered the house, knowing only that she would not be going back to the remand centre. She was surprised when David suggested that she cleaned up and changed. That fresh clothes were laid out for her in the indicated bedroom.

Using the en-suite was bliss – private and no need to rush. She could wash the memory of the remand centre from her skin and mind, make sure her hair was properly clean. Some of the black dye would wash out, but that could be remedied. She saw some of the dye beside the small wash basin.

Emerging finally from the bedroom, she looked across the lounge room and stopped and stared. Price Ali saw her, his eyes lit up, and he began to move towards her. She was rooted to the ground, expecting condemnation for the things she had done while helping him. He said nothing, just gave her rigid body a gentle hug, then whispered in her ear.

At that moment, the room might well have been empty of everyone else. Janna slumped into Ali's embrace, and her whole body began shaking. After a while, she drew away, and wiped her eyes on her sleeve.

"No, I can't. It is insanity. No one in your country will accept me."

"It would be wrong for me to marry anyone else, when I only love you."

"Then think of your father. If you force him to accept me, he will lose face."

"I will talk to him. Remember, he was charmed by you."

"When people hear what I have done here, they will never believe my child is yours too."

"Janna, light of my heart, don't you want to marry me?"

He could see the conflict in her moist eyes.

"I want you to be my consort. I want our child to be legitimate. I want you, no other. I love you."

Janna still couldn't speak.

"I will not promise you that our life together will be easy. I don't even know if I will have a crown to inherit. I will be placing you in even greater danger than you are already. I don't know what I did to deserve your devotion, and for saving my life, over and over. I can only honour you with myself, and I would be greatly honoured if you will be my wife."

Janna put her arms around Ali and whispered, "I'm such a fool, but yes! I will be your consort. I would give my life for yours, and if your people won't recognise our marriage, if they refuse to acknowledge that I exist, it won't matter, so long as I can continue to serve you in some way."

They kissed then, until Ali drew apart and announced, "How do people get married around here?"

Janna added, "Father, please find a celebrant, or a JP, before my sense returns."

Dupont sighed, accepting her choice. "You will need to give me some time to arrange that. Meanwhile, both of you keep out of trouble and stay here."

"Can you have Famira brought here? She will want to see Janna."

"I'm on it," David announced. "What about her boyfriend?"

"I suppose so," Ali said with some uncertainty.

"No!" Kane announced. "He doesn't need to know yet."

Ali and Janna moved to the couch where they sat close together. Janna put one of his hands on her just starting to bulge belly. The baby kicked, and an expression of awe suffused his face.

Dupont slipped out, and David sidled over to Kane. "You don't trust the boyfriend?"

"No. But I can't really say why."

"Well, my partner will be bringing Famira here. I will see what she thinks of him."

Kane's phone pinged, and he checked the message, then showed it to David. "Number of interest called from neighbourhood of house mentioned."

David murmured, "Any way to find out the boyfriend's phone number? I assume he has a cell phone."

"I believe he has one."

"Did he get it here, or did he bring it with him?"

"I can see if Martinez or Stephens can find out. Both of them could ask technical questions on some pretext or another."

"Good. And can you find out from the Group if they got anything else from the call? Was it answered? How long the call was?"

Kane nodded.

Voices from the front of the house heralded another arrival. David knew one was Wanda. She edged around the room, as Famira went directly to where her brother and friend sat. Janna stood and hugged the new arrival, whispering something that caused Famira to emit a squeal of delight.

David murmured to Wanda, "The boyfriend made a call after you left, to the number Jabir has been contacted through."

"Yes, he knows we were going to see Janna. And he may think Ali is with her now. He wasn't happy about being left behind, but couldn't get around the fact that Janna doesn't know him."

"What did you think of him?"

"He is supposed to be a scholar, but he acts like a spoiled rich brat. I am reasonably sure he understands more English than he is letting on."

Ali stated the expected question. "You did not bring Mohan."

"My decision," Wanda said quickly. "I thought the ladies would like a private discussion."

Famira turned to Wanda and said, "You were correct. Besides had I brought Mohan, he would have demanded more of my attention than I wished to give. Besides, he does not need to know that my brother and friend are to be wed."

"Are you going to keep other secrets from him?" Ali asked, surprised.

"Ali, I do find Mohan charming, and knowledgeable about many subjects that interest me. I like his attention and could do a lot worse than him in a consort I did not choose for myself. But I do not love him. He fought bravely during our escape, even though he is not a real soldier. In many ways, he is weak. I trust him only as long as no one tries to influence him."

"Like our uncle?" Ali suggested.

"No, Uncle hadn't been around for a while when I met him. Supposedly, Father agreed to our betrothal, but I have not been allowed to see him to confirm it."

"He never mentioned anything about getting you married off," Ali said thoughtfully. "It is still possible it is Uncle's doing. I wonder what Mohan was promised. Besides you of course."

"I don't know if anything was, but he said that if you do not have an heir, any child of ours will be heir after you."

"That could be thought of as maybe I won't be around," Ali considered. "I wonder that Uncle has no bastard children he'll bring forward. Or will he find some woman to have his own heirs."

"If any woman would have him," Famira murmured.

"It wouldn't stop him," Ali decided. Then he changed the subject. "Will you be staying in America now?"

"I do not know," Famira admitted. "I left because I was afraid for my life, and Mohan encouraged it. I didn't want to leave Papa alone, though."

"You could have done nothing," Ali told her. "At least here, our uncle and the general can't use you to force father to do something."

"They could, if they don't tell him I have gone."

David spoke from near the door. "If you remain, my lady, you might make your uncle believe your brother and Janna are still here."

"Yes, but...will you not be staying here?"

"No," Ali told her. "I think it is time that I went back and led the loyal forces and help to rescue father."

"And I will be going too," Janna asserted.

"No!" Famira wanted to argue, but she could see her friend was resolute.

"It will be the last place your uncle will expect me to be," Janna told her. "I won't be going at the same time, but it will be in the next two months."

"Why? Oh! Are you pregnant? Is it Ali's too?"

Janna nodded.

Kane inserted, "There is much you are not aware of, lady, but some people will insist it is not his."

"It is!" Janna insisted.

"Then before each of you go, we should get a DNA sample from you. I also know it is possible to get a DNA sample from the child, even at this stage," David suggested.

"We will do that," Ali stated, glancing at Janna as he spoke. "For me, that will need to be done tonight."

"You are going that soon?" Janna cried.

"Yes. Things are being organised as we speak. When I arrive back, I will have time to prepare a place for you."

More arrivals caused them all to fall silent. Dupont led an oldish man wearing a black cassock into the room, and introduced him to Ali and Janna. Wanda gestured to Famira and they went to where Dupont was watching the priest shepherding the young couple to a side room.

"Lady Famira, this is Frank Dupont, Janna's father." Wanda made the introduction, distracting Dupont from some thought.

"I am delighted to meet the father of my friend."

"Oh, yes. You are most welcome," Dupont murmured.

"He's heard why Janna left your country," Wanda commented. "It was such a thorough job of destroying her reputation that it is hard to believe there is no truth in it."

"Oh, but it was all lies," Famira exclaimed, reaching out to take Dupont's free hand. He had a suitcase in the other. "I cannot believe any of it. Not even for a minute. Janna has a beautiful soul."

"Maybe so," Dupont chose to agree, but he nodded at Famira and went to put the case in Janna's room.

Wanda knew he was thinking of what Janna had done since returning.

The quiet murmuring of the priest talking to Ali and Janna in side room became the focus of all, as silence fell. Kane's phone buzzed. He answered tersely, listened, but only said, "Keep me advised."

He said, "A call came from the number of interest to the phone in the other house."

Only Famira was ignorant of what the report meant.

"Well," Wanda murmured. "Whatever is being planned, isn't for here."

The Priest led the way from the side room. "I have spoken to these young people, and I am satisfied that their wish to be married so precipitously, is not a mere whim. They know what hardships they will face, and are prepared to accept them. Are there any preparations you wish to make before I begin?"

"I brought along a few things for Janna," Dupont surprised his daughter. "A more suitable outfit than that which was available here."

Famira didn't let Janna stay staring at her father. She began to pull Janna towards her room. Ali walked over to the men, and asked Wanda, "Aren't you going to join them?"

David winked and said, "Why aren't you?"

"I'm not sure..."

Famira decided the issue. She came and dragged her into Janna's room as well.

Dupont turned when he heard the bedroom door reopen. His daughter emerged, dressed in the same gown that her long dead mother had worn on her wedding day. For a moment, he seemed to see his wife there, then it was only Janna, as he led her to where Ali was now resplendent in a borrowed suit.

"Dad, can you forgive me for hating you?" Janna murmured.

"If you can forgive me for being so dense," Dupont whispered back. "I have to believe that you are not what was claimed when you returned from overseas. For I doubt your Prince would marry you if you were."

Famira carried a small wrapped bunch of flowers, which had also been in the case. Wanda made a show of carrying the train of the gown. She and Famira shared a smile that father and daughter were reconciled.

The ceremony was brief. Janna, with makeup done so well that no sign of her recent hardships showed, was radiant. Ali, looking so proud, couldn't take his eyes of Janna for longer than it took for him to sign the wedding certificate. He nodded when he was told one copy of the certificate would be kept safe, and took his copy when it was placed in his hand.

The rarely seen guards had come in to be witnesses as well. Then they returned to their posts.

After that, it seemed an anti-climax. Their couple's first kiss had drawn quiet applause, and now both received hugs or handshakes. Dupont stayed back, until Janna launched herself at him.

"Thank you for bringing the dress."

All that remained was the traditional toast, made after non-alcoholic cider was poured into glasses.

Dupont watched the new couple disappear into Ali's room. They would have little enough time to be together. Ali was to leave before dawn, and tomorrow, Janna had to become Nadia Shaston, for hopefully the last time. He looked around and saw Wanda and Famira disappearing back into Janna's room, talking low and intent. Kane was watching the street out the front.

David wandered over to him.

"You'll be going with the Prince, will you?" Dupont asked.

"Part of the way," David admitted.

"I'd be a lot happier if Ali's uncle was caught."

"So would I, but I fear he has too much power to stay caught. The best we can do, is keep him here, and distracted for as long as we can. Probably only a few days. That should be long enough for him to get back and merge into the populace. Once he is safe, word will be allowed to get around. I think then, Jabir will suddenly decide to leave."

"And forget his desire to kill my daughter?"

"I think a threat to his plans for world domination will be vastly more important. And we will allow rumours that Janna had no desire for anything more to do with that country."

Janna woke early, with Ali gently shaking her. "I have to go, my love."

She wanted to beg him to stay, but forced herself to be strong. She slipped form the bed, donned a long robe, and then gave him a long passionate kiss.

"Be safe," she told him. "I want you to be there when I arrive."

"I will, I promise. And I want you to protect our child, he or she is the promise of a better future."

Janna followed him from the room, seeing Kane, David, and the rest of Ali's guards looking like clones of each other in Marine camouflage fatigues. They wasted no time moving out through the passage to the garage, and a van waiting there. She returned to her room to get dressed, and found a message from Famira.

"For now, I will be with Mohan. I will not be telling him of your joyous union. I hope we may see each other again soon."

Wanda had taken her back, and stayed there until a female officer had come to act as a chaperone. Mohan had not been aware of Ali's other guards leaving. During the time they had been alone, Wanda had explained to Famira what they hoped she would do.

"We will have you and Mohan moved to another safe house. If you can let slip that Ali is having talks with US officials, and that you are very sad because Janna has told him there is no chance of anything between them."

Wanda returned after the men had departed, and found Janna

sipping coffee at the kitchen table. It was not hard to guess how she felt. Dupont must have suggested she redress in the remand uniform, but she had yet to fix her Shaston face.

"I don't know how I am going to do this today," Janna admitted. "I do not feel strong, like Nadia."

"Then be the strong woman Ali loves and needs," Wanda suggested. "Both of you have a battle to fight and win. Go and make up your face. That act in itself can remind you of who you need to be."

Janna left the coffee to go and do as suggested. At that time, she and Wanda and four guards were the only occupants of the house. When she returned, she found Wanda busy on a laptop computer.

"What are you doing?"

"Organising you a new passport and ID papers. Also, arranging for the papers you will need when you get to Ali's country. It won't do to go as yourself. As Nadia, I can use a photo of you for that ID. So just stand over by the white door."

"They will let me leave? I thought my old passport was cancelled."

"They will and they did." Wanda used her phone to take the photo, then went back to her computer. "In your favour, you have been prominent in assisting the capture of a lot of nasty men. Interpol is very impressed. I do already have an agreement from the higher ups in the State Department, that you deserve a second chance. So, you just need to get through today, and then Nadia Shaston will officially disappear for good. The press will never find out the full story."

"When will I be able to follow Ali?"

"Give him time to discover the situation over there, and to set up a place for you. Meanwhile, these new IDs will require time, and you will want to do the DNA testing and get the result. While we wait, there are more things I can teach you, and I have some audio courses to help you improve your fluency in Arabic."

It wasn't until after the newspaper arrived that John King realised he had lost a whole day. That thought triggered others. There was something he needed to remember. The what, remained elusive.

The nurse came in and helped him to sit up and take a call.

Dupont, asking how he was, triggered one urgent question. "How did things go in court yesterday?"

"The two cases were deferred until today. They brought forward the appearance of the four we caught at the house. They will be being deported to Italy."

The sense of something urgent to be said, increased in intensity, but King still could not recall.

Dupont kept talking. "The case against the three that assaulted Janet Delaney should be open and shut. As for Nadia Shaston, her appearance is only a formality. The judge has signed off on a deal. All charges will be dropped. The evidence against her for murder isn't strong enough in any case – particularly after the full story of what she was doing was revealed. They realised how she had helped us catch over a dozen Cobra sect members."

"So they know the woman's real name?" King asked. "I had the feeling both names were aliases."

"They were," Dupont confirmed.

"So who was she?"

"I'll fill you in when I see you later today," Dupont promised. "I need to get to the court house."

King accepted that there were things too sensitive to be discussed on an open phone line. His mind went back over the early part of the call. What had triggered his anxiety?

"Do you remember what happened to you?" Dupont was asking.

"Some. Jabir was angry about something. I just remember the bashing and being shoved into a large cupboard. I didn't know until this morning that I'd been drugged too."

He hadn't quite come to grips with his narrow escape from death. It was lucky the doctor here was familiar with the drug and its effects. He had to assume his half-brother no longer trusted him.

Dupont told him to rest up and get better, and he grunted a reply. He should, his whole body was painfully stiff from that beating. What had his half-brother wanted to know?

The conversation was a blank, but he could recall earlier ones. One when Jabir was gloating because Shaston had been arrested for murder. His malicious comments had caused him to reconsider Shaston as a threat. She was still a loose end. Jabir would want to be sure she could not tell anything she knew about him or his sect members. If she went to prison, that wouldn't protect her. He'd had his tattoo put on her. She was marked for death. But he still wanted Ali, and the other girl – Dupont's daughter.

"No!" he murmured aloud, as a truly horrible thought came out of the blue. "No! Nadia Shaston looks nothing like Janna Dupont." The thought paralysed him. Dupont hadn't even hinted at the possibility, but it explained so much.

King groaned as he leant to get his phone from the drawer. He tried calling Dupont, then Pearson. Neither answered. "Of course," he told himself. "They would be in court." And he had told his brother this was the day for the appearance, trying to trick him. But if he was right, and both Delaney and Shaston were actually Janna Dupont – "Oh, NO!"

Without asking permission, and by dint of ignoring the protesting of every muscle, King first yanked the drip from his arm, and ignoring the blood dripping from the puncture, eased himself out of bed. He moved with great care to the wardrobe and found his clothes. He didn't bother with anything except shirt, trousers and shoes. He only gave his hair the briefest of combing.

As he opened the door, he saw his police guard eyeing a disturbance down near the nurses station. He slipped out quietly and walked the other way. He found a lift to take him down, then walked through the foyer and out to the nearby taxi rank.

He hadn't thought of money, but when he checked his pocket, he felt his wallet. He gave the driver directions to the court house, and silently urged the driver to hurry.

Once there, he provided his ID, and asked directions to the chamber being used for Delaney vs the three men that he was relieved to recall the names of.

On the second floor, in the waiting area for later cases, he caught sight of a figure scuttling into one of the passage ways. The body movement was familiar, and the person's identity came to him. Quasim! He could only be there for one reason, and court 7 was down that passage.

King edged around the pacing people, and looked along the passage. He didn't see anyone, and wondered where the man had gone. He had noticed a clock downstairs, it had been half past eleven. How much longer would the court session last?

Dupont had said, "Open and shut". Then it occurred to him that prisoners leaving the court went out a different door to the witnesses and spectators. Delaney/Shaston was still technically a prisoner. In any case, Dupont would want her protected. How did one get to that back way?

As he thought that, the door to court seven opened and people began to emerge. He had a glimpse inside, over the heads of the emerging people. He edged in, forcing his way against the outward flow. He made for the rear door that also led to the judges' chambers. Dupont, with the woman known as Shaston, had just gone out, followed by two guards. He hurried after them, and emerged into a smaller, open hall just as movement from a stairway caught his eye. He didn't think, just reacted, shoving Dupont and the woman to the floor as something flew towards them.

Something shattered with the tinkling of glass, and acrid fumes filled the air. He thrust a handkerchief over his nose, and half dragged, half lifted the woman back into the courtroom. He went back for Dupont, but he was getting to his feet, and only needed shoving in the right direction.

King's eyes were watering, as he turned, he found himself facing Quasim. The man had clear goggles on now, and recognition was mutual. Quasim turned and fled. King was too stiff to try to run after him, and had little enough breath to try. If had been about to enact further mischief, he had changed his mind.

Someone in a suit, came and helped him back into the courtroom.

"What are you doing out of hospital?" Jim Pearson demanded.

"Had to come," King rasped. "I saw Quasim here. Are Frank and the woman okay?"

"We have help coming. Which way did the guy go?"

King gestured and tried to laugh. "He looked like he thought I was a ghost."

"You look like one and damn well nearly were. What happened?"

King managed a terse report. Pearson sent word to update the arriving fire trucks and paramedics. Then he gently urged King over to where Dupont was standing over the woman. He stood guard, while the other security people were helped by their fellows. Pearson dragged a chair over for Dupont and another for King.

"Where's Mrs Martin?" Dupont asked.

"She wasn't out in the hall. John, did you see her?"

"No. I was watching Quasim."

Wanda returned with the paramedics, and went directly to Janna. She had taken an oxygen tank and mask from one of them, and proceeded to slip the mask over Janna's face.

When her patient began to move, she said, "Just lie still, okay? We need to flush that stuff from your lungs."

"The baby?" Janna asked weakly.

Wanda placed a hand on Janna's emerging bump. She left it there for a while, feeling several kicks, and using senses few people knew she had.

"Well," she said finally, "I think the little blighter liked the excitement. However, you will be checked out properly to be sure.

One of the uniformed paramedics came over after checking the older men. "Special Agent Dupont mentioned this woman is pregnant."

"Yes," Wanda confirmed. "I have felt the baby kicking, but I assume you will want a doctor to check?"

He nodded, and Wanda moved to let him work. She went over to Dupont who was, like King, using a wet pad to ease the sting in his eyes.

"Where did you disappear to?" Dupont challenged.

"After the bastard. I got the police looking for him. He got a good whiff of his foul gas too."

"It is my fault," King moaned. "I told my half-brother the hearings were today, thinking they were yesterday."

Before he could berate himself further, Wanda asked him what a certain phrase meant. She repeated it accurately, and believed it was Arabic.

"Roughly, it means 'ghost from hell'. Where did you hear it?"

"That little bastard was muttering it. I didn't quite get a grab on him. I saw him see you and turn to run like a rabbit. Do his people fear ghosts?"

King appreciated that she wasn't lumping him with his half-brother's men. "Demons, yes. The ancient beliefs don't have angels like the Christian beliefs do. Those who do bad things are given to demons after death."

"Well, that guy must have a seriously guilty conscience," Wanda commented. "However, his aborted mission here, which was to kill Janet during the confusion, failed. But, it gives us an opportunity to end this. I will speak to the paramedic, and see if they will agree to take Janna out covered over. To make it seem like an unfortunate death. Maybe, John, you will let Pearson take you out like you are being arrested. We can put it about that you tried to finish that guy's job. You never liked Shaston, did you?"

"I doubt that will endear me again to Jabir. I think he no longer trusts me."

"So long as he decides you may still have a future use. We can make out that Janna had a concussion, from when you pushed her over, and she smothered while you lay on her. Something like that. Maybe we could have several conflicting stories. That blood on your sleeve could suggest things."

"You have an extremely convoluted mind," Pearson told her, and received a wicked grin in confirmation.

As part of the deliberate campaign of misdirection, Wanda went to visit Famira. She managed to tell her to ignore everything she was going to say, then urged her to the couch and began to speak softly to her, as if passing on bad news.

Mohan, seeing only they were talking and he could not hear, came over and asked, "What is wrong." He spoke Arabic, and became very solicitous of his betrothed when she abruptly threw herself, sobbing, into his arms. Famira didn't immediately tell him what was wrong, and then, all she implied was that Janna was dead.

Suspecting that Mohan was in fact in contact with Prince Jabir, this was Wanda's way of getting Ali's uncle to find out that Nadia Shaston, had actually been Janna Dupont, and to confirm in his mind that two threats to him had been neutralised.

With Famira pulling back from Mohan enough to ask, "Does my brother know?"

Wanda's reply of, "David will be telling him after his meetings," was, she felt sure, understood.

Famira spoke to Mohan, then went to her room. He would have followed, but Wanda advised, "Let her be for now." Mohan stopped moving and turned back to the television. She hoped the residual redness in her eyes from the gas, would be taken for her grieving as well.

The media coverage of the incidents at the court house was based on a media report read by Jim Pearson. It did not include all the details, mentioned no names, but gave enough tantalising hints for the sensation seeking papers to put their own slant on things. The main fact was that a visiting foreigner and a police agent had been killed.

Some more enterprising and less scrupulous reporters started stalking Frank Dupont, and followed him to the municipal crematorium, but were unable to discover what he did there. However, they had uncovered the fact that Nadia Shaston and Janet Delaney had been the same person, and had testified against some foreigners, who had come from a country Janna Dupont had been evicted from, and assumed the rest.

A few days later, they saw Dupont emerging from one of the crematorium chapels after a private service, and when Famira emerged, took a quick photo on their phones. They hoped Jabir would take that as proof.

During that time, Janna was under guard at a private hospital, but Dupont did not go near it. At first, she was recovering from the gas and the shock. Her pregnancy was monitored, to ensure the baby had not been affected. All looked well. While she was there, the procedure to extract a DNA sample of the baby was performed.

In another room, John King was recovering from some constructive facial surgery. His face had been altered subtly, to make it appear different. The rest helped him recover from his severe beating.

Janna had started to keep him company, realising now that he was not on his half-brother's side.

Their only way of keeping abreast of what was happening with Jabir, was calls from Dupont.

Chapter 23 – Last Days of Safety

Wanda Martin, Frank Dupont and his men, were all working hard to find where Prince Jabir had fled to. Wanda spent time with the Group, making suggestions to help find Jabir's new communication channel and to try to discover when he decided to leave the country.

Wanda had arranged for an opulent suite at one of Washington's top hotels to be put at the disposal of Famira and her consort. High quality servants tended them, a chaperone/companion was provided for Famira. Security was discreet, but strongly present. It was overtly to protect the couple from Ali's enemies, but also to watch Mohan, monitor any calls he made and observe anyone he spoke to. He had never experienced such luxury and the ready availability of room service, that he did not have to pay for, seduced him.

State Department agents with diplomatic training, accompanied the couple when they went out to explore the city, and the discreet guards were ever present.

Wanda was relieved when David called her to say he was back on American soil. He arranged for tickets to the upcoming state football match, and Mohan had eagerly accepted that invitation. Then, once Mohan had left, Wanda took a lightly disguised Famira, to visit Janna Dupont.

Famira was surprised when she saw her friend. Janna was wearing clothing of the style worn in her country, and had begun to take the pills that would darken her skin to a tone similar to Famira's. Wanda brought out all the clothing she had sourced and had Famira look critically at it. She pronounced it suitable. Then, she began tutoring Janna in the body language of her people, the expectations of women's behaviour – the little things that might betray her as foreign.

Amongst the clothing, and passed by Famira, were items that could also be weapons. She did not see the two slender palm sizes knives that could be slipped into a belt, a shoe or a narrow pocket.

The latter, Janna was already proficient at hiding and drawing.

Several more meetings were arranged, the last being, ostensibly, to allow Famira to buy some American gowns, and fabric to make some traditional ones on her return. At that time, David had taken Mohan shopping for formal wear, and some football merchandise. He was so hyped up that he was unaware of any thing odd about his fiancée.

David and Wanda returned to the hospital, to find Dupont visiting Janna. He as examining the new passport and identification papers Wanda had arranged for her.

"This looks totally genuine," he commented. "Dare I ask where it was produced?"

"The US one is, but as for the other, no, you shouldn't ask. I will say that it is genuine. The paper and ink matches what they use in Jakhabad."

That identity was for a Fatima Anzin, born in a remote village in Ali's country.

"The young man arrived safely?" Dupont asked.

"Yes, Sir," David confirmed. "Ali and his guards crossed the border and were met by loyalist forces. The 'all safe' message was sent on schedule and correctly worded."

Dupont gave his daughter a fierce hug, and spoke words for only her to hear. Her return hug was equally fierce, for unspoken between them was the knowledge that it might be the last time each saw the other.

When he was about to leave, he looked at David and said, "Keep my daughter safe."

"I will, Sir. Until I have to pass her onto others sent by her husband."

Then there was only the final briefing. Janna would be leaving the next morning.

"Janna, I know I promised your father to look after you, but I won't be going with you. Wanda will, but you needn't be concerned that she is any less capable than I am."

"I don't think that," Janna said immediately. "How will we be travelling?"

"Wanda will have the details, but initially you will be two

Americans travelling together, and later as natives of the Middle-East. You will be joined by some Americans recruited by Kane. You will also have John King with you once you enter Jakhabad. Ali will message us with the contacts you need."

"Are you coming in too?" Janna asked Wanda.

"No. I have to keep on the other side of the border. We can't get officially involved. It is dangerous enough for you to be going in."

"You know why I must," Janna insisted.

"Maybe not 'must go'," David argued gently. "At least in one sense. But, yes, we do understand. You and Ali belong together, and give each other strength. It may be a very long time, though, before you can be together as an acknowledged couple."

"I know that," Janna said, her face taking on a determined expression.

"Don't let the wait, or the circumstances, depress you," Wanda advised. "Think often on the future, when you and Ali are where you want to be. Think on that when the times are toughest. Sometimes, fate needs to be given a direction."

Janna gave Wanda a hug, and then did the same to David. "Thank you both for all you have done."

"You're welcome, Janna," David answered for both of them. "You have our best wishes."

Later, when Wanda and David were back in their motel, preparing for bed, David said, "I'll get you to the airport before five. You can read the details of the route on the way. Nicholas will meet you in Tel Aviv, and take you to the first relay point. He will have the gear you need to keep in touch with the loyalists. The most dangerous part will be from the last airport to the border."

Wanda nodded. "Got that. Any sign that Jabir has left?"

"Not yet. The Group are still picking up communications between his phone and another – possibly that Quasim guy. I am going to keep his attention as long as I can by allowing hints of what Ali is supposedly doing here to get about. The hints will be mentioned in the hearing of Famira's boyfriend. I have him thinking that I get a bit indiscrete when I have been drinking. He knows you and I have been dealing with Ali. I let slip today that my superiors have agreed to a meeting with him."

"I hope that is enough."

"So do I, but I am wondering about those conversations I mentioned. Quasim's phone has been originating calls from Washington DC."

"Send Erin a follow up call to mention that to Goldman," Wanda advised. "It might be related to the idea we had of Jabir being after some kind of technology."

Chapter 24 – In Danger

Wanda stayed at the hidden camp while her mentor, Jim Phillips, and another member of his covert mission team escorted Janna to the breach in the border security where, just over a week earlier, Ali had entered.

All the expected replies to their sent messages had come through, and they had to cross that night, since David had sent a message when Jabir's private jet had requested flight clearance. He would be back in the palace in the capital of Jakhabad by morning.

All she could do now, was send mental thoughts to the being she called 'the spirit of the Earth', to protect and nurture Janna and her child. Few people would believe that she had some kind of psychic connection to the Earth's aura, but that didn't matter. She had the sense that it would work to maintain peace, or work to return it. Already, the disturbance caused by the military coup was agitating the aura, and Wanda had only needed to picture Ali and Janna as the symbol of returning peace to the area. It was the only thing she could do for the couple. She hoped it would be enough.

Even aware of the dangers, Janna felt a stirring of excitement in her gut. She was going to join Ali, her prince, her husband, her lover. The father of her child.

It would not be her role to fight the rebel soldiers, or even make it known she was Ali's wife. Her rational mind said she shouldn't be there, but in spite of that, she needed to be. Of that, she was sure.

In the darkness, she and John King crossed the border. Before they had gone half a mile, they were joined by a group of locals, led by Kane. All had been handpicked by Ali. They had a farm cart, pulled by two placid horses. Within half an hour, they were hidden in a farm house.

They rested there during the day, and continued on once it was dark again. This time the cart was half filled with produce going to the market in the next town. Her guards acted like casual fellow travellers.

Three days later, Janna reached the village where she was to stay. It was nearly morning and she was tired, wanting only to sleep. When she entered the house, owned by an old couple, her eyes went wide. Ali was waiting for her, their eyes met, but he did not greet her immediately. Instead, he greeted John King as a friend, and introduced him to his loyal guards and the couple who lived in the house. Then, at a gesture, his guards went outside. When only the couple, King and Janna remained with them, he went and embraced Janna and introducing her, by the name she would be using, to the old couple.

The old ones had faint smiles on their face, but when he then told them she was his wife, and carrying his child, they sobered. As one, they bowed to Janna, and unprompted, they swore an ancient oath to protect her, and the child, with their lives. To Janna, he explained that Anilla had been his nurse, and Jako his tutor at arms.

Then, with Ali translating where Janna did not yet have the words, she told the couple her cover story. She was newly widowed, her husband had died in a clash between the two civil factions. She was a relative of a friend of another man who had recently died. She ended by saying, "I need to learn to be truly one of you."

"We will teach you," Anilla promised. "For now, you are in mourning and no one will be surprised if you stay secluded and speak little. If we go out together, I will talk for you."

As her pregnancy progressed, she got out more, and her command of the language and culture increased. Always with Anilla, she began to help with the old woman's work as nurse and midwife to the villagers.

News from Ali came infrequently, but it seemed that the loyalist forces were slowly pushing Jabir's army in from the border and closer to the capital. John King was a more frequent visitor and often the source of news from Ali. He never visited Janna directly but passed his news on through Jako.

The first sign of the reversals for the loyalists came when artillery fire started being heard from the village. Within days, rebel soldiers tramped through the village, and set up camp on the outskirts. By then, Janna was eight months pregnant, and when the soldiers began a house to house search, busy with Anilla, helping a woman having a difficult labour.

The soldiers burst into the house, at first ignoring the labouring woman and the two who were helping her. They demanded to see the identification of the father to be and then demanded he tell them of newcomers to the town, strange men. He claimed only seeing the soldiers, and before that no strangers since the last harvest festival. Then they demanded to know who the extra women were, already knowing only the man and his wife lived there. Anilla and Janna were ordered to show their papers and these were examined, and the pictures compared to their faces.

Janna betrayed no fear, she had been taking pigmentation pills and her skin tone matched that of the locals, and by then, her command of the Arabic dialect there was excellent. She was in the process of helping the pregnant woman to walk around, and her arms were bare to the elbows. Too late, she realised that the cobra tattoo might show up paler than her skin. She calmly turned the woman away from the soldiers, as if leading her back to her bed.

The soldiers left, but the father-to-be came over to her.

"Fatima, that soldier seemed to know you. Have you met him before? Perhaps in your former village?"

Janna met Anilla's eyes, as she said, "I think they saw this..." She pointed to the fine scars where the black lines of the cobra tattoo had been removed.

"You must hide," Anilla urged. "If they did see it and know its meaning, they will come back."

"Where can I go?" Janna asked. "And if they return, will they harm you?"

"Come with me," the father-to-be instructed.

With Anilla shooing her away, Janna obeyed. She followed the man to the back of the small house and outside and into a small shed. The man reached down and pulled up the cover of a trap door. Chicken droppings and food scraps dropped off it.

"There is a ladder going down and a torch just below the floor. Can you make it down?"

Janna nodded.

"Wait for me at the bottom."

He waited as Janna started down, guided her hand to the torch, and when her head was lower than the floor of the shed, closed the hatch. Janna kept the torch off, for she needed both hands on the ladder. The bulge of her belly was making the simple task difficult. Above, from beyond the hatch, she thought she heard someone sweeping. She sent a fervent prayer to which ever god would hear her. "Keep my child safe."

Once down onto the dirt floor, Janna used the torch to see what was around her. She saw a long low seat, some bottles of water and tinned foods. Not knowing how long it would be before the man returned, she sat down, keeping the torch off to preserve the batteries.

Soft scuffling noises woke her from a doze. She flashed the light on briefly, and her eyes widened when she saw a hole becoming wider, in the wall of the dugout cellar.

"Fatima, it is Jako," a soft voice called to her. "Can you crawl through?"

She went to the hole, and used the torch light to judge its size. It would be a snug fit, but she guessed they did not want to make it too big – possibly intending it to be filled in again.

It was awkward. If she were not so hugely pregnant, she would have commando crawled. As it was, she had to try doing that side on. Hands were helping to pull her through. In the midst of those contortions, she felt a strong contraction. Still pushing herself forward, she prayed the contraction was not the start of labour. She was not due for three more weeks. She stifled a cry, but even that smothered sound brought a warning. "We must be quiet."

She emerged into a large clay brick walled tunnel, high enough to stand in. As three men hurried her along it, she wondered why it was there and how old it was. They emerged into a wider area with several wooden doors and dim light that didn't seem to be coming from lamps or electricity.

Jako pointed to one and said, "That door leads up to our house. The bastards have already searched there. Even so, I think you should stay down here for now."

Janna went over to another of the long low seats, just as another contraction caused her to double over.

Jako swore softly. "Your baby is coming, yes?"

"I think so," Janna told him, once she could speak again.

"My wife has not returned from Mariam, and may not be able to leave for hours."

"I should be right. I'm told first babies take their time."

"I will bring her as soon as I can. Do you wish someone to stay with you?"

"I should be fine, but I should have brought some water."

"I will bring some."

Then Jako and the other two men each went out by different doors, and Janna could see nothing of what lay beyond, and didn't try. She hoped keeping still would not bring on another contraction. Instead she looked around, now noticing other low benches, several chairs around a table, currently pushed against a wall, and a separate chair, partly hidden behind a curtain. Her mind suggested it was a camode, and she tried to convince herself she did not need to use it. Yet its very presence suggested this place had been used before to hide people.

Janna, who no longer had a watch or a phone, or any other way to tell the time, tried to keep her mind on positive thoughts, as her mentor had advised. How she wished Wanda was here now, but it seemed that her friend had foreseen a time like this. So she made the best of things and tried to sleep. Her doze ended when another contraction coursed through her. She shoved the rolled up part of her sleeve in her mouth to stifle the cry of pain. As soon as it passed, she tried to keep a count of the time, but the need to doze - possibly a result of the airless place, again came over her.

She hoped Anilla would come soon.

Janna had lost count of the contractions, when a gentle hand shook her awake again,

"Fatima, how are you? Are you still having contractions?"

"Yes, and I think they are getting closer."

"Try to stand and walk around. I will fix up this bed."

Janna complied, but as soon as she did another contraction rippled across her belly.

"Lie down," Anilla ordered. "Let me look at you."

She first helped Janna from her underwear, then felt both her belly, and how much she was dilated. To distract Janna somewhat, she said, "Poor Mariam's child was still born, and she was bleeding badly. I needed to stay with her until the doctor could come. Even then, I could not leave. I had to help him too, for the soldiers had questioned him roughly."

"What else is happening?" Janna asked, wanting distraction.

"I should not worry you at this time, but they are looking for you. Showing a picture."

"What picture? Is it of me as I am?"

"No. If it is you, your hair is longer, your clothes are different, and you look like a woman of the streets."

"Did they give a name?"

"No, but I asked for a copy to show to the other women." Anilla drew a folded paper from her pocket and showed it to Janna. She cursed in English, and was quickly shushed.

"How could they have connected me with her? That was taken in the US. I left there in secret, after Ali's enemies thought me dead."

"I do not know, but perhaps it was that mark you showed us."

"I guess it has to be," Janna said after thinking a while. "Has there been time for those soldiers to have reported and got orders back?"

Anilla nodded.

Janna shuddered, this time from fear. "I don't want you to be punished for helping me."

"Do not worry for us, worry for your child."

"I do," Janna admitted, as she felt yet another contraction coming on. "Promise me, Anilla, if it comes to a choice between them finding me and finding my child, protect my child. Ali's child."

"We will hope you will both be safe. Those contractions are getting closer and you are almost fully dilated. I think this child is impatient to be born."

As the next contraction passed, Janna thought intensely, "Please come soon, little one."

"You said Mariam's child died," Janna said. "When mine is born, can you swap them? Does anyone else know?"

"Only Mariam's husband. She has been drugged to sleep. I said I would take care of the death matters."

Jako came into the chamber and whispered something to Anilla before leaving again.

"He told the soldiers he was looking for you as you were sent on an errand and haven't returned. He pretended not to recognise you in the picture, and asked them to look out for you. He will come back soon with some things we will need."

Janna didn't see what he had when he returned, but she felt his strong gentle hands supporting her as she was positioned over a blanket on the dirt floor. He gave her a thick wad of cloth to chew on as the contractions grew fiercer. He gave her strength, when Anilla urged her to push.

The baby slid out, deftly caught by Anilla, and Janna was eased to the floor, so the child could be placed on her belly. The boy, for she had lifted her head to look, gave a low mewing cry. Her two helpers stiffened, listening. Then Anilla went to work, cutting and tying off the cord, and urging her to push again to bring out the after birth.

As quickly as possible, the baby was cleaned up and wrapped snuggly in clothes and a blanket Jako had brought. "Take him to Mariam's house. She will be able to feed him. I have Mariam's little girl here. Go! Hurry!"

Janna was too exhausted to see the look they exchanged. She was aware of a quiet whisper, of Jako leaving and Anilla urging her to stand.

"You will need to hold these cloths in place," Anilla said, helping Janna pull her underwear back into place.

"In one thing you are lucky, Fatima, you did not tear and need stitching."

"What's that noise?" Janna asked, now more aware of a sound she'd been hearing for a while. Now she was also feeling the rhythmic thudding.

Anilla glanced upward. "They should not find us here. This cellar has been here for centuries and few know of it."

Janna continued getting dressed, and allowed her hair to be brushed and tied back, under the head scarf. Then one of the men from earlier trotted in through one of the doors.

"You must leave. They are trying to break the floor in Kulim's house. Come! We should be able to get past the dirt fall to the river passage."

Movement was painful, but Janna knew she had to stay free. She hurried her pace as best she could with the thick padding between her legs. The man led her to the far side of the chamber to where another passage led off. A section of brick wall had hidden that opening from Janna's former position. That passage did not go far, and seemed to be a dead end until the man shone a torch onto an excavated hole, like she had crawled through before. She crawled again, the process being easier now, but still painful. On the other side, she took deep breaths, while Anilla came through, and a man who had bundled up the bloody sheets and other signs of the birth. The last man reverently brought through the wrapped form of Mariam's dead child.

Then they all went on, as the passage sloped down to the river, and the trickling of water grew louder.

"The water comes from a spring, but when it rains, the water soaks down and it goes to the town well. We can travel along here at the moment and come up near the horse market," Anilla explained. "There is an empty house near there where we can go to."

They emerged, hidden within the night's darkness, and only had to walk 50 metres to the house. Even so, they were aware of the soldiers, still searching in the town. The horse market was quiet, and when they entered the house, they made sure all blinds were down, and the doors locked when the men departed.

Anilla helped Janna to a bed, then dropped the bundle of sheets, her bag, and more reverently, Mariam's child. Janna was immediately asleep, and Anilla watched the outside from a slight gap in the blinds. She hoped the search would be called off.

Morning came, and Anilla woke with a start, having dropped off after her long hours helping with two births. Loud voices outside must have woken her, and she saw her friend was also awake.

"Soldiers," she whispered after a quick check. "Rebels."

Janna whispered back, "If they come in, do not fight them. You have simply been doing your rightful work, helping me. You were not to know that I am whatever they will claim. Just make sure my son is cared for."

"I have already promised to do that for you, for the rightful prince, and our King."

The door was smashed open, armed soldiers ran in, weapons aimed. Neither woman moved.

"What is this intrusion?" Anilla demanded, with the dignity of her vocation. She was ignored as two soldiers went and dragged Janna from the bed and to her feet. "Fatima has just has a child. She is not fit to go anywhere."

"Child?" the leader of the group demanded. "Where is it?"

Anilla pointed to the pitiful small bundle. "The girl was still born."

The man went and unwrapped the bundle, roughly and callously, then let the body and wrapping drop to the floor. Anilla went to pick it up but was grabbed.

"You have been helping a criminal, a traitor, a whore and a spy," the leader claimed, then he ordered, "Bring her too."

They were both hustled unmercifully outside into the morning sun, and towards a small truck with high covered load bed. One of the men standing by the truck, watched them approach, his eyes fixed on the younger woman. Janna saw his face harden and twist with loathing. She recognized him, as someone who had visited Tozer several times. He should not have recognized her.

"Get in!" Janna was ordered, and she tried to obey, but she was still weak, and needed to keep the already blood-soaked cloths in place. A hard shove on her back only caused her to fall on the ground, in a near faint. She cursed him in her mind, calling down the wrath of any god that heard her.

The leader told that man to lift her in, and that one showed his resentment at her resistance by tossing her in and walking off.

Anilla scurried up and in, going to Janna and asking, "How are you, Fatima?"

"You do not need to concern yourself with that carrion, woman.

She is marked for death. Real death, not the fakery the American demons would have us believe." The leader gestured one of the others to get in the back.

"American?" Anilla exclaimed in shock. "You are wrong, she is a friend of a friend of Jaco's cousin."

"She duped you. She is an American agent."

The truck drove off with the soldier keeping his weapon aimed in the direction of both women. The road was rough and the truck's springs next to useless. Somewhere during the drive, Janna blacked out. She was still unconscious when her friend, Anilla, was dragged out. Then the truck drove out again.

Anilla spared some breath for prayers for the brave wife of Prince Ali as she was dragged to the city police station. There she was told to wait, until it was decided what to do with her. Later, she was pushed into a car and taken to a different part of the city. She recognised the route to the palace, and was proved right as she was dragged into the presence of Prince Jabir, and shoved down onto her knees.

She looked up, met the eyes of Prince Jabir, and her body recalled the many years she had worked at the Palace. She put on the mantle of her former position, and answered his questions. Jabir recognised her, but did not modify his anger. She spoke the truth as her whole town knew it.

Fatima Anzin is a widow, a friend of the cousin of one of the townsfolk. She had taken the pregnant woman in out of kindness. She had gone out on an errand, and when she did not return, was looked for. She had been called from tending at another birth, to look after her as she had gone into labour.

"It is well the child died," Jabir said callously. "Its mother will soon be reunited with it."

That told Anilla that he had received and believed the soldiers' report, and believed the dead girl was Fatima's child. She didn't know if he had thought it was Ali's child, or not. It didn't matter. The boy child was safe.

"Old woman, if you again help traitors to our country, you will die -painfully and slowly."

"I do not question those who need my help," Anilla said with dignity, standing straight and still meeting the Prince's glare. "Though I did not think a woman capable of being all the soldiers claimed. However, I am loyal to those who rule this country, and will endeavour to do as you request."

Her words seemed to be enough for Jabir to believe her scared into obedience. She was allowed to leave, and did so calmly, and without an escort.

She passed people she recognised, some flashed her a smile or a hand signal, telling her they were on her side, against the usurper. She nodded, impartially, to them all – her mind already considering ways to rescue the mother of Prince Ali's child.

Chapter 25 - Captive

Janna drifted in and out of consciousness, for a long while. Usually her head was throbbing, and her throat parched. Then, she woke and felt she was already in the fires of the demons of Jakhabad's hell.

The first time she tried to move, she felt her legs were glued together, and she scarcely knew why. But the sense of having something important to do drove her to try and sit up. Pain knifed through her.

A gentle voice told her to stay lying down, and there followed the feeling of a cool cloth on her burning head. She obeyed, for it seemed at that touch, the headache eased and the other pain subsided.

Her wrist was lifted and someone was taking her pulse. It was too dark to see more than a faint outline of the other person, and she moved her other hand to feel the hand that touched her. It was slender, unmistakably feminine.

"Anilla?"

After a pause, she heard, "No, sorry. I'm Erin."

"Where are we?"

"We are in some kind of dungeon."

The voice was American. Unbelievable.

"Why are you here?" Janna asked weakly, afraid to hope.

"I guess they aren't quite ready for you to die," the voice said. "They dragged me down here and said to make you better."

"Make me better so they can kill me," Janna translated. "They don't like Americans."

"That has been made quite clear to me. That and my being a woman who shouldn't be so intelligent. However, they desperately needed a computer expert and I was all they could get."

Janna tried to think why a computer expert was needed. The palace had just been starting to use computers three years ago.

"Don't worry about that," Erin suggested. "What happened to

you? Were you raped?"

"No. I had my baby." Janna burst into tears, and then felt the gentle hand squeeze her wrist slightly, as if in sympathy.

"Did they take your child from you?"

The thought that this woman was a plant, to get her to talk, made her lie.

"It was a girl. It died."

"Oh, no! I'm sorry. But that at least explains why you are bleeding. Did you have anyone with you?"

"Anilla, the midwife."

"Did she say if you tore at all?"

"She said I was lucky and didn't need stitches."

"You don't want them, I needed three after my daughter as born."

"If you are here, where is your girl," Janna asked, feeling that was safe to do.

"Back in the States. My dad is raising her. Long story. What's your name?"

"Fatima Anzin." Janna was still not going to admit otherwise. "Why are you working for them?"

"I didn't exactly get a choice," Erin said, keeping secrets of her own. "And while they won't tell me what they actually want, my usefulness is limited. Do you think you can take some water? I've been here most of the day, and I think you've been out to it since yesterday, at least."

"Yes, please."

Her hand was released, and Janna felt the movement of air as the other woman stood up and moved away. She heard the sound of water being poured, and the woman returned.

"Can I help you sit up? You are on a cot like thing attached to the wall."

Once she was up, she felt the cup held to her lips and she brought her own hands up to hold it.

As she drank the water slowly, she sensed that it was better that she did, Janna asked, "Is there a loo here?"

"Sort of. It's one of those long drop type. I will help you up, and I will change the towel I have soaking up the blood."

Janna needed the support of the woman for as soon as she was upright, she felt the blackness coming over her again.

"Take slow deep breaths," Erin told her. "You have lost a lot of blood and haven't been up for a while. Move slowly, when you are ready."

"Are you a nurse as well?" Janna asked as the dizziness receded.

"Hell no. My only experience is from having had a kid myself."

"Why did you give your baby up?"

"Well...I was going to be in jail for a while. I thought Gerry, my mate, was dead. And...I didn't think I would be a very good mother."

"Oh!"

Janna thought, she's some kind of criminal. Then she had a hysterical desire to laugh. Before she had come back to Jakhabad, they thought she was too.

"What's up? Are you all right?" Erin asked.

"No. Obviously," Janna admitted. She changed the subject. "I'm surprised Prince Jabir agreed to have you here, unless it is because you are a criminal."

"That may be part of it," Erin admitted, deciding not to deny the accusation. How could she know if they were being overheard? She didn't think the guards were that close, but there might be electronic voice pickups. "I don't think I was their first, or even second choice. I think I was meant to be the scape goat for the others. With my record, almost anyone would believe it. Still, they got me away from the people who were overseeing everything I did, brought me here, wherever here is, but I'm still being watched. I'm being treated better than you, but that is probably self-interest to keep me working hard. But that isn't saying much, the servants are better off than I am. Who is Prince Jabir? What's he look like?"

Janna almost missed the seat over the pit toilet. Needing help to such basic things roused some anger. She didn't answer the last question, because she again wondered if this woman was to report on what she said, or if they were being overheard. The person she was pretending to be, would not be expected to have ever seen the Prince.

Erin sensed the reluctance to answer, so went on speaking. "When I got here, I was dragged in to meet a hawk faced guy – richly dressed, arrogant, and a guy in a fancy military outfit."

Janna spoke very softly. "Jabir and his general."

Erin spoke again, just as quietly. "There has been a coup here?"

"Yes."

"Where is here?"

"Don't you know?"

"I was travelling prisoner class to come here."

"Jakhabad."

"Part of the UAE?"

"Yes."

"I see..." Erin murmured. "I sort of guessed that might be the case." In a louder voice, she went on. "You finished yet? Okay, stay put until I find one of the clean towels. And I want to put sheets on that bed."

Erin helped Janna get comfortable back on the cot bed, after positioning the clean dry towel to stem the bleeding. "I will try to get them to bring you some food."

"I'm not really hungry."

"You need to eat and keep drinking. Has you milk come in yet?"

"What?"

Erin explained in a low voice.

"Yeah," Janna admitted, realising then why her breasts seemed full and tender.

"I'll show you how to express some, since you don't have a little one to drink it. It will ease the soreness, and may help the bleeding stop. The milk will dry up soon if no one is suckling."

"No!" Janna protested, feeling tears in her eyes.

Erin didn't ask for the reason for the unexpected outburst, just explained what Janna needed to do. Then she softly hummed an odd tune before going quiet and seeming to be listening.

"Stay resting," Erin said quickly. "I think my escorts are returning for me and I don't know if they will let me back."

"I don't want you to go."

"I'd rather not as well, but I had better keep certain people sweet. They need me to do programming, but I don't I know their real plan yet. And I don't think they will let me nap first. Anyway, if I don't produce the goods they want, I doubt they will bother just tossing me back here."

Erin felt Fatima, or whatever her real name was, shiver. "Listen!

I don't know if they have a way to monitor this cell, except by peeking in, but it would be best to keep resting and sleeping and seeming weaker than you are. I put the bottled water where you can reach it, and the extra rolls of towel next to their idea of a loo. Do you think you can get that far by yourself?"

"Yes. I feel much better now."

"Okay, but like I said, don't act it."

"I can't stay here!" Fatima stressed, grabbing Erin's hand. "They will use me to get Ali here, to kill him."

"We can't do much. We are just two foreigners in the enemy stronghold. But, keep hoping for what you want. I am damn sure help is coming – don't ask me how – I just know they will not want me helping our hosts."

Erin drew her hand free and stood, just before the light came back on and two guards rushed into the cell. The point of a pistol was used to gesture her out. The man didn't look at Janna, just sneered at Erin.

"Bring out your rubbish, woman. The carrion is not to be allowed to kill herself."

Erin collected the bundle of bloody towels, and was then grabbed by the arm and hustled out. The man was not gentle. Janna watched, until the light went out, but the woman, and her manner, and that tune she had hummed, reminded her of someone else, and irrationally, she began to feel hope.

End of Part 1

The Serpent's Shadow

Part 2 – Thrust into Treason

The Serpent's Shadow

Part 2 – Thrust into Treason

Chapter 1 – Under Cover

Erin Mason put her phone down thoughtfully. David's message hadn't really told her anything. Yet his wife, her cousin Wanda, had insisted he ring, and she had moments of 'just knowing' things. Her instincts, were generally accurate.

Four weeks before, David had told her of an important foreigner who was interested in some kind of technology. His source had overheard the word "skywatcher". Neither he, nor her cousin, in spite of their high level security clearances, should have known of the Skywatcher Project. He had asked her to pass the message onto her current boss, the Director of the Scientific Intelligence Office.

Now, David had said that the important foreigner was getting impatient. Her own instincts were telling her that she should tell her boss, Magnus Goldman, right away. It might mean more to him than it did to her. She glanced at the clock, it was late, nearly 11pm. She had been about to go to bed, but she decided Goldman was likely to still be awake. She called his private number.

"Erin. What have you to tell me?"

She wasn't surprised when he recognised her number. She reported to him on an irregular basis, always to his private number.

"Sir, I have had a call from my cousin." Goldman would know who she meant. "Their person of interest has been communicating with someone in Washington DC. The person was the foreigner's 'procurer', as they put it. He sounded impatient, and they think he is likely to return to the Middle East soon."

She waited for Goldman to answer, picturing him sitting at his desk, considering how that snippet fit into a larger picture.

"That seems to confirm our earlier suspicions," he said finally. "I will arrange to increase security on the project, and I will let you know if your role needs to change."

Erin didn't try to prolong the call with questions. She only said, "Okay" and ended the call.

It was a well-kept secret that she was a covert agent for the SIO. Goldman had recruited her after she had completed a six month stint of marine training. That was the option that had replaced a longer jail sentence for some serious cyber-crimes. He had felt that her 'hacking' skills should be put to the use for the good of the nation – once he was certain she had reformed.

Initially that had been for short terms in labs doing diverse and often secret scientific research. Her title was program auditor, and her role was to trouble shoot computer programs and fix flaws that reduced efficiency. She had proved herself, over and over, rising to each new challenge.

Four months before, he had slotted her into the Skywatcher Project – still as a program, auditor. She was, in reality, the third most senior team member. Above her, in charge of the project, was General Charles Maxwell. His deputy was Stan Otway. Both knew of her criminal record, and each had warned her against stepping out of line. They had reservations about her, and had watched her for the first few weeks. Now, she was an integral part of the twelve person team that was intent on ironing out the bugs in the control program of a new intelligence gathering satellite due to be launched later in the year.

When she had passed on the initial warning, Goldman had directed her to make an addition to the firewall program to prevent incoming intrusions. After doing that, she had given him another to monitor the outgoing requests for information from the internet. He had told her to put it on the network.

Once loaded onto the mainframe, it identified the sites visited and recorded the data. It also recorded outgoing emails. The information was stored in a secure file, but she was authorised to access it and check over the data on a regular basis.

When she had produced it, Goldman had asked her if she had any suspicions of anyone on the team.

Erin reconsidered her decision to create it, and only said, "It is just a precaution."

Goldman had gone on to quiz her about it - how it worked, what it could do. He told her to see if anything came of it, but gave no hint of whether he would use it anywhere else.

So far, the program had yielded nothing suspicious. It hadn't really surprised her, because she knew that everyone in the team had been thoroughly vetted prior to being appointed. Her own position had come available when one of the women had left on maternity leave.

Nowhere in her job description was there a mention of some highly secret tasks. Her two superiors had no knowledge of them either. She was to be alert for any suspicious activity or unusual behaviour on the part of any member of the team, including her bosses.

It seemed to be a contradiction, considering the apparently faultless backgrounds of everyone, but obviously, things could change. After the latest warning, she would wait to see if Goldman wanted her to do anything else, and meanwhile keep on with her overt work.

The following morning, Erin arrived at the tall glass fronted tower that housed the computer lab, earlier than usual. She had decided she wanted to scan the monitoring program before her work colleagues and bosses arrived. There was also an addition she wanted to add to the program that she would need to program manually. It would have been quicker to bring in a USB, but she was not meant to bring such a thing into the lab.

Due to the highly secret nature of some of the programs they were working on, security at the building was ultra-strict. First, she had to log in at reception, then go through a scanner and have her bag scanned and quickly rifled through. That had become a source of strictly inner amusement for her, some of the other women resented it. She had simply shrugged and minimised the personal stuff she brought in with her. On the way out, they checked to be sure no 'work' was being taken out.

Then she was allowed to go to the lifts that serviced the three floors related to the planned intelligence satellite. Even then, she had to swipe her chip embedded ID card to open the doors, and repeat the process at the door of the lab. On the odd occasion they needed to bring in bulky things, security guards were with them.

Her plans, however, were thwarted. Both Maxwell and Otway were in the lab when she arrived.

"Must be the day for coming in early," Stan remarked when he saw her come in through the electronically locked door. Maxwell nodded and departed.

"Seems so," Erin agreed easily. "Don't laugh, but I think I was dreaming of that damn power unit algorithm last night. Some of the ideas I had still made sense this morning, so I want to try incorporating them."

"Well, you might as well get started," Stan told her. "It seems the top brass want to beef up security even further."

"What now?" Erin pretended the idea was completely new to her.

"Retinal scanners," she was told. "We are to expect technicians today, to organise recording them for each of us."

"Whatever keeps them happy," Erin said, glancing up at the ceiling then back at her boss. "I would have thought it more logical to beef up the computer security. Though, at the moment, they would need to get at all of our computers."

Stan grimaced at the reminder of the deadline they were under. There were still a lot of issues with the programs that needed ironing out. "Should have had us write it all from scratch, not modify an old one," he growled. "All the instruments are new, or more sensitive, and have added functionality."

"Aren't most of the systems needed basically similar to the last generation?" Erin queried. "That was what I understood – that we would just have to tweak the parameters."

A fleeting look of 'I know more than you' crossed Stan's face. "Even the instruments that are doing the same function are as different to the last gen ones as this year's smart phone to those of five years ago. Haven't you been up to the electronics and engineering labs?"

"Only briefly, on my orientation. Can I arrange a longer visit? The electronics lab might be fascinating."

"For you?" Stan seemed to consider. "Hmm, probably not. You

might get lost up there, and we need you here."

"Beast!" Erin grinned back. "But you are probably right as electronics is my other speciality."

She shrugged and headed towards her workstation to dump her bag in her drawer and turn on her computer. Having Stan pacing around like a nervous panther made it hard for her to bring up the monitoring program, but she could bring up her file list and check the size of the file she had created for the records. The size was the same, so looking wasn't imperative.

She set to work, writing the code she had claimed to have dreamt about. The rest of the team were used to her zoning out to everything, so once she started, Stan seemed to forget about her. This time though, something – like an itch – was distracting her. Every now and then, she glanced up to see what Stan was doing. Twice she saw him on the phone, once in the little side office that held the printer and a bench for doing minor computer repairs, or spreading out printouts or diagrams.

By nine o'clock the remaining team members, except for the injured Terry, had arrived. As each had come in, Erin had looked up, and used her little known empathic gift to see how they were. There was nothing really amiss, just minor things – Arwin had a slight hangover, Morgan had her period, and Joseph a twisted and bound up ankle.

At morning tea time, Maxwell called them all together. He mentioned the new security scanner and told them they would be called out, one at a time, to have retinal scans made. Then he went on with news that was even more interesting to them all.

"The electronics lab now have a working mock-up of the satellite's on board computer, and a means to measure the activity when our program runs. We can test the code, and they can see if it triggers the relevant systems. So, before you leave today, I need you all to upload the newest version of your sections of code, to be sent to Otway's computer."

"That's all very well," Erin remarked. "We might make the mock up turn on a system, but then what? It might only do that. How can we check if it begins to collect data and if the data is crunched to make sense?"

"That is a good point, and I have already asked that the next stage be for them to connect prototypes of the instruments - things like the cameras, the orbital position fixing...anything we can realistically test in a lab. The power unit won't be so easy. Do you have any ideas?"

"Yes. To see if my program can be fed information from an old mission – the actual trajectory data perhaps, to see if it predicts the actual power draw and usage."

Maxwell considered that. "I will give that some thought and see what Goldman thinks. For now, we will see if it does the basics, and gets data from the instruments mentioned."

Erin was satisfied with that, and let the others ask their questions.

At lunch, Erin went up to the Atrium, and indoor garden on level 5. She found a secluded area, away from the few other occupants. She called Goldman, to mention the idea she had given the General.

"You might have something there," Goldman agreed, sounding interested. "I will make enquiries. Anything else?"

"No. There was no unusual activity on the monitor program. The only people here after I go are Stan and the General."

"Keep alert. Can you send me a copy of your code?"

"Yes, Sir, but I haven't finished coding it yet." Erin wanted to ask why he had reminded her. She was doing that as a matter of routine, although her two immediate bosses had no idea of that.

When Goldman rang off, Erin pocketed her phone and used the quiet environment to refresh her mind, and to allow herself to be open to ideas that sometimes came to her. All she felt was the same trickle of alarm that she had felt that morning, and the previous night after David's call. She thought in turn of all of her work colleagues, and let the subconscious observations trickle up into her mind. Nothing new came to mind, except that both Stan and the General were stressed – but that might simply be because the project was to be presented to the Defence Department in a matter of months. That was obvious because the whole team was being urged to work faster.

Even though her break time wasn't due to end yet, Erin had the urge to get back to work. Wondering at the abrupt urgency, she eased the mental shields she had learnt to keep on her empathy – that extra sense she had. It was still a compromise, because she did not want the emotions of everyone in the building shoving into her mind.

For the next two hours, while she created lines of code from the rough notes she had made, part of her mind was monitoring the ambient emotions. Not all of the team were concentrating hard, but that was normal. Even she took short breaks to read over her work and relax her mind. Then suddenly, with no specific warning, a noticeable shiver ran down her spine. Immediately, she knew something was wrong. Even though she had still not become totally comfortable with her gift of empathy, she had learnt to trust warnings such as she had just felt. She stood up, as if just needing to stretch and move around. In doing so, she glanced around, seeing all the others in the lab in turn. The only oddity was Lauren Avery, sucking her finger tip. Was that all it was? Was that the source of her premonition?

A phone rang, and she heard Stan answering. Then, "Mason, the security guys are ready to do that scan business. You're up, want to be first?"

In truth, she didn't, but nothing else seemed wrong. "Why not. I needed a break. Where are they?"

"Meeting room B."

After checking she'd saved her work, and putting her computer into hibernation, she headed out.

The process really didn't take long, but she found it hard to stay perfectly still for the time they required.

On her way back, Erin felt her phone vibrate and checked the caller. She knew the number and paused in the passage to answer. Gerry, her soul mate, was calling her and she did not want her conversation overheard, or any hint that he was in prison to get around. He knew she was doing secret stuff, and they hadn't spoken for over a month.

"Just had to talk to you, girl," Gerry told her. "Had to know you were still waiting."

"Twenty-eight days," Erin said, and heard Gerry chuckle.

They spoke for a while until Erin heard the guard say, "Time's up, Rand."

Gerry said, "I'll find you girl."

Into the glow of pleasure the call had given her, Erin felt her other senses ramp up and she had an intense premonition that came as an intense shiver that settled in her gut and twisted.

Her electronic key card was in her hand, ready for use and while it activated the lock, she looked into the lab. All seemed normal...

Chapter 2 - Uproar

She was just about to sit back at her desk when she heard a chair fall over. She twisted, and saw Lauren, Instantly, Erin focussed her empathy there, and seemed to be seeing what Lauren was hallucinating. Creatures, terrible monsters, all around, gnashing teeth. Her own heart began pounding like a jack hammer, and her muscles paralysed, like they had been petrified. Her eyes met Lauren's, as she began to scream.

Erin forced shields on her mind, imagining throwing a thick rubber mat over herself. The emotion paralysis vanished and she began to move as Lauren began sweeping stuff of her desk, little things at first, then grabbing the edge of her desk...

"Lauren, NO!" Stan roared, but she could not hear him. He was trotting towards her, reaching out to grab her as she mindlessly fled for the door. He caught her arm, but Lauren spun around fighting back, hitting, biting, kicking – a virtual dervish. Stan released her, checking his bitten hand.

While everyone else was sitting in stunned silence, Erin was acting. Stan had slowed her, enough for her to position herself to block the door. They had to confine the trouble, and Erin, with her Marine training, had a grasp of the situation. Her empathy was already focussed on the other woman, and as she had once done for her cousin, she encompassed the terrified turmoil in Lauren's mind and clamped it down, and was ready to catch her.

Stan approached again, the others standing and seeming uncertain. Lauren's body was shaking, and she was sobbing uncontrollably. It looked like Erin was holding her up, but Lauren was hanging onto her like her life depended on it. Then she spotted Stan, and seemed about to struggle again.

"Let's go into the tea room," Erin suggested quietly into Lauren's ear. Then to Stan, she gave orders, reminiscent of herself as marine sergeant. "Stan! Don't let anyone leave here, and call the General. Get him back here, right now."

Stan stared at her for a long moment, stunned by hearing the voice commanding him. Then the relief hit – Mason knew how to handle the situation. He saw the strain on her face and pulled out his phone to get help. The others milled uneasily.

Erin, supporting Lauren's weight, for she was on the verge of blacking out, told the others, "Go back and sit at your desks."

Most did, except Mark who moved towards the dropped terminal and overturned chair.

Seeing the movement, Erin added, "Mark! Leave it. You can turn off the power at the wall, but leave everything as it is. It should be safe enough and I want to check everything before it is moved."

Mark straightened, shrugged and returned to his desk.

Stan moved closer, and helped take Lauren's weight. She had just enough awareness to move as directed towards the tea room. Once there, they eased her to the floor, and Erin began to examine her, checking her airway and breathing, and pulse before positioning her in the recovery position.

"I'll stay with her. Don't let anyone touch Lauren's stuff. Is the General coming?"

"He's on his way. He was in a very high level meeting," Stan told her. It was a subtle warning as well as a rebuke. "I also called a medical emergency. An ambulance is on the way."

Stan returned to the main lab and glanced around. All eyes were on him. "Is anyone else feeling strange? Ill?"

Head shakes or "No, Sir," came from the rest of the team.

"Did Avery mention to any of you that she wasn't feeling well?"

He received the same response, and it was all he had time for. The main lab door opened, and General Maxwell, Magnus Goldman and a man Stan had seen but not met, entered.

"What's the situation," Maxwell demanded.

"Avery had some kind of episode, potentially from her computer. Mason has her quietened in the tea room. She tipped over her desk, and was quite uncontrolled in behaviour. It was sufficiently concerning that you needed to be told at once. I have an ambulance on the way."

"Tell me everything," Maxwell directed more quietly, as Goldman began to study everything around the lab. The stranger, who was carrying a briefcase, headed for the tea room, where Erin was crouched over Avery. Stan was distracted, and only noticed that Erin didn't get up to greet the man, rather the man crouched down.

Erin recognised he third man with relief, knowing him to be a doctor. She was quite happy to let Stan act like he was in charge, as he should have been, and give the report. She could add her own view, through the doctor, while he examined Lauren and she kept her quiet.

"What happened, Erin?"

"Dr Wallace, I was sensing something off most of the day, but it was only when I was coming back from getting an eye scan done that it peaked. Lauren began screaming...but just before that, her expression seemed one of terror. I was feeling my heart pounding and my muscles seemed petrified."

Erin continued, giving Wallace all of her empathic impressions as well as visual observations. He accepted them as observable facts. "She fought while Stan was holding her, but I stopped her running out of the lab, and managed to clamp down on everything. I also think she was feeling like fire was burning inside her."

"What was she like before you went out?" Wallace asked.

"Normal. Wait...I saw her sucking her finger. You know, like you do when you prick it."

Erin watched as Wallace took a mouth swab and a blood sample. Then, he checked each finger carefully until he found one with a tiny scab. The finger was slightly swollen, and Wallace gently squeezed it – Lauren jerked, and Erin had to increase the intensity of her calming thoughts. He squeezed some blood out, and soaked it into a narrow strip of some kind.

"Will you be looking over her keyboard?" Wallace asked neutrally.

"I intend to, unless Stan or the General overrule it. I will insist on checking the computer too, though that is probably just junk now."

"Check for any tiny metallic fragments," Wallace said quietly. "I don't know how it might have been fixed, but the puncture mark is on the side of the little finger here. I would guess some compound was injected, and she may have sucked come into her mouth. It may have been a contact poison, but we can't be sure. In any case, it would be powerful or concentrated."

"I will take care," Erin promised, understanding the unstated warning.

Lauren began to moan. "Doc, you will need to knock her out. She would still be fighting if I wasn't holding her."

Wallace reached into his case again, and brought out a vial, then directed, "I will get you to release your hold, but be ready again to resume what you were doing."

At his nod, Erin began to ease her grip on Lauren's arm. She saw Lauren's eyes fly open; there was no sense in them now, and her arms flashed up to push Wallace away. Erin tightened her grip again.

"Some kind of hallucinogen," Wallace murmured. He took out a syringe and filled it from the vial.

Erin sensed when the medication began to work, by the lessening of tension in Lauren's muscles. When Wallace met her glance and nodded, she eased her grip again. This time, Lauren stayed quiet.

"Will she be alright?" Erin asked in a low voice.

"Leave her with me. I will see she gets the best care. It was lucky you were here. Your observations and empathy have given me a great deal of information. However, you will need to get back out there?"

Erin was torn. He was right, but she liked Lauren and wanted to help her.

Just then, Stan came to the door. "The ambulance officers are on the way up. How is she?"

Wallace stood up and turned. "I have given her a sedative, and will go with her to the hospital. We will need to do tests to determine the cause of the events."

"I'd like to be told if you find anything, Sir," Otway said then. "I can't think what might have brought it on, but I would not like it to happen again, to someone else."

Wallace nodded. "I will keep Magnus Goldman advised, and I am sure he will pass on the results."

Erin was still hovering after Stan turned way. "I can take things from here, Miss Mason."

Shaking herself from dark thoughts, Erin nodded at the doctor and headed towards her desk. She needed something to replace the energy she had expended keeping Lauren quiet. She had some share sized chocolates in her desk.

Stan came over. "Maxwell wants you to stay on after the others leave. He's told them to pack up ready."

"Won't we need to make statements?" Erin asked.

"Goldman is sending security up here to check us out before we go, but he wants the rest of us to write out what they saw before they go."

"Check us? How? More than the usual scamper past the metal detectors and x-ray machines?"

Otway shrugged. "We will find out."

"What about Lauren's computer?" Erin asked, glancing at where it lay.

"Maxwell said to wait. Goldman will have some forensic guys coming up. Once they've been over everything, we can clean up. He said to put everything in the side room. Someone needs to see what is damaged and if it's fixable. He is reluctant to let the engineering team go over it, but you know electronics, he said."

"I did say that. I have built a few computers from scratch, and know how to troubleshoot them."

"Good. Go and sit down. I don't know how long it will take those guys to get here and do their stuff."

"When will the rest of us get the eye scan done?"

"That, yes. With all that has happened, I'd forgotten that. Maxwell didn't mention it. It will need to be put off, I expect."

"Why not get them to do it before they go?" Erin suggested reasonably.

"I'll see," Stan told her.

Back at her desk, Erin tried to get back into her work, but she was still very aware of Lauren lying asleep in the tea room, and the concerned presence of Rowan Wallace. She picked up her written notes, so as to seem to be reading them, when in fact she was trying to sense the reactions of the other team members.

Strongest was the shock and after reaction to the events they had witnessed, as well as the questions of why and how it had happened. Those two questions were on her mind too, but she pushed those thoughts away. Now she wished that her special talent was more like that of her cousin, Wanda, who could pick up thoughts.

To cover her abstraction, Erin decided to print out what she had typed that morning and go collect it from the side room. She worked on a mind trick to exclude the dominant thoughts and emotions. Then she felt the slightest sense of "would they find it?" and something about the security, "A bit late for that now."

Had Lauren's misfortune been caused by the threat of more security?

That only made sense if some unauthorised person was coming into the lab unnoticed. One of the security people? Surely not, or not alone. What she was sensing was coming from within the room. And was there just the faintest trace of guilt?

The ambulance people arrived with the gurney, and Erin watched as they took Lauren out. She jumped when Stan spoke from right next to her.

"Are you okay, Mason?"

"Oh! Yes, I'm okay." She wasn't going to admit that her body felt like jelly.

"You look as white as that paper. How did you manage to quieten her?"

"I really don't know," Erin told him. She wasn't going to bring up her unusual talent. "I was whispering reassurances, and staying as calm as I could. I think she fought you because she sensed your agitation. I don't think any of us expected what happened. She must have recognised me on some level and after a while, the hyper reaction put her on the verge of passing out."

"I guess I was freaked at that," Stan admitted. "You did well, Mason, and I want to know what happened."

"Me too," Erin agreed truthfully.

The security team arrived as Lauren was leaving, and one ran some kind of scanner over the patient before nodding for the medical team to continue on their way.

Stan went to speak to them, then announced, "Everyone is to come over and be checked – bring any bags you bring to work, or intend to take home."

Stan submitted to the procedure first, even following the instruction to turn out his pockets. The devices, it seemed were even more sensitive than those at the ground floor entrance. She suspected they would detect more than just metal. Erin followed, making no fuss when one of the female officers expertly frisked her, even though the process reminded her of less pleasant times.

One by one, the others gave Stan their written accounts of the incident, and were scanned and allowed to leave until only he and Erin remained with the security team. Goldman and Maxwell had left earlier, probably to return to their meeting, and Erin assumed she would hear from Goldman later.

Stan slumped into the seat at Ed Tate's desk. It was nearest Erin's. "The boss won't get his updates today," he commented. "If the lab isn't cleared for us all to work here tomorrow, you or I may be cleared to access the other computers to get them."

"Do you know everyone's passwords?" Erin asked, as if surprised. "Or is there some kind of master password?"

"There's a master file stored somewhere, obviously, in case we forget our own. I think Maxwell has access, or maybe it's Goldman."

"I think it would be better to just wait," Erin said. "However, if it's that urgent, I guess we will be told."

Something Goldman had told her months back, made Erin think he would not be dismayed by the delay.

Erin tried again to focus on her work, to look at the logic in the flow of code, but it was useless. Her side vision kept showing her Stan's fidgety movements. She tried to sense anything he was feeling, but it seemed to be relate to a deadline, and time running out. That wasn't surprising, nor was his annoyance at having to sit around when he wanted to check out the damaged equipment, and feeling like the guards thought him a suspect. He was staring at the mess on the floor, with the sense of things needing to be done, Erin guessed he was considering how to replace Lauren's computer if it couldn't be fixed.

Stan jumped, almost guiltily when Erin suggested, "If Lauren's terminal isn't fixable, I might be able to take parts from it and fit them into that old one in the side room."

"What's that?" Stan spun to look at her.

"There's one in the cupboard we keep the paper supplies in. I could mix and match parts."

That interested him, Erin decided. "How long would it take to see if it's possible?"

"A day or two. I would need to check everything over first."

"It might be worth it. Maxwell didn't seem keen to bring an outsider in." Stan glanced at the guards, as if their presence contradicted his statement. "I think we are here to oversee the forensic people when they come, even as those guys must be watching us."

Erin emitted a quiet snort. "Do you want me to volunteer?"

"No, but I will ask Maxwell. He may prefer to keep you on that power unit program. That is the most complex part of the overall program. It's a trade-off though. Avery will need somewhere to work when she gets back, I can't guess when that will be."

Stan dropped back into silent introspection for a time then spoke abruptly. "Do you want a coffee?"

"No, thanks. I'm twitchy enough already. I might grab a hot chocolate later, before I leave."

Erin watched him as he headed for the tea room, and so did the guards, but he wasn't stopped. She turned her attention to the mystery. Lauren wasn't a programmer, not really. Her job was data entry – adding each new section of code onto the mainframe, proof reading, or occasionally research.

Was that why she had been targeted?

The forensic team arrived, she recognised the acronym on their jackets as being that of the Washington DC police department. Watching them work kept her mind busy, and their activities seemed of interest to Stan, too. He was intent on everything they did, particularly their inch by inch search of the floor around Lauren's desk, both where it lay, and where it had originally stood. They scanned everywhere with some device and even dusted for prints. Erin doubted they would find any that were not authorised.

Finally, after two hours, the leader directed the team to pack up. Stan stood, stretched and went over to talk. "Will you be sending Maxwell a report?"

"Our orders are to report to Goldman. I expect he will pass on out findings."

Stan nodded. "Good enough. I hope you can figure out what happened. Can we move the pieces into the side room now?"

"Yes, Sir. All but the keyboard and mouse. We will be taking those with us."

"I see. You will give a receipt for them?"

"Certainly."

Erin only had a glimpse of them, already bagged and labelled, but something caused her to jump up and ask, "Can I just get an equipment ID number from them?"

Her request startled Stan, she could sense him looking at her. She fetched a pen and paper when the okay was given.

"Thanks. I thought we'd better have it for our equipment register." She gave the team leader a quick apologetic grin, and moved so he could follow after the others. The security men left with them too.

Stan shook his head. "I should have thought of that," he told her. "We'll have to do an equipment damage report, and if we can't jury rig a replacement, put in a requisition." He sighed audibly. "I know where there is a trolley we can use. I'll go get it. That way we can put everything together. I won't be long."

Erin stayed standing, considering why she had asked for equipment IDs. If her sudden impression wasn't a trick of the light, the keyboard that was taken away, wasn't the one Lauren usually used, even though the mouse certainly was. The confiscated keyboard was dark grey, she was almost certain that Lauren's usual one was black. She tried to recall the last time she had noticed it. She had heard nothing about a change of keyboard, or of there being any problems, and Lauren hadn't made any comment that morning. She should be asked about that as soon as she was able to be questioned.

However, if it had been swapped, when had it been done? Everything had been okay prior to her leaving for the eye scan, even though she'd had that odd feeling. If it had happened during the confusion, was the proper one stashed nearby?

Moving quickly, Erin checked the desks used by Terry and Mark – the two nearest. Terry had been on sick leave for a week, after straining his back while moving house. His desk was neat, his drawers locked, but his keyboard was not plugged in. The fact was only apparent when she checked closely. It was black...

The rattle of an empty trolley alerted her and she quickly turned the board over and tapped it gently. She heard something like a pin drop. The quarter inch sliver had a reddish tip. With a pen, she pushed it out of sight under the mouse pad.

She was back staring at the computer when Stan stopped the trolley.

"Power's off?" Stan queried.

Erin moved to the end of the desk and checked that Mark had done that. "Yes." She pulled out the power cords, and released the few still clipped to the desk, so Stan could lift the computer unit.

"Something's loose," he commented. "How is the monitor?"

"Screens cracked, but at least it didn't shatter."

"Can you put it on the lower shelf?"

Erin did that as Stan collected the modem unit and the other bits and pieces. Then she collected all the scattered papers, now hopelessly jumbled, and put them all in an empty folder, and added the other folders after shaking the pages back inside.

In each case, she only needed a glance to know what each paper and folder was, but she left it a jumble to hide that fact. Then, when all the loose stuff was on the trolley, Erin helped Stan right the desk, and she checked he drawers before pushing them in fully. The forensic guys had checked in there too.

"I'll put the paper stuff in my drawer and sort it out," Erin said.

"Leave it for tonight," Stan told her. "Why don't you lock up and head home?"

"Will you be?"

"If Maxwell doesn't have anything else for me to do."

"I want a hot drink before I go," Erin said. "Do you want another coffee?"

"If you're making it," Stan agreed.

"Just this once," Erin warned him.

While the kettle was boiling, she considered how to recover the sliver she had found. She needed Stan out of the way, briefly. She decided to text Goldman, even if he might be at a meeting.

"Can Otway be called away for a bit? All others have now left."

There wasn't a reply, so she dawdled over her drink making. The lab phone rang and Stan answered it.

He hung up and headed to the door, but poked his head in the tea room on his way out. "Cancel the coffee. I'm wanted upstairs. If you leave before I'm back, lock up, will you?"

"Sure," Erin agreed, then sipped her drink.

As soon as she was alone, Erin found one of the sugar sachets and poured the contents in her cup. Then, she found the tweezers in the first aid kit and went over to Terry's desk to get the sliver and put it in the empty sachet. Then, returning to the tea room, she found a plastic sandwich bag and put the sachet within. This went into her handbag, as her phone beeped a message. "1900 @ office." It came from Goldman's private number, he undoubtedly wanted a reason for her request, and a report.

She had time, and finished her drink and left the cup washed and draining. She went to her desk and put all the lose papers from Lauren's desk in and locked the drawer. She left Stan's computer on. He would be coming back, but went around locking up to leave.

Erin didn't leave the building. Instead, she went back to the atrium to wait the two hours. She had been there twenty minutes when she received a text. "Room LG 1, Rutgers."

Curious, she considered how to get to the lower ground floor. Her first concern was whether Stan had left, and not being sure, decided to go via a route through areas she never usually went. At the indicated door, she knocked, and when asked, "Who is it", gave her name.

"Who are you to see," she was quizzed.

Erin made a guess, "Rutgers."

The door opened from inside, her ID card was scrutinised, and then she was gestured in. The grey haired man bypassed formalities. "Goldman says you know about this monitoring program."

Erin glanced at a nearby screen and confirmed, "Yes, Sir."

"He wants you to go through the logs for the past few days and see if anything strikes you as odd. You can work here."

"No worries, I'll get right at it."

Where she lived, she used her own personal computer each

night to check the past 24 hour's entries. Goldman had given her remote access to the storage file on the mainframe. So, she had already gone over all but the most recent day's entries. Goldman knew that, so he must have a reason to get her to go over that time period again. Maybe, in hind sight after the day's activities, there might be a clue.

About that...Goldman had only decided to beef up the security and install the retinal scanners the previous night. The team were told late morning. Lauren was affected just after lunch. That was a suspiciously short time frame if the events were to stop the extra security. No doubt Goldman had others looking at that, but she was looking at signs that the information had leaked from the lab. Had he someone checking everyone's phone use too?

Busily scanning the lines of data, mainly the web addresses and emails, she wasn't taking note of the data in the local originating or receiving columns, until the number '17' caught her eye. That was the ID number of her own lab computer. She stopped scrolling and read, "Café on the park." She opened a side window and accessed the address. It was a posh eatery and the menu page had been opened, as well as the reservation page. She noted the details, address, IP address, time, computer.

A week ago, she recalled, Stan had been planning to take his girlfriend out, but why had he used her terminal to check the place out? It had been done late, after she had left work...he had to have access to her password. She would suggest to Goldman that everyone be made to change theirs, although they were meant to do that each week anyway. She did. However, if Stan had access to the master file he'd mentioned – that would negate that bit of security. But, she couldn't see Stan as the leak.

Yet she noticed an email sent a bit later, mentioning a few of the exotic dishes the eatery offered, with an introductory, "What about these?" The destination email gave no clue to who it was. Stan might have sent it to tease his girlfriend.

She returned to scrolling and scanning, noticed some repeatedly blocked email domains, and then saw an outward email to one of the addresses. It came from Lauren's computer, but not from her account. It was an account Erin hadn't seen before. She noted that one too, highlighting it like the earlier unsuccessful emails. That one had been sent during lunch.

On a hunch, she went back to when her computer had been used, and looked only at the originating computer and the time. They were not denied access to the internet during work hours, but all requests went through the mainframe now. Almost everyone had accessed the internet at some time, but hers, Lauren's and Terry's were the only ones used after hours. She noted the details, but nothing stood out to her eyes.

She let the same data scroll past again, saw that unknown account once more, early – just before work.

A message had gone out from Stan's terminal, and his account. That had been three days ago. Erin recalled that morning, a Tuesday. Maxwell had insisted she take the day off, since she had been working on the weekend, straightening out minor glitches in Terry's section of the program.

Then her eyes recognised the time when a global update had been made to all the terminals that day – it showed up each time someone logged on to the mainframe. Her own computer had been accessed before 9 am, as had Stan's. It explained why she had not actually noticed the update. Then late that evening, an email had gone out from her computer. She had ignored it at first sight, since it was again to the Café on the Park, and a reply had come back. If she hadn't been alert to details, such things would have been unnoticed.

Was Stan up to something? It was beginning to look like it.

Erin reached that morning, after she had checked the previous 24 hours. A few emails went back and forward, to the unknown account from Stan's terminal, and his account. The timing was suggestive, but why would Stan be worried by the extra security? It wasn't her place to accuse anybody, that was for the higher ups, but Stan had ducked out for a while late morning. After that, there had been nothing suspicious.

Rutgers returned just as she finished. "Mr Goldman requires you. He said to go up to his office. Do you know where that is?"

"Seventh floor, somewhere."

"Yes, suite one. Have you anything to mention from the logs?"

Erin handed over her notes and said, "Odd ones, I highlighted."

"Good, I will prepare a report for Mr Goldman. You should go. He is a very busy man."

On the seventh floor, Goldman's office was easy to find, and his secretary knew to expect her. She was announced and directed to go right in.

"Sir," she greeted, before being directed to an armchair.

"I have heard what Otway had to say, and what you told Rowan. Have you anything more to add?"

"Yes." Erin rooted through her bag to find the plastic bag containing the paper wrapped sliver.

Goldman let it sit on his desk until she had finished telling how she found it and the rest of what she had to say.

"Otway," Goldman murmured, as he silently considered many things. "I will have him checked again. Good work. I will have that sliver analysed, and that other keyboard. Did you note the number on it?"

"It ended in ASL16," Erin told him.

"The one they took away for testing was clean. It seems we know why. Can you find a way to check it again tomorrow?"

"Won't you want it checked?"

Goldman smiled grimly. "Just tell me if it stays there."

Erin made a note of that request for further consideration, for Goldman was going on.

"Today's events tend to confirm that it is the Skywatcher project that is the target of foreign interest. I am sure you can think of ways the program you are working on can be used."

"Yes, even though it is not designed to work on new satellites. If they believe the hype, they might want to hack into mission control at the launch and take the new satellite over."

"It doesn't have to be a new satellite," Goldman told her. "Are you aware of how many operational satellites are currently orbiting the Earth?"

"Up around three thousand, I heard."

"Yes, and at least the same amount that are supposedly defunct."

"Dead ones don't count," Erin countered.

"Mostly, no. However, recently, an amateur astronomer got a response from one that had been out of contact since 2005, and was only expected to stay operational until 2018."

"It would be really iffy to expect to find another satellite like that," Erin argued.

"But still a possibility, along with spy satellites, commercial communications satellites, and those that map the earth," Goldman told her. "We hope to stop them before they get control of any though."

"So what else can I do?" Erin asked.

"Have a think about why your computer, Avery's computer and Ingram's were used for the messaging."

"Well, Terry has been away this week," Erin said immediately. Then after thinking, had to shake her head.

"What about those specific work stations?" Goldman prompted.

Erin shrugged. "We all have much the same equipment."

"Not identical?"

"No..." Erin wondered what he was thinking. "You can't tell what's inside by just looking at the casing."

Goldman smiled faintly. "What reason might there be for you to check each one?"

"Having to add something, or replace a board or card."

"Let's assume, that instead of installing the two programs to monitor internet access by Wi-Fi, like we did, we wanted to use a physical device?"

That really got Erin thinking. "Does the device really have to do anything?"

"Just look like it should," Goldman suggested.

Erin described what came to mind, ending with, "...looking like it can send and receive Wi-Fi, and plug into the motherboard."

"I will have something like that made up. Now, what are your intentions?"

"Well, Stan told me to go home, and lock up if he hadn't got back when I did. His computer was still on, though. He told me to leave any checking of Lauren's computer until the morning. I was going to check what can be fixed, and see if bits from an old one that's stored in the printer room, can replace the bits that can't be fixed."

"How long will that take?"

"Depends what I find."

"Don't rush the job," Goldman directed. "It will take a day or so for the devices to be made."

"Okay," Erin agreed, wishing Goldman would give out more information about his plan. He hadn't yet, probably wouldn't. She could guess a lot – like this was extra pressure – like mentioning the retinal scanners. That, had got a reaction.

"Tomorrow, come into work as usual. The other team members will be told to stay home for the day. I will have Maxwell give you the orders. This evening though, I want you to go back to the lab. Let's say I want a quick estimation of the state of Avery's computer – based on your suggestion. Otway is still in the lab, even though I told him to go home too."

"I am to try and see what he's doing?" Erin guessed.

A faint nod was her answer, then, "Perhaps you come back a bit under the weather, reluctantly. After all, dealing with your colleague and everything else is enough to unsettle most people."

"Like I went out and had a drink? I don't drink usually, they all know that."

"This can be an exception, but you don't have to drink – wash your mouth with it and spit it out, perhaps spill a little on you."

"Okay, so people will think my mind won't be on what I'm doing."

Another nod. "Just see what you see or pickup. You will get a call in half an hour – long enough?"

"Yes, there is a licensed café on my usual route home."

"Excellent," Goldman decided, his smile evident. "One last thing, how are you going with the power modelling?"

"Well, like I said about needing test data. I did have some new ideas this morning, started coding them, but I didn't get all the way through."

"I need that as soon as things allow. So far, the segments you have worked on have been very impressive."

"Thank you, Sir."

Then he surprised her. "What I am about to tell you is not to go outside this room."

Erin stared at him.

"The whole Skywatcher program has a multi-fold purpose. It isn't going to be the control for the next generation of satellites," he began, and Erin nodded. She already knew that. "Updating the old program to work with the new systems is one thing. We can try to relink to other older satellites. But mainly, it is to try to locate leaks from various departments. Except for your part, we really do have problems with the power modelling on the new satellites. So far, your segments are more efficient than those that came with the units and merge into the overall system without a hitch. Therefore it is vital that I get to see your work first."

"As always," Erin confirmed. "Though everyone else has their work ready to test."

"Don't let that worry you, just endure the extra pressure. How far off do you think you are?"

"Close – but I will need the test data."

"I'll organise that, and tell you when to have your ah-ha moment."

"Okay. Is that all?"

"Yes. Leave by the side door. I have asked security to log that you left an hour ago."

Chapter 3 - Aftermath

Erin didn't expect to see anyone from work at the little licenced café, and was surprised to see Mark and Morgan at a table in the corner. Thinking they were together, as on a date, she sat at the bar and ordered a double brandy. She pretended surprise when Mark spoke from behind her.

"Erin! I didn't expect to see you here. Why don't you come and join Morgan and me?"

"Thanks, I think I will, for a bit."

Naturally, once they were together, the conversation turned to the events of the day.

"Do you know any more than we do?" Morgan asked.

"Not a lot," Erin claimed, between sips of her drink. "I have been trying to find out how Lauren is, but no luck. Where ever that doctor guy took her, it isn't any of the major hospitals." That was purely a guess, but her two work colleagues accepted it. "I don't know if the forensic team found anything, but they took her keyboard and mouse away to check."

"Were you there when she got a shock off the keyboard?" Mark asked.

"When was that?"

"Not long before things went crazy," Mark told her.

"I was outside doing that retinal scan," Erin said, thinking also of Gerry's call and hoped she wasn't blushing. "Though I wouldn't have thought that was possible."

"That's what she said had happened," Morgan confirmed. "Maybe the cleaner dropped it and the plastic cracked."

Erin shook her head, "I doubt that. It was plugged in and the cable isn't that long. It shouldn't have fallen to the floor."

"No, but she only swapped it over again this morning. The day the update came through, Tuesday, she was having trouble starting her computer after it. The keyboard wasn't working, so I swapped hers for Terry's. That helped, but Stan still had to reverse the update. I didn't consider her mouse, but then she uses that weird ergonomic one – doesn't like the normal ones," Mark related.

"I saw her sucking her finger," Erin admitted. "But it doesn't explain what brought on that...fit, or whatever it was."

"Could an electric shock do that?" Morgan asked.

"I don't know," Erin said, not about to tell what she had sensed.

"Well, the way she went off really scared me," Morgan admitted.

Mark commented, "Interesting how you managed to calm her down. She looked like she thought Otway was the devil, trying to drag her to hell."

"She looked like that before he came over," Morgan retorted.

"She might have been reacting to his body language," Erin suggested. "I don't think he had a clue what to do."

"You did though," Mark persisted.

"Only that someone needed to stay calm," Erin told him. "That was something I had to learn last year when I did six months basic training in the Marines."

Two pairs of eyes widened, but Erin didn't elaborate. "Long story," she added, brushing away the unasked questions. "Anyway, after that, I figured I knew how to handle her, as Otway was hardly holding her."

Erin considered for a moment, the advisability of mentioning the metal sliver, pretending to sip her drink as a reason to stop talking. She had no idea why Lauren had been targeted, and the rest of the team might be equally at risk. "I probably shouldn't mention this, but that doctor that came in with the big boss, found a puncture mark on her finger. It bled a bit."

Let them come to their own conclusions, Erin thought.

"I am going to shake my keyboard tomorrow, before I start to use it," Morgan declared.

"I think I will too," Erin concurred.

"Are you two for real?" Mark asked. "You sound like you think someone is out to get all of us."

"Maybe someone is trying something," Erin shrugged. "Maybe they don't want us to finish the program on schedule."

It was a logical idea, even though Erin knew the truth was far from it.

Morgan changed the subject, when she saw Erin appear to take a huge swig of her drink.

"You should eat something if you're going to be drinking. Mark, can you order us something? Chips? Nachos?"

Mark shook his head and good-naturedly went to the servery.

"Can I have a mouthful of that?" Morgan asked, indicating Erin's drink. "Mark wouldn't get me anything stronger than lemon. He's s teetotaller, I've discovered."

Erin was happy to comply, since she didn't really want to drink much. Morgan took two long swigs, then poured some lemon to wash out her mouth.

"That's what I needed," Morgan whispered. "I'm less jittery already."

Erin saw Mark returning and feigned a large swallow. She echoed Morgan's sentiment as Mark sat the plate of nachos down. He glanced at her glass, would notice the reduced volume left.

"How are you getting home? You are not driving are you?"

"No, walking. I don't have far to go."

"Do you know how you react to that stuff?" Mark persisted.

"Yeah, dulls the mind," Erin admitted, again not going into detail. "Drank too damn much in college. Got into trouble because of it."

"Then start eating," Mark directed.

Just as they were finishing the food, Erin's phone rang. She answered formally, listened, then said, "Okay, Sir, I'll head back."

"What's up?" Morgan asked.

"The big boss wants me to do something," she told them as she stood up and subtly bumped the table. "I thought I had finished with work for the day, dammit."

She made her movements ever so slightly unsteady as she took out money to cover her part of the food. Then, grabbing her unfinished drink, headed for the door. Near the bar, in plain sight of the others, she seemed to swallow the rest of her drink, put the glass on the bar, and continue out. In fact, she took a small mouthful, and outside, spat it into the gutter when no one seemed to be looking.

On the walk back to work, she decided that the small amount she had imbibed, which was way less than the amount Morgan had taken, had not affected her. The mental shields she kept up to block ambient emotions seemed as strong as ever and when she eased them, emotions were clear, not fuzzy. Only when she was nearly at the door to her work building, did she again play at being slightly drink affected.

Some of the security guards on the late afternoon shift knew her well enough to comment.

"Should you be back here now?"

"Not by my choice. However the big boss told me to come back. It's been one hell of a day, and I thought it was over."

There were many security cameras in the building, so Erin continued her tipsy act. Her mind dredged up an old joke, something about, "one shot and you're loaded." It amused her, until she neared the lab. Hopefully Stan would smell her breath and notice the slightly unsteady walk, and think she would not be fully alert.

Stan looked up when the door opened, and Erin sensed he was startled. She changed directions to head his way, seeming to reel slightly into one of the desks. The contents of his screen suddenly changed as she approached, and he moved his mouse and clicked.

"How come you're back?" Stan asked, sharply.

"Maxwell called me. He wants more detail of the damage before tomorrow. I thought you must have gone home."

"No, I'm doing the damage report, so anything you can add will speed that up. And I have got to put in an injury report for OH and S. Thought it best to get it done before I forget details."

"As if!" Erin blurted, moving closer. "Do we have basic tools around here?"

"Have you been drinking?" Stan demanded, hoping Erin would not come closer.

Erin stopped as if expecting a rebuke, but aware he was trying to hide something. "Only one, and I ate half a bowl of nachos. Mark and Morgan can vouch for that. Besides, you've said often enough not to annoy the big boss. And I take that double, no triple, for Goldman. I think he's really the one behind this unwanted return."

Stan stood. "The tools are in the side lab. I got them out earlier."

"You must have had the same idea," Erin commented.

"True, but I decided I wasn't up for it. I'd just be guessing."

"Right you are," Erin said, way too casually when talking to her immediate boss. "I will just see what I can see. They don't want detail tonight."

"Which is just as well," Stan told her.

"Right again," Erin agreed, waving as she went off, and swaying slightly as she did.

While fiddling with the screws that opened the cover of the computer, Erin dropped one, cursed and leant to pick it up. She knew that a fidgety Stan was watching her. Her extra senses were telling her that, and that her presence was an unexpected complication as well as revealing his disgust that she had come back less than perfectly sober.

Erin unscrewed the next screw with exaggerated care, and thought strongly, "I am too drunk to pay you any attention when I need to do this."

After about a minute, Stan's emotions receded as he went back to his desk.

Once the side casing was removed, Erin saw that a number of boards were loose, and others warped out of position. She systematically removed each and set them down along the bench, knowing at a glance what each board did. Then she used the bright LED light on her phone to check the casing. She would need a better light to examine the boards for cracks or breaks.

When she glanced at Stan, he was intent on his screen and typing quickly. There was no need to see what he was doing, if he was accessing somewhere he shouldn't her monitor program would pick it up and the observer in the basement would know. For a few moments, Erin felt resentful...Goldman was still checking on her... but then, a full time observer could do more than she could.

Moving quietly, Erin emerged from the side room and edged towards Terry's desk. Stan was still intent on something and not happy. She was halfway back when Stan noticed her. Immediately, she swayed slightly.

"What do you need that for?" he called over.

She had the unplugged keyboard and her excuse for getting it ready to her tongue. "Saw this one wasn't plugged in, so I am going to see if it will plug into the wrecked one – the connections at the back seem okay, but they might be warped."

She wasn't revealing her real interest in that keyboard, but Stan seemed agitated again and was hovering behind her. One glance though, was enough to tell her it was the keyboard Lauren usually used. It had a tiny flower sticker on the base. So she went and tried to plug it in, failed, and took it back, still apparently oblivious. Well, who really looked at keyboards? This one was no different to her own and several others of the same make and style.

Stan moved away again, watching from his desk how Erin squinted at various parts, and scribbled notes. Finally, she emerged and went to her desk, turned on her computer and unlocked her drawer. She needed to lift off all the stuff from Lauren's desk to get to her time sheet. Just touching the pile gave her a sharp, "someone has been in there," awareness. She didn't pause or betray she had felt something odd, but when she had left, her time sheet had been on top of the pile, and her program folder had been on top of Lauren's stuff. She had not looked closely at any of the folders, but some had paper relating to the old satellite comm system. Was that important? Most of the program sections were ready to test, although some had needed modifying, and it was Lauren's task to update the master file based on highlighted code sections.

The thoughts occupied her mind as she added an extra entry on her time sheet. She dropped that back in her drawer as her computer came awake. Now she was the one to be typing quickly, an email to Maxwell, giving him the details she had noticed on the short inspection. She was aware of Stan looking over her shoulder, and yawned as she pressed send. He didn't ask who she was sending it too, he'd seen that, but she had sent a copy to him anyway.

"That's damn it!" Erin muttered to herself, as she turned her computer off. Then, turning to see Stan added, "Right now, the damn roof could collapse and I wouldn't care. I am going to turn my phone off when I get home, so no one can drag me back again tonight."

Once again, her attitude and subtle body language eased him of some concern. "Have fun with your reports. That's one job I don't want."

"I hope you'll be sobered up by tomorrow," Stan said, to remind her he was her boss.

Erin jerked deliberately, for Stan wanted her unsettled. "I told you, I only had one drink. Enough to make me sleep well. I'll be in tomorrow."

Chapter 4 – Increasing Pressure

Erin met Stan downstairs when she arrived and they went up to the lab together. They were both surprised to find Goldman and Maxwell there.

After respectful greetings, Maxwell asked, "Erin, how certain are you that you can repair that terminal? It looks bad."

"The various cards aren't the problem. If need be, I can swap them from the spare terminal – the one in the cupboard in the side room. I need to go over the motherboard with a magnifying glass. Same with all the other parts. But, except for the hard drive and the system drive, why not just use the other one?"

Maxwell glanced at Goldman before answering. "Let's say, I want to know if you find anything odd about that unit – other than it being dropped."

"Sir, that tells me nothing. What do you think I might find?" She met Maxwell's eyes and waited for more.

She wasn't going to play meek and dumb.

"A means to send information out that doesn't go through the main router."

"Like a wireless adaptor? Generally, they would be obvious. Unless someone has a USB WiFi thing that plugs in. Is that what you mean?"

Maxwell nodded. Erin set her mind to recall the loose bits she'd picked up. She hadn't seen anything that might be that, although Stan may have picked something up.

"I'll do a check," Erin promised. "What made you ask about such things?"

Again Maxwell glanced at Goldman, who inclined his head very slightly.

"We have proof that some of the confidential work we have been doing here has been leaked to an outside agency."

"Huh? How did anyone even know what we are doing?" Erin blurted, even though this wasn't news to her. "Like someone wanting to salvage a dead satellite? We haven't even finished the program."

Maxwell kept a straight face. "I am sure you can think of other reasons too. However, to explain, the first inkling we had wasn't definitive. That leak might have come from a number of places. The latest leak had to have come from here. It was one of the completed sections of code."

"So you are saying, that one of us," Erin gestured about the lab, to refer to all the team, "is knowingly or unknowingly passing on highly classified information."

"Yes, exactly," Maxwell confirmed. "However, we don't know if the business with Avery yesterday is related. Maybe she is involved, or saw something. Either way, when she is fit to talk, she will be questioned."

"And in the meantime, we are all under suspicion," Erin guessed aloud. "Not surprising, I guess, since we all have phones with wi-fi and data capability. And since we can't take printouts or data storage units out of here, we could still photograph stuff if that way inclined."

Every nerve in Erin's body suddenly seemed extra sensitive – and she wondered if someone didn't want that possibility discussed.

Goldman spoke into the silence her statement had caused. "Everyone working here has signed an official secrets document – if you recall?"

"I did..."Erin agreed, deciding not to say, "Someone could be paid to ignore it."

She wondered if Goldman had been the one wanting the possibility dropped, but he went on to say, "Tomorrow, or later today, I will be sending a man out to put a device on each of the computers."

"And what will that do? Tell whoever is watching how often we scratch ourselves?"

"I'm sure you want this business sorted out," Maxwell rebuked mildly.

"Of course I do, but all the security is getting restrictive," Erin complained. "So who is going to be watching us?"

"That is not something you need to know," Goldman told her.

"Though, in your case, you've been closely watched since you started here."

Erin blushed, then wondered why Goldman was bringing up her past again – and reminding her bosses about it. Damn it! He trusted her now, she was sure of it. Then she took in what Maxwell was saying.

"...was mad putting you here, but you have proved your worth."

"Thank you," Erin said in a less contentious voice. "So you realise that I have a damn good reason to keep my nose clean."

Maxwell smiled faintly, then changed topics. "Stan, how is the program coming?"

"I still need to go over all we've got, and I didn't get around to adding the latest updates – things got too unsettled yesterday, and no one sent their work through. I need to do a logic analysis – but it is nearly ready to test."

"Erin?" Maxwell returned his attention to her.

"Not so good. I realised I had not considered some aspects, and thought I had the answer. I forgot it when Lauren had her episode." That was the truth, mostly.

"I am to present the project to the Defence Department in just over two months," Maxwell reminded her. "The system framework you wrote is holding up well, and I expect the next lot of subprograms should integrate well. However, the power modelling aspect is vital, as is the power control module."

"Yes, Sir," Erin acknowledged. "I will be considering that while I am fixing the terminal. I have recalled a few of the ideas I had yesterday."

"Miss Mason, do what you can with that computer today and tomorrow. If you can't get it working by then, leave it. The programming is the real priority. Perhaps if you need to break, do a bit more then."

"Yes, sir," Erin agreed. As usual, she only gave Goldman a brief glance before looking away.

Once Goldman and Maxwell were out of the lab, Erin vented a mild expletive, then said, "Around here, it's getting to feel a bit like being back inside."

"It's a bit like that," Stan agreed. "I've got used to it, though. And you've been here what...four months?"

"Six," Erin corrected. "If you count Goldman having me in other places first."

"You don't like him," Stan commented.

Erin shrugged, rather than admit she respected him for giving her a chance. Her body language when he was around was deliberate to give just that impression.

"He's the one that caught me out at Uni," Erin admitted. "Got me expelled, along with the guys who put me up to it."

"So, how come he now trusts you?"

"You heard him say he's been watching me? He is using my brains. Plus, he thinks my stint in the Marines has taught me how to stand against people trying to inveigle me into more programming mischief."

"Did it?"

"I would really hate to admit he was right," Erin finished. "So, when did you find out we were all under suspicion?"

"Not until a few days ago."

"Well, if he expects us to figure out why and how, he won't get much help from me. I will be too busy."

"Do you want me to help with the repairs?"

"Don't you have enough to do? I doubt Lauren finished typing in the program sections, so I guess that makes you data entry officer by default – that's if you want to get on with your job."

Erin grinned, and Stan scowled, adding, "And finish the reports."

They separated and went back to work.

Erin could study the computer boards and connections, and still think about recent events. Lauren, she was sure, was innocent of any wrong doing. If anything, she may have seen something or said something to suggest she knew something that threatened to expose someone else. Stan? Maybe...he was twitchy, furtive for sure. She wasn't going to react to that or let him know she was aware of it.

Had he put a Wi-Fi adapter – a USB one – into Lauren's computer? He was playing at being hopeless as a computer technician, but plugging something into a USB port wasn't rocket science. Most likely all the computers in the lab had that capability. Might he have plugged one into her computer during lunch that day? If it flashed, Lauren might have seen it. If it came to that, Erin wondered if she might have seen it.

After half an hour, Erin wandered out of the side room and went over to Stan. He heard her coming and once again changed screens.

"What's up," he asked, stretching as if he'd been tensed up.

"I was wondering if we have the manuals and other stuff that came with that computer."

"I think so. Do you know the property number?"

"CC05," Erin told him.

Stan went over to a filing cabinet, unlocked it, and rifled through a number of zipped plastic folders.

"Here," he said handing her one. "What will that tell you?"

"The specs on each bit. Oh, that computer does have a place for a wi-fi adaptor. Two, actually. It has a dedicated comms board in it. Do you think I should put it back in?"

"Leave it for now. We can ask the boss later. Is it damaged at all?"

"A couple of loose connections. Easy to fix."

"I still think we should get a technician in," Stan grumbled. His face seemed tense. "You are being paid to program, not tinker."

"I like tinkering," Erin told him. "And I can probably get all that is fixable done faster than a technician could get a security clearance."

Stan ambled out, just shaking his head. Erin immediately opened up the zipped folder and took out the technical data booklets. She could sense Stan's eyes on her even without looking his way, so she leant back in her chair and began to read one of the brochures. Finally, he went back to his desk.

Next time he ventured to where he could watch her, she had the small soldering iron out and her eyes close to a small magnifying glass she had fixed to a makeshift stand. He would see her, totally intent on the task...and he had often seen her so intent while programming...and then, she usually was.

This time though, she was very aware of Stan's twitchiness. It was like he had something urgent to do, and her presence was in the way. Her ears were honed to pick up sounds out in the lab. In fact she had a fairly straight line of sight to Stan – partly her doing, partly his.

A faint thought, amusing, she wondered if he was watching for her to do something wrong, just as she was watching him.

It didn't matter, she just had to do as Goldman directed. She was pretty sure he had a plan to catch the traitors and their foreign contacts. Right now, he was upping the pressure making passing information even harder. All reasonable precautions of course.

The soft buzz of a vibrating phone impinged on her ears. She didn't look up, but to listen better, picked up the spec sheet again and seemed to be reading.

Stan's voice was a soft murmur as he answered, but his tension had increased.

"No I haven't," Erin heard as Stan's voice became a fraction louder. Then, "No! The bosses are upping the security. I know, but the computer was wrecked. Yes, one of the programmers is also a tech, she's working on it. We'll need to wait…It isn't that easy, the woman is damn smart and now she's on the lookout. No. If you want the whole thing, she's needed. She's got the power modelling aspects to finish. I will do what I can, now, don't call me here."

Erin went to get a multimeter, ignored Stan and returned to work. She let him come to her.

"You do work fast," he praised. "When can we try starting it up?"

She had all the checked components back in, but not made all the connections. "Maybe later," Erin estimated, but she was wondering if Goldman actually wanted it to take two days.

"Have a break, Mason."

Erin checked her watch. "Oh, yes. I didn't realise the time."

In the building's cafeteria on the second floor, Erin took her food to a table in the corner. As she ate, she went over the one-sided conversation she had heard. It gave her shivers. No longer did she have doubts that Stan was involved, but her question was whether he would try to implicate her. Trying to figure out why, was useless. There could be numerous reasons from greed to coercion. Instead, her mind went to the idea of their mobile phones as a chink in security. Goldman had 'covered' that idea by quoting the security act they had all signed. At first thought, it made him seem naïve, but Goldman most definitely wasn't. He probably had someone monitoring the calls from all their phones. Thanks to David, her cousin's husband, she knew what could be done. It wasn't foolproof. A person could have a second, untraceable phone.

Someone approached her table, but Erin gave no indication that she knew the blond haired woman who asked to sit with her.

"Go ahead," Erin invited, and went back to sipping a hot chocolate drink and staring into space. She was, however, heeding the woman's soft voice.

"My boss says to keep the unit inactive until after the techs leave."

Erin chuckled softly. "He must be starting to do my cousin's trick."

The blond grinned. "He also said to shred all notes relating to your other work."

"I usually do, and keep them locked up until then. I do wish I knew his overall plan, but I guess I know why I don't. Does he know how Lauren is today? When she will be back?"

"I don't know, but I will find out," Goldman's secretary promised. "What is your take on that?"

"Only that she might have seen or overheard something," Erin murmured. "The end result? Someone wanted her out of the way."

Until then, they had been alone, but now, two workers from engineering came to sit nearby. Erin decided it was time for her to go back to work. She rose, and apologised to her table companion. "Sorry, I wasn't very good company. My mind is on too many other things."

As she began to move past the table where the new arrivals were getting settled, on spoke up. "Mason! Wait up."

Erin turned. The man went on, "I heard something happened to Lauren. Is she alright?"

She recognised the man as Tom Knowles. He and Lauren had been dating when she first joined the team.

"Sorry, Tom. I haven't heard anything today."

"Can you let me know if you hear anything?"

"Sure," Erin agreed. "I thought you two broke up."

"We did, but I still like her a lot. Once the project is over, I intend to try again. It was just too hard to have a decent relationship with all the pressure we're under. Do you ever get to see your boyfriend?"

"You assume I have one," Erin said, with a faint grin. "I do though, but he will be tied up for a few more weeks on the west coast. And yes, I do want this project finished by then so we can have an ecstatic reunion."

"Well, if Lauren is going to be off for a while, and you need someone for data entry, Joanne from our lab hasn't much on at the moment."

"I will mention her to the boss. I assume she has had the relevant checks done and has the right clearance?"

"Should have," Tom agreed. "And it will keep her too busy to ask us all questions."

"Well, like I said, I will mention her."

On her way back, Erin wondered, "Was Tom involved? Was he trying to use Joanne to spy on them? Or was Joanne the spy – always asking questions." Shut up, woman! You will be suspecting everyone soon.

Chapter 5 - Suspicions

Erin found the lab empty and took the opportunity to glance through her monitoring file for that day. Only Stan had been active on his computer and he'd been very busy. She looked at the data stream he'd uploaded and recognised some of the data.

"Shit!" she exclaimed softly. It was part of her unfinished latest version for the power control program. She quickly closed the monitoring program and opened up her work file.

Had Stan accessed her computer? Did he know her passwords? He had to. She had not allowed anyone to see the program yet, and she had only started entering it that morning. Acting quickly, she saved her current progress under a new file name, and hid it amongst a batch of innocuous data files. She wondered if he had also accessed and copied her hand written notes.

When Stan trotted back in, she was staring at her screen with a frown, pretending to scan the lines of the originally saved file.

"Finished the computer?" he asked, as a reason to come over.

"No, just taking a break." Erin didn't take her eyes off the screen. "I was letting what I did yesterday stew in the back of my mind. Looking at it now...it's crap. It all seemed to hang together okay, but I don't know what I was thinking."

"You need to be working on it," Stan said, seriously. "Time is running out."

"I need a new think at it," Erin countered. "I'm just making a list of all the points about it, and then I'll be going back to work on Lauren's computer."

To distract Stan from his interest in her work, she added, "Oh, yes. Tom Knowles from Engineering was asking about Lauren. And he also said that their admin aide, Joanne, wasn't too busy at the moment. He suggested she could fill in for Lauren until she gets back."

"On which computer?" Stan pointed out.

"What about Terry's? Or is he due back soon."

"No, he's not. I might put the idea to Maxwell, though. He would have to get access to Terry's password."

"Whatever," Erin dismissed that idea and stood up. "I'll get back to tinkering. I might have it working by tonight and that problem won't matter. I can bypass the password security when I reset the system."

"Won't that delete all the saved information?"

"No...I'll not have the hard drive in the loop when I do it."

It took Stan a while to realise what she had admitted.

"Do you mean...hack it?"

"Hack! That's such a nasty word," Erin said, sounding demure. "I'll just be going in by a back door, until all is back working. Once I put the hard drive memory back in, then you will need the password."

She walked off, imagining his stunned expression. Surely he'd been told that little detail about her? Oh, for some of Wanda's ability to pick up on thoughts...

What she was sensing of his emotions, were confused. Her instinct seemed to tell her that he wanted her to finish her part of the satellite control program, and equally desperately wanted Lauren's computer operational, but not officially so. Interesting...

As she began checking the rest of the motherboard, her mind wasn't fully on the task. Officially operational? Working, but not so everyone knew it? What would that allow?

Erin found a broken connection and set to soldering it.

If the computer wasn't officially working, then would the techs put the 'fake' unit in it? Likely not...And since only she knew that was a ruse, this computer might be considered safe to use to send data...

She smothered a grim smile. If Stan was involved in the conspiracy Goldman was looking into, he deserved to be caught – preferably before he really sold out. He wasn't a bad person, or a bad boss. Human, fallible...and who was she to cast aspersions anyway?

At knock off time, Erin had reconnected all but the hard drive, and was using one of the unused backup drives instead. It would work like a new computer, and she had reset the passwords to factory default.

Now she wondered, did Stan really know so little about things or could he figure out the connection to the comms board, and how to swap the new drive for the original?

The report she gave Stan was, "I'll try booting it up in the morning."

He just nodded and asked, "Heading off?"

"Um, would it be a problem if I stayed on a bit? I would like to get down the flow chart that has been coming at me all afternoon."

"I'll okay it," Stan agreed. "I'll be here for a bit longer anyway. What say I get a pizza ordered in?"

"Are we allowed to do that?"

Stan grinned, "I'll have to go downstairs to collect it."

"Well, if you can...I am starving. So much so that I might faint before I get home to eat."

"What's your favourite?"

She told him and added, "With garlic bread."

Erin used the excuse of needing the ladies room to leave the lab. She needed to report to Goldman, and this was the time he preferred. He had become used to her "rambling" report style, for much of what she told him were empathic impressions or ideas from her subconscious, rather than hard fact. Sometimes, something she said or suggested resounded with other things he knew. Then she told him she was working back a bit, and why, mentioning the feeling that her computer had been accessed, possibly for the subroutine she had started entering then told Stan was crap. It wasn't the real routine, just something that would seem to be, to make it seem she was working hard to get the work done. The final routine was already complete and tested, and was just waiting for Goldman to give her the okay to have her, "Ah, Ha!" moment.

"Work an extra two hours," Goldman told her. "Let Stan lock up. You call me again when you get home."

Erin wondered why, but only said, "Okay, I'll do that."

The pizza's were huge, and Erin berated herself for eating too much. She couldn't help it. She had been hungry, and these were the nicest she had ever tasted.

"That was fantastic," she said, when she pushed a half finished slice away. "Where'd you get them?"

"Dom Pedro's. They are a block over towards the river. He does Mexican and Italian cuisine."

"I'll have to remember that," Erin said, meaning it. "And now that I am no longer starving, I had better get back to work."

This time she was working on paper, hand drawing the chart for the power modelling. It wasn't new, but a recreation of the one she had done two months ago, and the basis of her first draft.

When two hours were nearly over, she put her workings in a folder, slightly out of order, and locked them in her drawer. She then pressed a tiny piece of blutack across the slight crack between drawer and cabinet. If someone accessed her drawer, that sticky adhesive would be deformed.

Stan only waved at her when she announced she was going home. He seemed intent on something and Erin only sensed his mind was busy, and she decided that he had no idea of what else she had done with blutack in the short time he had been out of the lab collecting the pizza delivery. Now, the only computer with an external comms port that she knew of, that could accept a Wi-Fi adaptor, was the one she was fixing. Her computer and Terry's now had a tiny plug of blutack in the port where a USB Wi-Fi would need to be inserted. It would seem to plug in, but the connection would not work.

Erin enjoyed her smug thoughts as she walked towards her apartment. However, the longer she was walking, the more the bloated, full, feeling in her stomach increased. It had eased as she had been sitting, but now, it was intensifying into a strong ache. She slowed her pace, hoping that would ease it. It didn't. Speeding up didn't help either, but it got her to her building sooner. She just hoped that she was in her apartment before the feeling of nausea became too much to handle. Something in that delicious pizza must have been off, or was something that disagreed with her.

In trying to distract her mind, Erin played with the nasty suspicious idea that had come to her. Maybe Stan had added something to her pizza. She told herself it was unlikely, that there hadn't been enough time. It would have meant he had to have had some stuff on him, that he had planned it...

But why would he? If he was selling out, he needed her to finish her part of the program. Or did he not believe her claim that the last part she had done was rubbish?

Once up on her floor, Erin raced from the lift to her door, she was swallowing convulsively as she fumbled to open it. She didn't even stop to lock it behind her, just bolted for the bathroom. Five minutes later, after bringing up everything she had eaten, she rinsed her mouth and considered having some antacid. As she moved to the kitchen, the cramps returned, worse than before, and she doubled over in agony.

Vaguely, she remembered she hadn't locked her door, and then realised that the ringing wasn't the doorbell but her phone which was in her bag, wherever she had dropped it. She staggered towards the sound, realising she needed help. Her vision began to blur, and the colours of her carpet began to run together as they raced towards her.

Chapter 6 – Unprovoked Attack

Goldman rang off, thinking that Erin had not reached home yet. He decided to wait ten minutes and try again. As he put his desk phone down, his private phone rang. The call had come through direct, and very few people knew the number.

He answered cautiously, as was his habit, but recognised the voice.

"Miss Willard, what can I do for you?"

"Sir? Is Erin okay? My sister doesn't think so."

Magnus Goldman knew that Elisabeth Willard and her sister, Wanda Martin, were Erin's cousins. He knew of the connection between them – the psychic link. His concern peaked.

"She left work a little while ago. She is due to ring me shortly. If I don't hear from her, I will send someone to check. Was there something specific?"

"No, Wanda asked me to ring you," Elisabeth admitted. "It must be something, since Wanda felt it from out west. I'll leave it with you, Sir."

Goldman heard the connection cease, and immediately dialled Erin's phone again, marvelling at how her cousin, a continent away, could know something was wrong. When the phone rang out, he tried the landline in her apartment, and his alarm increased. He dialled another number and gave instructions. He couldn't go himself, to check on her, because he did not want anyone to know that she worked more directly with him.

He forced himself to relax, and tried to concentrate on other important matters, for the half hour before his private phone rang again. He reached for it quickly, snapped, "Goldman."

He heard, "Stev here, Magnus. I've called the paramedics. I found Erin unconscious. She had been sick before that and I couldn't rouse her."

Goldman didn't have to verbalise how he felt. Erin had been sure that no one suspected her of spying on her colleagues. She should have been safe. Had someone discovered her role?

"Keep me advised," he told his friend Stev Aldrin.

Goldman ended the call, and let his mind run through the plans he had in action to capture the traitors selling scientific secrets.

Goldman was still in his office when Stev Aldrin let himself in. He looked up, gestured for Aldrin to close the door and have a seat. His friend looked haggard. "Well?"

"She's okay," Stev reassured him. "The paramedics thought it was food poisoning. At the hospital, they pumped her stomach. They didn't get much. I organised someone from the local precinct to go and get samples from her apartment, and asked the police lab to analyse them. The doctors will be having other tests done, and haven't ruled out bad food, but the drug screen showed up something and they think it might be a strong emetic drug as well as a sedative. I mentioned the time frame, and whatever she got had to have been slow acting. I checked with the guards downstairs. Otway collected two pizzas, about two hours before Erin left. The doctor proposed that the drug was added as coated microgranules. The coating acting to slow the absorption."

"How soon will she be fit to work?" Goldman asked the most important question.

Stev didn't think it callous, as he was privy to the investigation Erin was working on.

"When I left, she was conscious, but not particularly coherent. They have admitted her and will monitor her overnight. I have left an officer from the local prescient on guard. They won't allow visitors, except for you and me."

"Can you go back and stay with her? It might be a few hours before I can get there."

"I'll do that," Stev agreed.

Erin finally realised she was in hospital and forced her empathic mind shields back into place. It wasn't hard, she already felt like a shipwreck survivor who had been washed up onto the land. It was close to what she imaged when she evoked her strongest shields. Half of the unpleasantness she felt went away, but she still felt abominable.

"What hit me?" she asked weakly, to the presence she felt nearby.

"Your apartment floor," Stev Aldrin remarked softly. "Good thing you had thick carpet on it."

"Yeah," Erin agreed. "How come you're here?"

"Magnus was concerned. More so after one of your cousins rang him."

"Wanda?"

"No. Elisabeth. Though Wanda probably put her up to it."

"Oh!"

Moments later, as Erin's mind began to function, "I only ate too much pizza."

"Perhaps, but there were things in your stomach that weren't natural."

"Yukky bacteria?"

"No, an emetic drug and a sedative. High levels of both."

"I did eat too much. I normally only eat half of a pizza that size."

"When you are feeling more alert, you will have to give me details," Stev told her. "What happened to the left over pizza?"

"Stan said he'd take it. His neighbour's dog eats pizza."

Stev made a mental note to have that checked. He told Erin, "Try to sleep."

He moved from beside her, to make a call, while still where he could watch her.

Erin did try to sleep, but she couldn't find any position comfortable enough. At best, she had short naps, and so was awake when Goldman came in around 1am. He spoke with Stev, too quietly for her to hear the words, then came over and saw she was awake.

"How are you feeling?"

Erin debated amongst the range of descriptions she thought of before settling on, "Like the end of the first week of basic training."

Goldman smiled faintly as he commented, "Then you will be back at work tomorrow morning."

He saw Erin start to say something, close her mouth, then turn to look at him. "I know you don't have a sense of humour!"

Goldman waited for her to say more.

"I am feeling better than I was. I will be there if the doctor okays it."

Erin felt him pat her hand. "Good girl. I will get Stev to get what you will need from your apartment. You can leave for work from here. I have someone at your apartment cleaning it up."

"Oh, yeah! Why did they want me to be chucking up everywhere? Do you think they know I am working directly for you?"

"You should be alert for that, but I really don't think so. Otway knows your record and that I am having you watched. He should have no reason to think you a spy. It may just have been to keep you out of the way. And that may be because I wanted both him and you around when your little devices are installed. How far did you get with the repairs?"

That question forced Erin to recall. "I have a spare hard drive in it, and haven't added the comms board. Told Stan I would try it in the morning."

"Good. I will tell the techs to ask about it, but to find a reason not to put the device in. I expect that won't be too hard."

"I did something else," Erin recalled. "Fixed the extra comms port on my computer, and Terry's. They won't work. Lauren's will be the only option."

"Excellent," Goldman murmured. "Keep your eyes, ears and all other senses fully alert tomorrow and don't let on how ill you were. I can't stress enough about being alert. The pressure is on, but Otway knows you are needed to finish the program. They won't want further delays. I will want you to have the finished program ready by the end of next week."

"Okay."

"Polish off the power control algorithm as soon as you can and let Otway pass it up to Maxwell."

"Yes, sir."

It was already finished. She had added a special subroutine that would allow access to the satellite's comm system, and get a position sent back then the system was pinged. If the program was run on a computer, it would search for a position locating program and send back the computer's location.

"Once you do, I will arrange for you to visit the archives like you proposed."

"Okay."

Goldman pondered the value of adding anything else, then

decoded he should. "Don't forget that you are a ready-made scapegoat if someone wants to switch blame."

"I haven't, Sir."

"Try to rest," Goldman said finally, before turning to leave.

When he was gone, Erin contradicted her earlier comment, "He is a comedian."

Stev chuckled. "What will you need me to get?"

Erin told him, then added, "And an hour out in the garden."

"Is that a good idea? It isn't that warm out, at the moment."

"The fresh air will help clear my head." Erin wasn't going to explain her full reason.

"Oh, yes. Right!" Stev remembered when he had first met her, and what he now knew about her and her cousins. "I will head out about sunrise. There will still be a guard out in the passage."

Lying with her eyes closed, Erin thought back over the part of Goldman's plan that she knew about. It seemed obvious to her now, Stan had to be one of the group Goldman was after. Was he the only one? Had Lauren been involved too? She thought about each of her colleagues in turn. No subliminal ideas surfaced – but then she hadn't seriously even suspected Stan.

Goldman had been controlling the timing of her completing each of her tasks. She never let on that she knew the project wasn't as important and hush-hush as the others believed. Most definitely, she had never intimated that it wasn't ever intended to be used – except for the idle curiosity of amateur sky watchers.

So, why had someone been leaking the program – piece by piece? How had Goldman even found out? And what did the people receiving it think they could do with it?

Her mind proposed ideas, some terrifying. The most obvious was to use it to hi-jack a satellite – they might think they could do that. Or, they might have a satellite of their own. Could the schematics for the new satellite been leaked already? Somehow, that idea didn't seem right either.

Then she suddenly recalled that Stan had accessed her computer, and the unfinished part of the near final version of the power control module program. She called to Stev and asked him to call Goldman.

Erin truly appreciated Stev's help, not just getting her things for work, but also driving her to a point only a block away from work. She still wasn't feeling back to normal, but she was functional, and better than her description of "day seven of basic training."

The visible signs of her indisposition were well hidden by a light layer of make-up. But it was just as well that she was not in for a full day of strenuous activity. The hour she had spent in the hospital garden had, as she hoped, helped. Her head was clearer and she was more awake. Her hope was that she could fool people into thinking nothing major had happened. It would be interesting to sense reactions when she arrived. The rest of the team would be back that day.

Some distance behind her, Stev Aldrin was also headed to her work building. He'd said he'd be visiting Goldman, at least for the morning. She took the lift before him, acting like he was a stranger.

At the door to the computer lab, Erin caught movement through the large glass window. Stan and Matthews were having an intense discussion. Face to face, rigid posture, with Stan making sharp, jerked gestures. She watched for a moment, wondering, before activating the door unlocking routine. When she walked in, the two men had separated and seemed to be merely having a morning gossip.

Matthews looked up and saw her. "Good! The techs will be here shortly to put some device on each of the computers. I want you and Stan to oversee them." He chose then to head for the door.

Stan gave her a quick grin, as he studied her face. "Everyone except Terry and Lauren will be in today," he said, sounding exactly like normal. "I'm going to get them to put their work into a sub-folder of the framework program."

"Have they done that before?" Erin asked. That was normally part of Lauren's duties.

"They have been shown, since they needed to give Avery the information in the right format. However, they have not actually used the framework program. I will get you to help them, if need be. You are familiar with it?"

"Not greatly, but if you have a user guide – I should be right once I've read it."

She looked directly at Stan, making him think he'd made a mistake, and not that she had blatantly lied. Of course she knew the program – she'd written it.

"Check Avery's drawer. I left it open."

"Okay!" Erin made her agreement deliberately cheery, and added a smile. What she was sensing as Stan went towards his desk came as waves of frustration. He had not expected her to be there, and didn't want her there.

Later, once the tech arrived, that state lessened. Erin was asking questions of the techs, seemingly wanting to understand what the devices did. The two guys had been well briefed, and their answers told Stan all he wanted to know. It didn't please him, but he was happier when the techs left without adding anything to the almost repaired terminal.

When the men left, he told Erin, "Get that working. When it is and all the programs open, let me know. I need to get the latest save of the framework program to give engineering before Monday. I hope to have everything ready to test. So I need you back to your proper work, ASAP. I will have to work over the weekend, and ideally, I want that power control program finalised."

"On it, Boss," Erin agreed cheerfully.

Getting the computer working took very little time. She let Stan know, and went back to her own work, appearing not to be interested in what he was doing. She glanced that way occasionally, usually finding him intent on something on the screen. She couldn't see what, as the screen was now angled away from the door.

No one needed to tell her that Goldman's plan was coming to a climax. She had the final, tested version on her computer, accessed from the mainframe, and was currently only adding some small "contingency" sub-routines. Unlike the larger program, these two small sections were unlabelled, and made to seem like part of larger sections.

Her phone buzzed with a text notification. "What is O doing?"

She quickly typed and sent, "Focus on L computer."

A reply came back. "Await instructions."

She didn't answer that. Stan had just jumped up, left the side room, and was heading for the door. He grabbed his jacket on the way. She didn't need to use her empathy to know he was agitated. He was barely keeping himself from running out the door. She sent, "O leaving lab, agitated."

Five minutes later, her phone rang. She was startled to hear Goldman's voice. "I need you to access Otway's terminal. Does he have it on?"

"Yes, but it hibernating."

"I'll text his password. I need you to see if you can find a message that would have arrived last night." He gave her details.

She gave a quick word of agreement and went across immediately. Once Stan's terminal woke up, she set to work, and hoped no one would mention her being there. She checked the email folders and sub-folders and found nothing that fit Goldman's criteria – not even in the junk or deleted folders. Assuming from the little Goldman said, the email probably wasn't just deleted. That meant it had to be saved elsewhere.

Putting herself in the mind of her boss, and being aware of his perfidy, she let her instincts guide her search. It took her twenty minutes, and all during that time, she expected Stan to return and catch her at it. When she found it, she forwards the email to Goldman and deleted the evidence of doing so.

The text made no sense to her, but she had found it was again sent from the Café in the Park.

A text followed quickly of her sending the message. "O on way back. Leave computer."

She did, but since she had needed to log in, she logged him off the mainframe. He would not know she had been on his computer unless one of the others mentioned it. However, before returning to her own computer, she looked in on the repaired one. Stan hadn't covered his tracks there. He had been in the email program, but hadn't hidden or erased the message. "Come now, or you dead." She sent that to the delete folder, then went quickly to her desk to send another text.

"Stay at work," was the return message. Then she quickly erased that message thread.

One by one, the other team members came over and mentioned

they had finished the task Stan had set them. To each, Erin said, "Send it through to his terminal by email," and went on with her own work.

Stan didn't actually return for over an hour, and when he did, he seemed little better than when he had left. She sensed his tension, and when he came over, the strong mint smell on his breath.

He's been drinking, Erin knew, but didn't challenge him about it. Instead, she reported that all the others had sent their work to his email, and that she needed another hour to check her work, and plug in the test data and check her algorithm.

"Tell me when you are ready," was all he said.

"Yes, sir," she agreed.

Stan seemed less agitated when the first three data sets gave the expected result. However, the fourth and fifth sets – more complex data - froze the program.

"Damn!" Erin thumped her desk. "I checked and checked the input."

"On the screen?" Otway queried.

"Of course! It saves paper."

"Try printing it out. Sometimes it is easier to see the problem that way."

The suggestion was counter to Stan's usual instructions and Erin felt her back prickling. Last time she'd had printouts in her drawer, he'd looked at them. Possibly even photographed them. Still, she did as he suggested, and took the pile of joined sheets to the side room where she could spread it out to scan read the lines and highlight some for rechecking.

Near knock off time, Stev Aldrin came in and caused a minor furore. The former astronaut was well known to the public. Even Otway was impressed. He led the celebrity guest into the side room where Erin was doing a good job of wasting time.

"Erin Mason?" Stev asked, as if they were strangers.

"Yes?" Erin put her finger on a line of text before looking up.

"Do you have a few moments?"

"Yes, but please just let me mark where I am up to." She reached into her pocket and took out a different coloured highlighter to mark her place. "Okay, how can I help you?"

"I understand that you need some technical information." Stev went on to mention what she had suggested to Goldman and Maxwell.

"Yes. I think I need to understand more about how the type of satellite works and have some real data to feed into the algorithm to check that it works."

"I have made arrangements to meet with Hugh Gallagher, the custodian of the NASA library archive. He is very knowledgeable and should be able to help you."

"Great!" Erin exclaimed. "What about actual data from something?"

"I should be able to get us into the section of the archive where that is stored. You will need to consider the type of data you need, before we get there."

"When?" Erin asked. The opportunity was not one she would pass up.

"How about Sunday?"

"Fine. I hope to have this part ironed out by then. Stan needs it so it can be tested on Monday. Not the final test, but how it works on a satellite mock up."

Stev turned back to address Otway. "Looks like it is all coming together. Will it be ready to present to the Defence Department on schedule?"

"We certainly hope so," Stan agreed.

With a word to her, Stev said, "I will see you on Sunday, then, Miss Mason. A car will pick you up. I will notify you of the time."

Stev gestured a half wave, half salute to the team as he left.

Erin decided to make herself a coffee. She was starting to feel really tired, from the lack of a restful night's sleep. Also, she was now feeling hungry again, after having nothing to eat all day. The 'stay at work' directive had not specified a time she should leave.

"You gone to sleep in here?" Stan asked, making Erin jerk awake.

"Ah, I must have," she admitted. "I didn't sleep well last night. My own damn fault for eating so much of that delicious pizza."

From Stan, she sensed a moment of confused guilt. "How long are you staying?"

"I will see how I go," Erin temporised. He was twitchy. "Did you get everyone's file? I told them to email it to you when they finished, since your computer had gone to sleep."

"Yes, thanks. How are you going here?"

"Okay. I found a couple of things. I'm just working the test data through manually...or I was. I have to start again. If I finish tonight, I won't have to come in tomorrow."

Stan wandered off, to deal with the other sections of the program. Erin watched him. She knew exactly why the last sets of test data had failed, and had it fixed, but was wasting time.

Her phone rang, and she answered it quickly. It was Stev, and she greeted him politely, not trying to keep the conversation private. Her part was cryptic enough, just yes or no answers to questions he'd been told to ask.

"Is the power control program ready?"

"Yes."

"Can you send it to Stan but make it undeliverable?"

"Yes."

"Is her version on her computer locked?"

"I can have that ready," she rephrased her reply, seeing Stan approaching.

"Is that the only copy?"

"No."

"Printout?" Stev guessed. "Can you shred it?"

"In theory," she said, and the asked, "What program will be needed to read the data?"

Stev ignored the irrelevant question, guessing it was misdirection. "If you can't shred it, let me know? Your friend is meant to be meeting someone tonight. We want to make sure we get everything."

"Okay, then. Is that all?" Erin asked.

"Yes. You finish up and go home."

When she saw Stan's questioning look, she said, "That was Colonel Aldrin, giving me a heads up of what I will need for Sunday."

"How's the program?" Stan asked, after just nodding to her.

"Done, I think. I was about to send it to you."

"You look like you could sleep for a week."

Erin yawned on cue. "No, just a whole day. No one had better need me because I am going to have my phone off."

While talking, Erin attached the locked version of her program to an email and sent it. "Done!"

Stan's terminal beeped. "Got it?" she asked.

"Yes, it's there. Thanks."

Erin quickly saved her copy of the program under an innocuous name, in an obscure folder and turned off her computer. She picked up her notes and the printout and headed for the shredder. When she tried to get it to work, the paper jammed. She cleared it and tried again. Stan came to see why she was swearing.

"I'll have it looked at on Monday. Lock that in your drawer until then."

"Alright! But only because I don't have the energy to kick sense into it."

Chapter 7 - Precautions

When she was a block from her apartment, Erin watched a car drive into the kerb just ahead of her. She slowed, fearing trouble, until Stev Aldrin stepped out of the driver's side and gestured her to the passenger side. She took the hint.

"Have you some other place you could go?" Stev asked when she was in the car.

"Why?"

"Just a precaution."

"I could go to Dad's place. I haven't seen Bree in a while."

"I'll drop you there."

"Is this related to what Stan's meant to be doing?"

"Yes."

"And should that be the end of it?"

"If nothing goes wrong. The people we are after are getting nervous."

"Sunday will still be on?"

"Yes. You still need to finish that."

Erin knew she would be greeted warmly by her father and step-mother, and they would have no problem with her staying overnight.

As it was, her 11 month old daughter Bree, was pulling herself up on the furniture when she went in. She saw Erin and tried to twist around to get to her, only succeeding in falling down. Instead of crying, she began crawling, then laughed when Erin picked her up.

"She is almost ready to walk," Loren commented. "You should come more often."

Her step-mother, who with her father had adopted her daughter, had said often enough that she didn't want Bree to think her mother had abandoned her.

"I should have more time, soon," Erin told her. Bree's parents knew the kind of work she was doing, but still persisted.

As soon as she had her hands free again, Erin put her phone on silent. It was good to forget about work at the moment. During dinner, she felt it vibrate, but ignored it, as she did with the message tone. If she had to make a guess, it was likely Stan having discovered her file was locked. Later, while preparing for bed, she listened to the message.

Stan's voice, pitched higher than normal, said, "What the heck did you do to that file, Mason? I can't open it. You need to get back here, right now, and let me get it."

Erin didn't get back to him, choosing instead to call Stev and have him pass the message to Goldman. She had to leave him a message, and wondered if she would get a reply.

Near midnight, when she was on the verge of sleep, her phone vibrated.

"Erin? I passed on the message. Magnus said to ignore the message and delete it. Monday, go in as normal and know nothing of the call."

"Okay," Erin said slowly. "Do I take it that things didn't go well?"

She heard Aldrin sigh. "No. The parties must have got wind of what was going on. Otway didn't turn up and the other party took off just as we were getting there."

"Who knew about it?" Erin asked.

"Very few people," Stev said unhelpfully. "We are looking into that. You just need to go on as before, but keep alert and be very careful."

"I will," Erin said soberly. "What am I meant to do about my program?"

Stev didn't know, and said he'd call back. Except the call, when it came, was from Goldman.

"What state is your program in?"

"Stan discovered the file I sent wouldn't open. That had the two contingency programs included in it. I had to lock my notes and the printout in my drawer as the shredder kept jamming. It's a good guess, Stan has looked at them. The printout has two vital algorithms missing, so it will only work on simple data."

There was silence on the phone as Goldman thought. Finally, "I know we have discussed this before, but if the buyers get the file and notes, could they fix it?"

"My notes were semi-cryptic, but if they have someone who knows the right algorithms, they might work it out from the printout."

Goldman went silent again. Erin broke it this time. "There are still the contingency programs. If they do manage to reprogram a satellite, and we know its contact codes, I could override any new settings they put in."

"We don't want it to get that far," Goldman said. "We are still watching Otway. This weekend, I want you to be out of contact. Monday...go ahead and let Otway have the program."

On the Saturday afternoon, Stev called and told Erin that Lauren was allowed to have visitors, and Goldman asked if she would find out what Lauren knew of the events earlier in the week. The driver of the car already knew where to go, and headed out of the city to a discreet private hospital.

She noticed the security, but as she walked in with Stev, no one challenged them. He led her to Lauren's room, which turned out to be on the second floor, and overlooking gardens, then left them alone.

Lauren was sitting in a chair, looking out the window. She jerked around, when she heard the door open.

"Erin! Thank God."

Before she had even come a few steps in, Lauren was with, her embracing her as if she was her lifeline. Sensing Lauren needed the contact, Erin returned the hug. "Are you better?" she asked after a while.

Lauren jerked away. "I don't know. I get nightmares, every time I sleep."

Fear of madness, Erin identified as Lauren went on.

"They won't let me out of this room. They have guards on my door and I can't even call anyone."

Erin led her back to the chair, and then leant against the window sill. "I would say, that since we don't know who caused your problem, they are protecting you. They will look after you here."

"But what happened to me? What caused it? I couldn't see anything but whirling swirling colours and horrifying faces leering at me – except you. You were the only stable thing."

"You were drugged, but I don't know for sure how or why or

by who. Sounds like some sort of hallucinogen or a psychedelic compound. What do you remember from that day?"

Lauren's face took on a blank look as she thought back. "Going to work...but I can't even be sure it was that day."

"Do you remember pricking your finger?" Erin prompted.

"Yes..." Lauren absently sucked her right index finger. "Is that how I was drugged?"

"I think so," Erin told her. "I found a metal sliver in your keyboard."

"But why? Why would anyone do that?"

"I'm not sure, but I found out that day that the higher bosses think one of us is leaking information – parts of the program – to someone outside."

Lauren's face darkened. "They don't think I did?"

Erin reached out and touched her arm, thinking of calm and peace. "No. Might you have seen something or overheard something?"

Lauren went rigid. "Yes! I do remember now. Some update had been done the day before. I couldn't get my computer to boot up. I told Otway, and he started it up from the operating system and reversed the update – or that's what he said. Then I couldn't open the database program. I didn't call Otway back right away – I did a quick scan, even though I hadn't needed to do online research for weeks. I thought a virus might have got through. It picked up and neutralised a couple of things. Then I did a file listing and saw some that were unfamiliar – they didn't use the naming format the big boss insisted we use. A couple were applications, but they wouldn't open, so I deleted them. I was going to ask Otway if someone had been using my terminal, but he'd gone out. So I went to Maxwell and gave him my observations and mentioned the problems I'd had."

"What did he say?" Erin asked, as her back began to prickle.

"Something about mentioning it to the IT guys, and having them check the firewall program. I never go online directly – always through the mainframe. I had the impression that he thought the odd files had come in with the update."

"Did you tell him you had deleted the odd ones?"

"Yes. He said, 'Good' and told me to reload the program and back up from the mainframe. He said he'd get Otway to check for any other programs that shouldn't be there. Do you think I was drugged because I found them? That Otway or Maxwell are involved?"

"I don't know," Erin lied. "I will let the higher powers look into that. But if I were you, I wouldn't be in a hurry to return to work, add I would forget all about the odd files."

Lauren nodded, and said, "That day really is hazy."

Erin decided Lauren couldn't tell her anymore, and turned the conversation to her intended excursion the following day. When Stev returned a short time later, to get her, Lauren was completely distracted by meeting him, and in a better state of mind.

When she had told Stev of her conversation, and the ideas she had from it, he promised to pass the information on to Magnus Goldman. He dropped her back at her father's place with a reminder of the outing the following day.

She had not checked her phone since the previous night and when she did, she found six missed calls – all from Stan – plus several angry text messages, and equally irate voice messages. Listening to them gave her shivers of disquiet, but she didn't reply to them.

Her visit to the NASA library archive, and her talk with the custodian, fascinated her for three hours. He was a repository of information about all the NASA programs. However, for her visit, he was concentrating on the various Earth-orbiting satellites and how they had evolved over the past quarter century. She took it all in, pleased that her modifications to the old operating program had been right on track.

With respect to the newest project, the new satellite, he had been permitted to tell her many of the classified aspects of the project brief. It was what she needed to complete the power modelling program for it. It also opened her mind to make it suit a wider range of space vehicles. A lot of the talk, though not the classified aspects, had been recorded on her pocket sized digital recorder. She was turning it off when her phone vibrated in her jeans pocket.

"It's Stan again," she told Stev.

"See what he wants."

"Hello Stan. What's up?"

His angry tirade didn't need to be on the speaker. She held the phone away from her ear until he paused.

"I don't know what happened," Erin lied. "I know I was tired, but I don't think I did anything without realising it."

"That last piece of the operating system is needed tomorrow, for the testing. Can you get in here today and resend it?"

Erin glanced at Stev, and he shook his head.

"Sorry, boss. I am with Stev Aldrin, heading down to the Aerospace Centre to get the data for testing the power modelling program. We won't be back until really late."

Something like a growl came through the phone. The next time he spoke, Stan had regained some composure. "Sorry, Mason. I was getting flak from Maxwell. I will tell him what's going on. Where were you all day yesterday?"

"At a friend's place, sleeping. Like I said I needed to do. I forgot to charge my phone until this morning and then I had to rush out."

"Okay, try and get in early tomorrow, okay?"

"Yes, sir." Erin said in her usual tone. Then she heard the connection drop out. She asked Aldrin, "Is Maxwell involved?"

Stev didn't answer at once. "I don't know everything Magnus knows. What is your gut instinct?"

"When Lauren asked me, I wondered if she was right. The other day, when I arrived at work, and as I was about to go into the lab, I saw Stan and Maxwell having an intense face to face. But that could as well have been the approaching deadline for the presentation."

"True. Let's leave it for now and concentrate on getting the data you need."

Erin wasn't reluctant to agree, preferring to anticipate the fascinating things she would see at the aerospace centre.

"Where do you want to be dropped off?" Stev asked, as they reached the edge of the city.

"My place, I guess. Although I still have stuff at Dad's place. Can I go home first and pick up a change of clothes for work, and then go to Dad's?"

"No problem," Stev agreed, and headed that way.

Erin was surprised when Stev followed her up to her apartment.

Her look was as good as asking a question.

"Just want to make sure it was cleaned up properly," Stev told her.

"Oh, yeah!"

However, the moment she entered her apartment, her back prickled. Her psychic side said, "Someone has been here." Her logical side said, "Of course! The cleaners."

Stev went off to do what Erin recognised as reconnaissance of her apartment. She let him. Her psychic senses told her no one else was around. She did her own careful survey, as a mental voice from her memory told her to check all her little tell-tales. Placing things 'just so' had become a habit.

The cleaners, should have had no reason to be anywhere but the main room and her bathroom, and indeed, all of her tell-tales in those rooms were askew. She went into the second bedroom, where her home computer was set up, and immediately had shivers racing up her back. Her chair was positioned differently – pushed right into the table. The mat, behind it, was too straight with respect to the wall and desk. The mouse was fully on the mouse pad, not half off it.

"Trouble?" Stev asked quietly, when he came up behind her.

"I don't know for sure. No one had need to come in here, but someone did." She explained her tell-tales.

"Check the other rooms and get what you need for tomorrow, while I call Magnus. He will get the police to come in and check things."

"I can quickly check the computer," Erin told him.

"No. Leave it," Stev advised. "Let it be thought that you don't know anything."

The shivers grew worse. Erin had to remind herself of the tricks she had learnt to turn aside fear. She might be a US Marine, but the only action she had seen was helping at one riot. But she was a Marine, and that thought steadied her. She told herself she was a spy in enemy territory. It really didn't feel far off that.

Stev picked her up on Monday and dropped her at work. "You know what to do?"

Erin nodded. "Send Stan the program, be abjectly apologetic, then get on with the modelling."

"The test run will be at 10," Stev told her. The two labs and the passages between will be under video watch. Do you have the copy of the data and the recording of the interview?"

"Oh, yes. I copied everything onto this USB," Erin took it from her pocket. "I will have to get Maxwell to okay bringing it in. Can you vouch for it?"

Stev grinned. "Okay."

Erin put it back in her pocket. She had the voice recorder there too, but its files were blank and the guards could check that."

Chapter 8 - Treachery

Erin was focussed on typing fast when Stan Otway arrived.

"Have you resent the program," he demanded without greeting her first.

"Yes. Tell me if you still have problems," Erin said, not looking up. "I couldn't find a reason to bomb last time, but just in case, I am trying to get it onto the framework."

Stan came over, and without asking, looked in the closed folder next to her.

"What's all this?"

Erin glanced to see what he was looking at. "Printouts of some data I can use for the power modelling. The figures are the raw data stream. I have it on a USB too. I didn't have time to upload it from home to here, so I will organise that later. I have other sections too, for checking some of the other systems – how it feeds back data and affects the power system."

"What are the squiggles?" Stan now had her hand written notes from her time in the archive and at the aerospace centre. "Did you sleep at all last night?"

"Couldn't. I had to write all the stuff down before I forgot."

Stan closed the folder, but his hand stayed on it a moment too long for just dismissing the topic.

"Will you be done by ten?"

"Hope so," Erin told him without pausing her typing.

At nine, the rest of the team came in, elated by the test to be run that day. It would be, they hoped, the vindication of all their work. Erin was sure Goldman's showdown would also come that day. Her nerves were telling her to be alert, even though she felt safe enough in the computer lab.

Even while maintaining her typing speed, Erin glanced frequently in Stan's direction. He was tense, so much so that when his phone rang, he practically fell from his seat. His face, when he glanced around to check if anyone was close enough to eavesdrop, was ashen. He spoke only twice, and when he pocketed his phone, he had to wipe his palms on his impeccable gray slacks.

He stared down at his desk, Erin sensed fear, that was nearer to terror, and that his mind was working furiously.

Erin's own phone was vibrating. She checked the message that just came in. "Keep the modelling data locked up." She deleted the message, and immediately secured the folder in her locked drawer.

She had just saved her typing, when the lights dimmed down and came up again. All the computers, judging by the exclamations of annoyance, had turned off. Erin's included. Before they all came back on, they were startled by the angry clanging of the fire alarm, and a seldom heard computerised voice telling all levels to evacuate the building.

Stan called orders, his voice initially stuck in his throat. Erin followed the directions, grabbing her bag and heading for the door. She brushed close to Stan, and when he was telling Mark to leave everything, she recovered her voice activated recorder from under the edge of Stan's desk – quickly hiding it and the adhesive blutack, in her pocket. Her near touch on Stan caused her to echo his emotion, and that was felt as an intense gut twisting feeling. She had the impression that he had just begun to feel relief from his earlier terror, and now knew he hadn't escaped it.

He was hurrying everyone out, doing his job as fire warden. Erin stayed in the middle of her group of colleagues, and headed down the stairs. Once down, and moving away from the building, Erin slipped a Bluetooth earpiece in her ear, and used one hand to rewind the recorder in her pocket, and played it through. The device was very sensitive, and she heard the voice of the caller, demanding, "Have you got it all?"

Stan answered, "I haven't the last piece yet."

"Tonight! Same place. If you don't show, or we see signs of an ambush. The deal's off."

"I can't get it until everyone has left."

"You said you'd have it two days ago."

"The damn woman has been playing cagey, keeping it protected."

"Excuses are worthless. We want what we were promised. You

have until 8pm. Then we will be gone and you know what that means."

After that, was silence, until the babble of when the power went off, and the alarm and voice over started.

Erin looked around for Stan, knowing that the evacuation would be the perfect time for him to get onto her computer, or into her drawer. She saw him emerge with one of the firemen, and decided he would not have had time to get into her computer. Still, she texted Goldman and then erased the message from her phone.

Once the all clear was given, Erin went back to work. She checked her drawer, and saw that pages in the folder had been subtly disarrayed. Her computer, already had the program she was using opened, so she checked the time of the last save and auto save. The latter had occurred while she was outside. The program might have auto-reloaded, but she couldn't be sure.

She had gone back to entering code, when the lab's main phone rang. After looking to see if Stan had returned, and not seeing him, she went to answer it.

Maxwell's voice barked, "Where's Otway?"

"He's not been back up since the alarm, Sir."

"When he gets back, tell him the test has been rescheduled to four pm. If he doesn't get back, I will want you to be there in case of problems with the program."

"Yes, Sir," Erin agreed.

"Otway said you hadn't quite finished putting the program into the frame work," Otway modified his tone.

"I have almost finished."

"Can you connect it to the rest?"

"No, Sir. I can upload it to the mainframe, that's all."

"Okay, do that. I will talk to the engineers. They will have to add it before the test starts."

Stan had still not returned when the test was due to begin. She could only shrug at Goldman, before being fully occupied by the matter in hand. When some of the subroutines failed, she took notes and sometimes was able to tweak the programming to make it work. The overall result, while not perfect, was extremely encouraging.

"What will I do with these notes?" she asked Goldman and Maxwell, who had both watched the full test.

"Put them on Otway's desk," Maxwell told her. Goldman gave a slight nod, indicating his agreement. She tidied the sheets of paper and began to head out. She sensed he was worried about something.

The unexpected summons, ten minutes later, made her hyper-alert. Goldman summoned her and she had to leave off telling her co-workers about the test.

She was directed to go right in when she reached his office on the 7th floor.

"I'm told you were able to calm Miss Avery the other day," Goldman got right to the point.

Erin nodded, and he went on. "Could I ask you to go out and visit her again? It seems that she is upset and the staff can't quieten her."

"Of course I will go. Can I get the address of the place?"

"I'll arrange a car. Go on down to reception when you are ready."

Erin felt the need to hurry, but while putting all her work away, she had qualms about leaving her notes on Stan's desk. He hadn't come back while she had been upstairs, and it was a strict rule to keep paper work locked up until it was finished with and shredded. She grabbed the papers and locked them in her drawer.

Moments later she was on her way down to reception.

Her sense of something wrong, she decided, must have been because of Lauren. Goldman was probably aware of her behaviour. However, she would have known that was not all, if she could have overheard a phone call between Stan and Maxwell, not long after she left the building.

"Where the hell are you?" Maxwell demanded.

"I don't know where they have me. They made me get what I had, but they want the rest – the test results and Mason's bit of the program. I wasn't able to send them that. I need it. Otherwise, they'll do horrid things to Janice, and they won't pay up."

"Calm down. I can get the test results and Mason's notes. I have had Goldman send her out of the way. The Avery girl called me earlier with some interesting accusations. I promised to tell Goldman, but also arranged for some more of that drug to be added to her food and drink. She is being very hard to calm down at the moment, so Goldman sent Mason out to talk to her."

"What good is that?" Stan's voice was high pitched.

"We can't put it all together, but I'd bet Mason can and she knows what else needs fixing," Maxwell said more calmly.

"She won't do it," Stan warned.

"I am sure they will have ways to make her cooperate. Talk to them. See what they say."

"They won't want a live cargo," Stan predicted, although he wasn't sure. They had already hinted at taking him and making him finish everything. But he was male. They hadn't much use for females.

"We can play this to the advantage of both sides," Maxwell went on with practiced calm. "With what you have, and the notes on what still needs to be done, it is as good as everything. As things are right now, they will have the jump on the government. The Defence Department don't have the full program yet, and without Mason, finishing it will be slower."

Stan considered all that, and finally said, "Maybe." He was too concerned with keeping himself alive, that he gave no thought to what Erin might have to suffer.

"She's gone out to the hospital. I will organise a couple of agents to go and pick her up – ones loyal to me. I will put word around that Mason has skipped. I know that Goldman still has a lot of reservations about her. She was involved in a million dollar fraud, just over a year ago."

"He was taking a risk," Stan blurted. He hadn't known the full story.

"He believes he has a way of keeping her in check. However, if she has vanished, and the evidence indicated she is involved, it will draw the heat off us. You can disappear as well, or turn up and recall nothing."

"I won't be sticking around," Stan vowed. "Although, if they agree..." He could feel hope flowing through his veins.

Stev hadn't expected her to meet any problems going in, and

Erin didn't think she would need his back up, so she watched him drive off before going inside. He had told her to stay there until he returned for her.

At the reception desk, she was challenged. "Do you have an appointment here?"

"No," Erin admitted, taken aback. "I was asked to come and speak to Lauren Avery, one of the patients here. I am Marine Sergeant Erin Mason."

The guard gave her a raking head to foot glance, but did not question her lack of uniform.

The receptionist stated, "Avery is not allowed visitors."

"I understand that she was being difficult, and the nursing staff called my boss, General Charles Maxwell. I was asked to come by Magnus Goldman of the SIO."

The caused the guard to raise his brows as he stared her down. "Maxwell? Is he related to Sister Maxwell, the head nurse?"

"I am not aware of any connection," Erin said, truthfully.

The guard did direct the receptionist to call up to the ward. Her story must have checked out, for the guard's tone changed. "It seems you are correct. I will need to see your ID, Miss."

The rest of the rigmarole, including being frisked and having her handbag checked, had not been needed when she had come with Stev.

Finally, she was cleared to go up, and an orderly was directed to show her the way. He introduced her to the nurse at the ward desk and was in turn dismissed.

"It was good of you to come, sergeant," the nurse greeted her. Her name tag read Vicki Harris.

"It's just Erin, and I work with Lauren. We're friends."

"Sister Maxwell, Vivienne, is in with her at the moment. Do you know the way?"

Erin nodded.

"Actually, I'll come with you."

The guards outside the ward just nodded, as Vicki took her into the ward. The screaming was abruptly louder as the door opened, and Erin had a glimpse of Lauren holding off two male nurses with a plastic dinner tray.

Sister Maxwell turned when the door opened, having noticed

Lauren's change of focus. She did not utter the sharp retort that came to her tongue, for Lauren made a dash for the door, and she went to grab her.

Lauren had ducked around one of the male nurses, and reached Erin just as Sister Maxwell did.

"Let me deal with her," Erin said quietly as Lauren clung tightly to her.

Sister Maxwell edged nearer the door, but nodded, for the screaming had abruptly stopped. One of the male nurses, strode closer. He had a filled syringe, and was bringing it up to inject.

Lauren twisted behind Erin, as she let her back to her bed.

"Please allow me a few minutes with Lauren," Erin requested of the nurse. "She will be quiet while I am here, and I need to ask her some questions. Now, not when that shot wears off."

"Five minutes," the nurse agreed. "Unless she gets agitated again. But she hasn't been making any sense."

Sister Maxwell shooed him back out of the way, but she stayed nearby.

"What happened?" Erin asked as Lauren settled into the visitor's chair.

"I don't know," Lauren protested. "I was feeling great, and I rang up work to see if I could go back. Otway wasn't around, so I was put through to Maxwell. He wanted me to take another week off. To stay here. But it's like a prison, and I'm watched all the time, like I was dangerous or insane. I had to sneak out to get to the phone. When Maxwell as good as ordered me to stay here, I got angry. I think I said something about wanting to keep me out of the way."

"I told you to forget all that," Erin chided very quietly. "I think he really wants to keep you out of harm's way. I suspect though, that he had another reason. Particularly if you get this angry about little things..."

"I don't want to stay here! It's a prison!"

"Lauren, this is not a prison. Believe me, I know!"

"They were angry when they found me out of my room. The two guards were really told off."

"Well, if you got out, they were slipping," Erin said wryly. "So what started this off? How are you feeling?"

"Awful. A bit like I was at work," Lauren admitted, in a low voice.

"After all the carry on, I was dozing, and they came in and gave me an injection. Said it was my usual med, but it wasn't."

"What time was this?"

"I think it wasn't long after four."

Erin's mind abruptly went into high gear. The timing was too coincidental. Stan was missing. He didn't have all the program, and had to get it. Lauren was potentially aware of the situation, that her computer was being used to get it. They did want her out of the way.

A more imperative reality occurred to her. The test wasn't a complete success. She could finalise it and she had a record as a hacker. As Goldman had warned, she was a ready-made fall guy. She put that thought aside to deal with Lauren, needing to calm her and allay her suspicions.

In a voice that was just audible, Erin said, "I don't know what you had in your system the other day, but when it breaks down, the metabolites might also affect you. My cousin reacts like that to sleeping pills – she doesn't sleep long, but then she goes hyper."

Sister Maxwell nodded, as if considering that possibility. Erin wasn't a chemist, or pharmacist, and didn't know if others than her cousin were like that, but Lauren wasn't either.

"When you were ill at work, the doctor gave you a sedative so you could sleep off the nasty effects. That's all they want to do now."

"No!" Lauren stated deliberately.

"The only other option is for you to be restrained. That's way worse, I know. I've been there."

"I don't want that guy near me."

Sister Maxwell suggested the two men leave and spoke quietly. "Doctor Wallace prescribed only a mild sedative. Will you let me give it to you? I will request a new vial."

Erin, with her senses not quite wide open, felt Lauren's distrust of Vivienne Maxwell. But her senses were giving her a different message – that Sister Maxwell was genuinely concerned for Lauren.

"Are you related to General Maxwell?" Erin asked.

"Yes. He is my husband. He insisted that I come here and work, because he wanted the best possible care for a member of his team. I had actually stopped working full time, several years ago."

While Lauren considered her words, Erin focussed her empathic senses on the speaker. She sensed nothing of guilt or underhandedness. If General Maxwell was in any way involved in selling secrets, she was sure that his wife didn't know.

Lauren was still leaning away from the still visible syringe in the metal tray, and Erin hoped she would agree soon. Something was building. She sensed it like she had the first time.

"Okay!" Lauren finally said. "Get a new dose."

Sister Maxwell took the tray away, and quickly left the room. Erin took Lauren's hand, and kept up a flow of calming logic, and even mentioned, "Besides, your computer still has a few things I need to fix before you can use it. I have had to concentrate on my program."

The sense of an imminent eruption had Erin mentally chanting a mantra to tighten her mind shields, and had just managed it when Lauren erupted out of her chair, shoving Erin off the arm. Marine training, allowed Erin to react fast, and regain her feet in time to grab Lauren's arm. She was ready for the fight, and was able to force a mind shield on Lauren, as she had the first time. The strength of the reaction halved, allowing her to restrain Lauren until the Sister returned, and while the injection was given.

The injection had been fast acting when Wallace had given it to her at work, but the five minutes seemed like an hour as Lauren kept trying to kick out and free herself. When Lauren began to teeter, Sister Maxwell indicated to get her to the bed.

"I will need to put restraints on for now, but I will remove them when she's quiet."

"I really hoped they wouldn't be needed," Erin said. "But how on Earth did anyone manage to give her more of that vile stuff?"

"I was told that she has been having these episodes since she was brought in, although this is the first since I have been on duty. I will talk to Dr Wallace, and mention it to Charles."

The sentiment was sincere, the bewilderment real, as far as Erin could sense.

"Are you alright?"

Erin started at the question. "Oh, yes. That was nothing compared to Marine drill sergeants."

Vivienne Maxwell managed a small laugh. "Do you want to have a coffee before you go?"

"I may as well," Erin decided. "I was told to stay here until I was picked up. I don't know when that will be. You may have my company for a while."

Erin expected it would be Stev Aldrin who would return for her, so when she saw the two men in suits heading towards the nurses station, she gave them no particular attention, just kept sipping her still very hot coffee. They were beside her, looking down at her, when one spoke.

"Miss Mason?"

She looked up. "Yes."

"We have to ask you to come with us."

"I was told to stay here until Stev Aldrin came back," Erin told them. She believed that was the truth, and in fact, this summons felt wrong.

"Mam, Colonel Aldrin is a busy and important man," the other spoke. "He had to go off on some important task. However, the matter in hand has now moved from SIO jurisdiction. You are required to come with us for questioning."

"Questioning? About what?" Erin stayed in her seat, wanting to sound out these men, put them off guard, see what she could sense.

"Mam, we were not informed. We simply have a directive to bring you in."

"Where are you meant to take me?"

"We are not authorised to tell you."

"Useful pair, aren't you," Erin said, keeping her sarcasm at a mild level, even as mental alarm bells were ringing in her head. I suppose, you both have names and identification?"

It was a perfectly legal question, but both suited men seemed to resent having their authority challenged.

However, they produced their identification wallets, and she took them to examine up close. They were State Department, and thanks to Wanda and David, she knew what real IDs should look like.

"Do you want me to call Charles?" Vivienne asked.

"No. I'm sure he will tell you this is all on the up and up."

She was sure of that, and just as sure that Goldman knew nothing of this...arrest. Though it was possible that the State Department had stepped in on this. It was even likely that this pair, O'Halloran and Ambrose, were ignorant of the full details, and were just obeying orders. Both were still young, ex-military, she decided, and likely newly inducted into the State Department. They were watching her as if expecting her to duck out on them. She was tempted, but it wouldn't be a good idea. She was almost certain that the 'fall guy', her, was about to find she had been set up. If the State Department had in fact taken over, Goldman would only have to say he'd had her working for him, and the matter would be settled.

She wasn't so certain that was truth, and for now, it might be wise to check the facts before causing trouble. Erin watched the men and decided she could probably overcome both of them. Neither were likely to have had the advanced unarmed combat training she had received, or expect her to be so skilled. Did they even know her marine rank?

With a sigh, that was to mislead her escorts, she pushed her coffee into the desk, collected her bag and stood up. Well, Goldman had warned her, and he knew she wasn't involved. He was a solid ally. So, she would find what kind of shit pile she was about to fall in.

Chapter 9 - Merchandise

Outside, it had become dark, but Erin recognised the way they were taking back to the city. As they got further in, she had the feeling they were headed for the building where she worked, and Goldman had his office. Contrarily, the sense that something was not on the level, peaked.

It was unlikely that there was anywhere in that building to interrogate anyone, and who would be the questioner? Goldman wouldn't need to, and if Maxwell had ordered her to be brought in, why didn't her escorts say so?

Yet, when her hunch proved correct, and she was led into the building where she worked, her escorts were obviously expected, for their IDs were ticked off on a list and they were waved through. They took the elevator to the fourth floor, the level where Maxwell had his office. Well, maybe he did have questions for her – about Stan, or herself. He didn't know she was Goldman's spy.

When they did enter Maxwell's office, Erin looked around, saw her boss and demanded, "What the hell is going on? Why was I dragged here?"

Maxwell's face hardened, no doubt due to her lack of respect, but he said mildly chiding, "Goldman wanted you on hand. There wasn't time for niceties. Make yourself comfortable."

Erin decided to sit, but glared back at Maxwell, while she jerked a thumb at her escorts.

"That's not what these two implied. They said I was wanted for questioning."

Maxwell glanced at the two men, then said, "Goldman is on the track of the people trying to get the satellite operating system. He may need you to answer technical questions. With Stan missing, you are the next best to know the program."

All very reasonable. Likely too, Erin thought, yet she felt sure Maxwell wasn't being completely truthful. If she wasn't increasingly becoming sure Maxwell was working with Stan, she'd have believed him.

Maxwell spoke to the two agents. "You might as well drag a couple of extra chairs in here and get comfortable. You are to stay on standby in case there is a need to get Mason to Goldman. You can get coffee from the staff kitchen, just down the passage."

So...was she a prisoner or a suspect? She distrusted the apparent normality and decided to test it. She stood and headed to the door.

"Where are you going?" Ambrose challenged.

Erin stared at him before answering. "To the ladies room, and to get some coffee. I didn't get to finish the one Sister Maxwell made for me."

"Don't be long!" Maxwell warned. "Things are moving quickly."

Erin intended to text Goldman, but no sooner had she taken her phone out, than O'Halloran pounced on her. "We'll have that!"

"You have no reason to take it, Erin challenged. "I am not a prisoner."

"There is a communications blackout. No outgoing calls are allowed."

"What if someone calls in? Can we answer it? You would be assuming a traitor wouldn't call in?"

"Don't get smart! Pass the phone, please, Miss Mason."

She held it until he drew his service pistol and aimed it at her. Ambrose arrived to back up his partner.

"I would like to hear what General Maxwell has to say," Erin challenged.

The weapon stayed steady, she was gestured back into Maxwell's office.

"Sir, Miss Mason refused to hand over her phone," Ambrose announced.

Maxwell, who was pacing the room, turned and said, "Do as they ask, Mason. I don't have mine either."

That seemed to settle the question. She had no choice. It seemed that the State Department had indeed taken over.

"I still want a coffee, and the use of the ladies room," Erin persisted.

She was escorted on both errands.

Time crawled. Maxwell still paced the room, and watching him made Erin feel tired. Yet she had learnt the value of not wearing herself out if there was likely to be a fight in the offing. She glanced at the two agents, standing stolidly by the door, and wished Stan Otway to hell.

No one in that room knew of her undercover role, and that she knew more about the investigation than she had been told at work. When Stev went to fetch her, he would learn of what happened – assuming she was right about Vivienne Maxwell. Even if she wasn't, they knew she would not have run off. They would know something was up. She considered taking on the two agents to get at a phone, but they were both watching her, not Maxwell. He was the one in charge here, and they were probably just dupes – obedient and ignorant.

Finally, near 9pm, the telephone on Maxwell's desk rang. He answered, gave no indication of the caller, but his posture became less rigid. "Right! I have that. What was the address? We're good to go."

He had written something on a notepad and tore the page off.

"Mason, they need you at this address." Maxwell gave her the paper. "An agent will meet you there."

O'Halloran said, "Come on then."

"I'll have my phone back then," Erin insisted.

"When we get there," was the immediate reply.

It was just possible that there was a valid reason, or rather a legitimate one, for their behaviour, but she had strong misgivings. Yet, she dared not step out of character and start accusations flying. She might be wrong.

If they really were legitimate, and thought her involved in the leaking of the program, why didn't they just arrest her and ask questions? If the State Department was not trusting anyone, that seemed more logical. However, if they were out to set her up, and knew she was innocent, this charade was so that she wouldn't suspect, and went along without giving trouble. Well, she wasn't clueless, and was ready to wait until that mental nudge told her it was the right time to act.

Meanwhile, she was invited into the back seat of a dark sedan with tinted windows. She managed, occasionally, to get a glimpse out of the front window but could see very little through the side one next to her. The driver was either taking a circuitous route, or deliberately trying to disorientate her, for he took a lot of turns.

Even when they stopped and allowed her out, she had no time to look around. They were in a narrow alley, with the buildings seeming to tower over her.

She could tell the buildings were old, and the smells in the air confirmed they were in one of the poorer districts. Then a door opened in front of her, and her fears crystallised the instant she saw Stan Otway. Without warning she twisted and ducked under the grasp of O'Halloran. Ambrose caught her, and she struggled to position him to disable him.

"You're not going to try and pin anything on me, you bastard," she yelled at Otway, and couldn't say more, because Ambrose grabbed her face, covering her mouth. She was hustled inside, where Stan said, "Erin, please! All I need to do is get you to access your computer and give me the rest of the program."

"No way!"

"Erin, please! If I don't get it, my girlfriend will be killed. They have her hostage."

"So you want to exchange her for me?" Erin yelled in disgust. "You should have considered the ramifications before you started this."

"I just need that bit of the program, okay?" Stan tried to insist. "One way or the other I will get it. Then tomorrow, you will be able to go. It won't matter if you go to the police, or Goldman. I'll make sure it looks like you were coerced."

"How much are these treasonous rats paying you?" Erin sensed his reaction and knew she was right, even as Stan continued his lie.

"They will let my girlfriend go."

"No. I have yet to be convinced I will be let go."

"How much do you want," Stan asked, changing his tactic.

Erin spat at him. "You are not going to get me double-crossing Goldman. He is the only reason why I'm not still incarcerated in a federal prison. He is a nasty one to double-cross. I know!"

Her conviction caused Stan to slump. A whistle from just outside the door, caused him to go rigid. A man came in. "They're coming."

Ambrose ran outside, to the car they'd arrived in and revved off. O'Halloran shoved her towards a door leading off the room they were in. Stan was shoving papers into a case, roughly. He followed out into a passage, and slammed the door behind him. He soon caught up to O'Halloran, for Erin was using every trick she knew to slow him down.

"Fool, you don't want those bastards after you," O'Halloran told her. "They won't help you."

"I'll take my chances," Erin claimed, being defiant stopped her admitting she was terrified.

A door opened to the left. Erin was dragged in and the door shut behind them.

"This is the woman?" a strongly accented voice asked.

Erin twisted around to see who had spoken. The man, looked to be a mixture or European and Asian.

"Yes," Stan confirmed.

"You had better not be trying to double-cross us," the stranger said. His voice held a subtle menace, and Erin wanted to hiss at him.

"She wrote that part of the program," Stan said quickly, ignoring Erin, as if she were not there.

Stan had gestured to several neat piles of paper on a table. "As for the rest of it, she knows as much about it as I do. Maybe more."

The Eurasian man, all five foot six of him, eyed Erin who was staring back at him, mind working furiously. She had to get away — should have tried harder before this.

The man's phone rang, he spoke in some other language, gave orders and ended the call.

"Bring what you have, American, and come. Somehow your police have found this place. We must leave. Your pet can bring the woman."

Stan ran to the table, gathered the piles and put them in his case. When that was closed, he grabbed a laptop from the floor.

The Eurasian came and invaded Erin's personal space. "Woman should keep to their place." His hand flew up and gripped her by the throat. She stood defiantly, since O'Halloran was close enough behind her to stop her moving away. The stranger's hand began to increase pressure, as if in warning, but then she felt a sharp prick, and alarm surged through her. She tried to push him away, but his bulk was too solid. He just smirked as his hand massaged his neck.

"Can't have you being a problem, Chickie."

Then he ordered, "Bring everything."

Erin felt O'Halloran release her, she wanted to run, but found her will would not make her legs work. She stood there until O'Halloran returned with a brief case, and shoved her into motion. She couldn't even resist the movement as she had before.

As they went out another door and along passages, Erin tried to remember the way, to notice details, but found herself forgetting from minute to minute. Quashing panic, for she still knew she was in deep trouble, she reached out with her mind, hoping the damn drug did not affect that extra sense of hers. While her mind felt locked within a small cage, and trying to batter its way out, she pictured a space between the bars, and sent out an intense emotion laden thought. A moment later, she felt a touch. Wanda! Yes! The deep link was still there!

A voice, maybe her own mental voice, told her to observe everything. She did, even though she soon forgot – maybe that mind, linked to hers, would remember.

They went down stairs to a concrete walled tunnel, and hurried along it. Finally going up into a building that was a very different style to the first. The Eurasian told O'Halloran, "Go bring the car up. Have it ready outside the door."

"Where's my payment," Stan insisted.

O'Halloran had put the case he was carrying down by the door. The Eurasian gestured to it. Stan ran to it, knelt down and would have opened it, except for the foot that the Eurasian planted on it.

"There is no need, Mr Otway. We are both business men and might want to deal again."

Erin, her mind getting foggier, wondered why he wasn't demanding to know where his girlfriend was, or wanting to see her.

Stan stood up, as O'Halloran returned, agitated. "The building is surrounded. They have the whole block sealed off."

The Eurasian backhanded Stan, "I warned you!"

"It wasn't me!" Stan protested. "It had to be her. Does she have a phone?"

"No," O'Halloran said. "I have it."

"Then that probably led them to us. It must have a tracker chip in it. Goldman hasn't ever really trusted her, except to do programming."

"Leave it here," the Eurasian ordered. "We must go deeper."

This time, when they returned to the passage, they only went a short way, then took a turn to the right. Erin only had a moment to notice that Stan hadn't followed, before she felt the floor of the passage tremble, and a muffled explosion – followed moments later by a pressure wave.

O'Halloran started an exclamation, but stifled it at the sight of the Eurasians satisfied smirk. He swallowed, convulsively, and his intense fear hammered at Erin. She knew, in that odd way she had of knowing things, even with her mind becoming more sluggish, that something had exploded.

"Carry that merchandise," the Eurasian ordered O'Halloran. "We need to get to the end before they find the door."

Erin couldn't protest, and the jerking motion of being thrown over a shoulder, overcame the last vestiges of her will to stay conscious.

Chapter 10 – Failed Raid

Stev Aldrin notified Goldman as soon as he heard how Erin had left the hospital. They had expected her to be safe there. However, knowing that she might be used as a pawn, they had placed an accurate tracker app on her phone. Within minutes, her location was identified.

They already knew where Otway was holed up, because of a similar tracker on his phone. There were people in place waiting to capture his contact. When it proved that Erin was headed to the same place, Goldman held off the raid, and called in more men so they could do a simultaneous attack on all entrances and exits to the building that were shown on the official building plans. The police were moving in to seal off a city block.

While they waited for the escape routes to be covered, Erin's tracker signal dropped out. Goldman ordered all teams to move in.

Twelve men went in through the door where Erin had disappeared. Finding no one in the room, they spread out to search. In the passage, about to check a side room, the door blew out with an intense fiery explosion, that caused the walls around to ignite into flame. Four men took the full blast, four more were badly burnt. The remaining four, although badly singed, helped their fellows out. The fire trucks, on stand-by down the street, arrived in minutes, and by then, the building sprinklers had reduced the flames.

As soon as the room was deemed safe, agents sent by Goldman went in and reported on the room.

The force of the blast had been aimed towards the door, and the worst damage was on that side. The other part of the room was fire damaged, but not so much that the man's body, scattered money and a phone were found. A second team found a room with vandalised computer equipment and no clue to there the operators had gone.

Goldman was angry. Somehow, the group had been warned to

leave. He gave orders for all equipment and other evidence to be collected. He heard the news of the men injured in the explosion, and felt responsible. He worried about Erin, where she was now, if she was alive or dead. His agents had identified the dead man near the site of the explosion, as Otway.

He gave orders to check for how the men had escaped, and then the man watching for the tracker signal said, "Mason's phone is showing up – the building that backs onto the target building."

More orders went out. Teams from the perimeter blockade moved up and stormed the building. The regular occupants, were herded into one area, and asked about strangers coming through. None gave any hint of knowing anything.

Back at the command post, Goldman's private phone rang. He answered in his usual cautious way, and recognised the voice that wasted no time on niceties. Wanda Martin's words, "Erin has been abducted by the people you are after," did not surprise him.

"We are aware," Goldman confirmed. "Can you tell me anything more?"

"Not much," Wanda admitted. "There was an Eurasian involved..." She gave as much of a description as she had received as a vision from her cousin's mind. "He injected her with some drug that disassociates the body from the conscious will."

"Then they want her alive," Goldman summarised. "That is to our advantage. That was all?"

"Yes. Erin can't send thought unless there is a lot of emotion behind it."

Goldman thought fleetingly, that there must have been a lot for Erin to reach her cousin across the width of America. "Call me again if you pick up anything more."

"Yes, Sir. No, wait! David has just been told that our targets are on the move – planning to leave. They have filed a flight plan for Egypt, via several waypoints. That's from DC. He's trying to get all the details now."

"I will see if I can stop all flights," Goldman promised, ending the call abruptly.

He called Stev Aldrin, who wasn't as confident of success as his boss. He had authority to call on various authorities including the defence forces to check all airfields in the capitol, and the surrounding areas. There were a lot of places a plane could land and pick up passengers, though not as many where a private jet could land. There were also ways for a pilot to change direction in the air, to remain unseen and lose followers.

The next report, of the lack of success in the other building, had Goldman quizzing the man at the tracking computer. "Did the signal from Mason's phone drop out again?"

"Yes, Sir. About five minutes before the team went in."

"And you still have nothing? If they went out before our men got there, via the street, would you?"

"Yes, if nothing happened to the phone."

"Keep alert. It dropped out between the two buildings..." He stopped abruptly, to make another call, and wasted no time before saying, "Get onto the local planning authority. There has to be a tunnel between those two buildings, and there may be more. Have the perimeter moved out, and cover all sides of the block. If there is a tunnel, it could come out anywhere. We won't get much warning if any."

The team searching in the building found the start of the tunnel, but could not move fast, as all of the fire doors had been activated. They had to manually disarm them before getting through, and then there were half a dozen side doors to force open and check. When they reached the street, it became obvious that their targets had emerged before the cordon had been replaced. Erin's phone was found just inside the outer door.

Even with proof that their targets had fled, Goldman stayed in the control room. After a time, Stev joined him.

"She's still alive," Goldman told his friend. "That maverick cousin of hers called me." He shared the information.

"And we shouldn't sell her short," Stev remarked. "They won't think she can send messages out, and that is our secret. Anyway, there were watchers out, because a street kid saw the car that brought Erin here. She was mobile then. Someone whistled, and they hurried inside."

Goldman told Stev all he knew, ending with, "The local precinct is examining CCTV footage, and questioning people just outside our perimeter. With the various cars racing around, we can't be sure one wasn't the targets. And it is beginning to seem like they have got away."

"Otway was expendable," Stev reported then. "It looked like the case they had the money in was booby trapped. The blast killed him, but it blew him across the room. We found some papers and a ticket to Mexico in his pocket. I sent a team to check that airfield."

"If the Martin pair are correct, the people we are after, are related to the ones they are after," Goldman reiterated, knowing Stev knew who he was referring to, even though casual listeners would not.

"Which means, if they have Erin, it is an unexpected move. Otway must have done a job convincing them of her skill. They usually have little use for women."

"Yes, but they might also think she can be dominated more easily than a man," Goldman smiled faintly.

Stev, returned the smile, but very briefly. "So what went wrong here?"

"Let's head back to the office," Goldman side-tracked the conversation. To the tracking officer, he said, "If anything important is discovered, I want to be called right away."

Alone in the back of Goldman's chauffeured car, where the back section was proof against being overheard, Stev asked again, "Who blew the set up?"

"Only a few people knew today was going to be the showdown. I trusted each of them. All of the arrangements were done by others, so I wasn't directly connected. I have a watch on each of the others that knew, except you."

"Even Maxwell?" Stev asked.

Goldman's expression was stony. "Yes, but he hasn't been located. I had his wife brought in for questioning. She is at the local precinct. We will head back via there."

"Do you think she is involved?" Stev asked.

"I didn't think Maxwell could possibly be involved," Goldman admitted. "Erin made a few passing references, but she only had vague feelings – nothing she could really point at."

"His wife did give us the names of the two supposed State

Department agents, and descriptions. Needless to say, no such agents are on the roster, but Erin checked their id's, and passed them as genuine."

"Which suggests high up connections," Goldman commented. "Maxwell could have recruited those two – Ambrose and O'Halloran, I know how the men he commanded idolised him. We need to find him, fast. Check to see if he was working late. There was quite some time between Erin being taken, and her turning up back there. She had to have been somewhere."

Stev used his phone to make calls. Finally he reported, "He was at his office. Mason and the two agents went there. The agents were expected. The time they arrived fits with coming directly from the hospital, and when they left there, it would be to go to the meeting. Maxwell signed out soon after Erin and the agents left."

"I want him picked up and held," Goldman said, betraying nothing of his personal regrets about a long time friend. "Have his phone and internet communications looked at, also his bank transactions, as well as the same for his wife."

Back in his office, Goldman resisted the urge to pace. He sat in his chair and let his mind go over the details of the plan he had orchestrated, and the outcome that seemed to be a fiasco.

The program was the bait. Supposedly, it could be used to take over a dormant satellite, which in turn could be used for espionage purposes. That was still a potential, but Erin had built in subroutines that could negate the foreign control – unless they had an expert as good as she was who could detect them. The communications subroutine, was the most dangerous part. It needed to be state of the art. They had covered that in part by offering a firewall enhancement to as many satellite operators as they could – but only within the United States. She and he, were the only people to know those things.

Now, it was obvious, the foreigners had all of the program segments, and notes to make the final few segments work properly... and Erin who could finish it all.

Otway could have finished it as he knew as much about the whole program as Erin did. Why hadn't they taken him? They would have been after a finished product, paid for it, and had probably not been prepared for a live cargo. Did they consider Otway unreliable? That he had become a liability? Or had killing him always been the plan? In any case, they wanted what they paid for.

Goldman considered the woman he had put under cover. Erin shouldn't have been involved in the hand over. She was simply his eyes and ears on the project, and her programming skill made certain contingencies controllable. He had been right to co-opt her skills, she was a genius.

What might happen now, he mused. With a very strong line on the identity of the foreign group, he could surmise that they believed they could control a woman, and make her finish the program. Until that was done, Erin would be safe. He had to stop them leaving the country. If they took Erin back to theirs, the chances of getting her away from them would be slim.

Finally his mind turned to more positive thoughts. Erin was a Marine sergeant, and had excelled there. She had taken a leaf from her cousin's book and learnt advanced self-defence tactics. She was strong willed, and not weak. His good friend Rowan Wallace had said, "Her mind needs to be challenged." He had been right. Now, her current plight was another kind of challenge.

Did he trust her?

The question was one he needed to be sure of. Particularly as the people who took her would want to have her cowed, and thinking them her only safety. Her background made that easy. He had made no secret of it when attaching her to the project. What he hadn't spoken much of was her time in the marines – except to imply it had been that or prison. A reluctant recruit would not embrace the training as Erin had done. So, a threat of all the powers of the American justice system being after her would be expected to scare her into compliance. In her role, she had always implied she preferred not to be near him, as if disliking him or afraid if his power over her. No one would expect her to have powerful protectors. And no one knew of her cousins and what they could do together. Yes, all was not lost.

He thought to himself, if he had to bet on the outcome, would be bet on Erin? Yes, he decided. She would look for her chance, but he needed to give her all the help he could. And be alert for contact from her.

Stev returned as he came to that decision.

"The police found Maxwell's car. It was in a deserted cul de sac down near the river. There were traces of blood on the car, signs of a struggle near it. The mud there was dry, but soft. Drag marks suggest a heavy body was moved to a second car that parked behind his."

"Was he alive, or dead?" Goldman mused aloud. "It is becoming clearer that he was in this with Otway. Was it reprisal for failing to fill a contract?"

"Or they want him for something else?" Stev suggested.

"Or he, or the foreigners, knew we were onto him," Goldman stated bluntly. "He might know who they are."

"Or he could have staged an abduction to cover his tracks," Stev continued the idea.

Goldman gave no reply to that, instead he rang he security office and asked for the phone records for the building since 6pm. He waited for the verbal report, then hung up.

"What are your thoughts about how Erin will handle this?" Goldman asked abruptly.

Stev considered all the times he had interacted with her. "She's had training that will stand in good stead. Her superior officers called her determined and resourceful, and she had that extrasensory ability. Not to mention more than a little disregard for what's right. I think she could play both sides equally well. She is a skilled hacker, and has ways to get information out that others may not suspect. And to program nasty little viruses, I expect."

Goldman actually smiled. "Yes, that program is full of them – but she has to get a chance to activate them and not be caught."

"Let's hope we find her first," Stev said.

The phone rang, with the first of the follow up reports. Airfields were being investigated, aircraft frequencies were being monitored. So far, no planes had taken off, and no private jets were known at the nearest airfields. As far as Goldman could determine, he had everything covered – but he didn't like waiting.

Chapter 11 - Prisoner

The lethargy was becoming worse, it now felt like her muscles were infused with lead. It took all her energy, just to breathe. Being pushed down into the back seat of a car, with no thought for her comfort, didn't help.

Erin couldn't tell where they were taking her. All she knew was that the streetlights had become less frequent, and now were few and far between. When the car finally stopped, she was only barely conscious. O'Halloran, if that was his name, had to carry her from the car, to the dark shape of a building.

The distance was short, but enough to give her the impression of open space and the whiff of fresh air.

Country? Her mind suggested, as she tried to draw in more of the fresh air.

The building might have been a farmhouse, but in the dark, slung over O'Halloran's shoulder, she couldn't see much. All she could do was count the three doors she passed through before being placed on the floor. When he checked to see if she was awake, Erin had closed her eyes.

Erin tried to move, but had no success. She was left on her back, but even so, she soon began to smell the fustiness of old, rotting carpet, and felt dust tickling her nose. When the door had been shut, it had done so with a solid thud.

Her mind was sluggish; she couldn't even rouse herself to be angry with the people who had taken her. Even trying to consider ways to escape, when she could move again, were hard to focus on.

I'm a Marine. Marines don't give up, she told herself. If she couldn't move physically, she could force her mind to exercise. She began by repeating the times tables from one to twelve, and when that became easier, she recalled a mantra for concentration – keeping that up for several hours.

When her mind felt nearly normal, she began to catalogue what she might be able to do. But most of that was conjecture – she would have to be ready to take advantage of whatever chance came along. And to tweak chances her way, her first plan was to try to reach her cousin. Back in the city, when she'd tried, she had felt a touch. Hopefully, Wanda would be alert for her to try again. Hours had passed though, and Wanda might be asleep.

Across the continent, in Crystal Springs, California, Wanda Martin woke suddenly. It was the middle of the night, but icy shivers were chasing around her nervous system. She rose and pulled on a warm track suit. Most of the shivers were not due to the chill of the night.

This sense of premonition bothered her. Her first thought was for David, currently back in Albany, New York. It would be almost morning there, so she took her phone from the charger and called him.

"Couldn't you wait another hour?" he complained when he heard her voice. He woke up properly when Wanda explained how she felt.

"I haven't heard anything," he told her, referring to the job he was on. "However, those Arab agents are in Washington."

"Erin?" Wanda posed the name as a question.

"She should be fine. Goldman was moving in on the targets last evening."

"Can you contact Goldman, or Stev? I told him hours ago, that she wasn't OK. Has he found her?"

David didn't answer immediately. "I don't know. He doesn't have to report to me, but our targets were agitated. Why don't you wake up your sister, and Tanya, and see what you can pick up. I think your sister is with your Dad at the moment."

"Yeah! Okay. But we aren't together."

"Don't let that put you off. You reached her from a lot further away that you are now. Don't forget that Erin is a Marine. She can take care of herself. More so if she has a private help line."

"You're right. Talk later!"

Wanda ended the call and immediately dialled her sister.

Elisabeth Willard's first words were, "Are you okay?"

"I am, but I think Erin is in trouble. Were you picking something up too?"

"I must have been. I don't usually have nightmares. Is this related to what you had me call Mr Goldman about?"

"I'd say so," Wanda decided. "David said he was to move on his targets last night. His plans might have got screwed, because Erin wasn't meant to be involved in that."

"What do you want to do?" Elisabeth asked.

"Try and reach her. Where's Tanya these days?"

"Here. With me." The answer surprised Wanda.

"Wonderful! Will you two try to reach her? I know you've done it before. I'm going to get a plane and head there. I will try during the flight."

"How will we contact you?"

"Text me. I will check my text messages when the plane lands. Otherwise, call David."

"Right!" Elisabeth said. "I'm on it!"

Wanda called David again and told him what she planned.

"You'll take six or seven hours getting there," David pointed out. "Is it worth coming?"

Her inner voice said, "Yes." She told David, knowing he trusted her instincts.

"Okay," he told her. "I will call the airport and roust our friendly pilot. You get your stuff together and head to the airport. Don't get a speeding ticket!"

"My name is not David Martin," Wanda retorted.

She heard David's chuckle. "Okay, Okay! Get going."

Erin was just starting to be able to move as a few narrow rays of light began to shine through cracks between the boards covering the window. She assumed that, from the three parallel bright lines on the wall. That gave her a rough idea of the time. It would still be night in California, Wanda was probably asleep. Still, she had little else to do, so she tried again, rousing all the emotion she could to force her message across the distance.

"Erin?" the return mind touch forced a surge of adrenalin through her.

"Elisabeth? Tanya?" Those minds were so familiar too.

"Yes, and Wanda is coming." Tanya sent words, more strongly than Elisabeth. "What can you tell us?"

The relief gave her thoughts power. "I think I am in an old farm house."

"Where?"

It was an obvious question, but she didn't know.

"Who is with you?" they tried next.

Erin pictured the face of the two supposed State Department agents, and the Eurasian.

"Three people?" Tanya's mind voice asked.

Erin didn't really know, for she had only seen three. She formed an image in her mind of a '3' and a '?'.

She took a moment to sense nearby people, and sent an image of her in a room, and one figure outside.

There was little more she could say, but knowing that her cousins knew her plight, gave her mind the kick it needed to shake the rest of the fuzziness.

I am not alone! I will survive this.

It wasn't much, Elisabeth knew, but it was more than they'd had before. She called David, since Wanda would still be in transit.

"I'll give you Stev's number," David told her. "Call him, okay? I'm busy here trying to pick up phone conversations. Goldman hasn't eased the pressure. All the airports and airfields within 100 miles have had to ground all out going flights. He won't be able to keep it up much longer, but it's only to be until the FBI get people to all of them."

Elisabeth wasn't upset by David's abrupt termination of the call. She simply dialled Stev Aldrin's number.

Erin pulled herself into a sitting position and looked around. More light was coming in around the window, and she could just make out the few pieces of furniture in the room. Mentally she cursed the man who had dumped her. At least he could have put her on the low cot bed, and its mattress. The floor was damn hard.

A round barrel like object occupied a corner, and there was an armchair in the middle of the room.

An idea came to her of the purpose of the barrel, and she had a really urgent need to perform that particular function – somewhere. The trouble was, she still couldn't get herself to cross the intervening couple of yards, let alone pull herself up.

That's when she sensed a faint chanting in her mind, listened intently and caught the cadence of that chanting. Of course! The mantra for healing.

She added her mind to the two she heard, and began to feel a faint breeze blowing within the room. She had felt that sensation before, welcomed it now, and imagined it blowing away the leaden feeling in her muscles. If anyone else came in, they wouldn't feel it and would never believe it was destroying the effect of the foul drug.

As soon as she could push herself along the floor, she did so. Moving the short distance still took a long time, and she hoped the silence from outside the room would continue until after she had performed her increasingly urgent natural function. It seemed too, that the more she moved, the easier movement became, even if only in small incremental amounts. Then, after time she hadn't counted, she sensed the third other mind in hers. Wanda!

"You betcha," came the acknowledgement. "You seen your non-friends this morning?"

In her mind, she thought, "No." She wasn't thinking about what she was trying to do, but did sense wordless sympathy. Then she heard, as if thought casually, "From what David is picking up, certain people are in quite a dither. There is an official block on overseas flights taking off. Not sure how long they can keep that up, and I can see ways around it."

Hey what?

"Do you think they will be taking me out of America?" Erin thought with another surge of adrenalin.

"I am guessing that might be their new plan," Wanda confirmed. "Since David and I are sure the case we have been on is related to Goldman's current concerns."

"And you know where they will want to take me?" Erin infused a touch of scepticism into her mental tone.

"General area, yes."

"And if they do?" Erin went on. She had reached the corner and was trying to decide how to stand up. The corner of the cot to push herself up, and the window sill to help her stay up.

"We are trying to prevent that," Wanda told her. "So when you have a moment, can you tell us more about where you are?"

"Yeah, okay. If I am still in here tomorrow, I might be able to tell you the time of sunrise. The window faces east and the early sun came in through cracks in the boards over the window."

"Can you hear sounds from outside?"

Erin listened, but all she could hear was silence. "No, but there may be nothing to hear."

"Well, if you do, think at us. Particularly if it sounds like a helicopter."

They are looking for me! "I'd be like the proverbial needle, wouldn't I?"

"Maybe," Wanda allowed. "But I don't think the haystack is in the city. It has to be in a more rural area."

Remembering the sense of openness and the faint earthy smell when she was being carried inside, Erin had to agree.

"And if they do start to move you again, you might see more," Wanda suggested with a sly mind tone.

Erin's relief when she was finally able to relieve herself, was sensed by her cousins, who for a time, faded from her mind. When she finished, she realised movement was much easier. She could stand up, although holding onto the windowsill made her more confident. Her mind returned to the thought, *Are they planning to take me out of America?*

She hoped her cousins were still mind linked to her, particularly Wanda. "So, what would you do? You're the expert at this cloak and dagger stuff!"

She sensed Wanda's chuckle. "Oh, I have a few ideas for you, Marine!"

During that day, Erin saw no one. In a way, that was a benefit, and they may not have expected her to be as active as she was getting. Yet, in all that time, she was no nearer to getting free. Every idea her cousin came up with had so far proved to be useless. Though Wanda seemed to have an endless supply of ideas.

She didn't let the lack of success depress her, the ideas were good, and might work somewhere else. And Wanda had stressed, she was a Marine, and she would be on alert for her chance.

One thing she was determined on. The people behind her abduction, and those they worked for, would not get a working Skywatcher program to use for their illegal purposes. If the police or other officials couldn't find her, and the stored files and notes, then perhaps she was the one to follow the trail...by being on it with them.

Sometimes, things did happen for a reason, even when she couldn't figure it out.

By evening, her stomach was cramping from lack of food, and her mouth was horribly dry. She told herself to ignore it. At best, it meant she did not have to use the barrel again.

She knew the room well by then. The door was solid wood, and the hinges made for heavy duty. There was nothing she could use to remove the pin. The window was made of thick and small glass panes, set in a metal framework like a checker board. It wasn't designed to open, even without the boards outside. The chair she sat in was old, the material on the verge of fraying – like the carpet that covered most of the floor.

The silence, which she had come to think was due to solid walls, bothered her. It seemed that even if she could produce sounds louder than a whisper, no one would hear her. She certainly hadn't heard the helicopter that Wanda's comment had suggested was looking for or her.

Just as she began to fear that she had been abandoned there, she did hear faint sounds and a shudder through the floor. She imagined doors being forcefully opened, or slammed shut. Extending her empathic senses gave her the sense of several distinct presences. After a while, she heard sounds that suggested her door was being unlocked.

She had already moved the chair so that it was facing the door, and now she sat in a casual pose, and prepared herself for any chance of getting free. She wasn't surprised when the man who stood in the doorway when it opened was the Eurasian. Beyond him was a stranger of similar heritage, wielding a gun.

Erin concentrated on the man she had met before. "Well, I see it's himself. Do you have a name? I can only think of ones you wouldn't like."

"Don't get smart, Chickie," he snarled. "I still have more of the stuff I gave you."

"Maybe you do, but if your bosses want me to do work for them, that stuff stops me being able to think and reduces my usefulness. After that first lot, I am not quite with it even now. You'd have to wait days for me to be able to work." Her voice was little more than a hoarse whisper.

The faintest of twitches in the man's cheek, was his only reaction to her comment. Perhaps speed in getting the program up and running, was an issue. More relevant to the present, though, was how her lack of fear and air of assurance, was giving him reason for thought.

"Who says we need your help," the man demanded.

Erin gave a short laugh. "Would your bosses have told you to bring me if they didn't need me?"

That was blindingly logical to her. "The way I see it, you or the people you work for, have all of the program except the part I was trying to finish, and you might have my notes for the modifications needed. However, when I made them, it was for my use. I didn't write down where the changes needed to go, because I knew that. I also reckon your bosses have a deadline, and need the finished program and someone who can access the computer at work."

"What else do you think you know?" came the belligerent counter challenge.

Erin decided she had nailed the situation, and merely said, "Enough."

"We will make you co-operate," was the blustering threat.

"There is a simple way to do that," Erin said, looking directly into his eyes as she spoke. "You try anything and I won't. However, I will discuss my fee with your bosses."

"I'm in charge here!"

"No you're not!" Erin disputed the yelled assertion. "Snakes like you are only found under rocks."

The hardening of the muscles around his eyes, warned her not to push him any further, but it wasn't any time to back down. She let him move towards her, gave no reaction when he grabbed her by the throat again. He wasn't affecting her ability to breathe, yet. When his other hand began to move down the front of her clothes, she grabbed his wrist with more strength than he expected.

She could still talk, and did so with icy calm and a warning intentness – despite her dry throat.

"If you mishandle me in any way, your bosses may just find that I have conveniently forgotten how to finish that program. Even if I did still remember, they will find I am capable of putting bugs into that program that are impossible to eradicate. Think about it, Chuckles. I will make sure they know it is your fault."

The Eurasian freed his wrist from Erin's grip, and dropped the other. He glared at her for a long hate-filled moment before stalking out and re-locking the door.

Erin slumped into the chair, letting out a long breathe of relief. "I reckon I won that round," she murmured. "And I can probably say goodbye to getting food anytime soon." The cramping hunger in her belly would have to be ignored and endured.

She scrambled up from the chair and went to try to see out through the thick glass and the cracks in the boards. Detail was impossible, but she could think of being outside, in the sun, feeling its warmth. The touch of the Eurasian had aroused revulsion – like something slimy had touched her.

A chuckle in her mind seemed to be accompanied by the odd sensation of a breeze in the room. She recognised it, and thought, "Are you any closer to finding me?"

The chuckle ceased. "No, unfortunately, and not for lack of trying." The mind tone had subtle notes of Elisabeth and Tanya. "Russell has been insisting on using every possible agency – but smarter thinkers have countered that. It is no use everyone running around like rabbits."

"Is he still considering me a terrorist?" Erin asked with resignation. Stan Russell, the Secretary of State was not a fan of her, or her cousin.

The chuckle returned. "No, more likely he thinks that since his daughter had returned to her former frivolous ways, you probably will have too. I think he'd change his tune if he saw how well you terrorised that creep, though."

"I remembered what you said about showing no fear."

"You're a natural," the mind voice of her cousin said.

"Or you corrupted me," Erin thought back. "But how can I help find out where I am?"

"You need to be out of that room," Wanda said to her mind.

"I can't see that happening any time soon. He'll probably try to starve me."

"And if you are too weak, how can you work? Low blood sugar can lead to all sorts of problems."

"I don't think he is smart enough to think of that. Did you pick up that whole interaction?"

"Most of it. David is tracing some calls – they might give us a lead on your location. I think you did rattle that creep, and he would understand the lure of money...particularly if he learns of your former reputation. His superiors may be comforted by that."

Erin sensed her cousin's attention shifting as her own senses were warning her of another visitation. The understanding was a deep two-way. She heard Wanda thinking, "We think we know the general area you are in."

The door wasn't opened right away, and by listening hard, she could hear the tone of a disagreement, but not the words. A surge of anger preceded the door being unlocked.

"Get out here!" the Eurasian ordered.

Erin stared at him for a long moment before pushing up from the chair. She wondered in passing what he would do if she refused. Just then, a flush was beginning to suffuse his face. Maybe he was getting the idea that her obedience was at her choice, not his. Then she looked away from him, and walked past him, out through the door. It would seem she was ignoring him, but that wasn't the case. In her mind, she was concentrating on the remembered sense of revulsion he roused in her. A fleeting brush as she went past, and she forced that emotion into his mind, but didn't seem to notice how he took three steps back from her. He wouldn't think she could cause that. He'd think the emotion was his own. In any case, her whole attention seemed to be on the other person in the room.

"Well, well, the chief himself," Erin said with veiled irony.

Charles Maxwell turned around and watched as she approached. He was noticeably unsettled when she held put her hand to shake his.

"So, you were a part of this too?" she continued, not betraying any sign of fear. "I must admit, it's a relief to see you. I'd rather deal with someone I know. People, like your friend Chuckles back there..." she shrugged over her shoulder, "...don't strike me as being overly intelligent."

Maxwell looked at the Eurasian and gave a head jerk towards the second door. That he obeyed the tacit command, told Erin a great deal. When the door had closed, Maxwell gestured her to a chair. It was the same vintage as the one in the room she had just left, but less dusty.

"I need a drink before we discuss anything," Erin told him. She sat, subtly forcing her boss to wait on her. He did, going off and returning with a beer glass full of water.

"Klaus says you won't co-operate," Maxwell said conversationally as he sat himself in another of the chairs.

"Co-operate with what?" Erin asked immediately. "All people have been doing to me recently is shoving me around. I have about reached my limit. And I can guess what you are hinting at, but unless I see some benefit for me, well..." she left him to guess if she was refusing.

"Klaus said you knew what was up."

Erin shook her head, as if sadly. "It seems Chuckles and I have a language problem," she told her boss. "People who try threats and bullying, before they try reason, or even ask nicely, really get my back up. Besides, are you saying I should take over from that traitor Stan Otway?"

Maxwell didn't answer that question, and he frowned slightly as if he thought he had read her wrong.

"I had you figured for an agent of Goldman's," Maxwell challenged bluntly. He was watching her for a reaction.

"And I was damn sure you and Stan had orders to watch me closely!"

"He told us your record, naturally. I argued against your inclusion on the team."

After a pause, Erin responded, "What you said. You were right." She gave a bark of a laugh.

"He has been telling me exactly what to do, and it suited me to do it, as it kept me out of a federal prison. The stint in the marines was so I could convince some of the hidebound that I would take orders. He needed someone with my aptitude, so I agreed to work for him. I had no doubts, what so ever, that if I didn't follow his directions I would end up back in prison. I know he was using me, and I hate being used, but I put up with it because the programming got me hooked. He said I would be being watched, and I took that as fact. He doesn't trust me a damn bit. I bet he has already got all the authorities out looking for me – and assuming I am a part of this already."

"Do you want to be?"

"Why are you?" Erin challenged him.

"I have reasons," was all Maxwell said.

"If it comes to selling secrets to foreign terrorists," Erin specified, "then no."

"That program was never meant to work," was the surprising counter. Erin didn't think he knew that. "Except that you proved to be so clever, that Goldman put you to working on one that was. Somehow, Otway got hold of both programs."

Erin let her mouth drop open as if this surprised her. "So how come you are here?"

Maxwell studied her before speaking. "I am trying to find out who is behind other thefts of technology. I became suspicious when some of the foreign students in one of my classes started asking odd questions."

A voice in Erin's mind, Wanda again, expressed disbelief in the perfectly logical reasons he gave Erin. She thought back, l can't sense that he is lying.

"That's because it's 90 per cent true, but twisted. If they aren't paying him, then they have something on him," Wanda proposed. "Ask him if Goldman knows what he is doing."

Erin did, but all he said was, "You were not meant to get involved."

Snippets of overheard conversations came into her mind, and she became sure her cousin was right and he was a traitor too.

"Shouldn't we be trying to escape then?"

"They don't have the program here," Maxwell said. "The only chance we have of retrieving it, is to follow the trail. You Mason, have a unique opportunity to serve your country – if you have the guts for it. I can speak up for you."

"Did you suggest that I could be proxy for Stan?"

"No, that was his idea. He was having second thoughts, way too late."

So, this is the sell, Erin thought, be a patriot by seeming to betray my country.

Wanda's mind voice retorted, "More like saving his own backside. Give you to them, and he can walk away all the richer and with his dirty secrets still safe."

Erin thought back, "He has a point about following the trail. I know how to make sure the program won't work."

"Do you have to be right there to do it?"

"No."

"Then we get you before they take you out of the country."

"Fair enough. But what about now? Should I play along?"

"Yes. It's the best way to try to find out where you are."

Erin returned her attention to Maxwell. "You organised to get me from the hospital, didn't you?"

"I had orders," Maxwell told her.

"Well, they can't think I took the program there, right? I mean, we weren't meant to take it out of the lab."

"I shouldn't think so."

"So you can tell them that I was taken when I was trying to get the program back?"

Maxwell nodded.

"Will these people pay me to finish the program? There has to be something in it for me."

"Won't that make you look guilty?"

"I don't really care. I have been itching to get a chance to be rid of Goldman. He is a nasty sort to cross, you know. I suppose I owe you one for letting them make me disappear."

"Does Goldman think I was involved?" Maxwell asked unexpectedly.

"I have no idea what goes on behind those calculating eyes of his. Lauren did say to me she thought you were up to something, but I didn't believe her – even after I found out what was going on. I did mention it to Goldman, but who knows what he thought. All I had to do was observe and report. I can't even guess at his overall plan. He told me to tell him when I finished my programs and not to put them on the mainframe until he told me. I still reckon he will think I absconded on my own."

Maxwell reached back to take a newspaper from a table. He tossed it to her, and she caught it deftly, then caught sight of the front page headline, checked the date then read the article.

"This is saying we were both kidnapped. You arranged your own disappearance then?"

Maxwell nodded.

"So, what's in it for me if I go along with them? I have no intention of showing up around here."

Erin sensed Maxwell relaxing, thinking he had her.

"I will tell them you want the same deal as they gave Otway," Maxwell suggested.

"No way! A suitcase of explosives is not my idea of a deal."

Maxwell twitched, her shot had been accurate. He knew what had happened to Stan.

"You tell them, that you have got me to agree to finalising things. That I was pissed off that I couldn't get to finish the program. Tell them, that my price is twenty five thousand American dollars, to be paid into an account I nominate, in advance."

"That's too much!"

Erin considered that his protest was just for show. She would bet he was being paid a whole lot more, or why would such a respected and decorated soldier risk being found out?

"Is it? To finalise that program, I need to access the work computer. That will be risky."

"You modified the fire wall. I bet you know a way through it."

"Damn right! But if my intrusion is detected, they'll know it was me. Anyway, I reckon they want the work done quickly. They won't find anyone with my skills, and knowledge, in a hurry. Particularly in knowing how all the pieces are meant to go together. I reckon your contacts are getting impatient, so the price is cheap."

When Maxwell asked, "Why twenty-five thousand," she knew she'd scored a direct hit on the truth.

"I'm not greedy, General. That much is enough for me to get out of the country, out of Goldman's reach, and make a start somewhere remote. All I will need is a computer and internet access. I have a few ways to make myself a nice little income. In fact, I am already. So, if your contacts agree, I will just need a computer or laptop, and internet access, to check the payment."

"What if they don't pay as promised?"

"Then, they won't have me working for them."

"They may kill you," Maxwell warned.

"Then they will have a problem, boss, because I don't think you know a thing about programming."

Maxwell shook his head, knowing Erin was right. "How long will it take you to finish?"

"A week or two, once I have access to a computer I can use to access the work one. And providing they pay me as I specified, and let me get on with it. Oh, and provide regular meals, and keep morons like Chuckles away from me. I won't take any more shoving around from him."

"Alright, I will talk to my contacts. Could you work from here?"

"Where's here? Can you even get internet?"

"Where doesn't matter. We can get internet and I will see about a computer."

"I can work anywhere then. Although I warn you, I'm still muzzy headed from that stuff Chuckles gave me."

Maxwell held out his hand, Erin shook it. She met his eyes, saw his were hard, as he commended her for her courage. His touch told her he was partly relieved, but also uneasy. She hoped his conscience was giving him hell.

When they stepped away from each other, Erin smiled, beginning to understand how danger exhilarated her cousin. If she was to work here, there would be ways to send out her location. And if they provided a computer, she could quickly transfer the payment out of her nominated account, to somewhere they wouldn't be able to trace. As for the rest, she'd have to bluff it out. She wanted a line on Maxwell's contacts.

"Do I need to be locked up again?"

"I don't think so. You would be a fool to go outside and risk being seen, and you have proved you are no fool."

"Then make sure Chuckles has that clear."

Klaus glared at her as she helped herself to a can of soup from the farmhouse pantry. Erin ignored him, and intended to do nothing to spook them. She noticed, without making it obvious, that all windows were boarded over. Only in the toilet did she try to see out, but she couldn't see enough. She decided to continue to ignore Klaus and his incessant watching of her. After a while she decided to ask him if he was sure the place was safe. He didn't answer, and didn't come near her as she prowled the main room. It seemed to be making him nervous. She smiled inwardly, and occasionally went close to places other than the kitchen, bathroom and her room. At those times, Klaus edged in her direction as if to cut her off.

After an hour of that game, she decided to chance having a sleep. Since Maxwell left, she'd only seen Klaus. The other man who had been with him, had not appeared, and was probably watching the place from outside. Erin did wonder what they would do if they saw the police watching the place, but she knew, that they did not have any idea where she was yet.

Before trying to sleep, Erin first made sure the door to her room would not lock, and then moved the solid chair to stop the door being pushed open.

She managed a few hours sleep, waking to catch the sound of Klaus and the other having a heated exchange. It stopped when they heard her moving the chair from her door. Both eyed her as she went back to the kitchen to rummage in the pantry. She wondered what Klaus and his mate were eating, surely something, even though they didn't offer her anything. She was about to eat the dish of tinned spaghetti she had warmed up, when a sound from outside impinged on her awareness.

Her cousin had mentioned a helicopter, and she recognised the sound of a Black Hawk, getting louder. When the sound seemed loudest, she sent a mental surge of elation, and continued to eat spaghetti as if the sound meant nothing.

When her cousin immediately sent to her mind, "Got you! That place has been boarded up for years, but the power company found an unmetered line going in there."

Thinking in her own mind, knowing Wanda was en rapport, "Maxwell is meant to come back with a laptop so I can check my fee and work on the program."

In the intense exchange that followed, Erin clued Wanda to

what she intended. The account she had given Maxwell to get her fee, would be watched and if possible the sending bank for the transaction traced. She also asked for someone to be on Maxwell's computer when she used it to access the mainframe.

Night came and Maxwell had not returned. She wasn't used to being idle, and had spent the time after hearing the helicopter, either pacing, sitting, or nosing into cupboards. It was the latter activity that bothered Klaus and his mate – as if she might find something. Like a hidden cellar, Erin thought.

She wasn't looking for anything in particular, just whatever it might be that was drawing power. The fridge worked on kerosene, the wall lamps worked, but were very dim. Not enough to account for the power use that had been observed. Whatever it was, had to be in the section they would not let her get near.

During that time, Klaus had occasional calls from someone – Erin assumed whoever had taken over watching outside – getting an all clear. He and the other guy had done little more than catnap since she had been let out of her room, and she decided they were due to crash. She kept emitting the sensation of being sleepy, and caught both yawning. She was doing the same, emphasising the need to sleep, and finally just upped and went to get ready to sleep. Repeating her trick with the door lock and the chair,

The house was silent when Erin woke during the night, sometime after Klaus and his mate stopped playing cards. She had risked leaving the door ajar, just enough for her to slip through the gap, but with the chair, have warning if one of them decided to try anything.

Now she listened, and heard snores coming from the couch in the main room. So, they were still keeping a close eye on her – maybe this one thought he would wake if she moved the chair to open the door.

Karma was on her side, as she slipped silently past the sleeper, and made it to the bathroom unobserved. She didn't stop there. Just along a bit was another room, where again, the sounds of regular heavy breathing were audible. She sniffed at the door way... Klaus.

Moving with the stealth she had learnt during Marine training, Erin made her way around the corner in the passage. Doors led off, and she glanced in the open ones and with the dim lamps on everywhere, saw only the dusty discarded remnants of the former owners. The door at the very end was locked, but a line of bright light shone across the bottom of the door. Instinctively, Erin increased her alertness, and carefully tried the door handle. It turned easily, but the door did not open. She tried the door on her left, just before it – that seemed to be a store room.

Some itch in her mind, suggested she had seen enough, and she began her silent retreat. She was just about back to her room, having past her still oblivious guard, when she heard sounds in the passage where she had been. She glanced that way and saw the flash of a torch, and hurried to get in her room. She was just peeking out when the torch flashed her way, just missing her, and stopping on the sleeping guard.

The time spent waking the guy, gave her time to get back in her bed, and feign sleep.

The whispers of acrimony, preceded the sound of her door gently hitting the chair. She had the dim lamp on, and felt sure someone was peeking around her door. They would see she was still there.

When the sense of being watched went away, she got up and went to her door, to see if she could hear anything. The first thing she noticed was that whoever had looked in had been wearing aftershave, so it hadn't been Klaus, or the other guy. They both reeked of Turkish cigarettes.

It raised the question of who had arrived, and how?

The question kept her from going back to sleep, and she considered that third man while hoping her cousin would reach out for her. He might have been the reason why she had been kept away from that part of the house. Maybe he had been in the brightly lit room. Or had he come in a back door? There had to be one, but in her quick foray, she hadn't found it, unless it was one of the other locked doors?

The door she had come in through was deadlocked. Any back door likely was too. These little mysteries only occupied her for a short while – her real interest being in discovering what was in the brightly lit room.

Near dawn, she felt her cousin's mind touch and gave her the info she had gleaned during the night. Then found out that the authorities now had the place under observation. Wanda didn't know who was calling the shots, but they were waiting for some signal to move in. Perhaps they wanted Maxwell to return?

Erin decided not to try to sleep more, and got up to go to the bathroom. The sleeper on the couch roused and watched her, and Klaus emerged from the room he had slept in. She didn't see the third man until later, when she went to find herself something for breakfast.

She eyed him where he sat at the table, then went to the pantry. She returned with a dish, a can of pears and the opener, and went to the sink for a washed fork and spoon. She had done some cleaning, more for her own benefit, and out of boredom the previous day. Klaus glowered at her, antipathy oozing out of his pores. Something had made him ramp us his dislike again.

Erin ignored him again, but not completely. She kept him in her peripheral vision.

"I don't trust you!" Klaus said, accompanying the statement with a hard thump on the table. "I saw you trying the door before."

"So?" Erin finished her mouthful and went on. "I wanted to make sure it was locked." She didn't look around until her unusual senses told her he was just behind her.

"I think you are spying on us!"

Erin put her spoon down, and glared. "Get real! You damn well brought me here." She sensed another presence closing on her from the other direction. She warned Klaus, "You had better not touch me, or your boss will have his plans delayed again."

"Our boss wants answers," Klaus leant closer.

"You could at least wait until after I finish breakfast."

"We want them now!"

"Fine, ask away," Erin invited, standing so quickly that Klaus teetered trying to back away. She twisted so she could see the two men, and only then spotted the third.

"Three to one? What do you think I'm going to do, huh?"

"We don't want lies," Klaus warned.

"Touch me, and that is all you will get." Erin paused, as the two men considered their response. "Well? Start asking. Then we can get this farce over and I can finish breakfast."

Erin allowed herself to rest back against the table, but she was ready to spring away if either of the two nearer men made a threatening move.

Klaus, from his questions, proved he had been listening to her talk with Maxwell. However, someone had been telling him other things about her and now he was growling accusations at her, and probably not hearing her calm, rational replies. Erin guessed he had caught some flak from someone, and wanted to have a reason to get back at her.

A subtle signal passed between the men, when Klaus was just out of arms reach of her. He lunged, but Erin wasn't where he had seen her.

"Under the table," the other yelled.

Erin was already out, and staring at the men from the protection of the other side of the table. They smiled, thinking her cornered. They didn't know how fast Erin's mind could compute speed, distance, angles. Klaus moved one way around the table, the other two blocking the other way of retreat. Erin watched his eyes, aware of the knife in his hand, and when he rushed, she sprang onto the table. The warning from the others came too late. Her foot kicked the knife from his hand, and when he reached for another weapon, she leapt forward, using her weight to knock him backwards. While he was still breathless, she punched him in the throat and again in the diaphragm – dirty tricks she had learnt from a street fighter. Klaus would be out of the fight for a while.

She didn't stop there, she grabbed the dropped knife and twisted in a crouch, inviting the others, "Next victim?"

They had been moving in on her, but stopped when they saw she was armed, and her stance suggested she knew how to use a knife as a weapon. The stranger was in a suit, not suited to a fight, but he and the other came at her together. Erin's mind analysed their movements in a fraction of a second. One was fractionally faster, and he was wide open to her counter attack. He narrowly missed landing on Klaus, and having his knife arm snapped when he was thrown against the edge of the table. The third man slowed his approach and took time to study her. Erin had the knife out, as if using it to protect herself.

Seeing that, the man changed his stance to a knife fighters couch and began a side to side swaying approach, thinking her to scared to move. He didn't know her well and should have considered her earlier unconventional moves. When she judged him in range, she sprung up and her foot caught him in the side. It did not have the force she wanted, and he was able to jump back as her knife swished across, just in front of his face. His return attack was swift, and he grabbed her wrist, the one with the knife, and forced it above her head. He leered at her, but only for a moment. Erin brought a knee up and jabbed it in his groin. He released her, falling to the floor and writhed in agony.

Klaus was rising to his feet, a manic look in his eye. Erin sprinted for her room, snatching up a second knife as she ran. The Eurasian came after her, growling like a rabid predator. The second man was also rising.

Knowing she was in a dangerous position, Erin felt her mind ramp up to a higher gear – almost prescient. It seemed she could see what Klaus was about to do. He was going to slam at the door, sure she was going to block it shut. He did, and stumbled forward when he did not meet the expected resistance. He hadn't even started to regain his balance when something sliced his leg and the blunt end of the knife met his temple. He slumped unconscious.

Erin was in a knife fighter's crouch when the second man came in. He pulled up, his eyes flicking from her to Klaus. That moment of indecision cost him dearly. It wasn't the knife he needed to worry about, she sprang at him, kneeing him in the gut and punching his head where it was oozing blood from the hit against the table. He too fell like a dead weight, and Erin pulled him fully into the room, then slipped out and bolted the door from the outside.

The third man wasn't in sight, but Erin heard a shuffling, dragging sound, coming from the passage. He was incapacitated, but something was making him force himself along. Erin wasn't intending him to be allowed to talk to anyone, and for the second time, she used the knife hilt to good effect. She stood a moment then, catching her breath and listening. If anyone was in that locked room, had they heard anything?

Some instinct nagged her to move this man in with the other two. She hoped the door would hold if all three men went at it together. This man wasn't as solid as Klaus and the other, but unconscious, he was still a weight. In the end, as the adrenalin effect wore off, she had to rely on innate stubbornness to finish the task. Getting the man into the room, took the rest of her energy, and she knew the other two would be stirring shortly. When she had relocked the door, she felt she needed to collapse.

"Way to go, cuz. Couldn't have done much better myself." Wanda's mental voice and a sense of new energy, helped Erin to steady herself. Erin thought of her concern about the door and an image came into her mind of an old fashioned door stop. She had seen some crude wooden wedges in the kitchen that would do and went to fetch one.

"One will do," she heard Wanda's voice in her mind. "Six would be better."

A laugh forced itself out. Reaction, Erin knew.

"Go finish your breakfast, Cuz, and make yourself a cuppa with plenty of sugar." This time Erin took it as a serious suggestion.

She did feel much better after finishing the tin of pears, and drinking all the syrup.

"What brought that on?" Wanda asked, putting the question in Erin's mind.

"No idea," Erin admitted truthfully. "But I reckon Klaus was behind it."

"Are you hurt?" Wanda asked suddenly.

Erin was about to think, "No," when her upper arm began to sting like it was burning. When she gingerly felt that area of her left arm, her fingers came away red.

"How did you know?" Erin thought, but answered her own question. "That deep link, right?"

A wordless sense of agreement was shared between them.

"Is there a first aid kit there?" Wanda asked.

"Not here in the kitchen, not even a Band-Aid." Erin forced herself to move on unsteady legs, as she thought back, "I saw spare towels in the bathroom. Probably not the cleanest, or freshest, but they will have to do."

After removing the light jumper she had worn under her work outfit, whenever that had been, Erin saw all the blood on the white shirt and decided that needed to come off too. Then, while trying to see the wound by twisting in front of the mirror, heard in her mind, "It doesn't look too bad. If it was, you'd have bled out."

Wanda went on to give advice. It reassured Erin to have a second opinion from someone who was training to be a paramedic in her spare time. But, getting clean bandaging wasn't possible. The towels looked to be thoroughly moth nibbled, but that made them easier to tear into strips with the help of the knife.

She used one strip to wash away the blood from the wound, to get a better look. Another strip, she made into a pad, and used the others to tie it in place. The result was bulky, and her shirt wouldn't fit over it.

"Take the shirt right off, and tie it about your waist," Wanda thought, just as Erin did. Their deep connection was gaining in strength. "Or give it a quick rinse," Wanda suggested. "In case you need more bandages later."

Erin decided that was a good idea, and also washed herself as best she could. At the same time, she was asking, "Should I try to listen at that door? To find out if I can hear anything?"

She felt the word, "No," and sensed Wanda was talking to someone else.

"Do you know when to expect Maxwell?" was the question when the mind connection came again.

"No. I thought he would be back by now."

"So did we. I think they were waiting for him to come. Do you want us to extract you?"

"I have managed so far," Erin thought back.

"Well, supposedly the place is surrounded," Wanda thought, but warned, "However, one of the locals mentioned the place was part of the old underground railway for helping escaped slaves, way back. There might be some actual tunnels we don't know about."

"Great!" Erin thought back with a degree of sarcasm.

"If we see anyone coming, we will warn you."

"And if anyone turns up here without that warning, I will tell you."

"Do that. But just keep up playing the expert who doesn't want to be found."

"And when Maxwell comes back?"

"He may not be alone. His contact may want to test you."

"So...they will discover the locked up goof-offs."

"And you will still be there – keeping a low profile. I'd make myself at home, and if you are asked about the goof-offs, be blunt. You made an offer in good faith and they tried to jeopardise the deal and cause further delays to the contact's plans."

Erin considered that. "And if anyone turns up that I don't know, I will be selectively dumb. Easy! Now I'm going to find something else to eat."

Erin did another quick, silent foray of the house while the contents of a can of hearty soup were heating in a saucepan on the old kitchen range. All she learnt was that possibly up to three men had been sleeping in one of the other rooms. The mysterious room was still locked, and she could hear nothing through the door. The same could not be said for her former prison room. Solid thuds were coming from within. The door didn't seem to be moving, but all the same, Erin hoped Maxwell would return soon.

She had finished the soup and was eating through the contents of a tin of beans when she heard sounds in the passage. She thought she heard Maxwell's voice, so she continued to eat, just moved to be looking that way. Three men appeared, Maxwell and two foreigners. They all had their eyes on her. She returned the scrutiny calmly, and only paused in her eating to answer Maxwell.

"Where is Klaus?"

"Chuckles? Oh, he and his two pals have a problem. They started something they couldn't finish."

At first her tone had been calm, mocking, but now it began one of icy threat. "And if you want me to finish that program, boss, you will keep them in there until I finish and have left this place. I can't work if I have to keep looking over my shoulder, and I won't work if I am threatened."

As if on cue, the banging noise resumed. Maxwell only glanced at the locked door before telling her, "Your money has been arranged."

"Fine. I will get started as soon as I have confirmed it." Erin pushed the rest of the beans and the dish away from her. "Where's the computer?"

"Come on," Maxwell directed, and he indicated the passage.

Erin's surprise at Maxwell's unexpected appearance, had resulted in tart comments in her mind. No one had seen Maxwell outside. Now, discovering that the area was not locked down as had been thought, and the farmhouse actually contained a very impressive computer set-up, was wordlessly passed along and the watchers would be informed.

On her part, Erin scanned the set up with quick thoroughness. "It will do. I gather it is compatible with the set-up at work?"

Maxwell nodded, and only had to switch on the monitor to have it ready to use.

Ignoring the close scrutiny of the strangers, Erin sat at the table and soon accessed the site where her account was located. The money was there, but only for as long as it took her to initiate a transfer. Her key entries were so rapid that no one could note the figures. Within four minutes, she was finished. She looked up at Maxwell with a satisfied smirk. "That should be safe now. Even if they were watching my accounts, they won't trace where that went."

Inwardly, she added, And those traitors can't retrieve it either.

"Ok. Do you want me to get started? You said you didn't have Stan's laptop or my notes here."

"Some of the program is on this system," Maxwell told her. "You said you could get through Goldman's firewall? Well, I have all the finished pieces on my computer and the latest versions of everything else."

"Okay! I'm on it."

Erin opened a new browser screen and began typing. Her watchers were intent, as she inserted her presence through the firewall. They gave her a collective chuckle when she announced, "I'm in."

"Goldman was right about you," Maxwell murmured. He then turned to his silent companions and challenged, "Satisfied?"

One replied, "Indeed."

Meanwhile, Erin was checking for the directory she wanted. Easy enough since Maxwell had insisted on a standard file naming protocol. Now I know why! Erin decided.

"I'm going to grab the latest versions," Erin announced. "Did Goldman put one of those monitoring things on your computer, boss?"

"No," Maxwell assured her. Erin nodded to herself, and thought, *I wouldn't bet on it!*

After a time, the strangers began to ask questions, which Maxwell translated. Erin didn't know what language they spoke, but their questions revealed they were well briefed about what the program was meant to do.

Without appearing to dawdle, Erin worked as slowly as she could, wondering how long it would take her cousin to contact Goldman and for him to get to Maxwell's computer. Long enough for Maxwell and the two strangers to get bored watching her typing. That suited her, for as soon as they moved away, she changed what she was doing and began to insert a virus onto Maxwell's computer. It would activate at a later date, or sooner if a specific email message was sent.

The warning premonition came instants before the door slammed open. Klaus barged in, oblivious to the other men present. Erin twisted to face him, and caught the change in his expression when he recognised the strangers. They spoke to him in their own language, voices calm, but deadly. He answered, defensively, but obeyed when they waved him out of the room. He had been full of anger and resentment when he had entered, but left, exuding an aura of fear. With a faint smile, Erin returned to her task. Now she had conformation that these men could be dangerous. They saw her smile and had one of their own – thinking her hard and ruthless. They lost much of their tension, feeling more confident that the woman they saw was not going to betray them.

It was getting dark when she stood up to stretch and move around. She went to talk to Maxwell. "Can you access my work terminal directly from yours?"

"No. Why do you need to?"

"I had a partial copy of the program I was working on in there. I wanted to get it. If I could go through yours, that monitor thing they put on shouldn't detect me."

Maxwell checked his watch. "Everyone goes home by six. If

there is no one else working, there should be no need to check the activity until morning. What's the issue?"

"I'm going to have to insert myself in through the firewall again. It would have been better if I didn't have to – that's all."

She shrugged, and went back to the computer, outwardly unconcerned. If watched, she would seem to be doing what she had before. There were no flashed up warnings, but she was sure her activities were being monitored. She wanted them to be. So she scrolled slowly through her files, looking for a specific one. In doing so, she saw an unfamiliar file name, 'Gotcha'. She didn't try to open it, just hoped it did mean they had managed to put a trace onto this computer via Maxwell's. Her file took a while to download, and when it finished, she disconnected from the internet.

"I need to eat," Erin announced. No one objected when she went back to the kitchen. So far, they were impressed.

Klaus was in the kitchen when she went in, but he did no more than glare malevolently at her. When she went to look in the pantry, he moved further away. She saw that someone had brought in bread, cheese and ham, so she opted for a sandwich. She began to walk away, munching as she did. She was watching Klaus too, while hearing her cousin in her head. She was so clear, she might as well have been in the same room.

"We're going to move in," Wanda warned her. "How many people do you know are inside?"

Erin took a bite as she thought, "Seven. Three guards, two foreigners, Maxwell and me."

"What are you doing?"

Erin knew she didn't mean right then, so she summarised what she had done. Wanda's mental chuckle came after the mention of the time sensitive virus.

"Fifteen minutes," Wanda warned. "We think we have found the way Maxwell got in."

Erin smirked in Klaus's direction, and took her sandwich back to the computer. In the next few minutes, she activated a program to lock the program she was working on, and make it impossible to open again without a complicated password. She would blame Goldman's new security for that.

She had just finished that when Maxwell said sharply, "Close down! No time for finesse!"

Erin began immediately then asked, "What's up?"

"There are people watching this place. I'll grab the hard drive, but you should go with Anko, now!"

Erin feigned alarm, and fear. "What about you?"

Maxwell gave her a quick grin, and said very softly, "I'm on Goldman's side, remember?" Then he spoke louder, "Get going!"

Anko grabbed her arm and half dragged her to the living room. Klaus had already jerked aside the old floor rug and was lifting a trap door. Anko directed Erin to go down an old wooden ladder, and he began to follow, having a small hand torch on to see where they had to go. Erin felt her feet land on a dirt floor, and quickly moved aside. The second stranger and Maxwell followed, Klaus bringing up the rear. When they saw a faint light up ahead, Klaus pushed past them all and trotted ahead. It was hard to tell how far they had gone when Erin felt Wanda's urgent question. "Where are you?"

"Underground. A passage from the living room. Going north – I think."

"We're moving in!" Wanda told her.

At that moment, Erin had a vivid premonition. "NO!" she screeched silently.

"What?" Wanda's mind question was a demand. Outside, Erin sensed her give the silent 'stop' signal, even as she picked up the same psychic warning she had. "Shit! They've got the place rigged to explode. What's happening where you are?"

"We seem to be waiting. Klaus has his head peeking out from up a ladder."

"How many with you?"

"Three. Chuckles, Maxwell and a foreigner, Anko. There was another foreigner with us – I don't know where he went. But Maxwell didn't return through the living room. There has to be another way out."

"I had a flash vision of this place going up," Wanda thought. "What did you see?"

"People walking in and the place going up."

"I think some power is on our side," Wanda's thought was sober.

"Pressure," Erin agreed silently. "We must be waiting for someone to set them off." She gave a moment's thought to wondering how far they had come from the house.

Klaus backed down the stairs, and spoke to his country men.

Erin asked Maxwell, "What are they saying?"

"They saw soldiers moving around the house. He's going to set off an explosion. When it goes off, and all attention is on the house, we move out."

Erin wanted to growl. Soldiers - men who probably looked up to the General – could be killed. *Didn't he care?*

Her revulsion was shared by her cousin, who yelled a warning just before a thunderous explosion rent the air, and shook dirt down from the roof of the tunnel. Before the echoes died away, Klaus was up out of the tunnel, Erin was being shoved up, and the others were following. Klaus grabbed her clothes and dragged her from under a hollowed out bush. Anko was close on her heels. Erin shook off Klaus's grip, and as he began to run along a particular path, Erin glanced back. They were a long way from the house, following a line of windbreak trees. Her direct view of the fiery inferno was partially blocked by an old barn. The ground was sloping down towards a small creek, lined on each side by scrubby trees. Anko had her arm now, as they sprinted a short distance to the cover of the trees. Maxwell was no longer with them and Erin wondered where he had gone, and where the other stranger had gone.

Somewhere nearby, Erin heard a car engine. It was moving slowly, with only its park lights on. It made her realise that it would be dark soon, and the others would have a better chance of escaping on foot.

Before she reached the car, she saw shadows erupt from cover to surround them and the car. Anko began firing at the dark figures, but they were protected by Kevlar outfits. Erin dropped when the first shot was fired, but Anko tried to drag her towards the car that was now revving ominously – until the driver was forced to get out of it. The attackers were economical with their fire. One returned fire and Anko gave a cry of pain, dropping his gun to grab at his wrist. Then the soldiers were on them.

Erin was dragged up, and treated like the others.

"Where are the others!" The demand was loud and shouted, meant to intimidate.

Anko swore. She only felt what he said was impolite. It was obvious though that he understood what the soldier had asked. Erin didn't know. She had assumed that Maxwell was to follow them.

She was held, as two soldiers held Anko, and a third was putting a field bandage on his hand. The car driver was struggling in the grip of two more figures. He came into the fading light, but Erin hadn't seen him before.

During the forced walk, back past the burning farm house, Erin felt the cut on her arm open up again with an intense burning sensation. She gave a faint vocal reaction, and the man holding her eased his grip a little. She didn't try to take advantage, for with some of the people still unaccounted for, she should still act guilty.

Goldman watched as the group neared. He gave her no indication of what she should do, just gestured the soldiers towards the waiting police cars. About him were several plain clothed men, a senior police officer, and four heavily armed soldiers. Anko and the car driver were forced into an armoured van, and one of the men in plain clothes approached her and gave a command. "Just a moment."

She didn't recognise the face, but her other senses told her who it was.

"Jim! Why are you here? Where's Wanda?" she muttered, so just he could hear her.

In a move that looked rough, Jim Phillips turned her towards one of the police cars, and when she reached it, pushed her against it. He went through the motions of frisking her.

"Who is still missing?"

"Klaus, Maxwell, and the other foreign guy he returned with. I didn't get a good look at the car driver to see if it was one of Klaus's two mates. I didn't see the other of that pair when we had to get out."

"We got two outside," Jim told her. "Are you alright?"

"I'm not feeling well, and my arm is bleeding again."

"You can sit in the car," Jim told her. "Goldman is pleased with you, but he said to tell you that you will be seen to be a prisoner until the others are caught. Is there anything else you need to tell us?”

“Maxwell was going to grab the hard drive from the computer in there. I had time to run the lock out program though.”

Erin grabbed for the car, and Jim just had enough time to grab her before she slumped to the ground.

“I don’t think I’ll be much use...”

Jim eased her to the ground, and checked her pulse. Then he felt the damp stickiness on her arm. He gestured one of the soldiers to come over and guard her and went to see if there was a handy medic. He ignored the mental voice in his head that he knew was Wanda.

He was only gone five minutes, and when he returned, Erin was gone and Wanda was there.

“Where’s Erin?” he demanded quietly, betraying his annoyance that she had disobeyed him. “You were meant to stay away from her.”

Wanda shrugged, unseen by Jim who was first checking in the car. She decided to check around the car, and found the soldier just stirring on the ground.

“Something got me from behind,” he groaned, bringing one hard to feel the back of his head. She helped him up, and sensed he wasn’t badly hurt.

She saw Jim looking quizzically at her and she shook her head. She could sense nothing of Erin. That meant she was unconscious, or drugged. “Her arm was hurting. The wound had reopened.”

“Enough for her to black out?” Jim asked, concerned. Wanda shrugged.

“We need to find her,” Wanda said after a moment. “I don’t trust that one she called Chuckles.”

“We will find her,” Jim stated confidently. “We need her to link Maxwell to all this.”

“Well, he didn’t take her,” Wanda said. “They stopped a car, two miles outside the inner cordon. He was in it. They are bringing him back now. No, I think it was that little foreign bastard, Chuckles. His name is Klaus. He doesn’t seem the type to forgive and forget. She got the better of him and was warned off her.”

Jim went and told Goldman of Erin's disappearance, and he set a search in motion.

Wanda wanted to go find her cousin, but she knew all too well that she could do little until Erin roused again. So, she stayed with Jim, while they waited for Maxwell to be brought to them.

Maxwell was handcuffed, as he was led to where Goldman had a command table set up. Wanda, keeping in the background, could sense Goldman was angry, but hiding it well. Maxwell, she couldn't read at all. Unusual, but not unique. Maybe that solid mind shield would slip.

Her phone vibrated in her pocket. She glanced at the screen, saw her sister's face and answered tersely.

"What's going on?" Elisabeth Willard demanded.

She gave a very brief mention, the asked, "Keep open for her, okay? I have other things on my mind just now."

In fact, something was niggling her mind. She went back over the impressions she had received from Erin. All were still in her indelible eidetic memory. Erin had shown her six faces. The two men who had been outside – one of those was one she'd locked up. The other unknown. She had re-bandaged the hand of one of the foreigners, and the other, the driver, wasn't one of the six either. So three of those had managed to escape, with Erin. She had a really bad feeling, as she turned her attention to what Maxwell was saying.

Maxwell was standing straight and erect between the soldiers holding him. He was answering Goldman's questions as if he was unquestionably loyal, and this arrest would be soon proved to be wrongful.

He expressed his role in the matter as being to try to recover stolen technology, and not just the program, that he had been playing apart. He even expressed his disappointment that Erin had been ready to change sides and go with the foreigners – mentioning that she had demanded a fee, that would let her leave the country and not be found.

Wanda held her tongue, although she wanted to yell, "Liar!"

Goldman berated him for not telling him what he was doing, once he had known of the plans to catch the traitors. He said to his friend, that he should have trusted him and been honest about what he was doing, and because he hadn't, he would be under arrest pending an enquiry. Maxwell had simply nodded acceptance.

Wanda did notice that Goldman had not referred to Erin's role, and she had the feeling that Maxwell believed that Erin had indeed turned traitor, and Goldman was not wanting that fact shoved in his face.

And that, might be all that protected Erin right now.

Goldman backed up and asked about Stan's laptop, and the other parts of the program. To that, he said he didn't know. He believed the foreigners might have them.

The sudden question of the computer in the house, came as a surprise to Maxwell, but he recovered well.

"Yes, Mason was getting on with finishing the program, but then the others caught sight of the watchers, and said they had to leave."

"Did they try to take the hard drive?" Goldman asked, although he believed what Wanda had told him she had picked up from Erin. It wasn't proof though, without Erin to testify. So when Maxwell professed no knowledge, and assumed it had been destroyed with the house, Goldman just pursed his lips and left it at that. He continued with other questions until directing the policemen to take him to the city holding cells.

Wanda had been trying to get impressions from him, but his natural mind shield didn't weaken. Perhaps, she decided, it had come into being over a lifetime of giving orders that might get people killed. A kind of self-deniability? And the deceitful bastard doesn't care if Erin ends up being killed. No doubt he did exactly what the foreigners wanted. Erin said he had the hard drive, but he hasn't got it now. He probably handed it over...but to whom?

She heard Goldman give orders for the area to be searched for the man known as Klaus, before he called for his driver. Her own idea was he would be well away already, since Maxwell had been well away when found. Had Maxwell actually slipped away from him? It didn't matter, except she'd like to tell him a thing or two. Instead, she found herself pacing. Heading towards the smouldering farmhouse, with the idea of finding the exit Erin had emerged from.

Jim Phillips walked up beside her.

"This whole show is a fiasco!" she blurted.

"Have you heard from David lately?" Jim said to divert her.

Wanda felt her pocket, she'd put her phone on silent. Now she checked it. Three missed calls and a message. "Call me when you are free." Hoping he had a lead, she did.

"Dav? Anything?"

She listened and told her mentor, "He said, all our targets received calls from the same number about fifteen minutes ago."

"Recalls?" Jim proposed.

"He thinks so too. He also found a booked air ticket under the name Maxwell Charles, Washington to Florida for tomorrow."

"I will advise Magnus Goldman. Anything else?"

"He's looking for trans-Atlantic flight plans for private jets, though he isn't expecting the one we want to have a true destination."

"Don't forget there are now watchers at the airports," Jim said, hoping to calm her fidgets. He knew what she was like when anyone she cared about was in danger.

"And the longer it is before they leave, the less alert they will be," Wanda argued. "Heck, Jim, we know where they are heading – why don't we just go and head them off?"

"We don't work like that," Jim reminded her.

Wanda wasn't pacified. She stalked off to where the fire units were still dousing the remains of the house. She wanted to go in and see what she could find, but knew they wouldn't let her. This was Goldman's operation. He would say to let the experts do their work. He'd be right – but she was in no mood to be agreeable.

Jim found her poking around the exit from the tunnel. "Have you calmed down yet?" His voice was soft, but none-the-less, chastising.

"No!"

"Then I suggest you do. I have seen you like this before, and I know you are concerned for your cousin, but you are more useful when you are not reacting."

It was like an instant cold shower. "Sorry."

"Have you found anything?"

"Only this." Wanda took a small object from her pocket. In the torch light, he recognised it as a micro injector.

"Well, that might explain why she blacked out," Jim murmured thoughtfully. "But not—"

"How someone could creep up on that soldier, knock him out and take her." Wanda didn't realise that once again she had read her mentor's thought. "Was the guy asleep?"

"I don't think so," Jim told her. "However, there is another problem. The car taking the General back to the city was found, broken down, and he is missing. The driver and guard, were both unconscious."

"Proper bloody fiasco this has been. Goldman is a damned bureaucrat! He should have let trained agents take over."

"Think carefully. What are your instincts telling you about the General?"

After giving consideration to all the little things she had sensed and noticed, she said, "I don't believe his story about trying to track stolen tech – if he really is a friend of Goldman, he knows that's the SIO's mandate. Unless, he was responsible for the loss of whatever he is referring to. Even then, that may have been at the start, but now...I think he is either being paid a great deal of money, or they have something damn nasty on him."

"Those ideas are being looked into," Jim assured her. "What else?"

"Well, I couldn't get anything from him – it's like he has a dense mind shield." She mentioned the idea she'd had a short time earlier. "But he did arrange to get Erin from the hospital, and told her to go with the fake State Dept guys. Then he faked his own abduction."

"Could there be another reason for that?"

"What? For selling her off to those bastards?"

"She's a United States Marine," Jim reminded her. "He's also—"

"A traitor!"

"Wanda..."

"Oh, alright. If he did think he was trying to get the program back, while pretending to be working for the other side, he should have stopped Otway! Okay, okay...It seems that when Otway began to get cold feet for some reason, they called the General's bluff, and yanked him by his dirty secrets to finish the deal. He did put the word on Erin that she had a chance to get it back...for her country."

Jim sighed faintly. "Do you think he doesn't care if Erin is killed?"

"He certainly wasn't trying to get her out of the mess, and at least he was using reason, unlike the one she called 'Chuckles' – Klaus that is. But he is used to sending people out to die."

"You are missing the point. Do you think he will try to keep her safe?"

"He will if he wants Goldman to believe him."

Wanda sensed the purely mental sigh, Jim didn't express. She knew she was twitchy, which usually meant she felt she should be doing something. "I'll be at the car. How much longer will you be staying?"

"Just until the fire investigators can give a preliminary report."

"Alright. I'll try to keep open for Erin, okay?"

Jim found her sitting on the ground, rather than in the car. At first, he thought she had dozed off, but her eyes flicked open, as soon as he stopped to look down at her.

"Ready to go?"

"Fine, Jim. Have you heard anything more?"

"Someone at one of the nearest farms saw a brown truck heading this way earlier. The police are looking for it. They will also be having a more thorough look around here in the morning."

"Surely we would have heard a truck start up," Wanda said as she stood up. "Wouldn't it have been riskier to carry her a longer distance?"

"Perhaps, but it is the only lead we have – unless your meditations have yielded something?"

Wanda jerked. "Maybe. When I had my eyes shut, I did sort of feel I was moving in the dark. But, if she's in a truck, where are they going? I thought this place had to be their fall back hideout."

"On the drive back, why don't you call David and see if he has more to report?"

"Yes...find out if our target rats are headed anywhere special. Maybe Florida, where Maxwell was headed."

"I will advise Goldman to increase surveillance on the airports there."

Her mentor was still on the ball. That they would go further away to get a flight, hadn't occurred to her.

Chapter 12 – Escaping the Roadblocks

Erin felt her body was made of lead. Opening her eyes felt like pushing a ton weight – even when she thought she had, she wasn't sure. It was dark, but then she became aware of the sense of movement. For a brief, panicked moment, she thought she must be blind, but then a light flashed through a window, down near her feet. Her mid began to fit pieces together. She was in a van, and its engine was humming at a steady tempo. They had to be on an open road, maybe a highway.

The last she could recall, was being with Jim, by a car. How long ago had that been?

The leadenness, that was familiar.

She had been safe! Jim had left a guard with her. How had Chuckles – it had to be him – managed to snatch her? Didn't matter, Fact was – he had. Where were they going? She had assumed they would have a plane ready, to leave fast. She had no way of knowing where she was, and they probably wouldn't tell her if she could ask.

Her head was buzzing, like she was hearing bees. It became annoying, so she began to count. That was until she heard a voice, nearby. She couldn't understand the speaker, or the one that followed which was loud and demanding.

A third voice spoke. "What is the problem?"

Erin understood that, and wanted to know as well. The answer wasn't spoken in English, but the third voice said, "If the police have road blocks on the main roads, you will need to use side roads. Turn off before you get near, and use the GPS to lead you around the blockage."

For a short while the van kept its speed up, and the first two voices grumbled. The third said something that pacified them, and the van began to slow, and soon turned left. Erin resumed counting.

"9415, 9416..."

The numbers morphed into words, and her mind took them up, and cool air seemed to blow over her face, as if someone had opened a window.

"How's the bitch?" the demanding voice asked.

A gentle hand felt the side of her neck, and then a tiny torch snapped on.

Erin told herself, "Close eyes," and hoped they had.

The light went off, and the hand gently patted her shoulder.

"Did you have to give her that vile stuff again?"

"We don't need her giving us trouble, soldier man. You neither!"

"You do need her to work for your masters. As is, she will be useless for several days. That stuff accumulates and takes time to disperse."

"No problem, soldier man. It will take a few days to get where we are going."

"That may be so, but she agreed to do the work. She won't think kindly of you treating her this way."

"The bitch needs to learn her place, soldier man. If she wants to dress like a man, and do a man's work, she has to show she's tough enough. And if she don't work, she'll be treated like one. You better not keep interfering, soldier man."

Erin was engulfed in a wave of overwhelming fear.

"My reason for being here is to keep your hired expert in good condition."

"When we get to the plane, your job will be finished little soldier. You can go off and forget we ever met. Be thankful my master was merciful about the delay. He might have been tempted to tell what he knows about you."

"Scurrilous lies!"

"Are they? Anyway, you've been paid."

The truck stopped and pulled over. The loud voice said, "Stay here!"

The man moved to the back of the truck, making the floor vibrate. The door opened and closed.

"Erin? You are awake?"

She could only move her eyes, and opened them – finding a light shining on them, that quickly moved aside.

"I'm sorry, Mason. I didn't have any choice."

He looked worried, Erin thought. And so he should be!

"I fixed your arm again. It was bleeding." He paused, probably hoping for a response.

"Look, if you do what they say, that bastard's superiors will uphold the deal. They will let you go when their satellite is operational."

And where will you be? Erin wanted an answer, but she had no skill at telepathy...not like her cousin.

It was like the thought had formed the connection. "Wanda?"

"Yes. Yes. Finally. Are you okay?"

"Being like a statue, is not my normal state," she thought, relief going through her.

"Do you know where you are?"

"No. Just that I am in a medium sized van. Parked at the moment, while they try to find a way around a road block. Going to a plane. Maxwell is here."

"I'd like to kick him where it hurts."

"No, he's...being coerced."

"He's still a weasel. Goldman trusted him."

"Leave it. What's happening?"

"Not enough!" The anger and frustration coming through the deep connection matched her own.

"I'll be okay," Erin thought back. "They definitely want me alive. And repeating the mantra helped last time. The effects wore off well before they expected. I'm already beginning to feel tingly. While they think me still helpless, I should get a chance."

Erin knew Wanda had doubts that she wasn't even thinking to herself. The truck rocked. The man had returned.

"Soldier man! Put the bitch on the bench there, and you sit in the corner."

Erin knew she was being lifted, and placed as comfortable as possible. She had a glimpse of light from outside, and heard the sound of a heavy crate being put in the truck. Then several more.

"Not a word, soldier man."

The van's back door slammed. Erin sensed that Chuckles had not returned. He must have decided to sit with the driver.

The distant mind read what was happening as Erin became

aware of it. She knew when the truck returned to the highway, when it pulled up and the load was checked, and when it was allowed to move off.

The distant mind swore. "They have road blocks on all the major roads. All this tells us is that they just passed one of them – passed the blockade. Damn! Damn! Damn!"

Erin began the healing mantra, in her mind, with desperate fervour.

Time seemed to stretch out endlessly, Erin could feel movement coming back and stealthily tried to move her arms and legs. It wasn't enough. When the truck drove into some echoing garage, she was still next to helpless. The heavy boxes were removed and Chuckles returned.

"Bring the bitch out. No! Wait."

Erin felt some kind of fabric come over her face. It wasn't tight, but she had no chance of a casual glance around.

Eventually, she was lowered to the floor, and the hood removed.

"Waking up already, are you little bitch?" Chuckles was sneering down at her. Erin felt safe thinking at him all the nasty things she hoped would befall him. "We will have to make sure you can't cause trouble."

"How are you going to transport a tied up person onto the plane?"

"Not your problem, soldier man."

Maxwell began to argue.

Erin thought, if he's trying to give me a chance, I haven't a hope of getting away yet. Instead, she ignored them, and slowly turned her head to watch the other men in her line of sight. One was the programmer type who had been with Anko, back at the deserted farm. He was checking the contents of a brief case, and she saw him lift several folders like she used for her notes, other thick Manilla folders, a hard drive, and a few small items, as he repacked the case. He spoke to another man, dressed in a suit, nodding as if satisfied with what he had seen. With them, was another that Erin classified as 'low brained muscle'.

Maxwell abruptly changed his tone. "If you have finished with me, I'll be going."

"Not so fast! Our merchandise is not safely on the plane yet.

You've another job to do."

"What is it?"

"Just being an escort. Our plans had to change. We will be leaving later."

"When will that be?" Maxwell demanded.

"The next plane heading in the right direction doesn't leave until 10.30 tomorrow," Chuckles sneered. "We will need you to bring our merchandise – a prisoner, being deported. We will have all the correct paperwork. You will add the seal of legitimacy."

"Well, what about letting her have some water? If you move her like she is, they will think she is ill. That's if she doesn't faint from dehydration."

"If you must. There's a tap in the en-suite. Make sure not to give so much she wets the floor."

The water was a relief, even if she could only sip it. Gradually though, she began to feel her centre thawing as the leadenness receded. She mentally thanked her former boss for thinking of it, and later pretended unconcern when Maxwell had to help her to the basic toilet and help her do what she needed.

"Can you move yet?" he asked her in a low voice.

She managed to slightly shake her head.

"I will try to get away. Tell Goldman where you are."

"Where...?"

"They said Florida," Maxwell told her. "I don't know more than that. They were supposed to leave from some airport in Virginia. We must be close to the international airport."

"I guess," Erin agreed, as Maxwell helped her pull up her rank looking business pants.

"I'll try to get us away," Maxwell said, almost like he was babbling.

In her mind, Wanda said, "If he's having second thoughts, he's left it too damned late."

Erin repeated what Maxwell had said to her, and knew her cousin would pass it on.

When Erin was able to stand and move around, Klaus ordered her tied to a chair. He smirked, but she merely treated him to a dismissive glance. She didn't let on how clear her mind had become, just leant back and stared vacantly across the kind of office room they were in. Already she had an excellent, detailed image of the area in her mind, and was actually watching each of the foreigners. There were six now, not including Klaus. Those were quietly playing some card game to pass the time. Klaus however, was talking animatedly, and bossily, into his phone. He thought that talking in his native tongue made it safe.

Erin allowed herself a faint smile, as in her mind, Wanda was saying, "David is trying to trace the call. He has already hacked into the signal and is recording the conversation. He's asked for an interpreter."

Sometime after Klaus finished his call, and while he was glaring at Erin who still had a faint smile on her face, yet another foreigner arrived. Erin heard Maxwell's intake of breath, but saw nothing on his face to suggest his full reaction. She stored that away to think on later. Right then, the interaction between Klaus and the newcomer was like that of two dominant dogs sniffing each other. She decided, that Klaus came off second best, and that told her this other stranger was dangerous. Then the newcomer gestured to a small man, who seemed to be greatly in awe of both.

Maxwell started to rise when Klaus drew a knife to slash the cord binding Erin's arms behind her. He grabbed her by the arm and dragged her up.

"Give no trouble, bitch. We're doing you a favour, so no one will recognise you."

"Great!" Erin agreed, as if welcoming the idea. "What about clothes too? These have probably been broadcast nationwide."

An unintelligible growl, suggested that Klaus hadn't thought that far. The other, however, spoke in Arabic and Klaus said, "You are going out as a prisoner, we will find something."

The little man, waited until Erin was seated on a metal chair in the en-suite before starting to explain what he was to do. His English was minimal, but Erin recognised some Spanish words and switched to that language. Klaus, watching from the doorway, growled, until Maxwell said in a languid drawl, "He's just explaining what he is to do."

That had been true initially, but Erin tried to sound him out, hoping he might be an ally. It soon became apparent that he was too frightened of those that had hired him to consider crossing them.

He knew his business though, and Erin wondered how often he changed the appearance of...well, criminals, she supposed. He began by giving her a barber cut, and Erin had wanted to protest, but quickly told herself that hair would grow back – and right then, her head was feeling better. More so when he used a wet towel and soap to wash the fraction that remained. When he had used another towel to dry it, he rubbed in a black dye, used a small hair dryer on it for five minutes, and then rinsed off the excess with her head leaning over the tiny basin. While it dried, he took some of the fallen hair, and dyed it too. Some of this, he glued to her face to give her a realistic looking moustache, and some he cut into tiny lengths, and glued to her face to give her the look of one who need-ed a shave. He finished by applying some "after shave" which was to set the hair to the glue. This had a distinctly masculine scent.

Klaus merely nodded when he saw he finished effect, but Maxwell stared intently. "No one will think you a woman from a distance, except for your shape," he critiqued. "You will need to walk more like a man too."

Erin nodded, it was good advice...if she wanted to be unrecognised, and he was assuming she did.

Klaus, it seemed, had found a pair of not too filthy overalls, and tossed them at her.

"Put them on, then get against that wall!"

It was one of two that was made of wood, not corrugated iron. He had moved a filing cabinet from the space, and turned over a map so its wide side showed. He took out a tiny digital camera, took several head shots from left, right and front angle. He tossed the camera at the Mexican. "You have one hour!"

Maxwell frowned, but didn't comment. He thought Klaus was simply being his usual overbearing self. From what he had been told, the flight would not leave for another six hours.

Erin had a different impression, that they might be leaving

sooner than that. She had no way to prove it. In her mind, Wanda told her, "I will get the word put out about a deportee. And I description or your new look. That little man is a genius – I'll tell Jim about him."

Erin knew that with all the men about her being armed, maybe with the exception of Maxwell, trying to escape wasn't realistic. Besides, she wasn't completely over the last dose of Klaus's drug.

She muttered to Maxwell, "I'm for a nap, okay?" He nodded, and when she had settled onto an out of the way area of floor, he moved his chair to protect her a bit. Erin appreciated that, and began to relax her body and to chant the healing mantra. She slipped into a doze, hoping she would have at least an hour's sleep.

A foot in her ribs woke her abruptly. She scowled. "You are pushing your luck, Chuckles," She warned. "I do not like how you have been treating me, and I am remembering it all. It is not enamouring me to your superiors."

"Get up!"

"I want a drink."

Klaus reached for a half full bottle on the table. "A drink!"

Thinking it was one that one of the others had put down, she pulled a face, but finished the bottle. Then, as soon as she put it down, her wrists were grabbed, and forced behind her. "You are a prisoner. You got to look like one."

She sighed as she was bustled out of the building, which now that it was becoming light, she could see was on the edge of an airport. A car waited outside, an official looking, dark SUV. She was shoved in the back seat and Maxwell followed. He had been allowed to change into a new smelling, formal suit.

The car moved off, exited the airport precinct via a rear gate, then drove around to a side entrance to the main terminal. From there, once out of the car, she was marched to the office of Airport security. Maxwell had her by one arm, and a well-dressed foreigner, had the other. He may have been one of the ones with her in the hangar office, she couldn't tell.

She tried to look like a reluctant prisoner, as the foreigner presented the legal papers for the policeman to scan read.

"They seem in order," was the determination. "They are holding the flight for you. This way."

At the door that led onto the tarmac, Erin saw the huge commercial jet waiting with a mobile stair going up into a rear opening. Nearby, were several smaller ones.

Just outside the door, a second suited foreigner thanked Maxwell. "You are free to go, Sir. We will handle things from here."

Maxwell stepped aside, as the man went onto say to the Airport Policemen, "Would you be so kind as to ensure no one has followed us, with the intent of freeing this prisoner."

All very logical and polite, Erin thought as she scanned the distance between her and the plane, looking for a place to break free. She saw the mini tractor with its train of cargo boxes, and was considering making a break there, where she'd be out of sight of the police. She never expected the abrupt shove sideways, or the hands that bundled her into crate on the trolley. She just had enough time to glimpse a figure, looking exactly like her new self, clad in identical overalls, walking between her two former guards. She only had an instant to warn the watcher in her mind, before a small canister in the crate emitted a colourless gas. She felt the effects immediately, but could fight it only long enough to see a wooden side wall fitted to the crate opening.

Maxwell slipped away from the foreigners as soon as they released him. He wanted to put a lot of distance between himself and them, in as short a time as possible. He found the taxi rank, and hopped into the first one, and simply told the driver to head into town. He didn't know which town was closest. He could tell the airport was big enough for the international jets, but it wasn't one of the two major airports in Florida that he was familiar with.

As the taxi moved off, he quickly considered what he had to do. He would get a message to Goldman, he had promised that much. Then his conscience reminded him that he had promised to help Erin get away. He should never have promised, but the woman had got to him. She wasn't like the thousands of young men he had sent into danger, never promising they would return, but stressing to remember their training.

She wasn't meant to be taken out of the country. She should have been able to finish that program for them before there was any need. Goldman had let slip that the program had been finished for over a month. All Mason needed to do was pull the bits together.

She didn't deserve to have to endure the degrading treatment Klaus had subjected her to. Yet she had, and to an observer, she had his measure, and when she wanted to, the better of him. Like back at the farm...No, she wasn't a helpless civilian. She had put her Marine training to effective use – Klaus had better remember that. Then his mind filled with face after face of men he had sent off to be killed. He had one chance to help Mason. If he could get to a phone, warn Goldman. They could get that jet to turn around.

"Driver, I need a telephone, the first one you can find."

There was a place within ten minutes. The driver directed him into a small shopping mall, and was in turn told to wait. Maxwell hurried inside, instinctively looking around, and seeming to see many foreigners. Just like he had at the airport. He knew nothing of the taxi that had pulled up behind his, or the man who had alighted and spoken to his driver, and was trotting into the mall to look for him.

He was too intent on finding the phone, to check behind.

Chapter 13 – Leaving the Country

Wanda Martin felt herself being shaken. She recognised the sense of her sister and was immediately alert.

"What's up? What time is it?"

Tanya, who had, with Elisabeth, been listening out for Erin, said, "A quarter past eight?"

Elisabeth said, "They found Maxwell in Jacksonsville."

"That's in Florida. A six or seven hour drive. They must have been really travelling."

"You're assuming he was with Erin all the way. He might have got himself there," Tanya suggested.

"No," Elisabeth countered. "Your warning about a deportee was circulated. Jacksonville airport did have one – they held the early flight for them. However, they swear the person was definitely a male, and the paperwork was in order. The agents on duty, had an excellent look at the deportee. Two had recognised Maxwell, but no one had seen a sign of anyone that might have been Erin.

Despite having less sleep than she had expected, Wanda was fully awake. "The plane was not meant to leave for another two hours. Why would they claim that? They couldn't possibly know Erin could reach us."

"Maxwell. They might have thought he would double cross them," Elisabeth suggested. "He was seen taking a prisoner to the Airport Security Office. He had two well-dressed foreigners with him."

"Then that prisoner had to be her! Disguised. Is there CCTV footage?"

"Yes, David said height wise, it could be her, but looks...."

"Irrelevant. I know what some of Jim's friends can do by way of changing someone's looks. That person is definitely on that plane?"

"Yes. They contacted the pilot. The pilot was ordered to return to the airport, he wouldn't until his company directed him to – but they are not impressed," Tanya reported.

Wanda reached for her phone and dialled David, hoping he knew more.

"Not a lot," was David's summary. "I was allowed to sit in on a discussion between Goldman, the FBI and the State Department. The watchers reported seeing a lot of well-dressed foreign business men arriving there about that time. Supposedly, they were part of a tour group. I looked at the CCTV, and many of them could well be citizens of Jakhabad, or from around that region. Their chartered flight flew out just after the commercial flight did."

"Where was that headed?"

"Bermuda, but it will be met when it lands."

"So, Erin might be on that plane?" Wanda suggested.

"It's possible, if they pulled a switch, between the terminal and the plane."

"You studied that footage," Wanda began, "Do you think the person who went on the plane was the same person who went into the Airport security are?"

"As far as I can tell, yes. There are cameras everywhere inside and I had a good view of the face just before they went out onto the tarmac. They had to go into the plane via the service stairs."

"And after that?"

"The cameras were further away – I can send you the footage and you can go over it too."

"Do that," Wanda agreed. "Was there anything else?"

"Only that all of our other targets have gone silent."

"I don't like that."

"It could be that they are all together, or have all left."

"Yeah, but..." Wanda decided to let her thoughts simmer. "Are they questioning Maxwell?"

"Didn't Elisabeth tell you?"

"What?"

"They found Maxwell behind a convenience store – unconscious and critically injured."

"Damn! I wanted a piece of that weasel. Like I told Jim, this whole affair has been a damn fiasco. He should have let me go in and get her."

"And you might have been blown to bits," David immediately snapped back through the phone. "I have alerted the Group, and asked them to get a message through to our agents in Jakhabad to look out for Erin."

Neither he, nor Wanda had doubts as to where Erin was being taken. "Ask them for news of Janna, too," Wanda said, calming down. "Her baby must be due any day now."

"Okay. I'll ask," David agreed, hoping his wife had settled down and wouldn't be planning anything rash.

The slow cargo flight from Jacksonville, Florida to Bermuda, was uneventful. Nothing about the flight, even its destination, had raised even the slightest of suspicions. Its manifest had been in order, and its cargo of farming tools, unremarkable. The customs inspection had not noticed that one box had a false floor, and was only half filled with tools. All the boxes had standard shaped holes to allow air flow around the tools – the consignee had said. The explanation went unchallenged.

Erin would have challenged it, but a small vial of gas had been tossed in with her, and once again, she had been sent to unconsciousness. Her unpleasant quarters, the box with the false floor, was the first to be loaded, so that it was right up the middle of the plane. When the flight was finally underway, the side of the box facing the small passenger section, was carefully opened. Erin, slumped in an uncomfortable heap, was gently lifted out by one of the passengers, dressed in a suit. He placed her on a fold down couch. When he looked at her, he called out in alarm. "This woman looks dead."

The co-pilot, a South American, who like the pilot was not averse to a bit of smuggling, left his seat and went aft. He had some basic medical training, and soon checked her breathing, pulse and overall state.

"Who is responsible for this? This woman is hardly breathing, and her pulse is slow."

Even as he was glaring at the passengers, he was pulling down one of the emergency oxygen masks and fitting it to the woman's face.

One of the less clean looking passengers called back, "Not your business. You been paid to be quiet."

The young man who had freed Erin, turned to the speaker and said, "If she dies, he will blame us!"

That led to a general growling exchange of words, and the name Klaus was mentioned.

To justify themselves, another of the rough looking men claimed, "She's female. It is not right that a woman takes the work of a man."

The near speaker spoke diplomatically. "In general, that is so. However, she is the only person who can do what is needed. We were told she had freely agreed to help us. It is a risk for us to keep antagonising her."

"We do not need to let her twist us to her whims! She must learn her place as a woman."

"It is not that, Ragnar. We will get better work from her if she is treated well. She will teach us what she knows before she leaves."

"Will she be allowed to leave?" a sly voice commented.

"Not until she is milked dry of knowledge," another low voice said, chuckling.

Erin heard the voices, some were not in English, but it was the individual feelings of the men that seeped into her mind. The sense of them, uncensored by her conscious mind, mixed with older memories.

Gradually, she became aware of her surroundings. The feel of the vibration of the engines through the frame of the plane, the straps that were restraining her, the mask and the flow of oxygen on her face.

Memories began to return. Being grabbed and forced into a crate, of expecting to be taken onto a commercial flight, of being handcuffed....but her hands were free. Something had changed.

She extended her senses. None of the presences had a familiar feel. Of the voices she now heard, all were speaking a language she didn't know.

The pure oxygen was helping to clear her mind, and her first cogent idea was, pretend to be asleep as long as you can. She wanted to be sure Klaus was not anywhere near. Once she was sure, she tentatively tested each of the minds she sensed. Some had a rough, uneducated feel – thinking thoughts that had a carnal feel. Others, were bright, intelligent, eager. These reminded her of the young men – Anko and the other – she had net at the farmhouse. They had been keen to learn what she knew. Shared with her a love of computing. Could she get these on her side? Get them to back her up if she encountered Chuckles, aka Klaus, again?

Gradually, the subconscious mix of memories and ideas brought forth more wisdom. She would need to be ultra-confident, diplomatic, and calm – reduce feminine behaviour to a minimum, so she could work with the men of Jakhabad. They would not trust her if she let them dominate her, and she would have to be careful not to sound like she considered herself their superior in intelligence.

Then she wondered, if she had been a man, how would they be treating her now? Recalling Stan's fate, came as a timely warning. Would they kill her when she had told them all they needed? It couldn't be ruled out, so she have to demonstrate other ways to make her useful – like knowing electronics.

Would they be silently spitting on her for being a traitor to her country? Or gloating because they had turned her into one? What would be her rationale be? Science deserved to be shared? Particularly if it benefitted the people of the country? A pedantic distinction that – since she was certain that the leaders of where she was going were not going to use the program for the benefit of the general population.

If it was a satellite they planned to use the program with, they could find warlike uses for it – spying for instance. She could pretend to believe they would use if for beneficial things like ground surveys, water surveys, seeking ore deposits. It also wouldn't hurt to let her disgruntlement with the US authorities show. It would minimise any ideas that she might be a spy, although surely they couldn't think that since she was a last minute fill-in, and a woman.

She didn't want them to treat her as a woman, and force her to obey any man that spoke to her. She was a consultant, contracted to do specified work, and she had pride in her work. They would have to treat her decently, or she would not be able to give her best – and that would not enamour her to her employer.

That, she decided, would need to be made clear from the outset – starting with this unfamiliar group.

Finally, she opened her eyes and tried to look around. She looked up into two pairs of concerned blue eyes. The men looked younger than she was, and when she woke, their faces cleared of strain and they actually smiled. One spoke, saw she did not understand, and switched to speaking American that had very little accent. Both young men wore American style suits, and might have just graduated from an American University.

"Can I get up?" Erin asked, testing the atmosphere.

They both sprang up to release the restraints.

"They were only to stop you falling – in case we hit turbulence," one explained. "Do you still need the mask?"

A quick consideration of how she felt gave her the answer. "No. I feel okay."

"Can we ask you about your work?" the other asked, obviously eager.

"I'd love to say yes, but my mind isn't quite back to capable of that level thinking. How about you filling me in about the project. What have you been told? I came in as a last minute replacement, and only have sketchy information."

A comment in the foreign language interrupted.

"He says we should tell you nothing."

"If I don't know what I am wanted for, I won't be any help, and the sooner I know – the sooner the real work can begin. I can be considering what is needed while we are still travelling."

This logic was translated, and the growling subsided.

What she heard, she labelled idealistic brainwashing. They were full of enthusiasm about the good things the project would do for their country. They hadn't yet seen the device that was to be run by the program but assumed a satellite, from the types of sensors it would have. Erin could think of other things, even robotic devices, or drones.

Well, Erin thought, if their leader intended to hijack a satellite, he couldn't yet.

"Can I have a drink?" she asked then.

Her two new friends were apologetic and one quickly fetched an unopened bottle of water. The other mentioned that plane had facilities, should she need them. She decided she did, and that the chance to wash her face would feel refreshing. When none of the lesser minds, that she assumed were guards, got up to follow her, she felt easier about her situation.

It came as a shock to see her face in the small mirror. She had forgotten her face change, and felt the fake hair must have been just dirt, from way back at the farm. In debating whether to try scrubbing it off, she decided to leave it as it was. It would help those with her to think of her as a man. Though she did test a small area under her chin, only to find nothing came off. She supposed then, that a special solvent would be need for the glue. While washing her hands, she studied how she looked, and considered how a young man, such as she looked, should act.

Nerdish and knowledgeable had already won over the young programmers. What about the guards? Pretend they were protecting her, not preventing her trying to get away? Were they going to be with her all the way to her destination? Where they going to continue the charade about her being deported?

Where was she anyway? She felt an inner chuckle. If she asked, they just might tell her.

They were heading for Bermuda! So, she hadn't been out all that long. Then they would be changing planes to go from there. When she asked if she was still to play the deportee, her new friends laughed. Yes, that ruse would continue – but someone else was playing that role. It would take the 'heat' off her. If the authorities suspected a trick, they would be looking elsewhere.

Erin had to admit the triple cross had been brilliantly conceived and executed, and was sure had not been devised by Klaus.

Once they had begun talking, the two young men were happy to continue. They told her how long it would take to get to their country, the route they were taking, where they would refuel. Then they told her about their country.

Erin soon had the feeling that these idealists, did not really know the full story of the change of leadership in their country.

Even though Erin had her mind open to chances for escape, she always sensed the eyes of the ones who were her guards. Shortly before leaving the cargo plane, several of her guards pulled on dark green overalls with a company logo on the front pocket. A pair was shoved at her, and the mime told her to put them on. To do so, she removed the brown ones. Under them, she still had some of her own clothes, particularly the cardigan and shirt she had kept from when she had first been taken. Around her waist, they made her look stockier, and disguised her female shape. When she had the new overalls on, the leader of her guards just grunted, and partially drew a gun from a hidden side holster – watching to be sure she understood.

One of her new friends, began to insist, "That is hardly needed..."

"We have orders to see our...guest...arrives safely."

After that, he shoved a clipboard at her, and told the young man to explain what she was to do.

"We must go through customs here. You are to be seen as part of the company exporting the farm implements, and will be seen overseeing the transfer. Later, you will also go through customs, under a different name, and as a student returning to our country. They will allow you time to clean up and become presentable. They say not to try to escape."

To keep with her intended persona, she said, "There's no damn chance of that! I need to leave the States, if I don't want to be thrown back in prison. I am more than grateful for your countries leader letting me help with his project."

While pretending to check the manifest as boxes were unloaded, Erin tried to reach out for her cousin's mind. That she could not, didn't worry her at first, as Wanda could be busy. Yet as the time passed, and the departure time for the next flight drew nearer, she began to think that something was stopping her from receiving her cousin, who would surely be worried about her.

As the last box was signed off, and the clipboard taken from her, Erin glanced around, looking for an escape route. Whichever way she glanced, there always seemed to be a wind in her face. She took that as a subtle hint that the direction was not safe. If so, no direction was safe. The wind, merely a faint breeze, paused to caress her face. She sensed a purpose, not her own. Did that mean she was meant to go with these people? The breeze brushed her again. Was that why she could not reach her cousin? The breeze swirled. Understanding came to her. A power older than all life on Earth, had a need of her. She stopped considering escape, and dropped fully into her planned persona.

Chapter 14 – Under the Serpent's Eye

Erin stood around in the passenger lounge, talking to the two young men. A stranger would see nothing odd. She was clad in neat casual, men's clothing, rather than a suit, but of equal quality, and likely would be taken for a student returning home.

Their flight had been delayed, and that was making the now spruced up guards nervous. They probably did understand enough American English to have caught snippets of the gossip around them.

The news was that an earlier flight had been forced to turn around and return, of the police waiting in the lounge just down from them, and out on the tarmac. Rumours abounded – the most common being that an attempted hijack had been foiled.

Erin guessed they had caught onto the deportation ruse that she had been told at first. The subtle signs of the extra undercover agents became obvious. She could have acted then…

"No!" seemed to be the command in her mind. It was not coming from her cousin, but from the ancient power she could sometimes sense.

Erin quickly thought soothing reassurances, but as she glanced at the activity, their flight was called, and her group edged her towards the flight attendants just opening a door. For one instant, between two of her guards, she thought she spotted David. He looked her way, seemed to meet her eyes, and then looked away. Then he was gone and she was being pressed into a passage – just another passenger on a charter flight to Madrid.

Almost twenty-four hours later, the final charter flight touched down at a modern looking Jawal Faizan airport – labelled in both Arabic and English glyphs. Despite sleeping during the flight, Erin was weary when she descended the mobile stairs to the tarmac. She had become used to the open friendliness of the two young programmers, Jiwan and Bisha, and the guards had stopped considering her likely to run away, so the arrival of uniformed and armed guards, was unexpected. More so when they come directly to her, grabbed her by both arms, and forced her off in a different direction. She caught the reaction of the young men, who were about to protest, until the guards with them hissed a warning. They became immobile, and their faces betrayed anxiety and fear. Inwardly, they were in shock. Their delight at being chosen to escort her and learn about her work, had turned sour.

The uniformed troop leader was courteous to them, and extended an invitation to meet with King Jabir, at the palace. But the invitation did not bring joy, but something like a lead weight settling into the pit of their stomach. Whatever they had been told about the change of leadership in their country, had proved to be a lie. The reality of the coup was now obvious. However, they were smart young men and hid their shock, by acting surprised by the honour just bestowed.

So, they went off in a stretched limousine, the guards in SUVs. Erin was led to an army type truck, as if she was the returning criminal they had claimed in the States.

Her escorts seemed to think she was a young slender man, and gestured for her to climb into the truck. Once inside, they indicated a bench seat. She sat there, one of the new uniformed guards sat opposite, and another stayed by the flap that was pulled closed at the back.

From inside, Erin only had occasional glimpses of the blue sky when the canvas door cover, flapped in the wind. The trucks engine seemed to be revving hard, and the suspension was rough, even on what she had seen to be a paved road. She braced herself against one of the cover struts, and sat up straight, recalling the importance of appearances. She began to wonder if, at her final destination, they would still have her impersonating a man. She certainly wanted a wash and a change of clothes after travelling for a day.

Conversation in the rear of the truck was non-existent, but that suited Erin. She went over in her mind the details of her planned persona.

When the truck was stopped at a guarded gate, passed through with what Erin assumed were directions of where to go, and finally stopped – she expected to be hustled out, not to have to wait in there, with the hot sun turning the back of the truck into a sauna. When they finally gestured her out, it was a relief to feel a breeze, and she straightened and decided it would be in character to be irritated.

As if in warning, thoughts of Gerry and her daughter, Bree, came to mind. It reminded her to be careful, and not to make her dangerous employer angry. The distant sound of explosions made her realise that 'killed while trying to escape' could so easily be arranged.

She didn't expect to have her hands grabbed and tied behind her, the instant her feet touched the ground. Still, she didn't struggle – just continued to hold herself erect and remind herself she had been invited to come...well, Otway must have been. Erin, keeping in mind she was a guest, and a contracted skilled worker, decided looking around would be expected, and she did so. They were in a paved courtyard of some grandeur, although nothing like the building beyond. All around, backed into walls and the sides of buildings, were other trucks – looking ready to be driven off fast. Her guess was that this was some sort of tradesman's entrance.

Inside though, as she was marched through various passages, she saw the décor increase from functional to grand. She entered a room with a portrait of a man in a magnificent gold frame, dominating the far wall. Then she felt a blow on her back.

One of the new escorts spoke in very poor English, "Eyes down! Infidels should not desecrate the royal palace."

Refusing to be intimidated, Erin asked, "May I ask the name of my host then, and how he deserves to be addressed?"

It allowed the man to flaunt his importance and arrogance. "This is the palace of King Jabir Fazir. You should address him as your Eminence. However, I doubt that foreign scum like you, who smells like the pigs that rut in the street, will meet him. You are to meet General Ishkan."

"Thank you," Erin said politely, and despite the warning, continued to study the picture, taking in more details and seeming to see the shadow of a cobra in the background. The eyes of the man seemed to catch any ambient light, for even the slightest movement on her part, brought a change to them.

If the wait was designed to intimidate her, she refused to let it.

However, the imminent presentation, arranged without giving her a chance to freshen up, would have her on a lower standing. She could smell herself, and also a smell that suggested the bandage on her arm urgently needed replacing.

Telling her mind that she was being honoured by this meeting with a high official, who was a busy man, kept her standing straight and feigning confidence. Though, after twenty minutes, she began to recall the early days of her marine training. It amused her that she sensed the approach of the personage, well before the two guards snapped to attention, and bowed to the arrival. She turned towards the door as the uniformed man entered. She copied he bow of the guards, but to a lesser degree, then met the man's gaze.

The medals and braid on the uniform seemed ostentatious, but were obviously to impress his power on the lower ranks. He was taller than the two guards, solid and powerful, and except for his ethnic origins, reminded Erin of the unlamented and long deposed African leader, Idi Amin.

His stare focused on her for a long time before he spoke – without preliminary greetings – and a crawling feeling began in her belly. This man, was a killer.

"Tell me about the program that cost us so much."

Since he probably knew what the program was purported to do, Erin was blunt.

"It is the operating system for an upcoming satellite. I don't know the specifications, but I can guess a lot from the instruments that will be part of the package. It has cameras that can focus on small areas of ground from high up, others that can magnify a distant area of space..."

The General's gaze stayed on her, as she outlined the instruments and their capabilities. He looked impassive, but Erin sensed the lessening of his hostility, and the surge of interest. Then, assuming he had already heard all the two young programmers had learnt from her – only the basics – she added more detail.

When she finally paused, General Ishkhan barked a command and her wrists were freed.

"I was disbelieving that an American woman," he stressed the gender, "could program so well."

"Sir, some highly placed American politicians think I program too damn well," Erin admitted. "I am grateful to you for accepting me as a consultant, to help finalise your King's vision."

"Ah, yes," Ishkhan said neutrally. "My agents checked you out. They mentioned the appropriation of a great deal of money. Why would you need this commission?"

Erin allowed a faint wry smile as she said, "I managed to convince people that the money all those businesses thought they had lost was actually misdirection. That they were simply being used to launder sums, that is to set certain parameters in the bank's programs to prove that the figures being transferred did relate to real money. Money that actually came from nowhere. My partner and I shared our profits and we each shunted it around, to hide it. He wasn't clever enough. I think they still think I have a stash somewhere, but I insisted that I only worked the program for the computing challenge. On paper, they can think I have a lot of money, but they could not find any accounts full of money, or traces of where I might have sent it. It would not be wise for me to try accessing that money for a number of years."

Erin sensed that she had aroused the man's rampant greed with the notion of 'money from nowhere.'

However, the General returned to the program and Erin was able to betray her eagerness to get to work to finish it.

"Come!" General Ishkhan snapped.

Erin scampered to follow him to a room nearby. Her first glimpse through the door caused her to stop and stare at the bank of computers. All high powered, top of the range units. Then she studied the units analytically and decided the capability of the set up would rival the control centre at NASA.

"Impressive," she stated. Her voice clear in the silence of the room. Her eyes slid past Bisha and Jiwan, who were standing rigid as statues, by two of the dozen workstations. They were not looking at her either, and that suggested they had just had a rude awakening to some aspects of their new job descriptions.

The General's low growl, broke her reverie. She moved quickly to stand opposite him at a table in the centre of the room. Spread out there were various folders, a hard drive and a laptop.

"What else will you need to complete the program?"

Taking that as permission to look over all the items, she reached for the folders.

Inside the first one, in Stan Otway's neat writing, was a list of everything in the printouts that followed. She checked all the folders before answering, cursing inwardly at how much of Stan's perfidy she had missed.

It was pretty much as she had figured. Stan had everything except her unfinished part, and the tweaks needed for the parts that were tested. He also had copies of her notes.

She looked up at the General. "I still have to finish the power control algorithm, and test the power modelling. Part of that will be to test all the subroutines – the programs that control individual sensors and instruments. I believe you are aware that this was written for controlling a satellite?"

The General did not answer, just stared at her and waited for her to finish.

"Just prior to my departure, most of the programming was tested on mock-ups of the actual instruments. The final stage of the testing would be to see how all the instruments work together and the individual power demands. I was provided with some raw data from past NASA missions to feed into the modelling program, to see if the program accurately predicts the power requirements. I will need to see if that data is on the hard drive. Ideally, we would test all the instruments in the lab before the launch."

"And what if the satellite is already in orbit?" the General drawled.

"Ah, well...if you have the satellite security contact codes, it would be a matter of updating its current programming with yours, and resetting the pre-set values."

"And what is the requirement for putting the program on our system?"

"I judge you have ample computing power here, so you would need to..." Erin itemised the steps and what would be needed for them to contact the hypothetical satellite.

General Ishkhan nodded and smiled as he said, "Excellent."

"Sir, may I ask if you have a particular satellite in mind to use?"

"Why do you...need to know?"

"Only because there are thousands of satellites, both active and defunct, orbiting the Earth. They are not all the same. This program may not suit more than a fraction of them. You may not be able to use it."

She intended to continue, and offer to ensure it would. However, it seemed that the General took what she said to imply he'd wasted money on the project. Before she knew it, he had circled into her personal space and slapped both sides of her face.

"My instructions are not to be questioned. I was assured that this program could be modified to suit our needs. You are to get it working as intended, and ensure my people fully understand it. Then – I will instruct you further."

Erin looked away from him, clenching her hands into fists to stop herself bringing them up to her stinging cheeks.

"That is – "

"Silence, woman! If you obey my instructions, and prove you can carry them out, you will be treated well."

He didn't mention alternatives, and Erin preferred not to know.

She looked back into his blazing eyes, once more subtly drawing herself up to near 'attention'. It worked again. Even though the General knew her to be a woman - her looking like a man, the men's clothing, and her military stance, distracted him on a subtle level.

"The reason I am here, General," she spoke firmly and calmly, "is to get the program finished and to adapt it to your use if required. I take pride in my work, so if I feel that what you want is impossible, or impractical, I will tell you – even if it is not what you want to hear. That does not mean that I won't suggest alternatives. I am sure you want the simplest and most efficient program possible. However, I do not dispute that you will have final say. When do you require me to start work?"

The brightness of the General's eyes dimmed, as he maintained his stare. That the American woman continued to meet his gaze, told him of her determination. However, the two young programmers had told him things about her - enough to control her.

"Tomorrow! You will be escorted to the rooms assigned to you, and brought back here then. By that time, I expect you to present yourself to a suitable standard and not like a derelict transvestite."

"Certainly, General," Erin agreed amiably. "And I agree with your opinion of my presentation today. It was, however, an ingenious disguise, and it thoroughly fooled the US authorities. However, the problem was that I was unable to bring suitable business clothes with me. Who should I see to arrange such things?"

General Ishkhan turned abruptly from her. To the nearest of the programmers he said, "You! Call a servant to attend to our consultant. And you! Get started on copying that hard drive onto our system. I will expect to see all of you hard at work tomorrow."

When the General left the room, even though two of the elite guards remained, the tense atmosphere remained.

Erin felt as if she had just run in a 1000m sprint, and wanted only to collapse, but she had a role to play.

"I do want a rest," she admitted to Bisha, "I expect you do too, but you heard the general's orders. What is the operating system here?"

Bisha had to ask the question of one of the other men, but the answer came without hesitation.

"Okay, that's fine. For us to start early tomorrow, you will need to upload the framework algorithm at least. If you transfer everything, I will check that nothing is missing."

She had nods from several others besides Bisha and Jiwan. Some of them understood English.

Erin risked a question, and asked in a low voice, "Am I right in thinking you are not to be friendly towards me?"

Bisha nodded slightly.

"Well, you don't have to seem to be. It's fine," she assured him. Then increasing her voice volume, she went on, "Amongst the paperwork on the table is a copy of the framework user guide. Read through it. You will need to understand that, before modifying it."

A servant, a middle aged woman clad in a brown tunic over ankle length brown skirts, came into the room. One of the elite guards pointed to Erin, and the woman gestured impatiently when Bisha nudged her.

The two guards followed, carrying their weapons casually, but made sure Erin was aware of their presence.

If they were there to deter her from any idea of escaping, they needn't have bothered. Where would he go anyway? Besides, she didn't intend these people to have full use of the stolen program.

At least, Erin decided, they didn't insist on blindfolding her, or anything like that. She tried to memorise the route, but what worked best for her was to treat the route like a maths vector problem.

When they finally arrived at the door, the fourth in a series of identical doors in that passage, the woman opened it and gestured her in. She followed, but the guards remained outside.

Inside, the woman went to a curtain on the right and pulled it aside. It covered an alcove with a bed, chair and table. "Sleep here," she said in basic English. She turned abruptly and crossed the room to a closed door. She opened this as well. "Wash here." She went in. "Soap, towels, what you need, in there." She pointed to a cupboard.

"How can I clean my clothes?" Erin asked, plucking at the wrinkled suit.

The woman took a moment to understand. "Leave here." She pointed to a basket. "You have case?"

Erin shook her head. "Only what I have on."

The woman looked exasperated. "I come back."

With that, she bustled from the room and Erin began her own exploration, quickly deciding that her room was better than she had feared. The bed felt comfortable, even if it wasn't elegant. A cupboard held extra sheets, pillows and blankets on a top shelf. The drawer below the hanging space was empty.

With the curtain drawn closed the rest of the room still looked clean and airy. She had a table with three chairs – the fourth being near the bed – a window that overlooked the yard with the trucks and it had thick drapes to block out the sunlight. The walls were of light yellow painted stones, and the floor a mosaic of light and dark woods.

The only oddity, with this being a guest room, was the ten centimetre square glass panel set in the door. Her first thought was that it was there to check on the guest, and that caused her to look around for evidence of electronic monitoring. She found none.

Finally, needing to use the toilet in the wash room, she checked in there as well, finding only hygiene necessities and spare toilet paper.

All in all, the room was much like a motel room and wondered who, in what she assumed was the royal palace of Jakhabad, usually used it. Hearing the soft nick of the door being unlocked, warned her of the return of the servant. She had a neat pile of men's clothing, and a second servant had a neatly pressed pair of trousers and a white shirt. Both women turned to leave, the original one telling her, "Food come here."

When the room was quiet, Erin laughed softly. She couldn't make out if she was a prisoner or a guest. The supplied trousers were brown, and she suspected they came from the stock that supplied the servants. That wasn't an issue. She preferred them to the outdated skirts the women wore. It also implied they had thought her a man. She had seen a grooming and shaving kit in the bathroom, but that wouldn't remove the fake 'five o'clock shadow' which was beginning to itch. Maybe a good long shower might help. It would certainly make the rest of her feel better. With that in mind, she checked the door. It had a safety bolt on the inside, and she quickly slipped that into place. Since she had not been given the key to the lock.

A clock on the table by the bed gave her the local time, a little after noon. She adjusted her watch after noting the time difference between there and Washington. Then she collected clean clothes, a towel and soap and headed for the shower. The cubical was one that had a base that could act as a rudimentary bath. It gave her the idea of using it to wash her own shirt and jumper that was still around her waist. She could use a hangar from the cupboard to hand it in the shower to dry. She also unwound the bandage from her arm, to wash that as well as to see what her arm looked like. She didn't want it to go septic.

Half an hour later, Erin emerged from the shower and examined herself in the mirror. It was a shock to see it so short still, but it was no longer dark black – she had noticed some of the colour washing out in the shower. But the soap and shampoo had also faded the fake face hair to a light grey.

For want of an alternative, Erin made use of the male aftershave in the cupboard and discovered this loosened the sticky material that held the facial hair. She persisted with a soapy cloth alternating with the after shave until her face was rid of all that part of her disguise.

Lastly, after letting her healing wound air for a while, she used a clean face washer as a pad on the wound and tied it in place with two strips of the long bandage, cut off using the tiny scissors in the grooming kit.

Then, intending to nap for a couple of hours, Erin lay down on the bed and fell into a deep sleep, not even rousing when her lunch was slipped in through a flap near the door.

Erin woke when it was near the time she would have expected was dinner time. It was growing dark outside, but she didn't close the curtains, or put on her light. There was still some light from outside, and she pulled a chair near the window. The sleep had refreshed her mind and now she was able to objectively look at her situation and consider how to proceed.

Goldman had told her all the scenarios he feared, and now that she had met General Ishkhan, some of the more frightening ones seemed ominously likely. How could she slow the completion of the program, without making it obvious? If the director of the SIO knew enough to make those guesses, surely he knew where she had been taken. And Wanda and David, she was sure they had ideas too.

So she had to slow things for long enough for them to work up a plan to extract her. She would need to be ready for that, and be able to make the program unworkable when she was gone. The groundwork for that was already in place, with the little extra pieces of code she had added. The problem now was how they could be triggered.

The sound of a loud explosion, and the eruption of an orange glare that changed the colour of the light in her room, startled her to her feet. She was at the window, looking out as yelling erupted from the yard below. A stampede of booted feet preceded the appearance of many soldiers, and it was followed by the revving of truck engines. The trucks left as soon as they were filled with armed men.

Where ever the explosion had been, it was not very far away. It reminded her, forcibly, that the country was in a state of civil war, and the leaders now, had not pacified it. They may have usurped power, but it was not a popular change. Her employers could use a satellite to locate the bases of the loyalists, and then target those locations. If those forces were doing damage this close to the palace, would they dare to damage the palace? Maybe not, but it would anger the General and the usurper King.

That would probably make them impatient for the program, Erin realised. How would they react to delays?

The sudden leaden feeling in her stomach, at the thought of the General's anger, was a warning that she would need to be sure of her logic when talking to him. He didn't know programming, but the group of other programmers, might be totally loyal to the new regime – even if Jiwan and Bisha were not. If any of them knew English, her logic twisting to the General might be challenged.

Erin sighed, and turned from the window when the last of the trucks could be heard roaring down the road.

The sound of something sliding on wood near her door caught her attention. She had been told food would be delivered to the room, but had fallen asleep. Now she saw they tray just about to nudge an earlier one of a shelf, and she ran to catch it – just in time. The dinner just delivered, smelt delicious, and she turned on the light to see what was there.

Taking the two trays to the table, she took out the wrapped cutlery and started on the hot food. Lunch had been sandwiches, wrapped fortunately, and she decided to keep them for later. As with the bottle of water. She did drink most of the second one that came with the dinner, and decided to keep the bottle so she had something to use to drink from during the night.

It was only when she was stacking the two trays for the servant to collect that she found the small folded piece of paper under the sandwich plate.

The writing was unfamiliar, which wasn't surprising, but it had to be from one of the two programmers she had befriended on the trip here. She read through it, sensed the apprehension that had prompted the warning, and she didn't need to be told to destroy the paper. It came through as the General wanting to prove her help was not needed. In the tiny little printing, she knew that the

General assumed if a woman could do what was needed, the men could do it as well or better. The older men thought they knew it all too and would not listen to those who read the information and translated it from English.

Erin could already picture the following morning...and decided the General would be his own worst enemy. If he had made the programmers slot in all the subroutines, out of the correct order, they likely triggered some of her nasty surprises. She would have a real mess to sort out in the morning, and there was nothing they could blame her for. She had told them to read the manual. Maybe she wouldn't have to invent problems, just keep fixing them.

No, she had to seem to be truly dedicated to getting it working... one way would be to have a group meeting first thing, so all the programmers would understand things about the program. Not everything, enough so they had to accept her authority, but how much would be too much?

She went back to the window, and tried to open it to get some fresh air. It didn't budge. That suggested she was a prisoner...she sighed.

Just before she decided to position the trays to be collected, it occurred to her that it was a pity the current rulers of the country were so bloody-minded. What she had been abducted to come here to do, could be used for much better purposes than fighting a civil war.

Chapter 15 – Dangerous Defiance

The moment she was escorted into the computer room, there was bedlam. Half a dozen angry voices began shouting at her, each getting red in the face because she was just standing there uncomprehending.

Jiwan trotted over, and began waving his arms around, and trying to be heard, until the others took in the sense of what he was saying.

When there was an angry silence, Jiwan turned to one of the older men, bowed slightly and asked a question. He listened to the answer and translated.

"Senior programmer Yusif wishes to know why the program crashed."

"I will need to know what was done before I can answer that," Erin said, keeping her tone impersonal. "If the subroutines were uploaded, there is a particular way they need to be linked to the framework. Was the manual consulted?"

Jiwan's answer was equally neutral, and in itself true, but implied something else. "The senior programmer does not read English."

Her mysterious note writer, probably Jiwan, had implied that they didn't see the need. Erin saw an immediate way to waste time.

"Ask if I may use a terminal to check the code as it is."

Very promptly, she was escorted to a work station, and Jiwan translated the invitation. "You will work here."

Her courteous, "Thank you," led to Jiwan being instructed to show her how to start up the workstation and access the system to access the underlying code.

That was an immediate problem. The instructions were in Arabic, although Erin memorised the process, and the keyboard also had the foreign glyphs. However, the real problem had Erin wanting to gape, for what started to scroll down the monitor screen was a mixture of English and Arabic. That in itself was enough to make the program bugout.

Trying to sound interested, not absolutely incredulous, Erin asked, "Did you use a translation program? I am not familiar with how they work."

Jiwan stared at her, but his eyes widened as he realised that trying such a fool thing had caused the problem. Erin guessed he hadn't heard of any such concept either. With his face flushing faintly, he managed to translate the question and give it the same tone of innocence that Erin had. He let his superior answer, not Yusif, but one of the others, and merely translated.

Erin listened, nodded at places, and prepared a completely civil reply. "Your logic has merit, Sir. In fact, I am cautiously in full agreement. It would make it better for your people to be able to debug the code if it was in their language. However, if I may explain, the program is written in English, and the majority of satellites have American based programming. If you have a purpose built satellite available, programmed here, in your language, then I would advocate working through the code and translating it – but I would need help. As things stand, I am not privy to such information, and to finish the program, and test it, I will need it all in English, and have an interface that shows English."

Erin was watching the man's face as her answer was translated, and she saw the man glance at the door, and then take on a pinched look. Beside him, Yusif became poker faced. Erin had warning from that of the entrance of the General behind her.

His voice barked a question, one that Erin sensed the Senior programmer was reluctant to answer. Jiwan quietly translated the exchange, but when the General glared his way, he stepped back. Erin only had her extra empathic sense to guess what was being said after that. Her guess was that the man she had been speaking to, had been told by the general to do something that Yusif had disagreed with. The other man had insisted and the mess was the result. However, it seemed that man had switched the blame to her.

"You, woman, are not in charge here," General Ishkhan said loudly, challengingly.

"No, I am a consultant."

The general's hand flashed out and struck her face, adding to the residual soreness from the previous day.

"I want that system, finished and ready to be used by the end of the week."

"Sir," Erin began, trying not to clench her teeth or betray anger, "that is what I came here to do. I know what needs to be done, and I need to teach your team the intricacies of it, so that they can maintain it in the future."

"They do as I tell them!"

"They cannot do their jobs effectively if they cannot do it the right way."

Erin expected the stinging slaps and did not try to avoid them. She believed he would not do anything to disable her, just to humiliate her. She was not going to back down. "I know what to do. Do you?"

The General's eyes blazed. "You have one week!"

He turned and strode from the room.

Erin muttered, "I thought not!"

Jiwan wouldn't look at her, and the other men were, mostly, equally uncomfortable. The exception was the man she had been talking to. His intent look was vengeful. No doubt he, like the General resented that an American, a woman at that, knew more than they did. And to make it worse, that woman was in a position to dispute the orders of a powerful man.

Erin didn't want to see what her face looked like, but she wiped a dribble of blood from the side of her mouth, straightened, then looked around the group.

"I know I'm a woman, but I do know what needs to be done. I am not claiming to be better than you, just show you what to do. I did not know to expect you to be ready to proceed so quickly, but the process required was outlined in the framework program guide."

Jiwan translated that. Bisha, who had fetched the user guide, told her. "They don't dare disobey the General. He is King Jabir's right hand man, but they are impressed at how you stood up to him. We were warned he is nasty to disobey."

"Yeah, I got that much," Erin murmured, then raising her voice again, told them, "I have no way of making the program work as it is. What I think should be done is to reset your main computer to how it was before anything was done, then start again – keeping everything in English."

After the translation, Yusif issued orders and then came closer.

"Can you do it? Have it finished in a week?"

"I can finish it to what it is designed to do in that time. It all needs testing, but I can only use the test data I was given. If I knew exactly what he wants to use it for, I can prioritise the relevant functions and buy time to finish the rest. It would save a lot of unnecessary work."

Bisha and Jiwan looked to Yusif. He was licking dry lips, clearly undecided. Finally he shook his head. His comment when translated was, "We must get it working first. I will see that you get an English workstation. Will you tell me what you require to test the programming? The most important aspect is the cameras and the detection of metals."

Erin nodded tersely. "I will prioritise those things, and while the framework is reloading, I will get onto the power modelling. Will you tell me when the framework is up and operational?"

She received a terse nod in return, and Yusif appropriated Bisha to translate the manual.

Jiwan watched Erin return to her assigned workstation, and begin to write her code on paper. He went to the table, checked the folders there, then took one over to her. That way, it would seem he was discussing the contents.

"We must talk quietly, like strangers," he warned. He passed her a sheet, Erin glanced at it then reached for the folder and began to sort through the sheets. "Is one of this group a pet of the General?"

"You can guess one that might be – either of him or King Jabir. Yusif is not. He gave you as much information as he dared. Can you give me the requirements for a test camera?"

"What distance and resolution is required?" Erin asked. "To test the program - something like the ones found on a recreational drone would do. We can bypass the default programming with ours – and have the computer here set up to receive from it on whatever frequency the satellite uses."

"Could you test it at a different frequency and change it later?"

Erin nodded, cursing the direction the conversation had taken. If they could program and control the more readily available drones, he may not need a satellite. Which was good, but also bad. If a drone did what was wanted to find the loyalists, they wouldn't need a program. They could go out and check places from a safe distance...her stomach lurched. She promised herself, "Not if I have any say in the matter."

To hide her dismay, Erin said, "We might be able to modify a commercial metal detector for one of the sensors. The rest I will need to think on."

Jiwan straightened, saying, "I will see what I can arrange for these."

Erin turned her attention back to her program, but was aware of eyes on her and after a while, casually looked up, making sure she wasn't looking at anyone, though the man she had spoken to about the loading fiasco, was watching her. He wouldn't think she'd noticed, but from now on, she'd be watching him, even while seeming intent on her work.

When the framework was up and ready, Yusif came to tell her.

"May I call everyone together?" Erin asked him. "If you have a blackboard or a white board I can use, I will explain the next stage to everyone."

During her presentation, Erin noticed the man she had nicknamed 'Mole', slipping out of the room. A short time later, General Ishkhan came on and listened. His face was red, set in a scowl, but he did nothing more than glare at her. If he could have taken offence at what she was doing, she guessed he would have, except that she was showing his countrymen the knowledge they needed.

Chapter 16 – The Serpent's Work

Three days passed. Erin was increasingly sure that the General planned to use drones to seek out the forces opposing him. The idea made her feel wretched. More so when the mole must have told him that the camera subroutine was ready for testing. He came in demanding proof that it worked. His attitude bordered on tyrannical and Erin was dragged from her purposefully slow code-making.

Shaking off the rough hands of one of the General's body guards, Erin assumed her subtly military stance, and her neutral consultant expression while waiting for his request to be translated. He was demanding more than she was ready for, which meant there would be more trouble for her.

"General, Sir, I have data files available to test the program. The difference is that one computer will send it by Wi-Fi to another, to simulate receiving it from the sensor of the satellite. There is a small amount of setting up to do to enable the video stream to show up on one of the available screens."

"How long?"

"One hour, Sir."

Daringly, Jiwan spoke up. Erin noticed he was adopting a similar attitude and stance to her own.

"General, Sir? I have obtained several small drones, fitted with cameras, that will be the next step in this part of the test."

The General's eyes blazed again, but this time there was a feral smile on his face. "Test with that! No more time wasting."

She shrugged, nodded, and turned to Bisha to have him pass on instructions. She hoped the General was not going to stay watching until it was ready.

One of the other programmers came to ask a question, and it was one she did not want to answer with a feral listener nearby. She breathed in relief when a messenger came in, and the General hurried out.

Bisha murmured, "He wants to find Ali and thinks this drone can help. He will want many, in many places."

The other programmer nodded, he apparently knew some English.

"Well, each of the drones will need a different frequency," Erin pointed out. "If they haven't come that way, do any of you know how to do that?"

They both shook heads.

"Okay, I will need the specs for the drone, to see if it tells us the frequency, and if it can be changed. But we will need to add that figure to the program. If he wants more than one drone operating at a time, I will have to duplicate the camera part of the program and have more than one monitoring station."

Two nods.

Erin went on, "However, drones like Jiwan found, have a very limited range, usually line of sight, and won't be useful beyond 50m from the transmitter. And too much power from the transmitter will burn them out."

She knew she was mixing truth and fiction, but she was trying to think how to thwart the General.

"Bigger ones have bigger ranges?" the other programmer asked.

Erin nodded, suddenly itching to get back to her work station and add a range limiting function to the program. Bisha abruptly said, "I'll get the frequency."

The other asked, "Show me where to change the frequency."

"I will," Erin promised. "When I get the data, I will tell all of you together. I want to quickly check the algorithm to see if any other input needs adjusting."

That did the trick, the man nodded and went back to watch the drone being unboxed, and join those keen for a trial flight using the hand held controller."

That was something Erin had no answer for – if the General went close to a suspect area. In theory, they could use an iPad or tablet to see the video stream. Oh, things were likely to get out of hand...it would all depend on whether the General preferred to spy unobtrusively from the safety of the palace. If so, that would require bigger drones...was that where that other question had come from?

Exactly on the hour, the General was back and immediately focussed on the monitor screen showing the view from the drone zipping above the heads of the people in the room. He wasn't alone, however, and the person with him had all of the locals turning rigid and bowing low. One glance at that figure, dressed expensively in a mixture of western and traditional garb, sent shivers through Erin. She quickly put her head down, pretending to be zoned out, but she glanced up as the personage was looking her way, and talking to Yusif.

The tableau suggested she was the topic of conversation, but it was the wicked red scar, that she glimpsed as the head covering moved to uncover the left cheek, that made her want to arch her back and hiss – like a cat seeing a snake. Very quickly, she finished what she was doing – an unauthorised message to go off through an anonymous webmail service. It was a risk, but if anyone came across it and tried to read it, there would be nothing to see. They would assume it was an accidental thing, not a desperate message written in white on white. She cleared that screen and quickly brought up the camera algorithm.

General Ishkhan was almost at her workstation, "You will bow to his Eminence and answer his questions."

That, Erin decided, was excellent advice in the current situation.

"I see that you are honouring your contract, Miss Mason." The personage, who had to be King Jabir, spoke excellent American, though with a noticeable accent.

Straightening, Erin dared to say, "I take pride in my work, Your Eminence."

"It seems that you do," the suave voice agreed. Erin sensed a 'but...'

"You will be helping to root out the insurgents that threaten the prosperity of Jakhabad."

He was watching her for a reaction, and a voice in her memory reminded her not to react. In truth, all she really knew was that this man had usurped his brother's position, and not everyone agreed with it. Her imagination could fill in the details, but it wouldn't be wise to protest.

"I don't need the details, Your Eminence. My challenge is to perfect what the program needs to do."

"Indeed? Like the ability to defraud a lot of companies?"

Erin allowed a faint smile. "They only thought they lost money," she said, with a faint shoulder shrug. "In fact, I just told their computers I was giving the company a certain amount of money from person A for reason X - then sent it on from their account."

"You are a very unscrupulous woman, Miss Mason. Why should I trust you?"

"As I said, I take pride in my work."

"And I have been told you've been working for the US Government."

"That's a fact, Your Eminence. It is closer to the truth to say they were using me, and I allowed it because it kept me out of prison. This contract, was a very welcome 'get out of town' opportunity."

"How much more is needed to finish your contract?"

Erin, pretending she still thought she was programming for a satellite, answered with apparent candidness. Her earlier admissions were a risk, but some instinct told her she would be safer if they thought they had a hold over her. Besides, they were not lily white innocents themselves.

"Perhaps there will be other contracts for you after this one."

"That will be your decision, Your Eminence."

"Naturally. Now, however, men need to do their work."

Erin hadn't seen him make a gesture, but she was immediately grabbed from behind, by guards she hadn't even sensed behind her. They forced her to move from her workstation, and Erin didn't resist – intending to remain dignified as she was hustled from the room. None of the programmers were daring to look her way.

At first, she assumed she was being taken back to her room, but they didn't go that way. They went along passages unfamiliar to her, down two stairways, into a stone passage, and along it until they came to a partly open door. Inside was dimly lit until one her escorts touched a switch in the passage. They pushed her into the cell.

"What's the meaning of this? Is this how your eminent leader treats people who help him?"

Erin didn't expect a verbal answer, and so was surprised to hear, "His Eminence does not trust women. Particularly American women who try to emulate men. It is immoral."

"You reckon?" Erin snarled to herself once the door had slammed shut. She waited until she felt the men should be well away, before saying softly, "They had better be prepared to grovel, when they find their damn program crashing, or their damned drone drops out of the sky."

After five minutes, the light went off, leaving the only light what little was coming in at the high window. By then though, Erin had seen all there was to see of the 2 metre by 2 metre square cell. A covered bucket in one corner, a mattress on a frame that was attached to one wall, woven floor mats over the stone slab floor, and a stoppered flask that was empty except for a small amount of fusty smelling water. She had smelt enough too, but was gradually becoming inured to the various odours – urine, mildew, and who knew what.

"Bastard!" Erin exploded. "How long does he think he can keep me here? Until his precious, petrified programmers work up the guts to tell him they don't have the answer?"

She paced the room, too full of angry energy to sit down. She was thinking that she should have tried to get free, shouldn't have let them lock her in this dungeon.

"Bastard," she muttered again, before recalling the sensation she had felt when she had first seen the supposed king. For a while, her mind was distracted, wondering what had been done to the former king. Was he dead? Was he in another of the rooms like the one she was in? Could she do anything?

Then she laughed at herself, the mirth displacing the smothering darkness she felt encroaching. Even after having therapy, she still did not like enclosed places. How could she do anything from within a locked cell? Maybe her cousin had ways to get out, but she did not.

The sense of smothering dark, surged again, until a faint cool breeze caressed her face, and she thought, "They think they know it all now, but they don't. That program was written for a satellite, in space, not for a drone being flown around a settled area. It was amazing that it flew the drone so well, but that was inside, above everyone's head. It really wasn't a proper test. A satellite, in a proper orbit, wouldn't be expected to have to dodge trees, houses, pylons..." Erin laughed, adding to herself, "Just a lot of man-made space junk."

She hadn't worked on the guidance module, but it would have a subroutine to react if sensing something on a collision course. Here...well...birds ought to have enough sense to avoid a drone, even a tiny one, and if the operator was paying attention, he could steer it around trees and other things but...if the power was getting low, the image stream might drop out, and the operator might be flying it blind. Then what? She had done some research on-line about drones, some time back, and recalled that some were programmed to go to a safe height and return to the start position if signal was lost. Some were set to land, possibly some had other options, but a satellite...it would have to return to its programmed orbit. The drone, using the satellite programming, would likely return okay if it had a clear flight path and was told to return home. However, if something messed up the radio system, maybe an electrical storm, or being too close to telecommunications towers, or amateur radio transmitters, those might affect it.

The sense of the breeze went away, but Erin had her mind on the difference between directing a satellite and directing a drone. Unconsciously, she went and sat on the cot bed, to consider the differences in programming terms.

The intense crack of thunder, followed by a long rumble, woke her from a trance-like state. She could feel the rumbling through the floor of the cell, following every brilliant flash. She used a subsequent flash to read the time on her watch, and was surprised to discover two hours had passed.

Not the weather for a field test of a baby drone, she smirked, or any bigger one either. She wondered if they had a chance to do it, as in who would control the drone...she could picture the General demanding things of the programmers, and perhaps taking over himself. If so, he would need to practice a bit to get the hang of it.

The storm had passed, and was only faint rumblings in the distance, when the light came on and the door to her cell opened.

Gestures indicated she was to come out, and once in the passage was bracketed by the two guards. This time, they did take her back to her room. Outside, one guard said, "Clean up fast."

Not at all loathe to wash the stench from her skin, and get in clean clothes, she obeyed. Though after changing into more of the servant type outfits, she only rubbed a face washer over her face neck and arms, and as an afterthought, over her short hair. Some of the after shave removed any lingering smell.

That the guard knocked, when giving her a hurry up, put her in a slightly more civil frame of mind. It seemed not all of the elite guards were rude or bullies. They still hustled her back to the computer room, where all eyes were on her, and she sensed a palpable sense of relief that she had returned. None of the other programmers spoke to her, but in the General's presence, they tended to be mute, unless spoken to.

"Well? What happened?" Erin asked, just before the General exploded with fury.

"It crashed!"

"The drone?" Erin asked, pretending she had no ideas of the bugs in the programming. "Were you testing it when the storm went through? That little thing you had in here hasn't a very long range, or battery life."

Actually, Erin realised, the timing of that storm had been amazingly providential.

The General turned to Yusif, whose face was pale.

"It appears that the feed from the drone stopped, then the program crashed."

Erin quizzed him on various aspects, and during that time found out they had been using a much larger drone. They handed her the English version of the information supplied with the drone.

The General, irritated by being ignored, stated, "It must be working by morning!" and strode out.

Everyone in the room, it seemed, breathed easier when he had gone. Erin knew she did, because he had found no flaw in her logic, or any hint the problem was in the program. Now she dared to point out, "If you were flying with it in a wind or storm, it might use up its power more rapidly, and the static in the air might have affected it. Did it fly back?"

"It was found several kilometres away," Yusif told her.

Erin had been glancing through the drone information, and now said, "According to what's here, when the battery charge gets down to a certain point, it is pre-set to return to its start point. That's not something a satellite needs to do. They are programmed to return to its pre-set orbit. If we had been given time to test it fully, we would have discovered the issue under controlled conditions. The program will need to be modified to include aspects from the factory installed program. But the other point, if it was being blown off course, say, it will have to work harder to get back to the start point."

Yusif was nodding, impatiently. "Can you fix it?"

"Depends if I am allowed near it. Does it look damaged?"

"No, but something is wrong. We changed batteries, and it still doesn't work."

"Try resetting the program," Erin suggested. "Other than that, how did it go? I wasn't completely sure how the program would work with a drone. I was giving it quite a bit of thought while I was in time out."

"We could only get it to go 20 kilometres away."

"I didn't see a mention of that in the information, did you?" Yusif shrugged.

"Can I look at it?"

The senior programmer considered for a moment, then nodded.

The distinctive smell of burnt electronics was the first thing Erin noticed. She thought it might have been hit by lightning, but there was no obvious damage to the outside. She still thought that storm was unnatural, and she hid a smile when she felt the faint breeze. Should she tell them what she really thought? That someone, the operator, had pushed the drone too hard, or too fast, and when her distance limiting subroutine had activated, tried to force it to go further.

No! Erin decided smugly. Let the General figure out he was the problem.

"I think the motors have burnt out," she said, stating only the fact. "I can't tell about the wiring, without getting in to look."

Yusif, abruptly decided to hustle Erin away from the drone, back to the computer room. She sensed he was on edge – probably taking the blame for the General's ignorance.

"It would be better to set up the other one," Yusif muttered, not realising he was speaking aloud. "If the General wants it working by tomorrow."

Erin wanted to ask, "What's so important about tomorrow?" except she didn't dare. These people she worked with, knew things they didn't like knowing, and were being made to do things they did not want to do. Yusif, wasn't the only one projecting fear.

Her own position was, perhaps, more precarious than theirs, but now she knew drones were being used, she could program more contingencies.

"If I am allowed to stay," Erin asked tentatively, "I'd like to try the power modelling tests. They won't be suited to a drone, but when you have use of a satellite, you will need it."

She received an absent, 'go ahead' gesture, and went quickly to work. She wanted to be finished there, but still had doubts they would let her go. It occurred to her that she had been locked away during the drone flight so she wouldn't object to what they were doing. She had been told, by the King. Had she given herself away, or had the king other reasons for thinking she would protest?

Well, she would finish, and point out her contract didn't include being distracted by drones, and suggest it was time for her to leave.

Hard on the heels of that thought came one of her 'just knowing' moments. Now was not the time to insist on leaving, or to leave. She could rationalise the feeling, but not the power of the certainty. It felt like she had to stay...and that made the feeling of dread intensify.

That evening, the General was in a particularly foul mood, and even Erin's report that she had finished testing the power modelling algorithm for the satellite, didn't please him. He simply dismissed her for the day, with a terse, "Leave!" A command she was pleased to comply with.

Back in her room, Erin allowed herself a smug smile, but only said aloud, "Of course he doesn't care about the satellite modelling.

I doubt he even realises how important it is not to overload the power system."

While having a shower, Erin continued the thought. The main thing the General wanted was the aerial camera, and if he had always intended to use a drone, he really didn't need the program, he could have used the remote that came with it – except that might mean the operator getting too close to the target. A satellite would cover more area, but unless it was geo-stationary, it would have down time when it couldn't be used. She hoped whoever he was after stayed more than 20 kilometres from the palace.

The servant who brought in her meal, seemed to have caught the same feeling of dread. Was the General's foul mood affecting everyone? The woman had begun to be friendly, and smile when she came in, instead she was grim faced.

"What's the matter?" Erin asked, after getting up to take the tray.

The woman merely shook her head and hurried from the room.

Chapter 17 – Deadly Warning

Next morning, no one came for her, and her door was locked from the outside. Erin began pacing.

"I don't like this. No breakfast, no summons to work..."

There was an intercom to summon a servant, she had never used it, but now she tried, and was half surprised to get an answer.

"What do you require, Sir?" Most of the servants still thought her a male.

"Is there a problem with breakfast today?"

"No, Sir, we will bring it at once."

"Would it be possible to get something for a headache too?" Erin asked, feeling a bad one coming on.

"Yes, Sir."

"Thank you."

When the breakfast arrived – fruit and cereal, not eggs and bacon as usual, she was convinced the servant's minds were elsewhere. She ate quickly, since it was past time she went to work. If she was summoned, they would want her to come immediately.

Eating had eased the incipient headache, but she put the headache powders in her pocket. She patted down the two towels around her middle that helped disguise her body shape. And went back to pacing or staring out of the window.

All that day, and all the next, Erin was confined within that room. Her guesses at why, were becoming more and more fantastical even as the sense of dread was almost palpable. The evening servant was red-eyed, but might as well have been mute, when she came to collect the tea-tray. She hurried out before Erin could try again to find the reason.

Later, at sunset, she heard a fusillade of shots, and looking down from her room into the lit court yard, she saw bodies being carried out to one of the covered trucks. Two had white shirts, and wore suit pants – others were clad in rougher clothes. Her eyes though, went to one - and involuntarily, she drew in a breath, and hoped she was wrong. Yusif! No! She tried to see the other white shirted figure, but she could not see the face.

Panic rose within her. Was the other man one she had been working with too? Would they be coming for her next? What could she do if they did? Where her friends coming to get her out? Surely they were, but would they be too late? Were her friends already in the city? Was this the reason for the murders?

For a time, she didn't realise she was projecting her terrors, then when she did, she took herself firmly in hand. Her great-uncle, had taught her better and she began the mantra of calm, and began to project that.

She would not give in easily, whatever happened.

On the third day, Erin still dressed as she would for work, prepared to show she was a professional. So far, appearing to be a man had helped, but she had no idea who would take over in Yusif's place. His death was a simmering memory, another strike against the General and his master.

It was still early, not quite time to be sent to work, when the door to her room was opened, quietly, furtively. Her usual servant beckoned her to the door.

The woman had a smattering of English, but the reason for her visit was hard to understand. After getting her to slow down, Erin thought she had the story.

"They have a prisoner, downstairs, a woman. An American, Ali's friend? She's really sick."

The woman nodded, and quickly scurried away. Erin's mind was in high gear. "Could it be Wanda? No. She would know if it was. Ali's friend? But who? What? How?"

She knew of Prince Ali. He was believed to be leading the troops loyal to his father, who were fighting King Jabir's troops. Where had this friend of his been? She'd been told all foreigners had been ejected from the country, or killed.

With sudden force, another of her 'just knowing' moments hit her. An inkling of the truth, a reason why she had to come to Jakhabad. Well, she didn't know how she could get to the woman, but irritating the General might do it.

Abruptly, Erin turned and surveyed her room. Found the headache powders and pocketed them, she'd not needed them after all, but they might be of use now. She fetched some face washers from in the bath room and in the bed recess, she quickly stripped the two pillows of their outer coverings. She had just finished adding the pillow cases to the wrapping around her middle, and was returning to the outer room when she sensed her escorts coming. She happened to see the tiny pair of scissors on the floor near the door, and swiped them into her pocket as a loud knock made her jump out of the way. The door had not been relocked, and the heavy fist had shoved it open.

The two guards who entered were not the usual ones, and for a moment, she felt another surge of panic. Would they be suspicious of the unlocked door? They didn't seem to be, for they just gestured peremptorily for her to follow them.

In the computer room, the man she had dubbed 'the Mole' was strutting around and giving the others orders. Erin studied the body language of the others and guessed the new senior programmer was not greatly liked. He turned, saw her and came right up.

"I am in charge here now," he said in accented English and with a nasty sneer. "You do what I say or you treated like disobedient woman."

Erin felt her body tense, as if for flight, but she maintained a neutral façade.

"The men you corrupted have learnt their lesson. You go, show me that this expensive program works. And I won't be tricked by subtle lies and illogic."

"Yes, sir," Erin agreed promptly. "Would you like me to bring over a chair for you?"

"You do that," the Mole agreed, leering at her when she turned away.

Without seeming to do so, Erin looked around. She could see neither Jiwan, nor Bisha, and only counted seven others.

"Gods, I hope they are okay," she thought to herself, but the memory of the other white shirted body tormented her. Was she the reason they died?

Bracing herself for a difficult time, Erin reactivated her work station – it hadn't been shut down at all. Had someone else been using it? Checking on what she had been doing? Well, they wouldn't have found anything, she was smarter than this arrogant bastard.

"You recall all I have shown everyone?" Erin asked without giving any honorific.

"Yes. Everything, and I will know if you contradict yourself."

Liar! Erin thought, recalling he was always ducking out when she was teaching the others.

"Good," Erin said immediately. "Then I will go through the results from the power modelling. This program, being written for a satellite installation, won't produce results for the drones, but if you require it, I can rewrite it to suit them."

"Get to the meat of the report, woman."

"Very well. Each of the sensors on the satellite, requires power to operate. The power comes from solar panels on the satellite that are positioned to catch the sun's energy during the charging period. The energy is captured and stored in batteries." Erin ignored the sneer on the Mole's face, and proceeded as if presenting to a hostile audience. After a time, she knew she had his full attention. He was fascinated in spite of himself. She had also subtly suggested what he would need to explain to the General, guessing that he was out to impress his superiors, and would hog any glory he could.

In his favour, he did seem to understand all she was saying, and would probably not mangle the explanation he passed on. She showed him the list of limiting parameters that needed to be slotted into the main program.

"And are these the same for every satellite?" the Mole demanded.

"There will be a small degree of variation with respect to the figures for each individual sensor, and that will depend on the exact model in use. However, if the actual usage stays within the median values, the power should remain sufficient for general use."

"Well, you are finished then?"

"Unless there is a need for a similar model for the drones. I had not been aware of them."

"It's not right that a woman be so smart," the Mole snarled. "But since you think you are, why do you reckon the drone ditched itself?"

Erin gave a list of possibilities, including being pushed too hard, and caught the slight nod when she mentioned that. And she slipped in the idea that the distance limiting effect was due to the strength of the signal it was receiving during the storm.

"Could be," the man muttered as if to himself, and he seemed unaware he was muttering. "Himself was trying to push it."

Abruptly, he stood up. "You do that thing for the drones as well, woman. Sooner you do, the sooner you can go back home."

"I plan to go somewhere other than that," Erin told him.

"That can be arranged, woman, and I be pleased to help you."

Again, he leered at her, and again she felt a shiver of revulsion. "Get to work."

Erin's mind kept wandering to other things than the program she had offered to write. She had to stay there, not let the Mole find a way to say she wasn't needed. So she forced herself to concentrate, and forget, when it was mealtime, that she was hungry. None of the programmers came near her. It was like she was poison. When the Mole slipped out, she relaxed a little but wondered at the covert glances her way and the half heard mutterings.

Silence fell again when General Ishkhan strode in and went to where Erin was pretending to be oblivious to him. He slammed a hand on the desk to get her attention, and she couldn't help jumping at the unexpected action. The feral smile when she saw her face gave her a feeling of dread. He held up a USB drive.

"Run these programs, and use the data in the spread sheet to fill in the settings."

"Yes, Sir," Erin prudently agreed. "May I ask what it should do?"

"You should get a signal back and when you do, reset the programming on the satellite with yours."

Erin widened her eyes and asked, "Are these codes for old satellites?"

"Not that old." The general began to look like the Cheshire Cat in the classic Alice story. "The American's recent spy satellite. I am told it is up there, watching us. I want to send it back to watch them."

"It will have protections," Erin began.

"You have the key – go and do as I said! For all your talk of storms hitting drones – it was the American devils doing it. Do the same for any other return signal you get."

Erin grabbed the USB as soon as the General released it. She didn't give him another glance as she trotted over to the nearest monitoring screen – the man sitting there standing and moving away. He had been watching the graphical grid on the screen which showed moving objects. Was that how they discovered the watching satellite? Was that program another stolen one? That wasn't good news. And if the codes were for the newest satellite – they could only have got it from Maxwell. She spared a moment to wonder if they had caught him again, before hoping fervently there had been time for Goldman to warn the satellite operators and add extra protection to their firewalls. He wouldn't have a chance to cover all of them, though, and this program might still find an unprotected satellite to hijack.

While she sat watching the screen, waiting for a response that might come, the tension in the room was increasing. Her back prickled, like all eyes were watching her. When her computer beeped, she became aware of the others crowding closer. On screen was a flashing box, "awaiting update".

Her hand moved to the mouse, but another came down over it. She looked up and saw the owner was glancing around.

In terse, almost threatening tones, the man said, "You pretend that didn't happen."

Erin sensed his conviction, buttressed by that of the others. "Four of us are no longer here, because of you. Yusif was a good man. Jiwan, my brother's son."

"I'm sorry. Really. I liked them both and I don't know why you blame me." Erin spoke softly, but at the same time, she had cancelled the connection and said audibly, "Phew! I didn't expect that! The bastards! I just managed to block the counter attack from their firewall."

The prickling of her back eased, and she dared to look at the man. Only the faintest of smiles was her thanks. The other men had eased away, and Erin said to the one who spoken, "There is a very real chance of such an occurrence. I don't know what sort of protection this computer has, but I do know that the protections on the newer satellites were upgraded just before I arrived."

She felt the hand gently squeeze her shoulder, then move away as the sound of the door being shoved open alerted them.

The Mole strode over to Erin and demanded, "Any success yet?"

"No," Erin lied. "But the right satellite has to be in range when the appropriate code is sent out."

The Mole wasn't listening. "You! Take over here." He grabbed the man who had spoken to Erin. "This piece of American filth has another job to do."

Erin likened it to being arrested, for she was pushed out of the room and half dragged along various passages. She really hoped she was not about to be taken to confront Jabir, or that his was a prelude to a firing squad. However, when they reached the downward stairs, everything fell into place.

The American woman, the one who was very sick, must be down in one of the cells. Why had they not had a doctor look at her? What would they do to her if she died?

Erin began to hasten her steps, oblivious to the surprise of the Mole who probably expected resistance. But she was reacting to an urgent need, and the effect of someone's, misery, fear, helplessness and pain.

As soon as the door was unlocked, Erin was drawn to the wall cot. The slender figure there was unmoving, and Erin reached out a hand to feel for a pulse. She felt the heat first.

"She's burning hot!" she exclaimed, just as the Mole was about to leave. "If I am to do anything to help her, I'll need medicine for fever, a cup and several buckets of clean, cold water. Also some clean sheets and blankets, and...Shit! She's been bleeding. I'll need towels too."

The Mole just glared at her, and Erin snapped, "If you left it too long to bring her help, it won't just be me who is in trouble! She wouldn't be here if the King didn't want her alive, and for a very important reason. Has that occurred to you?"

The man snarled, but he understood what she said, and it resonated with him. She was right, and he hated that. He promised nothing, and definitely wouldn't bring the things himself, but Erin hoped he would arrange what she needed. He stalked off in a fury.

Well, Erin thought to herself, there were things she could do, and thanked all the gods that the servant had been brave enough to warn her. Without further thought, she unwrapped the two pillowslips and the towels from around her waist and found the tiny scissors dropped by the servant, on purpose Erin decided. She put the pillowslips aside, and used the tiny scissors to cut the hem of the towels so she could rip them in half and quarters. She rolled each quarter to make narrow pads, and stacked then handy, then set about to remove the saturated and leaking roll of cloth that had been placed to stem the blood initially. It reeked of infection, so it was no wonder that the woman had a temperature. She was a mess, but for now, Erin had little she could use to clean her up. Someone had left a plastic water bottle, and it was still unopened, but unless clean water came, that was all there was to drink. So for the time being, she placed one of her clean makeshift pads in place and considered how to hold it in place – finally deciding to sacrifice the shirt she had on, and without caring, took it off so she only had a man's vest for modesty.

All through the process, the woman didn't wake, just groaned in her sleep.

Erin sat back, and considered using the bottle of water to dampen the face washers in her pocket. Though the need was negated when she hear a loud, worried voice exhorting someone to hurry. The door opened, and as she had guessed, the Mole hadn't returned, but must have put the fear of hell into the guard who came with the servants. Everything she had asked for and more, came in – carried by three servants. One was the one she knew. In addition to her requests, there were six more water bottles, a fresh mattress, and more headache powders, but her servant whispered, "These for fever, kill germs."

She wanted to hug the woman, but already they had deposited their loads and were being hustled out, and Erin needed to move things so she could find them quickly if, more likely when, the light went out.

With the extra supplies, Erin could do more, and she began at once – using one face washer as a cool compress, and the other to start cleaning the woman to remove oozing and dried blood. As she worked, she considered the empathic sensations she was receiving, and having trouble shutting out. The pain, the ache, were like they were in her own body. They were so very familiar.

To be sure, Erin crouched beside the woman, and touched her gently. Her state appalled her – the heat was coming off her like a furnace was emitting it. She took the cleanest face washer and refreshed it in cool water, and went back to sponging the woman's skin and letting it cool as the water evaporated.   Then, abruptly, she thought of another idea, and ripped off her shoes and socks.

Thinking to a past time, when this had worked for her, Erin thought of the odd breeze she had felt down in the dungeon level. She thought of the woman, and the need to get her temperature down, to kill any infection. Until the woman was conscious, she couldn't give her the medicine to help. Then she held the woman's hand, and began to chant a healing mantra in a very low voice. She had to do all she could, now, before someone decided to drag her away.

After a time, the light went off, leaving them in darkness.

Erin alternated between the chant and sponging the woman down, and slowly began to sense consciousness returning, even before the groan, and the limp hand becoming stiff. She moved to dip the washer in water again.

The woman groaned and tried to sit up. Erin shared the pain that knifed through her.

"Don't try to get up," Erin said, gently pushing her down and replacing the cool cloth on her forehead. Then she lifted the woman's wrist to check her pulse. She felt the woman's free hand feeling hers.

"Anilla?"

Erin was startled, and took a moment to realise that was a name. "No, sorry. I'm Erin."

End of Part 2

The Serpent's Shadow

Book 3 – Deposing a Dictator

The Serpent's Shadow

Book 3 – Deposing a Dictator

Chapter 1 – Itching to Act

"Erin has been gone over a week, Jim. Is there anything we can do?" Wanda demanded as soon as the apartment door was closed behind him.

"What brought this on?" David asked, having come in first and was setting his laptop case down on a table.

"I woke early this morning, in a right panic – nothing I could figure – and I am sure it had to have come from Erin. You know – it was like it used to be."

"Did you get any other impressions?" David asked. He'd seen his wife in this mood when her sister had been in trouble. Often, she received more than just the emotion.

Wanda considered that question, her eidetic memory recalling the dream as if she had just woken. "An image of bodies being taken away in a truck. She was looking down at the scene. I think she felt she knew who they were."

Jim asked, "Have you received any recent reports from your group?"

Wanda glanced at David. He was the liaison with the group of computer geeks who were monitoring events in a distant Arabic country.

"Not for several days," David admitted.

"Perhaps you should follow up with them and see if any of their foreign contacts have heard about a computer expert. As yet, we have no solid proof that Erin is in that country."

"She is there, Jim," Wanda insisted. "I know you think so too. Can't we just go in and get her?"

"No!"

Wanda was silenced for a moment. His tone was firmer than she had even heard him use.

"There is more going on than you realise," Jim said, moderating his tone. "And I don't have any leeway to act in this instance. However, let me assure you that your cousin's reputation as a hacker is of major concern to those who do not realise she was working for Goldman in a covert capacity. Also, while there is a powerful push to have her hauled back, it is likely that those who have her have an equally powerful desire to use her skills. What do you think she will be doing?"

"She won't do anything that will help them act against the US," Wanda stated with certainty.

"I agree," Jim told her. "She is also resourceful and in a perfect position to discover what is happening there."

"But how will she contact us?" Wanda asked. "And all I have sensed from her is that moment of panic. She could be dead now for all I know."

"I doubt it," David disagreed. "You would know if she was." He was booting up his lap-top. "Besides, like Jim said, they need her. Otherwise they wouldn't have gone to all the trouble they did."

"Okay, you're right on all counts."

"So why don't you get together with your sister and Tanya, and see if you can pick up more?" David proposed. "I mean, you aren't wonder woman. Erin is half way around the world."

"They won't be free until this evening," Wanda admitted, as she saw his faint grin.

"Well, I don't believe that we need to panic," Jim said calmly. "However, in the interests of being prepared, and all information is useful, why don't you go and talk to Princess Famira? Ask about the layout of the palace, and any secret ways she might know of. Ask if she has heard anything from her country."

"What if that weak-chinned consort of hers is around?"

David suggested, "Give me a bit of time to call the Group and then I will come too. I know how to distract Mohan."

"Excellent!" Jim commended. "I have to get back for a meeting. Let me know what you find out."

He rose and let himself out.

As David finished his call, Wanda asked, "What do you think,

Dav? Will they get him to go in?"

"I can't say," David admitted. "I do know that the Commander's in Chief are concerned, knowing how provocative it would be if America interfered in events over there."

Wanda growled in frustration.

"Let's wait and see what we learn, okay? It maybe that the powers are waiting for confirmation of certain things. They do have other agents besides our group, and no one has reported seeing Erin."

"They haven't mentioned anything about Janna either. Her baby must be due by now."

"You know that won't shift any minds," David reminded her.

"Yeah, yeah. She made the choice to return there and knew the risks," Wanda admitted. "But what about her kid? Ali's child?"

David just shrugged in shared helplessness. "Let's go see what we can get out of Famira and Mohan."

Chapter 2 – Rising Stakes

Jim still hadn't returned from his meeting when Wanda and David returned to the apartment. They had just settled for coffee when David's message tone beeped. He fetched it from his pocket and read the message. Then he made a call.

When he ended it, he told Wanda, "The FBI picked up a Mexican guy. He's known to be a whiz at disguises, and he admitted to being paid to make a woman look like a man – the one on the CCTV that was taken out to the plane."

"But that plane was told to come back," Wanda argued. "The prisoner on it was definitely a male."

"So, they pulled a swap somehow," David shrugged.

"What about that later flight you mentioned? The charter?"

"Let me open up the airport security file," David suggested, as he was opening his laptop.

He brought up the date on the flight, Florida to Spain and points beyond. Not counting the pilot, co-pilot, and two stewards, the information gave the details for ten passengers. Then, he opened up the site where he had stored relevant security footage for that day. They both studied it as it played through.

"That one! Not in a suit," Wanda pointed. "Did you get a face on look at him?"

"No, this is all I have. As you can see, all the others keep around him. Though, I think I did get a glimpse when I was headed down to meet the other plane. It had to be a man – looked college aged, and had the look of needing to shave."

"Anyone seeing that would assume male, alright. But now we know about that Mexican."

They were still watching the passengers in that group boarding, and when the last had entered the passage, Wanda said, "Go back to where they are still huddled, and count them. See if you agree with me."

"Eleven," David said Wanda nodded.

"None of those looked like pilots or stewards," she confirmed.

"Okay," David agreed, reaching for his phone again. This time he hit the speed dial for "The Group".

"Hey bro," he said, using the usual greeting to the person who answered. "Something else to add to what I said before. Any mention of an effeminate male in the relevant places?"

The voice on the other end, said, "You're joking, bro. You know what the guy would do to that sort, don't you?"

"I think so, so if there is one, it's significant," David pointed out.

"Fine, we'll add that," the voice promised. "Haven't much else yet. The capital there rocked a few times – our friends managed some useful action. Nip in, duck out."

"That is promising. Call me if you get more."

Wanda had heard the call, and only asked, "When is the next scheduled contact?" She knew it wasn't regular, and tied to some convoluted randomising.

David considered. "This afternoon, our time."

With a grunt of frustration, Wanda asked, "Can you bring up the plans for the Jakhabad Royal palace? I will try to work out where the way out is that Famira went through."

Wanda put a plate of pasta beside David, who gave her a quick glance before continuing to scribble notes. Through headphones, he was listening to a report from the Group, as well as recording the report.

He finally took off the headphones and put down the pen. He took a few mouthfuls of the pasta before saying, "Things are heating up over there. There is a report of a massive explosion, somewhere just out of the city. Most people think it was weapons, but no one can be sure which side controlled it. Not so nice is the word that our target is having a cull. Eliminations, was what they said – supposedly traitors and informers. Confirmation that two had been programmers. Both were older men, known to have been loyal to the deposed King."

Wanda swore. "We have to get Erin out."

"Well, on that," David said after another hasty mouthful, "there were mentions of an American guest, and an American woman prisoner. That came from two different sources. However, the 'guest' was dragged down to the dungeons at least twice. The first time was when they were doing some kind of testing. As for what, one source mentioned seeing a large drone flying near the palace."

"Drones?" Wanda said thoughtfully. "Not sure if that fits with what Erin was working on, but one way to look for your enemy or his troops."

"It may be. I put it to Goldman to tell me more about that Skywatcher reference. That is related to what he had Erin working on. It is still a bit far-fetched that our target can get control of a satellite, in my opinion. However, according to Goldman, a part of the overall program could be modified to control a drone from a greater distance."

"Which a satellite could also do, but not 24/7," Wanda nodded, understanding. "I agree with you, they want to find the loyalists. Did you have the Group pass a warning?"

"I did, as it happens. Anyway, if the American guest was taken down to the dungeons, it was probably so she wouldn't protest or try to sabotage the test."

"I reckon that confirms Erin is there," Wanda decided. "That woman prisoner has to be Janna."

"Likely," was David's answer. "The Group is trying to contact their palace source – assuming he is still alive. Anyway, I need to pass this on."

"Eat first!" Wanda ordered.

"What about you?"

"I'll be eating when Elisabeth and Tanya get here."

Wanda saw the change in David's expression and waited for him to finish the call. He didn't keep her guessing.

"No word about Erin," he said quickly. "But as they hustled her to the palace, it isn't surprising. However, the word is that Janna was taken prisoner by Jabir's elite troops."

"What about the baby?"

"Only rumours," David summarised, as he reached for his jacket.

"What do they say?"

"That she had a girl, but it was still born."

"Poor Janna."

David agreed, but he had a lot more that he needed to tell Jim.

He gave Wanda a wave before leaving.

"Who is Janna?" Elisabeth asked.

"She is married to Ali, the heir to Jakhabad. His Uncle, Jabir, has seized control of the country." Wanda explained. That was all they needed to know. "Where are you off to, Dav,"she sent mentally. He was used to her mind in his and just thought, like to himself, "I'll fill you in later. This is urgent stuff."

"Oh," Elisabeth exclaimed softly. She was oblivious to the communication between her sister and brother in law.

"They won't send anyone to help her," Tanya said bluntly. "She is not important, like my father was."

That she had unwittingly reiterated the official position, didn't help any of them. Tanya, sensing that went on, "But Erin is different. They won't want her helping those terrorists – surely. Has Jim heard anything?"

"Nothing he is sharing," Wanda admitted. "The whole situation is dicey. Personally, I had hoped Ali would have freed his father by now. Instead, his Uncle has Janna a hostage – probably to use her to draw him out."

"Then I think she would be in the palace," Elisabeth considered. "Erin probably is too."

"That could be a good thing," Tanya suggested.

"It should have been me!" Wanda argued. "She shouldn't even be in this."

"You can be so dense at times," Elisabeth exploded. An unusual enough occasion to startle her. "You are not Erin's keeper! She has had all that marine training, and she is more like you that either of us." She indicated herself and Tanya. "Plus, I think there is more at work here than we've considered. The reason why those traitors kept getting Erin."

"Incompetence of our authorities?" Wanda suggested.

"No, silly! I mean the aura!" Before her sister could go off again, she said, "You wanted to help Janna, right?"

Wanda, startled that Elisabeth had thought of that, nodded.

"Well, how much do you know about caring for just post-partum mothers?"

"Enough!"

"Text book learning!" Elisabeth snorted. "With Vera always

having babies, I reckon I know more about that than you do."

"What's your point?"

"Erin is the only one of us that has actually had a baby herself!"

Most of Wanda's irritation vanished, but she still felt she was meant to be doing something. Surely they would have to go and get Erin out.

"You are right, Liz. I did ask that Janna, Ali and their baby would be kept safe. I hope Goldman can hurry up and convince the higher ups..."

"I bet he won't like the idea that all the stuff ups were caused by some invisible power," Tanya laughed. She went on, "Yes, but if they do agree, I bet they will get Jim involved. Then, you will get your chance."

Wanda fiercely wished just that – so she could help Erin and Janna, and to get rid of the Serpent, Jabir. Almost at once, an impossible breeze began to caress her face.

"Come on then," Wanda decided, "let's go outside and see if we can do anything."

Chapter 3 – Clandestine Orders

Jim Phillips grabbed his phone as soon as he heard the beep tone. He read the message and immediately felt the familiar adrenalin surge of excitement. The text was just a place, a time, a pass phrase and a check phrase. The usual anonymous arrangement that distanced the message from the sender.

After all, who would think a casually dressed man, in no obvious hurry, who stopped to chat to an attractive woman who was picnicking alone in a park, no where near the White House, would be embarking on a world changing mission.

All the same, Jim never took chances. Before approaching his contact, he carefully looked around, checking for observers or potential eaves droppers. As he strolled closer, he already had the pass phrase inserted in his casual chatter.

The woman, startled for a moment, looked up and laughed. She stood up, leaving a tatty looking lunch box on the ground. She pointed to a rotunda, then walked off – her job done. Jim watched her for a moment, then glanced down as if just seeing the box, looked at the woman, and stooped to pick it up. He headed in the same direction, towards the rotunda, but stopped at an empty seat, a little off the path.

The park wasn't deserted, but at that time of day, no one would think it odd that he was watching something on a 5 inch tablet. Jim, with earbuds in, activated the screen. The familiar voice, accompanied a series of photos.

"Good afternoon, Jim. Jakhabad is a small Kingdom within the Arab States. The hereditary ruler, King Rakhal Fazir, was removed from leadership, six months ago by his half-brother, Prince Jabir. During the military coup, led by General Ishkhan, Jabir had his brother arrested for treason. He is currently imprisoned within the palace. While the loyalist forces, led by Prince Ali Fazir, Rakhal's son, are fighting to regain control, Prince Jabir is working to consolidate his position. He has brought in a computer expert and has stolen technology aimed at creating a guided missile network. It is believed he intends to hijack a satellite to use to locate his intended targets. This will threaten not only his neighbours but any country in the world.

Prince Jabir is also the leader of the terrorist group The Cobra Sect, and this group has been responsible for many acts of terrorism the world over. It is said all were the direct command of Prince Jabir.

Your mission, Jim, should you choose to accept it, is to discredit Prince Jabir, so that the sect members no longer follow him, and to enable the loyalist troops to retake the palace and prevent the completion of the computer weapons system. As usual, should any of your IM force be killed or captured, the Secretary will disavow any knowledge of your actions. Good luck, Jim."

Jim slipped an envelope of photos and other data on a USB, into the pocket of his jacket as a minor explosion caused the tablet's LCD screen to turn black. He returned it to the lunch box and disposed of the box in the nearest waste bin.

As he walked back to his car, he was already adding detail to plans he had begun making over a week ago. Some parts of those plans could be implemented immediately, and be put in action while he was briefing his team. He began the first of a series of calls, ending with one to two of his team who were staying locally. Wanda and David would guess immediately what was up when he told them to expect visitors.

Wanda handed David the phone as soon as Jim said to expect guests. Now her husband was writing furiously, and didn't stop until the call ended. She glanced at the list of numbers and notes and wrinkled her nose.

"What can I do?" She knew how Jim worked and that David was like his personal assistant. She wasn't so interested in the admin side of things, until the stuff was needed – like now. The numbers were related to aspects of an upcoming mission – information that may be needed.

"That plan of the palace – bring that up for a start," David requested. "And set up your laptop to send to the display screen."

They both worked quickly and efficiently, so that when Jim returned, the pieces were ready. David had also spent a lot of time on line, or the phone, organising a collection of equipment and supplies for them to collect.

Jim didn't tell them the details of the actual mission, but Wanda knew as soon as he returned that they were to be going to where she believed her cousin was. The details would come when the team assembled. That would be by early the following day. Before then, he went over everything David had done, caught up with the latest from David's informants, and asked Wanda, "Did you and your relatives get anything else from Erin?"

She'd had to admit, "No."

"We will take that as a good thing," Jim told her. "And when we get close, you should be able to contact her."

Wanda nodded.

"Good. Now, both of you get some sleep. We will be moving out as soon as I finish briefing everyone."

The group would consist of six active members, including Jim and Wanda, but David would be working in the background passing on intelligence from various sources. Wanda waited to have her role explained, but she knew Jim would make use of her well-honed, otherwise illegal, skills.

"Nicholas, you will be going in as a doctor – a plastic surgeon. King Jabir recently received a very nasty face wound during an attack aimed at killing him. Word has it that he has not ventured out of the palace since then. He is seldom seen within the palace either," Jim explained. "The loyalists have started rumours that he is dead and the General is in control. He is going to have to appear in public soon to retain his hold on the soldiers. He is known to be very vain, and will not want to appear scarred."

Nicholas glanced through the notes he had been given. "That scar would be very hard to hide with make-up, but I can make a cast of his face."

Jim nodded. "Casey, you will be working as his nurse and assistant."

"So, I am to be a protégé of Albert Moro," he confirmed, glancing through some magazine clippings.

"Yes, and Doctor Moro is primed to give you a personal reference. Casey, you will need to keep a low profile. King Jabir dislikes Westerners, and has a low opinion of women in general. But you have another important task. We need you to talk to these two women."

Jim put up images of Erin Mason and Janna Dupont. He explained who each of the women were. "They don't know we are coming to help them, so you must warn them to be ready."

Casey nodded, and heard Wanda murmur, "Erin, the treasonous programmer, is my cousin." That settled the lingering doubts in Casey's mind that she could be trusted.

"Grant, you'll be going in as a security expert. King Jabir has become paranoid about his security since the attack that damaged his face. You will be installing security devices all through the palace and linking it to a computer monitoring set up. Have you been over the equipment?"

"Yes, Jim. Rather unusual devices. The sound and movement sensors will also emit sound, and likewise the cameras will record pictures as well as projecting holograms.

"What will I be doing?" the final team member asked. Max was a blond haired, rugged Australian. A total contrast to the dark skinned Grant and the dark haired, English complexioned Nicholas.

Jim grinned. "You will be walking around the streets at the perimeter of the palace, in the guise of a Temple priest. You came from a distant city, drawn by the sense of demons here. You will be preaching to be aware of demons and demon possession. You will have had a vision that someone at the palace has been possessed and that an exorcism must be undertaken."

Max grinned as Jim went on, "You will have an assistant," he nodded at Wanda, who he had only just met. "We have worked together a number of times and she has some very useful and unique talents."

"Like I am a damn good thief," Wanda interrupted, knowing Jim wouldn't reveal her classified talents.

"While I am playing your sight challenged acolyte and wandering around the outside of the palace, I will be looking for ways in, security vulnerabilities, and a couple of secret ways Princess Famira knew of. Famira wanted to help us because Janna Dupont is her friend."

Jim added an extra warning, "Our mission does not include rescuing Janna Dupont, however, she is being held in the palace, and she is secretly wedded to Prince Ali. When Ali returned to his country, Janna followed – already pregnant with his child. She should have been safe with the loyalists, but King Jabir's troops found her just after her child was born. I doubt she has had medical attention since then. Ali's troops would give their lives for her if they knew. So, she is also an important part of this. "

"What of her child?" Casey asked, concerned for the mother and child.

"We haven't had more than rumours," Wanda admitted. "And they suggest she had a still born girl. I am hoping otherwise. My gut says that rumour was deliberate because if it became known to the wrong people that she had given Ali an heir, well, you can guess the reaction."

Jim told his group, "We intend to get Janna out, and have Wanda impersonate her. The overall plan is to convince everyone that King Jabir is demon possessed so even his fanatic followers will leave him."

"He has instigated enough acts of terror to be a demon," Wanda said. "His followers of the Cobra Sect are all like-minded. Following him means being well paid in this life. Following a demon, only promises things in the next."

Max gave a low chuckle. "I wouldn't want those kinds of rewards."

Jim went on briskly, "Nicholas, Jabir's General will meet you in Istanbul tomorrow. You will need your references, and all the equipment you will need is waiting for you there. David has the details."

Nicholas glanced at the so far silent attendee.

"Max, you Wanda and I will cross the border into Jakhabad from a neighbouring country. There will be a guide there to take us to Prince Ali's camp, and then onto the palace. We need to brief the prince."

"How will we know the guide is reliable?" Max asked.

"Wanda knows him."

"What will you be, Jim?" Casey asked.

"The loyalist forces are slowly pushing Jabir's army back towards the capital. They have had strategic successes, in blowing up two of his armouries – one of which had stolen missiles stored within. I will be posing as a South American arms dealer, since Jabir will be wanting to replace what was lost."

After summing up the final details of his plan, his team left for Jakhabad.

Chapter 4 – Opening Gambit

Grant Collins flew into Jakhabad in a privately chartered Lear jet and was met at the airport by an impressive array of military personnel. That they were there for security purposes, not just to greet him, was not mentioned. When he descended from the jet, a man dressed in a highly decorated uniform stepped forward.

"Mr Collins, I am Colonel Kazim. His Eminence King Jabir, has asked me to meet you. May I see your identification and your letter of contract, please?"

Grant withdrew his passport and the requested letter, and kept an expression of superior distain on his face. While the Colonel examined the documents, he made no secret of looking around the airport – what he could see from out the back of the terminal.

"All is in order, Sir. If you will come with me, Mr Collins."

"Certainly, Colonel. However, my equipment is still on board. I trust no one will interfere with it while I am away? All pieces are delicate and I am sure His Eminence will not be impressed by delays due to careless handling. My pilot will be staying with the plane and will keep in touch with me."

Grant flipped open a small communicator, and gave the pilot instructions, pausing to ask, "Colonel, I will need to refuel before leaving. May I have my pilot attend to that now? Good. Will you be needing payment in local currency for that?"

"No, No, Mr Collins. We will take care of that for you. I will have one of the airport staff assist your pilot."

"Thank you, Colonel." Grant finished his call to the pilot, which was to subtly deter anyone from trying to misappropriate it. The pilot was no ordinary one, but a highly trained soldier, well able to deal with any trouble.

Only two of the guards followed Grant and the Colonel to the latter's limo. And once they were underway, followed in a second vehicle – an ordinary SUV.

Grant refrained from talking, except to give terse answers to the Colonel's unsubtle questions. In turning to answer one such question, he glimpsed a tiny cobra on a chain around the man's neck. Even with this proof of allegiance to the usurper King, Grant didn't open up. His instructions from his client included keeping the reason for his visit strictly private. The questions might be a test.

The ride was smooth, and half an hour later, the car arrived outside the palace. Grant was asked to wait with the car while the Colonel took his papers inside. It was a further half hour before Grant was escorted into the presence of His Eminence King Jabir. His escorts bowed low to their leader, but Grant, as an outsider, gave only a cursory bow with head and shoulders. King Jabir scrutinised the new arrival from deep within the folds of his traditional head gear.

"You have studied our requirements, Mr Collins."

"Yes, Your Eminence, and I have been able to source everything discreetly and at an acceptable price."

"How quickly can the work be done?"

"I will require six days to install all the units, three to install the ones marked as priority. Then probably three days to hook everything up to your security computer. If you are able to provide local skilled workers, that time can be shortened. However, I am not fluent in your language, and any assistant would need to understand me."

Jabir's head nodded slightly. "I do not wish everyone to know the security arrangements, naturally. What skills would be required?"

"A knowledge of electronics and computers, and deft hands for the installations."

A faint shake of the folds of cloth was the only sign of annoyance. "There may be someone. When can you start?"

"As soon as I can bring everything from the plane. I will need a car that can carry all the boxes without jolting them. And if you can spare someone to direct me to the places where you would like me to begin..."

"Colonel," Jabir glanced at the uniformed man, "Place yourself at the disposal of Mr Collin's."

It was a tacit dismissal, the Colonel bowed, Grant repeated his earlier gesture, and followed the Colonel from the room. Then, with commendable efficiency, two well-built lower ranking officers were dispatched to collect the boxes - Grant giving them a signed authority, and warning the pilot they were coming – and a small suite was arranged for him to use for storing the devices and sleeping. Grant declined the offer of food and rest, in favour of beginning immediately.

If the Colonel resented being the guide for the American, he hid it well. For the King had trusted him with the task. He took Grant on a tour of the palace closest to the King's suite, where the priority locations on his job list were located, and enabled him to order the installations efficiently. At each site, he waited patiently as Grant took measurements of distances, angle and made other arcane notes.

In each of the places, Grant kept his interest business like. He showed no particular interest in the décor, except where it would affect his work. When he came into the computer room, his outward single-mindedness continued. Even so, everywhere he went he was memorising the layout, and his quick sketches were less for the installations that for information. In that room, he was hoping to see Erin Mason, but the only workers he could see were Arab men.

Later, when his equipment and the devices had arrived and he was bringing everything to his suite, he did notice a slender male figure, being dragged along a passage by a weasel faced man. As if sensing his presence, the younger figure glanced his way. It was enough for Grant to recognise, Erin Mason's current appearance.

Chapter 5 – The Serpent's Weakness

General Ishkhan recognised the man he was to meet by the sight of his white clad companion. He assumed she was the nurse, and his interest went no further. The two were drinking tea together in the small café near the transit lounge of Istanbul Airport. He took his time studying the man, comparing him to the details that had been sent to him.

Inwardly, he scorned English men, who insisted on wearing typical English suits, in spite of being unsuited to the climate, and unworthy of an audience with a king. His hat was beside him at the table –so comical looking.

Ishkhan went to the courtesy desk and had the doctor paged. He waited near the telephones. He watched the doctor rise, and look around for the phones. He left the woman to mind his hat. As soon as the doctor reached the phones, he drew nearer, asking the question, "Dr Farnsworth?" just as the man answered the page. It amused him to see the slight hesitation as the man was torn between two conversations.

"Excuse me, Doctor. It was I who had you paged."

Nicholas spoke tersely to the operator, and hung up. "Er, and you would be?" he said in an English accent.

"I am to be your escort to Jakhabad. I am General Ishkhan, advisor to His Eminence King Jabir."

"Oh yes. Thank you for meeting me. We will be leaving now to go to my patient?"

"Yes. I have a plane waiting. You have some equipment, I believe."

"I am to understand it will be in the custom's shed, as I am in-transit. If you would be so kind as to notify them of the details of my next flight, they will transfer everything there. I have told them to be careful with everything."

The General's expression hardened as he decided the English could be as arrogant as Americans. However, he smiled politely, as he returned with the doctor to the table to collect the nurse, and to go on to the plane, after giving one of his body guards instructions for the customs people.

The large trolley stacked with sealed boxes was unexpected.

"You have a lot of equipment, doctor."

"Yes, my dear General," Nicholas agreed. "I ensured I was prepared with all I would need, as I understand the procedure was not going to be done in a hospital. It means I have needed to bring a great deal of sterile supplies."

Since he had set the conditions himself, the General couldn't argue. He didn't dare give the eminent physician a reason to refuse to go on. He simply directed his two bodyguards to oversee the stacking of the boxes in the plane.

On the arrival at the palace in Jakhabad, the General whisked doctor and nurse inside. He had driven them from the airport in a limousine, with the equipment following in a large van.

Nicholas insisted on being shown the room chosen for the operation. It was a big room, with places for watchers to observe all activities. He left the General standing near the door and stalked around, finally returning with a frown on his face.

"A hospital would be much better," he began, but seeing the General drawing breath to speak, added quickly, "However, since this is what is available, it will need a thorough scrubbing with strong antiseptic soap. All those drapes and carpets will need to be removed..." He continued to list more things that should be done.

"I will see to it immediately," the General promised. "Was there anything else?"

"If you can have your people bring all the boxes up – carefully – and have them stacked by the door. My nurse can help oversee the cleaning. When can I see my patient?"

"His Eminence is a very busy man. I have sent word of your arrival and as soon as he can make time on his schedule, he will send for you. He is eager for this procedure."

Nicholas nodded. "I will start preparing this room. I will need to be assured that when I have deemed it suitably sterile, that no one other than myself and my nurse and the patient go in. Can that be arranged?"

"Certainly, although it is protocol that His Eminence has two of his Elite Guards with him at all times."

Nicholas frowned. "It is most irregular to have non-medical persons attend an operation. No, General, you don't need to insist. I will permit two only, and they must scrub up and dress as I will. I have no wish for His Eminence to pick up an infection during the procedure."

"You are most thorough, Doctor. I will see to all that you need." He beckoned to the two lower ranked soldiers that had followed him and issued instructions. One went off and returned with the servants and the cleaning equipment.

Over the next hour, an observer would only have seen busy activity. Unneeded furniture was removed, the tapestry hangings taken down, and the luxurious carpets rolled up and removed to reveal the polished wood floor. Then, Nicholas had the servants find a long narrow table that would be suitable for an operating table, and a flattish mattress that could be cut down to size, and re-covered.

As sections passed his inspection for clean, Nicholas assembled frames to drape sterile sheets over, to hide the walls. He let the cleaning women leave, and put covers on his shoes before going to the door. He guessed there would already be a guard, and was right. He asked the man to request a dozen towels, as his attention was drawn to a woman being dragged past, moaning, her face puffy and grazed.

Even a layman could see she was in a bad way.

"Stop! Where are you taking that woman?" Nicholas demanded.

The soldiers didn't take any notice, they didn't speak English or take orders from foreigners.

General Ishkhan, returning to check on progress, had Nicholas turn on him.

"That woman needs a doctor!"

"Such trash does not need a doctor. That creature is a criminal and a traitor against the crown."

Nicholas opened his mouth to protest, but was forestalled. "His eminence will see you now."

Casey, hearing Nicholas's raised voice, had come out of the room.

"Is there any reason why I can't do anything for her?" she asked, looking to Nicholas, not the General.

"Go if you wish," the General said off-handedly. "The doctor will not need you for a time." He gestured for one of the guards to follow her.

Casey walked quickly in the direction the soldiers had gone with the woman. She knew to turn right at the end of the passage, but not after that, until she heard raised voices.

"I am going to help Fatima, dammit." Then, "Of course he knows! She is no use to his Eminence if she is dead! Why else did they bring her here, and not just have her killed."

Casey heard the sound of fist hitting flesh, and hurried. The sound of her hurrying steps alerted the unpleasant little man that had a younger looking one in a tight grip.

"And you had better hope I don't mention this to anyone," the loud voice threatened. "I am entitled to a break, three actually, and today I have worked since 5am. I am catching up now."

The younger figure, with a distinctly feminine voice, yanked herself free.

"Well, if you won't be in your rooms, I will tell the kitchen you do not need lunch today."

"Is that the best you can do?"

"I will tell the General if you are not back in twenty minutes," the older man threatened.

"I am due 30 minutes," the other countered, not backing down.

"Well I think the General has other things on his mind today."

"Anyway, you needn't worry. I work faster after a break."

Casey came closer, and the short man favoured her with an ugly leer, before stalking off. Casey heard, "More trash." As he went past her.

Casey ignored him, and ran to help the apparent young man lift the woman who had slumped to the floor.

The guard who had followed Casey made no move to help, and simply stood stoically.

"Let me help," Casey offered.

The young man looked up and Casey beheld the face of Erin Mason.

"Are you're a nurse?" Erin asked.

Casey nodded, this was no place to claim otherwise.

"Good. You can help me support her weight."

With the guard watching, Erin told Casey how to position herself to best effect. Casey was amazed, but made no comment and asked no questions.

Erin explained, "We are headed downstairs to the deluxe dungeon apartments." Her sarcasm was unmistakable. Indeed, the stairs appeared on cue, and Casey came to realise the full benefit of the unusual hold. They were holding the woman upright and supporting all her weight.

When the cell door was firmly shut, Erin led the way to the wall cot and eased the woman down. During that process, Erin asked, in a low voice, "Who are you, really?"

"A friend of your friend, Jim," Casey told her. "I am not really a nurse, but I have done first aid."

"Then help me. She's bleeding again. His royal foulness doesn't care if she has no chance to heal."

Erin began to move the woman's clothes, and drew out a blood soaked roll of towel. Casey exclaimed softly in dismay.

"Yeah, real gentlemen aren't they. Around here, if you can't walk, you get dragged. I'd say that's how she was taken upstairs. I'll wash the grazes, and if she rouses enough, I will give her some antibiotics and something for pain."

"They let you help her?"

"Sometimes. When they think she is too ill to torment. At least the fever she had when she arrived has gone down."

Casey was surprised when Erin drew out some towels from under her shirt, rolled them up, and put them in place somewhere under the woman's skirts. The woman moaned softly.

"Relax, Fatima. They have finished with you for the day. I will try to do what I did before, okay?"

With Erin sitting on the edge of the cot, holding her hands so they cupped the woman's face, Casey watched and wondered at the sudden look of concentration on Erin's face. She stayed quiet and watched.

After five minutes, the moaning had stopped, and the woman

seemed to be sleeping.

Erin's face eased of the strain as she stood up. "So, Jim is here," she remarked softly. "Sorry. In spite of how I look, I'm Erin Mason."

"I know. I recognised you from a photo. I'm Casey. I am glad I was in a position to see you. Jim will be here tomorrow. He needs you to be ready to help. We will tell you what to do."

"Jim knows I will be in that, but you tell him that I won't leave without Fatima."

"That's not her name."

"I know it's not, but it is what she told them it was, even though his foulness, damn him, knows it too. Anyway, Fatima knows I won't hurt her, but I'm not sure she completely trusts me."

"We do plan to get you both out, but will your friend be well enough?"

"I will do what I can," Erin promised.

"Like what you just did? Whatever it was you did?"

"That and more if I can. Is my cousin around too?"

"What? Oh, yes, she'll be around."

Erin chuckled. "So, where did you just spring from?"

"Nicholas, Dr Farnsworth for now, will be repairing the King's face."

"I see. Nasty wound he got. No, don't tell me any more. The General would love an excuse to question me – we are not exactly friends. So if the question arises, I am a right arrogant, typical American and I didn't trust you to help."

"Right!" Casey understood immediately. They should not appear to be friendly.

"You should go back," Erin suggested. "I can do what's needed here. Just ask the guard to show you the way. I'll stay here until that little weasel sends someone for me. I always guessed he was a snitch, and now he's admitted it."

"Won't you get in trouble?"

"Nothing major. They need me. For now, they only dare to threaten. Anyway, I want to see if Fatima can take the medicine before I go."

Casey did as suggested, calling the guard outside and politely asking help. Erin noted that she had a knack for getting the man to co-operate.

Chapter 6 – The Prince's Permission

Jim Phillips, Wanda Martin and Max Hart crossed the border into Jakhabad at a prearranged security blind spot. They were met by John King, a former FBI expert on terrorism, who had arrived there a month before. He took them in an army truck to where Prince Ali currently had his base. It was approximately an hour's drive in from the border. They were quickly ushered into his presence.

"Your Highness," John announced. "These are the people who have come to help you."

His eyes lit up when Wanda, outwardly dressed as a man, grinned at him. "You are certainly welcome," he greeted informally. "But how do you expect just three people to end this obscenity of a war?"

Jim bowed slightly and suggested, "If we could talk privately, your Highness."

Ali rose from his low seat. "We can talk in there." He pointed to a door that led off the large room they were in. The house was once the abode of a family loyal to the king. They had fled to relatives in a more remote area of the country.

Two servants who were cleaning in what was apparently Ali's sleeping quarters, were abruptly dismissed, with added instructions to bring refreshments for his guests.

As soon as they were alone, Jim began to explain his plan. He stopped when Ali raised his hand for silence, a moment before the servants returned. Max had taken a position near a window, which had a narrow slit in the curtains and was watching outside. Wanda lounged against one wall, studying the prince, and sensing the changes in him since they had last met. She approved. When he had left to come back to his country, he was still more of an idealistic boy. Now...he had grown up.

Ali nodded when Jim mentioned the need to prevent the finalisation of plans for a guided missile system.

"I think we blew some up," Ali told them. "A lucky fluke with one of our raids. It is what must be done, but how exactly do you plan to do it?"

"Your highness, the exact details need not concern you. It is best, I am sure you will agree, if it were not known that foreigners are helping you. However, our first priority is to free your father. I need to have his permission to proceed."

"Yes...my father is the true hereditary leader. And I know my uncle has violated more than one international agreement. The neighbouring countries all fear what he may do. They are too frightened to actively support my cause. They do help in small matters that will not be discovered."

Jim smiled, thinking, "*Like helping people across the border.*"

He went on to prompt, "Our sources tell us your father is imprisoned in the palace."

"Yes, but he is not in the dungeons. My uncle still needs him alive and well. However, I should warn you, my father has twice refused the offer of escape. He has his reasons, not that he has shared them with me. No doubt he still thinks me a callow boy."

Wanda spoke up. "Let's hope that your Uncle does too."

Ali glanced at her. "Maybe he does, and he puts my successes down to good and lucky advisors." He gave a wry smile. "My father is being reasonably well treated, and is probably safe as long as I am free. If I were to be caught, my uncle would kill us both, and I doubt my sister would be safe for very long after that. Was Quasim ever caught?"

Jim glanced at Wanda.

"He was allowed to roam free, until just before we left the states."

Ali fell silent, as if debating to ask a question. "I have a personal request..."

Wanda came forward and crouched next to him. "We plan to rescue Janna too, although our instructions only mention another American woman. One they have in the palace, working for your uncle on a computer program."

"That woman, if what you say is true, is an enemy of the crown." Ali didn't sound impressed by that aspect of the plan.

"Erin is my cousin, a gifted programmer – very inventive. It wasn't her choice to come here – she was abducted by your uncle's agents. He needs her skills, so she does have limited freedom, and

I know she has been able to help your friend a bit."

"But you have just arrived here! How could you know that? Is she alright?"

Jim told him, "I have an agent already in the palace."

Ali rose from his seat, "Is Janna alright? Have they hurt her?"

Neither Jim nor Wanda wanted to risk him rushing off to try to rescue her. Wanda spoke before Jim could. "This is war, your Highness. Janna is tough, I know. She will stand more than a few bruises for your sake."

In a low voice, Ali asked, "And our child?"

Wanda decided to lie, or rather, oped she was. "We don't know. But she had the baby before she was found by your uncle's men."

Ali just nodded, and said no more on that subject. Instead, he straightened, and took on the full dignity of his position. "As my father's true heir and son of the rightful ruler, you have my permission to proceed. What help can I give you?"

"A letter, from you, to take to your father, explaining who we are," Jim began, "I will tell you what to say. And we would like to take some special film of you."

Ali nodded, eyes gleaming. "And then?"

"We will need you to be near the palace, the day after tomorrow, and to be ready to challenge your uncle to a duel. We will have a means for telling you the exact time."

"I note you said I had to be ready – not that I would actually need to duel with my uncle," Ali commented. "I do not think that I am so expert yet that I could beat him."

Jim merely smiled, so Ali said, "I will do that letter right away. This country needs my father, and this war must end soon, or the people will face famine and ruin. We can no longer trade for goods with our neighbours, and Uncle's troops care not that they are destroying harvests and killing breeding stock. He must be stopped. Surely father must realise that."

Ali called for writing materials, and listened to Jim's dictation. He translated it into Arabic as he wrote. When he was finished, he sealed the letter in a small envelope and sealed it with a blob of soft wax. He pressed the top of one of his rings into it. "It's the royal seal," he explained. "Father gave it to me when he told me to flee. He did not want my uncle to have it."

He passed the letter to Jim, then asked, "Tell me about this film."

Wanda spoke up. "Before we left to come here, we were speaking to your sister, and we have film of her. We will need the same from you – I will tell you what to do and say. You will need to pretend you are talking to various people."

Ali was an apt pupil and the filming only took half an hour. Wanda switched topics while Jim uploaded the film to a site Grant could access.

"What can you tell me about the secret ways into and out of the palace?"

Ali looked at her for a long time before answering. He had no reason not to trust her, and his friend, John King had told him what was said of her.

"You will be the first person, not of the family, to learn of these," he explained, before telling her all he knew. He guessed she was memorising everything he said and described. He answered the questions she asked, and it gave him an interesting idea of what she intended.

"Why must I challenge my uncle?"

Jim only said, "If our plans work as intended, your uncle's followers will be feeling very uncertain about him. Many of his lesser soldiers will be ready to switch sides. Your challenge will be seen as a sign of strength and confidence on your part. We do not intend to risk you unnecessarily. Max..." Jim nodded to the silent watcher by the window, will give you the signal to proceed, if our plans have worked."

Ali decided not to think about the alternative. "I will go and give orders for the move to the capital."

Chapter 7 - Acting in Plain Sight

"Your Eminence," Nicholas spoke with patient deference. "I am aware that you are a very busy man. However, if I am to work to improve your face, I should begin at once." His tone took on a touch of exasperation. "I have explained what I need to do with this new technique, and it will only be two days, not two weeks before I can remove the bandages. The sooner I start, the sooner your schedule will return to normal. I would like to start tonight."

"You will not make me unconscious," Jabir directed emphatically.

"Your Eminence, the procedure will be exceedingly uncomfortable, if you are conscious. It will be impossible to do if you are awake and moving at all. I will, reluctantly, allow two of your personal servants to attend at the procedure. However, they must be washed and gowned as if they were to actually help with the procedure. They must, for the sake of keeping the operating area sterile, keep well back from the table. If you were to allow an anaesthetic, you would be asleep for no more than four hours."

With ill-grace, King Jabir conceded. "Very well! Eight o'clock." He then gestured that the audience was finished.

Exactly on the time she had promised, Erin arrived back in the computer room. The first person she saw was General Ishkhan, and he was watching her. She ignored him and went directly to her workstation.

She knew he had followed her, but he would be trying to dominate her, as usual. As she reached out to reawaken her computer, he said, "You are to work elsewhere for a time."

She turned around, keeping her stance business like, and asked, "How can I get this work done, if I cannot be here?"

"Oh, it is only for a day or two. I am told you know electronics."

"Yes, but..."Erin began, as she tried to think what he might want her to do. "With respect, General, can I just check that the file I was uploading has finished and save it?"

General Ishkhan was not a programmer, but he did know the King wanted the work done quickly. "Two minutes" he snapped, before moving back to the door where his aides awaited.

Erin breathed a sigh of relief when he moved away. She hadn't told him the truth, for what she intended was to activate stage one of a virus program, if she was not back in three days to stop it, it would go fully active.

She joined the General at the door, before he thought to send an aide to get her. He stalked off, expecting her to follow and since he was going into areas Erin had not seen before, she tried to memorise the route. The decor and carpeting was more opulent here, and that gave Erin a degree of apprehension. She had no wish to confront King Jabir.

He stopped at a door guarded by two of his junior officers. "In here."

The room they entered was fit for the king himself, but to her relief, only occupied by two of the elite palace guards, another of the General's junior officers, and a slender black man who was up a ladder, installing some device. He was the man Erin recalled glimpsing earlier.

"You will help Mr Collins, and do as he directs. You are not to speak to anyone about this work."

"As you say, General," Erin said, as she turned her back on him and assumed an expressionless face. "What can I do for you Mr Collins that no one else here can?"

"I understand you have a knowledge of electronics," Grant said neutrally, he judged that Erin's attitude was not endearing her to the General.

"Yes. I might even know more than you," she told him, testing the stranger.

"I doubt that, but it is irrelevant. I simply require someone who is deft, and knowledgeable to assist me installing a number of security devices. You will help me."

"So I have been told," Erin put a hint of annoyance in her tone. "So we'd best get a hustle on. I am meant to be doing other important work. So, tell me what I have to do, you can check me doing the first one, then you can flutter off."

Collins turned and passed her a unit, newly taken from its

packaging and passed it to her, observing as she looked it over. When she glanced around the room, she pointed to a spot in the corner. "Over there, right?"

Grant gave a faint smile that only Erin saw. "Yes. I will help you set up the ladder."

As soon as Erin's hand brushed that of the stranger, she knew that his attitude was as much an act as hers, and also to impress the General. He watched as she scampered up the ladder, and put the device in the general position she had indicated.

"No, no, no!" Grant said fussily. "Higher! And turn the device 180 degrees. Yes! There."

He gave Erin a wink, and watched as she drilled the holes for the mounting plate, attached that to the wall, and then sat the unit in place. "Okay, see the power outlet for the light? You need to add the adapter so it gets power from there. That will charge up the backup battery too."

Erin knew some of what the man was saying was just verbiage to impress the watcher, but she said nothing to contradict him. One look had told her all she needed to know about the device. She did let out a breath of relief when the General took himself out of the room, even if he did leave one of the ubiquitous guards watching them. She'd stopped paying attention to him after the second install, as this work was fun and a refreshing break from the tense atmosphere of the computer room. She didn't need to be told how to do the testing and linking of the devices to Grants laptop – she could have done that in her sleep.

He was doing a running commentary, using highly technical jargon, and the guard was already bored. He perked up when they had to change rooms, and then looked bored again.

They were both installing units, Erin knew hers were passive and IR movement sensors, but his were different. When they were doing their fifth location, one of the passages around the first room, he handed her one of the devices he was installing. He watched as she again examined it, and when she glanced at him, brows lifting to show she knew what it was, he nodded faintly. It was definitely not a security sensor.

He twisted to take a schematic out of his tool pouch, and dropped his voice to just audible. "I have to finish my job by tomorrow night.

The day after that, Jim wants you out."

"I won't leave without Fatima. She is too sick to be left alone," Erin's voice was just as low, and she didn't look at Grant. "Every time his foulness talks to her she is worse."

"How is she now?"

"When I left her, just before I was dragged here to help you," Erin specified, "Okay, but only just."

Grant nudged her to point to something on the schematic, and continued talking as if discussing the diagram. "His Eminence will be unavailable tonight, and his brother will be spirited away. By morning, there will be rumours of his death and of a demon possessed entity in the palace. They will come to believe it is you."

"They won't be far wrong," Erin muttered. "They don't realise I am already their worst nightmare."

Grant grinned. "You will be taken out of the palace, and appear to die. This is important. That night, we will be coming for...what did you call her?"

"Fatima Anzin. I know it is not her real name, but it is what she is calling herself."

"We will get her out and have someone impersonating her."

Erin refrained from asking questions just then, for the guard was idling over. Aloud she said, "Okay, I've got all that. I just hadn't seen this model before."

They returned to their routine, with her up the ladder most of the time, and Grant pinpointing the precise location he wanted things. When they had finished in that location and linked the devices to the program on the laptop, Grant directed Erin to carry one of the cases to the next position – another room, one that had the feel of being used regularly, but no one was in sight.

As they walked, carrying their tools, and the bag of devices still to be installed, Grant said quietly, "In that case is a protective garment. When you go behind that table, put it on. Have it on tomorrow."

Pretending to be looking for a power point for the laptop, Erin did as directed. From the weight and feel of the vest, Erin guessed it was Kevlar. When she stood up, she just gave him a querying look. He just handed her the next device, and had the guard help him with the ladder. Grant thanked him again, for he had been helping move the ladder between places, and when he moved away, he said quietly, "We don't expect them to try and shoot you, it's just a precaution."

Erin considered all this stranger had told her, and when they began to install a camera at the head of the passage leading to the cells, she hissed, "What's the catch? What haven't you told me?"

He waited until he was holding the ladder for her to get down, to reply. "Tomorrow, I will give you a capsule to swallow."

"Why?" They were heading downstairs now.

"It will make you freak out."

"Charming!" Erin had a sudden memory of her work colleague 'freaking out'. "Why?"

"At this point, Jim said to tell you to trust him."

"At this point, I start to get a creepy feeling in my gut."

At the level with the cells, they stopped to install one to cover the corridor.

Erin said, as they were testing the device, "Fatima is in the fourth room along. On the right."

Grant nodded, and said audibly, "Our next is to go at the far end." Then quietly, "Jim thinks you should be able to tell if the other rooms are occupied."

On the way back out, she told him, "Six in all, and I think I know who two of them are."

They went up the stairs and heard the bells that indicated the servant's meals.

"Finish here, now," their guard escort insisted.

Erin added, "Or we will miss dinner."

Grant pretended to be reluctant. "Oh, very well! I will start again after that."

As they walked back upstairs, Grant said, "So, you are also a programmer. That will be helpful. I need to put the security program on their computer."

"I wonder if they will get me to do that too?" Erin considered. "Maybe not though. My other work is urgent."

"So is this," Grant insisted, adding more arrogance to his tone.

"Argue it out with the General," Erin told him. "I just do as I am told..."

"It's going well?"

"Yeah, coming together." Erin dropped her voice, "I have set a timed virus for the day after tomorrow. If we need longer, I will have to change it.

"Tell me about it. With you off the scene they might get me to look at it the computer."

"You know the background?"

Grant nodded.

Erin just said, "Later. I'm starving."

While working after they'd eaten, Erin managed to whisper the details of her virus program – how to stop the temporary one and how to activate the overall blackout one. She said she had locked the program on the original hard drive, and said that anything added afterwards would be fragmented.

"Excellent," Grant has said, but the watcher might have thought it referred to how the device was working.

As they continued working, they noticed the extra security around some of their first locations, but made no comment. When they finally finished, both were glad to get back to their guest areas.

Chapter 8 – A Secret Way In

The procedure involving King Jabir's face had been underway for an hour, and the four observers were all in various states of stupor or nausea. Nicholas's earlier manoeuvres with blood capsules had sent one into a faint, a second to retching, and the other two, also fighting nausea, were now as far away as the room would allow. That, and finally convincing the patient to accept light sedation, now made it possible to do what they intended.

As Nicholas was no kind of plastic surgeon, all he was really doing was fitting a realistic plastiskin mask over the King's disfigured face. It was the same procedure as he used for his disguises. The only difference was that he would be sprinkling a power over the face, that would make it sting for a while. It would give the impression of residual pain.

The fabulous new technique had already been explained to the patient, who believed the mask was in place to protect the new grafted skin below, and it meant that he would only need to be bandaged for a few days, not some weeks. However, during those initial few days, the face needed to be kept as still as possible, hence the bandages.

When told the mask would be moulded to his features, and look exactly like his new face would be, Jabir nearly purred with satisfaction. That he could soon appear in public was vital to him. The stretched out period, had it been done the traditional way, was unacceptable.

When the face was finished, Nicholas also put plastiskin, and bandages over the area where the graft had supposedly come from. All that remained to do was drag the procedure out for a while longer and then get his nurse to clean up and make the patient comfortable.

During this time, and from earlier in the day, Max Hart, clad as a temple priest, was circling around the palace, walking up and down the nearby streets, warning people about demons. He was saying how they liked to possess people, and then giving out ways to recognise if a person was possessed.

He was doing such a good job of scare mongering, that the begging cup in front of his blind acolyte needed frequent emptying. Passers-by stopped him and asked for blessings, for their god to keep the demons away.

The stops enabled Wanda to examine sections of the wall around the palace, and the area in front of it, for signs of where a tunnel might emerge. Outwardly, she was blind, and when he stopped, Max simply touched her left shoulder. Wanda would stand and move her head this way and that, as if listening to the people talk. If she sat down, staring at the walls, Max knew to talk longer. All the time, the dark sunglasses hid the fact that she was interested in the near surroundings – comparing what she was seeing with what Princess Famira and Prince Ali had told her.

Members of the elite palace guards watched from the top of the walls, and on each section, one followed their movements. She already knew they were listening to the temple priest and becoming edgy. At the time of the shift changes, Max contrived to be near one of the gates used by the off duty guards to get back to the city. The men were just as susceptible as the lesser workers and when Wanda went into a prearranged 'fit', where she sprang up from the ground, and became aware of a 'demon' and pointed to

That her words were mainly gibberish to the listeners, wasn't important. They heard 'demon' and 'exorcism' and that's all they took in. Max, each time, had to calm her. An exercise that took nearly ten minutes, and had donations piling onto the ground – noticeably from the wealthier merchants.

Of most importance, were the guards who were going on duty, who would spread the word inside the walls.

Wanda would finally slump to the ground, while Max collected the donations. Then he insisted she get up and continue their work. By evening, they would often have people following them, so every now and then, Wanda feigned stumbling, so that if she finally found what she was looking for, her falling down would be related to her earlier 'fit'.

Finally though, Wanda did find what she was looking for. All the observations fell into place. This time, when she fell, and Max crouched beside her – all outward concern – he was looking to where her feet pointed. The only place directly in line was a dairy seller's stall.

This time, he hefted his moaning companion over his shoulder and went directly to the stall. Going in without invitation, he found a clear place on the floor and crouched to place his acolyte there, then rose to greet the store owner.

Wanda had told him the people there were loyalists and had helped Famira get away. However, the man, hearing all the followers outside, was getting nervous – and began contesting the intrusion. Max held up his hands in a familiar religious gesture, and asked for blessings on the humble abode of the dairy seller.

The man subsided when several coins passed his way, but his head jerked up on hearing an unexpected sentence.

"Send a man to the house of Mahmand for his son to come here."

The man jerked his head at the crowd outside, and Max nodded, "I will see they go to their homes."

On his re-emergence, the crowd seemed to want to swamp him, but he calmly raised his hands for silence, was obeyed at once, and began addressing them. "My young acolyte, is sensitive to the effluvium of demons, it is becoming stronger. All of you should go to your homes, draw together with your loved ones, to be strong enough to fight off the temptations the demons offer."

In minutes, the area was clear, and the dairy seller himself went to do the requested errand. Within ten minutes, the man was back, accompanied by a lithe, slender figure in a voluminous hooded cloak. He first ensured his windows were fully shuttered and his door locked.

When he turned around, he stopped still in shock, until he remembered traditional courtesy and bowed low to the young man he now saw to be Prince Ali.

"My friend, be at ease. You are a loyal friend and we again need your help."

The man's eyes widened as Ali explained what they hoped to do, and readily answered Ali's questions.

Switching to English, Ali said, "The tunnel is here. He will show you now."

Max gestured for Wanda to look and he waited in the shop while she and Ali followed the seller.

The man went down stone stairs into a cellar where the air was crisply cool. He drew aside a think rubber curtain, letting them into the chilled room containing milk, cheeses and other dairy products in varying styles of container. He moved between neat stacks to the rear where they edged through a slit in the thick rubber insulation, and passed between two humming refrigerator units. They emerged into a passage, and soon reached a corner, around which the noise was muffled.

The man spoke quietly and Ali translated, "Hussein says he will leave the shop unattended tonight and the door will be open for you."

Wanda shook her head. "No. Tell him to lock the door. It will not be an obstacle. Even better, if he could bring back some friends for a party that goes on until after midnight."

Hussein nodded, and grinned enthusiastically.

Ali continued, "He said the passage leads directly to the hidden door, but he does not know the secret to opening it. I do however."

"Okay," Wanda decided. "Let's get back. There's work to do."

Ali replaced the hood on his head before leaving, and Wanda assumed a limping gait, while holding onto Max. As they walked towards where Jim was staying, they again began to attract followers. These had heard the warning of the priest from friends, and they too wanted the blessing of the temple for their families. Some wanted reassurance that the temple could rid people of demons.

The short stop for the blessing, with all the followers hanging on Max's every word, enabled Ali to slip away to there he was lodged. When they obeyed the direction to go home to their families, Max and Wanda continued on in the direction of the Temple. As the sun set and the sudden darkness fell, they both seemed to vanish between one moment and the next.

In half the time it had taken them since leaving the dairy sellers shop, they were back there. Everything was solidly locked up, Wanda had the door open in less than half a minute, and they were as quickly inside and out of sight. Max was impressed, but he knew that was one reason why Wanda was on the team.

Wanda relocked the door, and pulled out a tiny torch. She flicked it towards the steps, and led the way down to the cellar and through the cool room into the passage beyond. They were both moving carefully, and their sandalled feet were making only a faint scuffling sound on the stone floor.

All the way, they were alert for sounds that might indicate another presence, even though they did not expect anyone to know of the passage, or their presence in it. Wanda, also had her classified extra senses wide open, and that confirmed they were alone.

When Max estimated they had traversed a distance equal to half way between the shop and the palace wall, Wanda suddenly stopped, and he ran into her.

"Sorry," she told him. "Wait a bit."

What she wasn't about to tell Max, was that her wide open extra senses had caught the full impact of her cousin's sudden panic. She needed to sort out all the impressions she was receiving. Until then, she had, at Jim's insistence, kept her mind fully shielded from her cousin. He had not wanted her presence to distract Erin from her own attempts to thwart King Jabir.

Chapter 9 – Caught

Erin reached her room with a feeling close to relief. Her ordeal was almost over, but as she began to review the day's events, panic inexplicably grew. She was to place her life in the hands of strangers. Jim had sent them, and she trusted him, but these others? She didn't know them, didn't know if they really comprehended how evil the king and his general were. It was not like relying on fellow marines, her troop mates had become like family.

They strangers had just got to the palace. She had been there long enough to know her own danger had never been so great. She was sure Collins hadn't told her everything, and that was okay, but if the general discovered what she had done to the program, before they got her out, she would probably need the Kevlar vest. Having that was reassuring, but it only covered her chest.

Once, her intention had been to get out as soon as possible, until it became clear that she was always well guarded, even if she couldn't see the guards. Then she found out about Fatima – she would not leave without her! The General or King Jabir, were intending to kill her, she knew that from the way they felt to her empathy when they mentioned her. They were anticipating the time.

Then there was the fact that the General resented having to accept a woman to finalise the program. He'd have killed her right away, but he was sure of his king's anger if he had. That program was more important than being led around by a woman. He didn't trust her one little bit, and when she finished what they wanted her to do, they might make it seem she was being honoured with a charter flight out of the country. Her own intuition told her she would be lucky just to be alive and dumped like rubbish over the nearest border. Fatima would be lucky to live.

Now there were other people stirring things up and the delicate balance between them hating her and needing her was teetering wildly. She could not control events.

"Steady, Erin!"

The mind voice was clear and distinct. Bracing, like a sudden cold wind.

"Wanda!" She put all her relief into that thought.

"I am not far away. Everything is going according to plan."

"I'm scared," Erin admitted, knowing her cousin would not be critical, and would sense the thought.

"Of course you are! Being scared means you take more care. We have both been there before, and come through it stronger. Besides, if you are dead, you don't have to worry about anything."

The tart last sentence did the trick. It broke the cycle of panic and helped Erin get her shields back up.

Wanda sent, "Tomorrow! Be ready!" before she broke the contact.

Erin found she was able to relax enough to sleep.

In the hidden tunnel, Wanda said, "It's okay, we can go on."

However, they hadn't gone much further when she hissed, "Someone is coming. From behind."

Max didn't hear the faint sounds until later, and spared an instant for the thought that Wanda must have ears like a rabbit.

There were no alcoves or passages off the tunnel, so they lay next to the wall, one after the other, as the walls were only four feet apart at best.

Whoever was approaching had a dull torch, and the holder slowed when the two odd bundles were caught in the light. The steps approached with greater caution. Wanda tested the mind, but it was unfamiliar. She was ready to spring up, when the figure paused to investigate the bundle that was Max. He was completely surprised by the attack that took his legs out from under him. The unmoving form in the disguising cape, erupted into action, twisting to be ready to fight. He cursed, when he heard Wanda hiss.

"Ali, you fool! We could have killed you!" She was annoyed enough to omit the usual honorific. "Why are you here?"

"I know my way around my home, and I though my father might not listen to you, even with my letter."

Max added his own caustic comments. "If you are caught, you and your father will quickly be dead."

Before Ali could contest that, Wanda grabbed his wrist and

whispered forcefully, "I hope you don't have any ideas about trying to see Janna!"

Wanda felt his start of surprise. He had been thinking that. "Please, Ali. Don't do anything to jeopardise what we are doing. Tonight, our only target is your father. Tomorrow, we will bring Erin out. When it's night, we bring Janna out, and I will take her place, okay?"

Ali kept silent.

"I know what Janna is to you. Last we heard she was still okay, even though ill-treated."

It was old news. She hadn't heard an update all day, but Ali had to believe it. "We have agents in the palace. They have seen her."

"Very well. I will come with you to my father."

They went on, stopping when the tunnel seemed to dead end. Famira had said that the door swung on a central axis. Wanda examined the stones where the door should be, but Ali was examining the floor.

He lifted up a palm sized stone that wasn't quite flush with the floor.

"Here!" he exclaimed quietly, as he reached his hand into a hole for the activating lever.

"Wait!" Wanda spoke sharply, like a hiss of breath.

Ali stopped, and both he and Max stared as she seemed to be listening through a stone wall.

"Now!" she said after a few minutes.

Ali pulled on the lever, and the door seemed to move towards then by an inch. He then began pushing on one side until the gap was wide enough for them to slip through. Wanda pushed it almost closed, preventing it from locking by slipping a slender file, from a toolkit the others had been unaware of, at the point of the locking mechanism.

A quick look around was all Ali needed to orientate himself. "They were keeping him down in the cells."

That was logical, Wanda decided, but her instinct was telling her otherwise. She had a hunch, that after the first two attempts to free him, they had moved him somewhere unexpected.

"Max, go with Ali. I'll check upstairs."

"Jim said to stay together."

"If I am wrong, and you find him, I will know." She wasted no more time disagreeing, and headed further into the palace. Max shook his head at her cryptic comment, and gestured to Ali to lead the way to the cells.

Wanda let an inner instinct guide her. She trusted these hunches, just as she did when her instinct warned her of people approaching. As she moved inward, she had to duck into doorways, or beside tall decorations or furniture, on more than a few occasions. The increase in guard activity was not unexpected, and seemed to confirm she was getting close. This area wasn't near the king's suite, or where Nicholas was keeping the king out of the way. It was, judging by the ambient opulence, possibly an area for important guests. She moved until her instinct said to stop. If the door next to her was where the proper king was being held, there should have been a guard. Wanda retreated and watched from behind a pedestal with a large urn on display. A glimpse of a man approaching from the other direction put her on high alert. She expected him to stop at the door, but her danger sense had kicked in. He was still coming.

As he was about to pass, Wanda sprang at him, grabbed his neck and before he could call out, squeezed firmly. Under her hand, a strategic press of her thumb, stopped the carotid blood flow, and the man dropped. Nearby was another door, And Wanda opened it, listened and sensed for anyone within, and when sure of no one, dragged the guard in. She quickly frisked him, and found the keys she'd hoped he had. She had very little time, for the man should rouse in five to ten minutes, but having the keys made things quicker.

All senses on alert, she went out and tried the keys on the lock of the door where she'd sensed someone. The third key opened it. She stepped in quickly and closed the door behind her. A quick glance around, showed her the haggard man sleeping in a chair. She was about to move forward, when her danger sense flared higher. She spun around, and found the source of the threat, and herself staring at the barrel of a military issue pistol and the malicious smile of General Ishkhan.

Chapter 10 – Rescuing a King

Max and Ali moved quickly along the double row of closed doors, glancing in through the small window, seeking the face of King Rakhal. They had no time to listen to the pleas of the few prisoners that noticed them. Even if it was safe to do so, they didn't have the means to open the doors. Ali gestured them to silence, and he and Max returned to where the secret door opened. And squatted down behind pillars, so the guards heading to the cells did not see them. The guards were not being silent, but were discussing reports coming from all parts of the palace – odd reports. Not just the ones about demons in the palace, but reports of people seeing Ali, Famira, and even King Rakhal. Their jerky movements as the glanced around, suggested edginess, like they didn't quite disbelieve the rumours.

Once the guards were past, Ali gestured for Max to follow him, whispering they would go to where his father's suite was. A minor commotion, from somewhere nearby, had them hiding again. This time within a cleaner's cupboard, from which Max peeped through a crack.

He saw Wanda being half dragged, half pulled past them. She wasn't talking, and only struggling to keep her feet. He saw one of the guards had her neck in a dangerous grip, but before his mind decided to try to help her, he seemed to hear a voice in his head. "Go back to the passage! Wait!"

But of course, she couldn't have spoken...then he remembered something Jim had said. "She's good with locks, used to be a professional thief. She has other unusual talents. Telepathy! I have experienced it."

Max recalled he had still been sceptical, but Jim had just compromised by advising, "Then trust your hunches." He had not elaborated further, and now Max thought, telepathy or a hunch?

He decided to obey the words he heard, and directed a protesting Ali back to the passage.

"What of your friend? They have Wanda?"

"Don't think her meek and helpless," Max told him. "She will join us later, so we had best stay out of sight in the passage."

After the initial shock, that her danger sense had not warned her in time, Wanda schooled her face to an expressionless mask, and began looking for an escape route. The old looking man was awake now, and watching from his chair.

"Who are you?" the General snapped in Arabic, but then repeated in English.

He got no answer. Wanda stared, not at him, but at a point behind him. Between him and the passage door, were four more armed guards. When the repeat of the question still didn't get a response, the General slapped her face with deliberate harshness.

The pain brought tears to Wanda's eyes, but she made no sound and did not move. Sensing then that there would be more physical violence, her mind retreated into a dark place of sanctuary. Aware of her body, aware of what she had to do, but feeling nothing, hearing nothing.

"Why are you here?" No answer, SLAP.

The General quickly realised he was not going to get anywhere, and debated making this intruding female into a lesson for the equally stubborn deposed king.

"Search her!"

Two of the guards shouldered weapons, and began roughly patting her all over. They found the other guard's keys, a few lock opening tools, and nothing else. No personal items, no ID.

"So we have a thief, or a spy," Ishkhan commented, eyes avid. "Let's see how long you hold out when I start questioning you. It won't be just my hand you feel. And if you still don't answer questions, you will deemed a traitor, and treated as such."

He was speaking mostly in Arabic, but Wanda guessed his meaning. He may think her a local woman, but if she spoke, he'd know she wasn't. He nodded to one of the guards, who came and wrenched her arm up behind her. Before he could instruct him more, a messenger arrived with an urgent message. He read it and scowled.

"Take her to the cell for dangerous prisoners."

Wanda sensed malicious amusement from him, and a sharp sense of dismay from the older man.

She heard the General mutter, in English, "Let's see how clever you are at opening locks, without keys."

In spite of that, though, she sensed he wanted her to try. That impression came with fleeting glimpses of the effects of some nasty traps. Concern from the older man suggested he'd spent time in that same cell – a place meant to break a man's spirit.

Wanda, in her dark mind sanctuary, wondered. Had he been broken? Was that why he had not tried to escape? Why they felt it safe to keep him in relative luxury now?

The guard holding her arm released it, but only long enough to force it next to the other. Some kind of restraint device was applied. It felt like two bars clamped somehow.

Wanda had her awareness back in her body now, and despite the residual pain, flexed her wrists to make them rounder – a trick of the legendary Houdini. She was pushed and shoved unmercifully, and when she lost her footing, they dragged her. Most times, she managed to regain her footing.

As they neared the place where Max and Ali were hiding, close to where the secret passage emerged, she aimed a thought at the tall blond Max and hoped he'd hear her.

"Go back to the passage! Wait."

The cell was barely large enough for a person to stand in. Any one over six foot would have needed to crouch. It would be a very tight fit for a man.

They pushed her in, very quickly slamming the door shut behind her. It was locked before she had sidled around to look at them. The walls of the square cell were made of glass, reinforced with thick steel rods. The only opening was a small cut out area, at about head high for an average sized local man. The floor was an open space, covered with a metal grating – the residual odour coming up from it, told its purpose.

Charming! Wanda could see the two guards were laughing, she didn't need to read their thoughts to know they were crude. One grabbed the chair that was in the outer area around the cell, and turned it so its back was to her, but then sat astride it, resting his arms on the back, and leering at her. The other left her sight, but she heard another door shut.

Wanda began to smile, her gaze met his. With his mind fantasising about what he could do to her, it was like saying, 'come into my mind' to a telepath. Her mind sent insidious little voices into his mind, and used his lewd fantasises to gain control. When she broke eye contact, the guard continued to stare, straight ahead, but obliviously.

Moments later, Wanda's hands were free of the primitive handcuffs. She had pulled them out, scraping her wrists, but without undoing the clamps. That just left the lock. Warned of traps on this cell, she reached out her hands to the door and quickly drew it back. Her nerves tingled, telling her there was an electric current running through the bars.

A minor delay, for Wanda still had much of her basic tool kit – though her guards thought they had found it all. She pushed up her left sleeve to reveal a soft leather gauntlet, sealed with Velcro. Opened, an array of flexible tools were displayed. She selected a couple of non-conducting items, and some narrow strips of gum based adhesive.

There was no real skill needed to open the old style lock. Wanda had glimpsed the key used on the lock, and knew from that what to expect. With a pair of non-conducting pliers, made rigid by sliding the two parts together, she had the lock opened in moments. The next stage, the electric circuit required care in case it was connected to an alarm. For that, she fiddled with her belt. Short pieces of insulated wire were built into it and could be pulled out to use. She joined two together by twisting the exposed ends together. One free end was pressed against the frame with a ball of gum. The other end was pressed onto the door, maintaining the circuit, now there was a gap, just wide enough for Wanda's slender form. She repeated her actions in reverse on the outside of the door, before removing the inner bypass. Once the door was relocked, she removed the second one.

While the hypnotised guard continued staring, Wanda closed up her gauntlet toolkit and covered it with her sleeve. She shoved the coiled wire and adhesive into her pocket, and muttered to the oblivious guard, "You can tell your General – I do much better without keys."

Wanda didn't know when he second guard was going to come back, so she wasted no time leaving. Her escape had taken no more than five minutes. She recalled the way she had travelled to get there, and began to retrace her steps, alert for guards, and always finding cover before they were close. Their nervous energy was easy to pick up on. The numbers of guards were increasing, as she neared where the former king was imprisoned. She played on their nerves, making some think they had seen something or heard something. In their favour, and in spite of their high strung nerves, they went to investigate each time.

Outside her target room, was the same guard that she had outwitted before. His face was reddened, either from the General's discipline, or intense humiliation. He looked determined not to leave his post.

Then Wanda saw something that nearly made her laugh aloud – an image of Ali, walking up the passage. The one image guaranteed to break the guard's resolve. At first, his mouth just gaped open, then he seemed undecided whether to challenge the intruder, or shout to bring others. He grabbed his gun and strode towards the very realistic hologram.

Right on cue, the hologram appeared to duck into a side passage or open door. The guard began to run.

After he went past a room further down the passage, Grant peeked out and gave Wanda the 'all clear' sign. She waved back, and took a cellulose card out of her pocket and had the door open in a flash, then quickly stepping inside.

This time, no sense of danger assaulted her, but she wasn't assuming there was none. King Rakhal was not in the main room, so she crept to the open door that led to a bedroom with a bed ready for occupation. She saw another door, slightly ajar, and enough of the interior to know it was a bathroom.

Wanda sensed the king's presence, felt a touch of her danger warning sense, as the hand she was reaching out to open the bedroom door further, was suddenly clamped in a vice-like grip.

It pulled her into the bedroom, and is strength belied the

haggard appearance of its owner.

"Who are you, woman?" King Rakhal demanded in a whisper. He spoke in English, seeming to know she was a foreigner.

"I am Wanda, and I bring a message from your son."

"Does my son now consort with thieves and brigands?"

The polite enquiry brought a redder flush to Wanda's cheeks than had been there already. For some reason, she wanted this man's good opinion, not just for her mission, but as a person.

"I am no longer a thief, your Highness," Wanda told him, and then to King Rakhal's amazement, used her free hand to reveal the leather gauntlet on her held wrist. She undid the Velcro to reveal the letter with its visible royal seal. "That letter empowers me to deliver the letter to you, and bring you out tonight."

The king took the letter, examined it carefully, then broke the seal. He began to read the short missive, then looked to her gravely.

"Unlike those who have come before, you seem to hold a charmed life. I did not expect you to return, or even be alive in the morning. After seeing those earlier brave men tortured to death before my eyes, I gave my word not to try to escape. This letter from my son changes that. I can no longer believe my brother will care for the people of my country. How do you propose to get me out of my palace?"

"Though the tunnel your daughter used to escape."

"And you believe you can spirit me away unseen?"

Wanda didn't react to his deliberate reminder of her earlier visit. "Sir, I know I can," she told him soberly, but with mentally crossed fingers. "But we must leave now. Before they discover I am not in their escape proof cell."

The king smiled faintly. "I admire your courage. Yes. It is time I resumed my rightful place. Let us proceed."

Wanda gestured for the king to flatten himself against the wall, while she cracked open the outer door. The guard was back, as she had sensed, thoroughly spooked by Grant's hologram and staring stolidly at the opposite wall. Wanda pictured Grant and thought carefully, "Make him look left."

There was a faint sound, enough to make the guard's head swivel, in spite of his determination not to be tricked again. He began to react, just as Wanda reached out and repeated her trick. He dropped to the floor with a dull thud, and Wanda gestured the king out.

Trusting that Grant was keeping the majority of the guards busy elsewhere, she led the way unerringly, around the unconscious guard, along deserted passages, to where the secret passage opened. They had only to avoid two pairs of guards, and Wanda had sensed them well before they might have spotted their escape. At the wall, Wanda removed her lock jammer, and the king helped push the wall back so it would swing open. She sent Max a mental warning, and when they were in the passage, saw Max and Ali alert for trouble.

Max came to help her close the door and put the locking stone back over the lever. Ali had run to embrace his father, although the gesture was short. Already they were deep in conversation, too quiet to be heard a metre away.

"I was getting concerned," Max admitted.

"Sorry, just a minor delay."

Max went over to the two royals and urged them to get going. He was keeping track of the time and needed to be back in the dairy sellers stall before the last of the party guests departed. It didn't stop the two of them talking as they trotted along. From the occasional phrases she heard, Wanda knew they were discussing the political situation. She didn't need to eavesdrop, so all her attention was on sensing for dangers ahead, other presences. The King's anger had become a simmering furnace.

Gradually, the sounds of laughing and loud voices reached them. Ali told his father what was going on, so when they emerged back into the diary seller's cool room, he knew what to expect.

The owner waited for them, and his eyes widened when he recognised the second man. He bowed to both royals, and straightened when Ali requested, "We need a change of clothes for this man and the woman."

He nodded, and trotted off, returning quickly with some freshly laundered and ironed clothes.

"I'm sorry I cannot offer better, Your Highness. These are rough wear. They are all I keep here."

King Rakhal said gently, "I am grateful for your generosity."

Wanda thanked him for the clothes he had found for her and quickly drew off the male clothing she'd been wearing for the mission and drew on the skirts over the black sneak suit she had worn underneath. The king went to one side to change, with Ali acting as his valet.

Wanda donned a hood cloak to complete her disguise. They all went upstairs, mingled briefly with the guests, then moved out with other pairs. Ali left with two of his loyal followers, Max and the King moved out with a group of several men, all high on some local illicit substance. Wanda left on her own, aware there was an unofficial curfew for women. However, there were very few other people out in the streets, thanks to the rumours of demons. The noisier home going party guests were the focus of the night guards' attention. Wanda returned to the building being used by Jim with no one noticing her stealthy route in the shadows.

"Good work," Jim praised her. "Max said you met some trouble."

Wanda gave him the facts of all she had done, and was then more than ready to get some sleep.

Grant periodically played his holograms throughout the night, sometimes adding sound and light effects. He was aware, through a sensor placed by Nicholas, when the usurped king, Jabir, woke and demanded to be able to get up. He grinned, Nicholas and Casey were going to have a hard time with him – but then, that's what they were relying on.

It was after eleven when Jabir summoned his General and about half an hour after that when he heard Wanda return to King Rakhal's prison rooms. Jabir was livid when the general reported the presence of an intruder. His inability to speak caused him to thump the bed he was in. It brought Nicholas back at a fast trot.

"Your Eminence, please, I need you to stay calm and rest quietly or all my work will have been for nothing."

General Ishkhan explained, "A very dangerous woman managed to enter the palace – it is an urgent matter."

"I hear that woman had been taken to a secure cell. Surely she can keep until morning."

Jabir, chaffing at the restrictions, subsided with ill grace, although he was touching the bandages on his face. He dismissed his General and growled a dismissal to his doctor.

"We will just be in the next room, your Eminence, if you require anything, the bell unit will summon us." Jabir waved them out, impatiently ignoring Nicholas's bow.

With the adjoining door shut completely, Nicholas took out his communicator and reported to Jim.

Jim, while Nicholas was still listening, said, "Grant, are you listening in?"

Receiving an affirmative, Jim went on, "Max has just arrived back with the target, and Wanda should be returning soon."

"Right, Jim," Grant spoke, "I will begin the next stage."

In his room, with the outer door locked for privacy, Grant opened his briefcase, removed a false bottom, and pressed two buttons. One activated the hologram projectors and the other a voice relay. His job now was to ensure Nicholas's patient became even more difficult.

The room where King Jabir was now resting, and trying to sleep – he had rejected all offers of sedatives or analgesics – became the next location for Grants ghostly images. Through a tiny camera, set up as Nicholas was preparing the room, every time Jabir appeared on the verge of sleep, an image would appear with voice pitched to just barely audible, and gradually getting louder until it disturbed the room's occupant. These images were of Jim, disguised as King Rakhal, berating his brother for various ill deeds, and looking younger than Rakhal looked now. The voice was Ali's.

The first time it happened, Jabir let out a strangled yell. The bandages precluded the option to open his mouth and let out a full bellow. Nicholas, having the voice call monitor beside him, came racing in to calm his patient yet again, and to discover what was wrong.

Unwilling to look like a fool, Jabir blamed noises outside his room, or Nicholas's equipment. The demand, "Can't you hear it?" had Nichols looking confused.

"I was asleep," was the only polite answer.

Several more times, during the night, Grant played variations of that hologram, and each time, Nicholas came in, offered a sedative and was refused. By morning, Jabir was in a really foul mood.

Grant did manage two hours sleep, and when the palace servants began stirring, he could act as if he had slept solidly since midnight.

His escort took him to see General Ishkhan, right after breakfast. Grant noted the signs of a sleepless night on the man's face, and hid his inner glee.

"I want you to set up your central security monitors today. There is a room next to the computer room with computers and monitors already set up."

"If that is what you wish, General. "However, I still have four sections where you require sensors, that I have yet to set up."

"They can wait. The most important ones are set up and I need to settle a lot of rumours and hysterical claims. I need that monitoring capability set up as soon as possible."

"Well, then, you had best send that effeminate creature to help again, He/she is at least competent – that's all I can say."

"That one has been told to do as you direct or feel my displeasure. I will send someone for her."

Colonel Kazim brought Erin about ten minutes after Grant had started work.

"You could have told him to let me finish breakfast first," Erin complained, as soon as she saw Grant.

"This work is important," Grant snapped. "Now, I have loaded the security monitoring program. We need to be sure every unit is linked to it." He went on, giving highly technical instructions, until the Colonel yawned and retreated. Then he lowered his voice and changed topics.

"I left a number of units in an inoperative state, all in strategic places. It means we are going to have to go and check them. Now, take this capsule and put it in your mouth. When I signal, bite it and swallow it. Erin nodded, and stalked off, as if annoyed. She didn't want anyone thinking she was friendly with him.

Chapter 12 – The Demon

The knowledge that King Jabir was in a right fury began to circulate with the other rumours, and they were putting everyone, servants and guards alike, into a state of nervous tension.

Grant listened to the talk of the programmers, soft voiced and furtive, as he spoke to Erin about their work. She wasn't sharp with them, and encouraged their gossip, stopping them if she sensed the General, or the Mole coming near. The stories had grown with the telling, but the basis was that a female thief had been caught, but had escaped, and the former king had too. Only now, that woman was supposed to be a demon, who had killed the former king, and his successor was the demon's next victim.

When Erin told them there were no such things as demons. They only became more certain.

Jabir would not stay confined to his bed, or to the sterile rooms Nicholas had set up. He demanded the removal of his bandages, until finally wearing the doctor down.

Muttering his concerns, Nicholas gave in, just before lunch time, and began carefully unwrapping each layer of bandage, all the while hearing veiled threats from his patient. When the last layer of bandage was removed, Casey passed Nicholas a mirror so the patient could see his face.

"That of course is the layer of synthiskin," Nicholas reminded his patient. "You must keep that on for the full four weeks, to allow the new, delicate, natural skin to regenerate over the place of the scar tissue. If you take it off sooner, you risk tearing off the new skin."

Jabir, however, was pleased with his temporary appearance, and more so when Nicholas assured him his new face would look as good.

"How soon must you leave, doctor?"

"Really, I should go soon, but as there are no local doctors to attend you during this critical time, I will stay until the mask can be removed."

Jabir merely nodded and left the room. Then, as soon as he had, Nicholas and Casey began to pack up their equipment. What had seemed cumbersome and bulky to bring in, would take very little time to take out.

King Jabir's entrance to the computer room created an instant uneasy silence when everyone had bowed in respect. The only two who did not were Grant and Erin, busy in the little side room.

When addressed by the King, Grant stood, turned and bowed, then gave a terse but detailed report of progress and the current status. When Erin turned around, he told her to keep working.

Seeing the American woman being ordered around, mollified Jabir's glare of distaste.

"Show me how it works," Jabir ordered.

Grant had Erin move and he took over, beginning the demonstration. When he came to one that didn't come up, he had Erin make a note of the unit number and check its location on the schematic. The arrival of General Ishkhan with a message, halted the demonstration. Although the two men moved away to talk, their voices were not quiet.

Grant whispered, "Can you activate the virus from here?" When Erin nodded, he went on, "Get ready to do it."

"I do not believe it!" Jabir snarled. "My enemies would not rescue him only to kill him. His bastard, traitorous son, would not have the guts for it. Is there proof?"

"No, your Eminence, but the word is all around the city. All anyone is talking of is his escape and death. Everyone has heard that your nephew will call challenge on you for his death."

Jabir laughed. "That wolf-whelp cannot think he can challenge me and win. No, he's planning something else. Have him found, he has to be close by. Use all the new drones to look for him, or his men."

"People are also saying he was seen here in the palace last night," Ishkhan reported.

"Superstitious nonsense," Jabir snapped. "That boy is a coward and a traitor. When you find him, I want him brought here. And if my brother is dead, I want to see his body."

Grant gave Erin a nod, and while all attention was on the General and King Jabir, she sent an activation code to all the other computers.

Anticipating the General's next orders, Grant nudged Erin and said quietly, "Let's go and fix one of the sensors."

He took Erin's notes, and his installation schematic, and slipped out behind the two personages. He told the guard nearest the door where they were going by pointing to the relevant place on the diagram.

Orders for the launching of the drones was being given as they left, and guards were sent off to bring the units. The programmers were sent to activate the linked computers, and get them ready to oversee the search.

Grant had Erin go up and partly uninstall one of the units, while he called up information. The usual guard had followed them and was again looking bored. They were not far from the computer room, and heard the uproar when the monitors went blank. Erin had planned for her virus program to do that when the third drone began sending data. The delay meant that when the computers crashed, and two guards were sent to find the Americans, Erin was up a ladder with a partly disassembled sensor, and Grant only had the schematic in hand. Neither was near a computer, not even Grant's laptop.

Erin, up the ladder, saw Grant's next signal, and bit down on the rubbery capsule in her mouth, and swallowed the contents.

As Grant argued that Erin had been up the ladder all the time, and had to finish what she was doing, she was feeling the effects of the drug. Her vision blurred, her hands became weak and the camera in her hand dropped to the floor.

Grant spun around, and yelled, "What the devil are you doing?" He ran to the ladder, and grabbed Erin, as if intending to drag her off it. In fact, he was ready to catch her when she fell off. Just his gentle touch was enough to set her off.

Erin felt as if everything around her had exploded. She was kicking, clawing, biting, trying to get free. Her body did not want to obey her mind and disassociated with it completely. For a time, she was outside of her body, watching herself fighting and screaming – getting free and letting no one back near her.

Servants and more guards raced to the source of the noise. Most soon fled, and began spreading the word of another demon in the palace.

Grant grabbed the nearest guard. "Go get that doctor. Tell him to bring a tranquiliser."

One guard went for the Doctor, another for the General, who arrived with King Jabir just as the doctor was injecting her with something.

"That much should stop a horse," Nicholas claimed, while Erin was still struggling in the grip of two hefty guards and showing no sign of a lessening of her struggles.

There was an uneasy shuffling around the edges of the room, as the guards and few remaining servants thought about demons.

Grant reached into his pocket and activated a remote control. A faint reddish glow began to encase Erin's body, as she suddenly collapsed in the guards' grip. It grew brighter, and Erin seemed to wake and try to talk, but nothing came out.

General Ishkhan caught the sudden intake of multiple breaths. He spotted the red glow, and barely stopped himself copying the action. Some of his men were edging to the door, the General grabbed the nearest. "If you cowards really think there is a demon here, go to the temple and fetch a priest."

It was an order, the caught guardsman was willing to obey. He took off at a run, leaving the other nervous guards moving edgily. Only that guard had no intention of going to the temple. The priests there were unapproachable. Instead, he went out the servants' gate, and to the market to fetch the roving priest who had predicted this and knew how to exorcise demons.

Within the room, time might have stood still. The foreign doctor was still trying to calm the woman, and General Ishkhan was smiling faintly.

As Max was led into the room, he was gently swinging a palm

sized censor that emitted fragrant smoke. Everyone except Erin went quiet as the smoke filled the room. He stopped in the centre of the room, eyeing the struggling woman, and scanning the rest of the room.

"There is a demon here," he proclaimed, merely confirming what most of the already believed.

The two guards holding Erin released her and began to back away. Erin made a dash for the door.

Max called out, "Hold the possessed. The demon must not be allowed to leave this room."

Only the General moved. He reached out and took Erin by the throat.

By then, Erin had felt the drug effects wearing off, but had been continuing the earlier behaviour. Prudence told her to stop, but she only looked at the door, not any of the people. Max had immediately begun to light braziers and set them in a hexagon around the General and his captive. The whitish smoke, which was rapidly adding to that from the censor, was making the red glow more noticeable.

"Sir, you should step away now," Max directed. Erin stood like a statue as if the smoke and incense had lulled the demon.

The General obeyed, but as soon as he was outside the ring of braziers, turned and pulled out his handgun.

"This is ludicrous! There is only one solution for this."

Max moved fast, pushing down the arm that had the gun.

"No! If you kill the body inhabited by a demon, you release it. You cannot catch it. It will find another to inhabit. You can, while the body lives, subdue and destroy the demon, for it will cling to that body until it dies."

"We'll see, will we, priest," the General challenged. He shook his hand free and aimed the gun at the woman, then fired."

Even with the Kevlar vest on under her shirt, Erin felt the bullet hit and it was like an express train had hit her. She fell backwards, hitting her head on a desk, and knocking herself out. In the next moment, the red glow separated from around her still form and flew at a fearsome rate around the room. Even the General ducked reflexively and had to control a primitive terror.

When all eyes were on the glow except his, Grant turned off the projection just as it seemed to exit the door.

The General looked around the room, saw no sign of the glow, and ordered, "Remove that body, priest, and burn it."

Max spoke in dire tones, "The demon is not gone. It has found another host. You must let me perform an exorcism, to sanctify this royal palace."

"No!" the new voice startled everyone. "Demons cannot overcome a strongly opposed mind. Get out of here, Priest, and dispose of that rubbish. Doctor, I want you out of the palace today! You can return in three weeks unless I summon you."

He turned to the people he had pushed past in the passage. "Back to work! All of you."

Most of the watchers obeyed immediately.

"You!" he pointed to the recently appointed Chief Programmer. "Get those computers working and the drones back in the air."

The Mole turned pale. "Your Eminence, that was what I was trying to tell you. It is like the program was wiped."

"Impossible!" Jabir thundered. "The program must be ready to show my guest later today. Go!"

The man went, almost tripping over his feet to get away from the furious king.

"You!" he indicated Grant. "Was your computer wiped too?"

"Your Eminence, I do not know."

"Find out! What do you know of computers?"

"I know a great deal," Grant claimed. "Did your people try to reload from the back up?"

Jabir looked blank, and only said, "Finish your work here and go and advise my programmers. I would have blamed your assistant," he spat at the body, "except too many people have confirmed she was nowhere near the computers."

The King strode from the room, making his body guards trot to keep up.

Chapter 13 – Temple Blessing

Nicholas was kneeling beside Erin. When no one was looking, he took a small vial from his pocket, and squirted a dose of a counter drug for the hallucinogen into her mouth. He had already ascertained that the vest had indeed stopped the bullet, and although her heartbeat had been uneven for a time, it had returned to a regular rhythm. She had a lump on her head, but the thick carpet on the floor had cushioned her from exacerbating it. He gave Max and Grant a nod, before standing up and shaking his head.

Continuing his charade, Max asked Nicholas, "Will you carry the body to the temple. There, I must cleanse it so the demon cannot reanimate it."

Casey, keeping out of sight in the suite provided for the doctor, kept track of events through the well-hidden Wi-Fi headpieces they all wore. As soon as she heard the king order them all out, she summoned two servants and instructed them to take the no longer needed equipment to a storage room.

"We may need to return and use it," She told the one who understood some English. "When we come back in three weeks, we will remove everything."

She took up the two small cases of equipment that they dared not leave behind, and left via the servant's door, to where she knew a disguised Jim was waiting. However, she couldn't answer the questions that concerned him most. "Was Erin okay?"

The solemn procession, Max and Nicholas carrying Erin on a makeshift litter and guards ahead of them and behind them, walked towards the temple through streets that were completely deserted. News from inside the palace had already spread outside the gates. Even the market stalls had been hastily shuttered.

Nearing the Temple, Max turned and dismissed the guards. They had been becoming increasingly edgy, the longer they were in the open, and were pleased to return to the palace. Nicholas and Max continued right up to the temple gates, which opened for them by a no less high personage as the Senior Priest.

He did not let them proceed more than a few yards inside, but he did greet them with a solemn nod.

Although he was meant to be beyond involvement in the affairs of men, the priest was an advocate for peace. For almost a year, ever since Jabir had usurped the throne, he had heard of the evil things his men were doing and what the usurper himself wanted to do. That very day, following a visit from King Rakhal, he had, for a time, agreed to be involved. He had only needed assurance that the charade would not result in mass bloodshed. When Jim's plan had been explained, he just shook his head.

"We are still primitive at heart, but perhaps it is best that the evil is thought to be from an outside source – and not in the blood of Kings."

When the strangers had arrived, he went immediately to Erin, where Nicholas and Max had placed her carefully on the ground. She was coming around and when she opened her eyes, realised she was not in the palace and saw the kind eyes of the Elderly priest.

"Who the heck are you," she managed to say, although breathing and talking hurt.

"Friends, Erin," Nicholas assured her.

Erin's eyes widened in surprise when the priest, in his ochre yellow robes, placed a wrinkled hand on her forehead. Unbelievably, he seemed to be summoning the cool, healing breeze she knew of as the aura of the Earth. His hands were gentle as he explored the bump on her head, and it seemed his touch drew the pain from it. He moved his hand to where a large patch of red soaked her jumper.

Max said, "She is wearing a bullet proof vest. The blood is fake!"

Erin asked for help to get her jumper off, and then undid her shirt. Looking innocently like a decorative button, the squashed bullet was jammed into the vest.

"Wow! The damn thing worked. I thought that bullet went right through me." Erin felt hysteria rising in her. "When Jim said to trust him, I knew there had to be a catch. He said, they'd probably not shoot. And this vest may have stopped the bullet, but its momentum went somewhere. I think I will have a bruise that goes right through me."

Max asked, "Can you walk?"

Erin considered asking the priest to help with the pain under the vest, but she could do some of that herself. "Can you let me have a few minutes?"

The little priest took one of her hands, as she placed the other on the ground beside her. She thought of the mantra for healing she had learnt from a stranger to earth, and felt the cooling breeze coming quickly and fast. She thought it might be due to the holy ground, but then she felt the priests hand tighten in surprise. Their eyes met, and the priest nodded knowingly, like he was uttering a prayer, he murmured, "Now I am sure you are good people."

Erin, feeling that understanding, knew they had a willing ally. When she finally stood up, she asked if she could borrow an acolyte's robe, to cover the state of her clothes. He had merely smiled, and summoned a member of the temple, as if by telepathy, then sent the man to get the requested item.

"Are you to take the place of this roving one's acolyte?"

"I thought for now it would be a good way to hide. Since the people in the town are used to seeing my cousin playing that role."

"Cousin? Yes. May all the gods be with you."

They went out of the Temple in a small group, but Nicholas went off in a different direction to get to their base. Max went another way, keeping to a pace Erin could maintain.

As soon as she was inside their base, Wanda ran to her to be sure she was alright. They didn't need words.

Max and Nicholas were reporting, and when they finished adding to what Casey had told them, Wanda introduced them properly to Erin.

Then Jim asked, "Erin, is the program destroyed?"

"Totally," Erin assured him. "They will have to reformat the master drives of those expensive computers before they can use them again."

"Back ups?" Jim prompted.

"You know, Jim, I don't think it occurred to those fancy experts to make one. I implied the original hard drive was enough and that is password protected. In any case, if a copy was made, it wasn't by Yusif, and the Mole, well, he will find his copy is blank. My solution was a right nasty piece of work."

"Good job," Jim told her. "Go get some rest. Will you be able to help us tonight?"

"Try and stop me," was her verbal reply and she glared at Wanda, warning her not to say anything to counter that.

In truth, even after having the counter drug, she was still aware of the effects of the strange hallucinogen. Not to mention the physical aftermath of the way her body had acted when not under her control. Then there was the way her chest still hurt when touched.

"I fixed a bed for you," Wanda told her, then pointed to a small side room where she also had water and pain killers.

Erin fell asleep quickly, but her dreams were troubling and full of fears for the woman she knew of as Fatima.

Later, with Grant still in the palace, and Max and Wanda back to their routine as priest and acolyte, and Jim off to his appointment with King Jabir and General Ishkhan at an exclusive restaurant in the town, only Nicholas and Casey were around to hear Erin moaning in her sleep. Nicholas had to concentrate on the masks he was making that would be needed later that day, so when Erin woke up crying, Casey was the one to help her forget the dreams.

Jim returned from his meeting confident that his part of the plan was proceeding to plan. He had been able to confirm that the stolen program had indeed been destroyed, and the usurper Jabir, was in the right frame of mind, for what was to come. He was to meet the General again the next day, to go over the secret catalogue of weapons that he purported to supply. That was exactly as he intended, since he was to be Wanda's back up. He mentally reviewed the rest of the plan.

Grant would leave early next day, after the final systems check for the security devices. Too late, however, to have prevented Janna's escape. Janna would be free, with Wanda in her place. Ali had gone to bring up more of his loyal troops, and have runners go off to start more distant groups heading for town. The majority would be in the square, outside the palace, by dawn.

Wanda and Max slipped back into the house and collapsed into the nearest chairs.

Wanda asked, "Everything ready for me, Nicholas?"

"Yes. Do you want me to run through it?"

"I'm listening," Wanda confirmed.

She went over the details while she ate a high energy snack, then allowed herself a half hour power nap before allowing Nicholas to help prepare her face. This was a more complex task, than usual for she would have not one, but two, of the synthetic skin, moulded masks on her face.

The inner one would be held on by a strong gum, and would need a softener to remove. That was to ensure that the outer mask, Janna's face, could be removed without disturbing the inner mask. The top one, unusually, was only held on by a narrow strip of adhesive placed at the outer edge of the mask.

While Nicholas was applying the first mask, and adding the intricate fake tattoos of a temple priestess to the cheeks, Wanda was startled by a scream from the inner room.

"That's Erin," she said, trying to stand. Nicholas pushed her down. "She's been having bad dreams all afternoon. Casey can handle her."

Wanda subsided, but inexplicably, she was worried.

Chapter 14 – Premonitions and Apparitions

Erin woke, content for the moment to lie awake, knowing she was safe, with friends. The vague memories of waking from nightmares unsettled her, because she was sure those dreams had been important. Frightening, but important. Then those scenes came back to her, caught her awake mind in vivid intensity and she moaned.

This time, Jim went into her at a run and caught her wrists as she began to flail around. She didn't even recognise him, only the feeling of being trapped. Slowly though, his calm reassurances seeped through and the terror loosed its grip. He took her in a hug as tears began to stream down her face.

"Tell me what's wrong." Jim urged.

"It's only a dream," she insisted, trying to believe that, and praying it wasn't foresight. She tried to describe the images, but they melted away. "It's no use, they are like chimeras. But I know they were important."

"You've been under a lot of strain," Jim told her. "I bring you out of trouble, then ask you to go back in without time to adjust. I will send Max in with Wanda tonight."

"No!" Erin denied frantically. "No! I have to go. She doesn't know to expect anyone else."

Jim studied her, thinking hard. He couldn't risk her unintentionally jeopardising the mission. "No, it would be better if you stayed here."

Erin slumped back on the bed, facing away from Jim. He went out and spoke to Casey. "Go in and keep her company. I have told her to stay here, but she might try to follow us."

Casey did as asked, but she was back in moments. "She's gone, Jim. Out the window."

Jim uttered a rare curse and went to the door. He looked each way along the street, and set his lips in a tight line.

"Jim, I'll go look for her," Max offered. He was still garbed as a temple priest, and already known to the locals.

"If you can't find her in a quarter of an hour, come back."

Max nodded and slipped out the door.

Jim went to where Wanda was nearly ready. "What is Erin thinking of?" He didn't spell out the situation, he knew she would pick it up. He wasn't surprised when her face went blank, he was used to that when she was using her extra senses.

"I can't pick anything up, she's shielded. Probably guessed you would ask me. But something is driving her."

"Do I need to worry about her sabotaging the plan?"

"No, I don't think so. Some of that stuff you gave her is still in her system, but I only sense purpose."

Jim took her word. They were out of time to go find her and drag her back.

Max returned alone, and Wanda realised that she had been hoping he would find her. However, the mission came first and she had to concentrate on that and trust Erin could look after herself and keep out of trouble. It was time to go.

By the time they had finished slipping from shadow to shadow to reach the dairy seller's shop, Wanda knew they were being followed. But, as her danger sense was quiescent, she felt sure she knew who the follower was.

"Erin is following us," she told Max.

"Jim didn't want her to come," Max reminded her.

"I know her better than he does," Wanda told him soberly. "And yes, I am worried about her and those dreams she was having."

"Good reasons why she shouldn't be with us," Max suggested.

"Yes, but ... oh, I can't explain. Sometimes I just know things without logic. I feel that her dreams are a kind of presentiment. Distorted perhaps, by the traces of hallucinogen, but, if we are going to run into danger, I want her with us. I think, when she sees her dream beginning to unfold, she will reveal it. I will recognise the signs."

"What if she is just hallucinating?"

"You may not believe this, Max, but Erin is at her most sensitive when she is half zonked."

"Telepathy," Max asked, remembering that Erin was Wanda's cousin.

He sensed Wanda's calculating look, even in the dark. "No," she finally told him. "Empathy."

The slipped into the stall, but left the door unlocked. A few minutes later, a stealthy form opened the door and came in. Wanda grabbed her cousin's wrist. Recognition was mutual. Erin made no sound, but sent her gratitude for letting her come along.

"Come on," Wanda directed.

As they traversed the secret way, Wanda quickly explained their task. "We are going to get Janna out, and I am going to take her place."

"Janna?"

"Her real name is Janna Dupont, or Janna Fazir now. She was using the alias Fatima Anzin."

"Oh! And she said her child was a girl and it died."

"That's the rumour," Wanda confirmed.

"Is it true?"

"We have someone checking," Wanda told her. "Anyway, Max knows the way to the cells, and he will be watching while we get Janna ready."

When they were about to leave the passage, Max called Grant. He could assure them the lower levels were practically deserted – only two guards outside the door of the passage leading to the cells. Most of the guards were in the more occupied areas of the palace.

Grant was manipulating his holograms in the main parts of the palace where the servants were spooking at shadows. Certainly the superstitious ones were in a high strung state of nerves.

The three of them had begun descending to the lowest level when both Erin and Wanda stopped and seemed to be listening. Max heard nothing, but he recalled Wanda doing this before.

"Back upstairs," Wanda hissed. "There is more cover."

Max decided not to argue about how she knew whatever she was sensing was going to the cells. He and she flattened themselves into two closed doorways. Erin though, remained in the middle of the passage, lightly marking time with her feet as if walking slowly.

Two of the elite guards came into view, and stopped abruptly, raising their weapons in her direction.

Erin didn't react to the threat. Instead she raised an arm and pointed at them. A woman's voice spoke.

"I curse you and all your Master's servants. You will die and rot in the hottest of hells, and I shall laugh as I watch."

Erin did laugh then, a wild, almost hysterical laugh.

The guards, whose minds had been on the fun they planned to have torturing prisoners, glanced at each other. They both recognised the woman, and had seen her die. When they looked back to where the vision had been, the woman had vanished. Erin was now hidden in a third doorway. Next instant, the two guards were racing out of sight.

"Quickly," Erin urged, and she led them unerringly to Janna/ Fatima's cell.

Max and Wanda quickly overcame the two guards, who had seen Erin and gone to find out what she was doing. The men were now in one of the previously unoccupied cells, tied up and gagged.

Max waited near the guard's post, and watched the two unusual women trotting along to Janna's cell. Once again, he was impressed by how fast Wanda had the door open.

Erin's only thought was for the woman she knew as Fatima. In the light of a tiny torch, she could see fresh abrasions on face and arms, and when she touched her to rouse her, she was again feverishly hot.

"Fatima, its Erin, We have come to take you out."

The response was barely a whisper.

"Can you stand?" Erin asked, urgently. She watched her friend try to get up, but it was obvious she couldn't walk. Wanda went and gestured to Max. He came at a run, alerting some of the other prisoners to their activity. They all tried to get attention, but sensed the need for silence.

Max took in the situation, and without being told, picked up the sick woman and began to retreat with Erin beside him, reassuring her friend.

Wanda stayed in the cell, using a tiny light and mirror to see her face, and was about to add fake abrasions. She hadn't locked the door, so when she sensed her team members were about to run into trouble, she shoved her torch and kit under the mattress and ran to where she knew Erin to be. She sent to Max, "Put Janna out of sight."

Ahead of her were the two guards who had run from Erin's ghostly apparition. With them, and giving them orders, was General Ishkhan. They were searching room by room, and the next one was where Max, Janna and Erin were hiding. Time for a diversion.

Wanda walked out into the passage, stumbling and reeling as if weak, and moaning as if in pain. The sounds were low, but enough to make the spooked guards spin around. As all three men reacted to the unexpected sight, Max carried Janna across the passage and into another that would lead to the secret way.

Where was Erin?

Wanda knew she was close.

"Whoever let that woman out, must be close!" the General roared. "Find them!"

The two guards, currently more fearful of their superior's wrath, than they were of ghosts, thundered past Wanda, who timed a stumble towards the wall.

As the General strode towards the apparently dazed woman, Wanda thought strongly, *"Erin! Get away now!"*

"Not yet!" Erin thought in her own mind. *"I have a score to settle with the bastard."*

"Erin! Just go!"

"Can you manoeuvre him so he is looking towards the cells?"

"Oh, alright!"

Wanda pretended to faint, and the General turned part way and caught movement in his side vision.

The hologram was Erin, larger than life, doing as she had before, pointing at the General.

The voice was the same, matching the motions of the holograms mouth. Wanda realised that Grant must have used the film from the security monitor and turned it into a hologram. This time though, there was more – an undeniable aura of dread and terror. She hid a smile, realising it was Erin projecting, and her own senses told her it was having an effect. The General's mind was in turmoil, trying to believe what he was seeing wasn't real, and failing. He was telling himself it was a trick, and if he hadn't killed the American bitch himself, he'd blame her. He could think of no one else who would try such a trick.

It was a wedge for Wanda to insert thoughts into his mind, for his naturally strong shields were eroding. She made her mental voice like an echo of the hologram ghost, adding hints of fear, and finally hitting the jackpot when she suggested that King Jabir hated failures.

Yet the man wasn't a coward, he drew his gun and fired at the illusion of Erin. "You're dead, and I'll see you stay dead."

The bullet went right through the ghostly figure. He took a step backwards in shock, and his face paled when the ghost smirked and began to approach him. His mind was telling him to run, but he dare not let the unconscious prisoner go free. He ignored the apparition and called the other two guards back. When they arrived, the apparition had gone, and he told the men to get the prisoner back to her cell, and check all the other prisoners were where they should be.

He forced himself to stay where he was, until his breathing returned to normal, then carefully scanned the passage. He saw the security monitor and decided to challenge the American technician. He stalked off without going near Erin's hiding place.

Wanda, dangling limply over the guard's shoulder, sent, *"Erin, sometimes you positively scare me."*

"He deserved it, and I felt you meddling too."

"His mind is like an open hell pit. Those two were going to rape Janna, he knew it and didn't care. They were going to do other things to some of the other prisoners too."

"I think that was what I dreamed, but I knew Grant was likely to try one of his holograms. I didn't expect him to have recorded me the first time. I really just intended to put the fear of hell into them."

"Now will you go?" Wanda urged.

"Like the wind," Erin promised.

Wanda continued to feign unconsciousness until the guards left her in Janna's cell. While the light stayed on, she finished making her face seem grazed, and hid her kit. She also explored the small area, and only returned to the cot when she sensed the General nearing. At the moment, his mind was an open book, and he didn't deserve the respect of her keeping out of it.

He was still very nervy, but he had checked with Grant, seen no one anywhere down in the cell area, and was satisfied he would see no more ghosts. He was convinced the hologram had been a real person, and ignored the disparity in size. He could not explain why Grant's time stamped footage of that period showed no sign of the ghost.

Muttering angrily as he left, he gave orders to have the palace searched for intruders, and decided to question the woman prisoner some more. In her condition, she would surely break this time.

However, slapping, shaking and threats did not rouse the woman, and he knew he dare not over do things. His king needed the woman alive and able to walk. He uttered a vile curse and left the woman alone.

Chapter 15 – Palace Siege

Erin was too busy caring for Janna, for Jim to give her the sharp edge of his tongue. He could see Janna was in a bad state, but he had no way to bring a doctor in until morning. Erin and Casey were taking turns sitting with her, placing cool damp cloths on her forehead and rubbing moist cloths over her face and arms.

Erin's main concern was that she wasn't still losing blood from after the child birth. The new and angrily red abrasions were still worrying. When it was her turn with Janna - she was beginning to think of her by the name the others used – she concentrated on summoning a healing wind, having it flowing around Janna, cooling her damp skin, healing the abrasions, giving her energy.

Three hours later, after Casey woke from a short sleep, she was just in time to see Erin toppling sideways onto the floor. She was so deeply asleep, that she didn't rouse when Casey eased her into a more comfortable position, placed her head on a spare pillow and covered her with a rug.

Erin had probably only slept for two hours when Janna awoke, and sprang up in bed. Her movement startled Erin awake, and brought Casey to her feet.

"Where am I?" Janna asked, her voice hoarse. Her eyes were on Casey.

Realising she had been sleeping on the floor, Erin stood up, and said, "You're safe. My friends came for you."

Janna broke into a fit of weeping, and Erin would have gone to her, except when she began to walk, she collapsed.

"Are you alright?" Casey asked in alarm. Janna too, looked concerned, distracted from her relief.

Erin knew she had over tired herself, but seeing Janna now, she considered the effort worth it.

"Yeah," Erin claimed. "Sleeping on the floor, my foot went to sleep." She began rubbing one of her feet to make them believe her lie.

"Why don't you find the other bed," Casey offered. "I'll keep an eye on Janna until morning."

Grant completed his work early in the morning, having already assured King and General that the system was working perfectly. It certainly seemed to do everything he had claimed it would. They just didn't know it could do even more.

It was the test of the final cameras, the ones that scanned the outside courtyards, that caused them to dismiss him abruptly. It was an instruction he was only too pleased to obey.

While leaving, although he did not openly acknowledge it, he saw Jim had arrived for his follow up meeting with King Jabir and was being escorted by General Ishkhan.

The King had flown into a rage when he saw Ali and his loyalist army camped on the palace doorstep, and was in no state for polite company.

The camera had easily zoomed in to also show that the elite guards who should have been guarding the area, were nowhere to be seen.

However, Jim, after being courteously requested to wait, was now exactly the man the King wanted to see. He was led into the large chamber on the first floor of the palace, and his mental map told him this had the balcony overlooking the courtyard. Instinctively, he was reading the body language of the King and terrorist sect leader. The plastiskin mask hid the angry flush that was characteristic of the man when he was angry, and the fabric headwear hid the neck, but the eyes were blazing, and his movements rigidly precise.

"My General tells me he has given you a list of our requirements, how soon will they be here?"

Jim bowed and said calmly, "Your Eminence, they are in transit. Your deposit was received, and delivery will be made when the balance is in our account."

"If the balance is sent at once, how long then?"

Jim checked his watch, then said, "Just over eight hours."

"Can that time be halved?"

"I will need to contact my associates," Jim advised. "If I may have a moment to make a call."

"Go!" Jabir waved him away, seeing the man already reaching for his phone. He went to glare at the crowd below, but from out of the direct view of those below.

"Your Eminence, it would be wise to keep away from the window," Ishkan advised, and the King, growling angrily, took his advice.

Both men turned when hurrying boot steps became audible. A soldier slowed only a little as he neared the King. He had only begun the expected abasement, when ordered to, "Your report! Quickly!"

The man looked up. "Your Eminence, General, it is indeed Prince Ali, and he requests you come to the balcony so he can talk to you."

"Have him arrested! He is a traitor to his bloodline!" the King snapped.

The messenger began to tremble. "Eminence, he claims that all of your troops have surrendered to him, and all the officers are his prisoners."

"What do you know of this?" King Jabir challenged his General.

"All reported as normal, with correct passwords, no more than an hour ago," Ishkhan told him.

"Contact them again!"

The General pulled out a sat-phone and began to dial number after number, and getting no response until one answered, but that unit was too far away to be of use, but the leader was ordered to regroup at the palace anyway. The only others that answered were also distantly placed. His face paled as he admitted that the claim may well be the truth.

Jim Phillips had moved back between two of the floor to ceiling ornamental pillars that were situated around the walls of this presence chamber. As Prince Ali had told him, the walls were mirrored, and he used that fact to his advantage. At that moment, he believed that his South African arms dealer character was far from their minds. More so when a massed roar came from outside, and seemed to shake the glass doors that led out to the balcony.

The General approached the window, from the side, trying to see the crowd. The cause of the roaring and cheering was out of sight. To see it he would need to be on the balcony.

When he did, he saw Prince Ali as a very tempting target on a raised dais. He began to raise his gun, but Ali said, "General, my greetings. Please tell that traitor who pretends to be king, that I challenge him in my father's name."

The sound of Ali's voice was picked up by a nearby microphone and relayed to speakers around the courtyard, on the balcony and in the presence chamber.

King Jabir's response, a roar inside the chamber, was clearly heard outside, also relayed from a hidden microphone to the speakers. "The throne is mine by right! The traitor Rakhal is dead, and his bloodline tainted."

Ali's voice, still calm and conversational, replied, "Uncle Jabir, spawn of the devil, you are the real traitor, and in no way the rightful ruler. However, if you truly believe otherwise, then let us settle it by invoking the Temple Ritual."

That announcement sent an audible ripple through the crowd. Many had never heard of it. Those that had, explained it in detail, even as Jabir told his General, "It is superstitious nonsense. The stronger man always wins and I am a better swordsman than he is."

However, the elite guards, all high ranking and fanatical members of the Cobra Sect, began to edge further away from their assigned places as his body guard. They were all glancing at each other, and murmuring prayers against demons. The primitive dread, was stronger than fanatical devotion.

It had been King Rakhal who had suggested invoking the Temple Ritual, and had facilitated a meeting between Jim and the Temple's Chief Priest to learn of its history and the ritual itself. And Jim, seeing the benefits, immediately changed his strategy to include it.

It was an ancient rite, dating back centuries, but seldom invoked once the tradition of male primogeniture began. If there was no male to inherit, only a female, the ritual tested the worthiness of contenders for the hand of the Royal Princess. The legends though, told of bloody retribution for those who were merely power hungry, or unworthy.

From outside, Ali's voice was again heard, "I shall send for the Temple arbiter then, Uncle?"

Realising that somehow, his voice was being heard outside, Jabir whispered to his General, "Have the woman prisoner brought up."

"Traitor! Would you hide behind a woman?" Ali challenged again.

Jabir looked around, trying to discover what was transmitting his voice, not realising that a tiny microphone was embedded in the plastiskin mask. He refrained from further comment until the officer sent on the errand, returned with the woman he believed was Ali's whore.

In most ways, Wanda looked like Janna. Hair disordered and dirty looking, clothes unwashed and rancid smelling, face tinged with bruises and the reddened areas of recent abrasions. The effect was a masterful job.

The General took over dragging the prisoner to Jabir when he strode out onto the balcony, after having first checking his face. It was his first public appearance in days.

"Are you willing, traitor spawn, to gamble with the life of your whore?" The words came out like a screech of fury.

On the dais, Ali shook his head and assumed a sad expression. He wasn't about to concede, as Jabir hoped, but to say, "Uncle, you are truly deluded. My beloved friend, Janna, is here with me."

All the attention of King Jabir, the General and the fanatical Cobra sect members was fixed on the square below, where a hooded woman was ascending the stairs. Some of the elite guards, lower ranked and less fanatical, and already spooked, were the only ones to see Wanda's quick change of face, and her rapid throw of the Janna mask away to the side.

One was about to challenge the woman, until she turned and he saw the intricate cheek tattoos and turned sheet white.

Jim, emerging briefly, gestured to the door, those handful of guards abruptly and silently turned to flee. They had no wish to face the wrath of the temple, or the sacred power of the priestesses that was only invoked in extreme circumstances.

Looking outside, Jabir saw a woman's face emerge from under the hood – smooth, unmarked, as seen from the distance. He spun around to see the prisoner, and was momentarily stunned to find instead a temple priestess. Ishkhan dropped his grip as if he was holding a dangerous insect.

Wanda's formerly dirty brown servants garb, now looked a

pristine tawny yellow, and as the General's hand reached for his gun, Wanda raised her arm and pointed. She spoke deep into his mind, "Do not challenge the power of the Temple."

Ishkhan stared, unaware that he was moving backwards or that Jim was close enough, pipe in mouth, ready to send a drugged dart at him if he recovered enough to threaten Wanda.

Jabir was still on the balcony, eyes fixated on the impossible sight approaching him. As Wanda neared the glass doors, and came nearer her target, a murmur of awe ran through the crowd. Most of the crowd dropped to their knees.

"Shoot them!" Jabir ordered, but none of his guards appeared to obey. Seeing that, he drew a gun of his own and fired at the two figures taunting him. Each of the eight, high powered projectiles hit an unnoticeable sheet of armoured glass and ricocheted off. He threw the gun aside, as Wanda began to spin and twirl, moving closer to him, and ready to throw the liquid contents of a vial at him.

Before the false king could reach out and throttle her, Wanda released the liquid with an aim that was uncannily accurate. Her voice rang out, amplified by the microphone pickups.

"This is the creature that calls himself King. See him as he really is."

The people nearest the balcony looked up and saw the synthetic skin dissolving into a reddish goo, and emitting a yellowish vapour around Jabir's face.

A voice from below, screamed out, "Aieeee! A demon." Other voices joined in.

An insane roar from Jabir coincided with him seeing his reflection in a section of mirrored glass. He turned, intending to kill the woman, be she priestess or not, but his eyes were filling with the yellow fumes, and watering. The woman had moved, was no longer on his right, but at the edge of the balcony. Into his mind, came the thought, "Ali will die for this!"

Wanda risked a quick read of his unshielded mind, and withdrew even more rapidly. The roiling evil there made her nauseous. She began the rapid and meaningless twirling she had done before. Jim, watching Ishkhan take a short but wickedly sharp display sword from a display wall, thought a warning at her that he was coming her way.

"Wait!" she sent back.

Jabir, his hands outstretched to reach for the neck of the woman, suddenly saw Ali there instead, and his mind fixated. He sprinted forward, oblivious to the balcony balustrade, and before anyone could have prevented it, went toppling headfirst to the balcony below.

Ishkhan, realising that his protector could not possibly survive the fall, turned the sword on himself, slashing his own throat.

Jim watched without remorse, betraying nothing, as he observed the gory scene in the chamber. He watched the body fall, waited for it to stop twitching and the blood to stop spurting, before checking the man was dead.

Wanda hadn't finished her act yet. Jim knew that the initial reaction to the body falling outside, was alarm, by the change in the sound of the crowd. They would be seeing the red hologram glow around the body, seeing it rising and starting to swirl and circle, gaining speed as – people would assume – the demon looked for a new host.

He moved a small brazier out onto the balcony, and quickly lit the tinder dry starter fuel which soon ignited the other material that created copious smoke. It was needed for the people below to see the red glow clearly.

Wanda's voice rang out again, was artificially amplified, so those at the front were silenced, and the silence moved like a wave to the back of the crowd. "Demon! Come here! Now!"

Her arm was pointing at the glowing hologram, and it was visibly slowing. "Demon! I order you – come here! You are powerless to disobey me."

No one with a clear view could doubt the reluctance of 'the demon' to approach the priestess. , but it came to the tip of her outstretched arm, and hovered there unsteadily. Wanda moved her other hand to one side of the glow, and a flame hologram replaced the red glow. An amplified tortured shriek, convinced everyone the demon had died. The flame died down, and the priestess, not waiting for an ovation, turned and re-entered the palace.

Her voice was heard one more time, as she spoke to the remaining fanatics – still in shock at the death of their two most senior superiors.

"Pray, you deluded men. Pray as you have never prayed before.

That your souls will not be dragged down to hell for rejoicing in the thrall of a demon."

Seeing that they were all in terror of such a fate, Wanda saw the opportunity to save innocent servants a particularly distasteful task.

"Begin to redeem your souls by removing these unblessed remains to the crematorium for burning, and removing all trace of its contagion here. Do the same for the contagion below. Then go to the Temple, offer all you have to them, to come and re-sanctify this palace."

As if hypnotised, and Jim wondered if Wanda had managed that too, half of the guardsmen raced out to go to the courtyard. Wanda followed the men, sedately, serenely, oblivious to cautious servants who bowed as she passed, and did not notice the tall white haired man who followed her.

Near the door to the courtyard, Max was waiting and the two men provided cover for Wanda to remove the yellow robes and the priestess mask. For her next task, she needed to be overlooked, anonymous, and the servant garb allowed that.

Outside, some of Ali's soldiers were overseeing the men preparing to remove Jabir's body. There was no doubt he was dead. Priest, servant and stranger, edged around the courtyard as Ali was moving towards the palace steps, circled by loyalist soldiers, who were clearing a path for him through the still stunned onlookers.

Once on the top step, and visible to the crowd, Ali raised both arms and all remaining murmuring ceased. His voice, still being amplified, carried to the edges of the crowd and beyond.

"People of Jakhabad, today, the rightful ruler of our country has been returned to his rightful place. All kneel for the true king, Rakhal Third."

As the people obeyed, they looked to their Prince and saw a tired, old-looking figure, his arm around a woman, slowly ascending the steps. The first surprised statements of, "The King, he is alive!" spread through the crowd that as one, surged to its feet and began cheering and punching the air. This time, the older man raised an arm for silence.

Chapter 16 – New Understandings

Earlier, in the dairy sellers shack, Nicholas, Casey, and Grant when he arrived, were close enough to be aware of what was going on. They knew Ali's troops had taken over the square once the mercenaries, who had protected Ali so faithfully, took out the elite palace guards. For now, they were watching for unexpected trouble coming up from out of the town. Inside, Erin and Janna were huddled together for mutual reassurance.

When two men came to the house and were let in by the owner, Nicholas had Janna look to see if she recognised them. She gave a gasp and seemed about to faint. Erin rushed to catch her.

"What is it?"

"It's the king, Ali's father. Oh! No!"

Erin nodded to Nicholas to let the men into their inner room. She sensed nothing but concern from the two strangers. Only one of the men entered. Janna glanced up, relaxed marginally, but offered no greeting.

With a polite gesture, he urged Janna back to the couch where she and Erin had been sitting. He squatted down to talk to her.

"Why did you bring him here?" Janna's voice was unsteady. "He knows what I am. I can't see him."

Tears were streaming down her face. "You know what they said about me."

"Janna, you need to talk to him. You don't deserve to be less than an honoured wife to Ali. After all that you have done to protect him, to help with the salvation of this kingdom, no one should dare treat you with contempt." The voice spoke English with little trace of an accent.

"You don't understand! What I did was immoral. No one will ever accept me."

"Yes, in this country, you would be correct," John King said. "But you are American, and have learnt different ways. Was there ever a time, while you were here, when you broke the laws of the country?"

Janna shook her head, saying, "But no one will ever believe I didn't."

Erin, sitting beside Janna, took her hand. She added her own advice. "I, too, think you should talk to him. Ali, I think, will not give you up. He would never be happy if he did."

"No, I can't. I don't ever want to see the contempt in his eyes."

"Janna, he has had long months to consider his brother's actions," John spoke again. "He told me he thought our brother would care for the people, and since he wanted it so much, he would step aside. Too late, he realised that his brother only wanted power, and that one country would not be enough. He was on the verge of despair, for his brother had told him that both Famira and Ali had died in America. He had produced convincing evidence."

Janna met John King's eyes.

"He did not believe it when one of your friends, Wanda Martin, told him that Ali was alive. He thought it another trick until Ali himself was waiting for him in the private tunnel. Talk to him. Don't be afraid to tell him everything. He needs to know how strong you are. To show him that even the women here can be strong."

"Wanda is here too?" Janna asked, and she felt Erin squeeze her hand in confirmation. "I thought I imagined her."

Erin sensed the change in Janna. Somehow, the knowledge that her former mentor was nearby, recalled the belief she had in her, and her courage revived. Wiping her eyes, Janna straightened and nodded.

"Okay. I will see him."

John rose, and went to the door, opening it and letting Rakhal come in. At that moment, he was simply an aging man, not a monarch. Janna looked up and John saw the fleeting look of pity on her face, before she dropped her gaze to her lap. John gestured to Erin to leave the two alone.

Once back in the outer room, John King introduced himself and went on to say, "I know what your friends are doing, and his majesty already knows much of Janna's story. You need not worry for her. The showdown is coming and I will not mourn for my half-brother, Jabir, or any of those misguided fanatics who followed him." He turned to Erin and asked, "Will you stay with Janna until it is over? I will meet you at the palace, later, with a special gift for Janna and his Highness."

In a moment of sudden clarity, Erin knew what he meant. "Oh! Her child. Janna said she had died."

John was startled, but admitted, "It was to protect the boy, and I think perhaps, Janna believes the lies. It is time they were reunited, and unless Janna mentions it, his highness does not know of his grandson."

"Thank you," Erin told him. "I'll do as you ask. Those two in there, both need something happy to think on."

Chapter 17 – Mission Completed

John King returned to the fringes of the crowd, watching the plan of the American covert team play out. He hadn't really had a chance to see Wanda Martin at work, only heard of her competence. In the final moments, before his brother's inexplicable...well you had to call it suicide...when his brother was explosively angry, her confidence had been astonishing. Or was it her trust in her colleagues? All of them, were frighteningly competent.

He saw Jim Phillips and Wanda Martin edging his way and went to meet them.

"Come with me, Mrs Martin," John urged.

Wanda glanced at Jim, knowing he'd had something he wanted her to do, but he just nodded and shrugged to do as he said.

"Where are we going?"

"You'll see. It is to be a surprise for three people who really need something happy to contemplate."

"Janna's baby!" Wanda said at once. "We thought it was dead."

"First Erin, and then you? How did you guess?"

Jim was smiling faintly.

"I knew it was due about now, and I guess...I was really hoping it was okay."

"Well, he is. The couple who were looking after him arrived last night. They are not far away, but we need to fetch the boy now."

Wanda was glad to help, but she was also concerned for Janna. "Do you think King Rakhal will let Janna stay?"

"Rakhal is a fair man, who has made his share of mistakes. I told him about her, and Ali made his feelings abundantly clear. However, he is still the ultimate authority in Jakhabad and must satisfy himself about her before he will acknowledge her."

Wanda accepted that, then said, "They belong together."

"Because they are in love?" John asked lightly.

"Not just that, but because they complement each other. Like David and I – I knew what he was to be for me, the moment we met. Just like Erin and her mate."

John didn't relate to mystical things, he dropped the subject after saying, "Time will tell, I guess. Just up here."

John knocked on the door of a private residence in a prearranged cadence. The face that peeped through the crack before the door opened fully, recognised him. The owner spoke briefly as they came in and then called for someone. A woman emerged with a closely wrapped baby, and without fuss, handed him to Wanda. John spoke to her as well, while Wanda was looking into the purple blue eyes of the baby. Something inside her just then, envied Janna her child, envied Erin her little girl.

Then John nudged her. "Come on. We need to hurry."

Once free of the moment of reverie, Wanda knew he was right. She was receiving from Erin, knew that the king had just reached the fringe of the crowd, been recognised by members of his loyalist army. No one had questioned the presence of a woman with him.

Ali was letting the crowd celebrate, waiting for the right time, when his father returned from his errand, to announce him. Janna had gone off, reluctant to face his father, so it was a surprise to him when she returned with him. He raised his arms and the crowd went silent.

His announcement met with cheering as his loyal troops cleared a path for his father, allowing him and Janna to ascend the stairs.

At the same time, Erin, hearing Wanda's summons, edged herself out of the crowd. She noticed the little group because Ali's soldiers had formed a silent ring around them, but she approached and was allowed to enter. Her eyes went at once to the baby in her cousin's arms, and she was suddenly homesick, wanting to feel Bree's little arms around her.

Wanda whispered, "You take him to Ali and Janna. As soon as this crowd understands who you have, any doubt about her will be gone. And if you get a chance, tell Janna I wish her well."

"Can't you stay?"

"No, but you can if you want."

"No, well, I'd like to, but well, you know Gerry is due out soon. I want to be there when he walks out."

"Of course you do," Wanda said, understanding perfectly.

John King suggested moving closer to the steps as the King had begun talking.

"What is he saying," Erin asked.

"He has been denouncing the deeds of his brother, promising all in his power to help those affected by his tyranny. Now he is expressing pride in the man his son has become, and telling these people how he has been fighting against Jabir's evil. He has begun talking about Janna. We should start moving now."

Janna was staring down at the stones of the step, listening to Ali's father saying, '....a true friend to my son, a woman of great courage, worthy to be his son's consort and the mother of a future king.'

In the moment before the king mentioned their marriage, Janna heard, above the murmuring of the crowd, the sharp cry of a baby. Her head went up, Ali moved around to stand by her, and said to the crowd, "Janna has always put my life above hers. The importance of my country as well. That is why she let herself be caught, so that our son could be safe."

Only the king really comprehended that last sentence. He gave his son an inscrutable look, but Janna's cry of joy drew his attention to the woman carrying a wrapped bundle and being escorted by loyal soldiers. It took the crowd some moments longer. Even the prospect of a royal wedding paled into insignificance compared to the moment when Janna took her son in her arms for the first time, when Ali saw his son for the first time, and King Rakhal saw the redemption of his realm.

Janna moved her son to one arm and drew Erin into a hug with the other. "Thank you! Thank everyone who made this all possible."

"I will," Erin promised.

"Can you stay?"

"Not now. I have a long overdue date with my mate."

"Then you and Wanda will come to the wedding? And David too, and ..."

"Gerry," Erin supplied. "I wouldn't want to miss it. Now, you get well. Wanda said she wishes you well too."

"Tell her I will be in touch."

Janna pulled away, becoming aware of the concern of Ali and his father. She let Ali hold his son and her heart lightened at the joy in his eyes. She turned back for a last word with Erin, but she was gone.

Even with tears in her eyes, Erin made her way unerringly to where Jim and his team waited. She climbed into an anonymous looking van, and sat beside her cousin. After telling her of Janna's parting words, she fell into silence. Not unexpectedly, Wanda sensed her thoughts.

"It's not long now until Gerry will be free. And you did a masterful job here."

"It was all a waste – because the technology they stole, could have been put to other uses, ones to benefit this country. And I feel responsible for Bisha and Jiwan. I don't even know if they are alive still or killed like Yusif. He was a good man, and it's my fault he – "

"No! It wasn't your fault. But if it will make you feel better, I will get a message to John and he can investigate. And when we come back for the wedding, perhaps you can talk to King Rakhal about your ideas."

At the airport, word had already reached the workers and they had left in droves to join the celebrations in the city.

The concourse was deserted, but their plane, the one Grant had arrived in, was fuelled and waiting ready to take off. The flight plan filed.

No one answered the radio in the tower, but they took off anyway – relaxing at the conclusion of mission successfully concluded, a job well done.

The End

WANDA: FROM BAD TO WORSE

If she was going to die young, like her mother, Gwen Willard was determined to die rich and she had very few years to do it. Her first step was to leave home. She met Hooch, who taught her some exciting and illegal skills. She was the Draco's lucky mascot until she came to the attention of the police. Then her uncanny knack for predicting trouble, warned her to flee to the city and change her name.
Life wasn't easy. She was 15, had little money and no regular job, but her new skills came in handy. Then she crossed the path of an evil and unscrupulous man and she didn't want him to have his way.

WANDA: CHOOSING CRIME

Wanda was free. She was never going back to jail. But she was homeless, almost penniless and Harrison Franklin had a long and vengeful memory. Jim Phillips had a long memory too, and Wanda had saved his life. Could he save her from Franklin?

WANDA: RISKING LIFE TO LIVE

The euphoria of successful heists were what kept Wanda Dean alive. At 23, she was crime boss Harrison Franklin's top agent – well paid for absolute obedience. That's all that mattered. Until she met Mike Johnston and her boss ordered him killed. For that, the Franklins were going to pay. In Risking Life to Live, justice conflicts with loyalty and the penalty for betrayal is death.

WANDA: A NEW LIFE - HIDDEN SECRETS

Even before beginning as a covert agent for the US Government, Wanda is abducted by a foreign operative. After being rescued, there are signs that she had been subjected to hypnosis. With an important government gathering imminent, her handler must ensure she is not a security risk. Can Wanda's psychic extra senses help her recognize and resist the implanted commands and clear her for secret work?

WANDA: A NEW LIFE - FIRST MISSION

On her first covert mission for the US Government, Wanda calls on the skills that made her a skilled thief to convince a revolutionary general that she's an ideal recruit. When her team mates' covers are blown, it is up to her to ensure that two missing scientists and confidential Government documents are not smuggled out of the US.

WANDA: FULL CIRCLE

Three generations after the alien Kumatan left Earth, their own world is suffering from alien invaders. In desperate hope, one returns to Earth seeking help - little knowing they had left one of their own behind. Wanda, a child of the third generation, answers the call.

ERIN: THE FORCING OF WISDOM
For years, Erin has used the intricacies of cyberspace to banish unwanted emotions. Others call what she does hacking, and her manipulations criminal, but now her skill was exceptional - in, out, traceless. She was wrong. Someone betrayed her.

Travis has dangerous plans. He needs an electronics expert – one he can coerce through fear. Erin was perfect.

With the inescapable threat of prison looming, Erin accepts his offer of sanctuary. When she realises his intentions, she is in too deep. But the terrifying of innocents is unforgivable. She cannot walk away. She is an empath and shares their distress. She has to help them, even if it means prison, and insanity...

ERIN: THE CALL
(including ELISABETH AND TANYA: BLOOD CALLS TO BLOOD.
Elisabeth's sister, Wanda, had been missing for half a year. Multiple authorities had found no trace of her, or her two colleagues. Yet she knew her sister was still alive and had answered a call for help from an alien who had once lived on Earth.

Elisabeth, along with her newly found cousin Tanya, have started to sense things from her missing sister. Enough to know that she is in dire trouble, but not enough to help her.

While looking for traces of the aliens, Elisabeth makes some unexpected discoveries about her family. Yet even with the help of a second newly discovered cousin, she fears she is not strong enough to help her sister and the others to return.

ERIN: THE CALL
Convicted cyber-criminal, Erin Mason, is startled into awareness in an unfamiliar place, with no memory of escaping and only vague memories of getting there. Voices in her head were urging her to go west, and they were getting more urgent.

After a chance meeting with covert agent, Jim Phillips, when she helped save his mission, he realised that she might be the key to another, more personal quest – to find three missing state department agents.

All he must do is keep Erin safe, and hide her from an intense police search, until he can introduce her to cousins she was unaware of.

However her uncontrolled psychic gifts conflict with a logical mind that prefers the ordered intricacies of computers and electronics. She only wants to shut out the voices and the madness she sees looming.

Can Phillips convince her to help him, before the forces of the law find her?

KORVU: THE BEGINNING

The prequel to The Wild One

Jai Ansuni was the first female Atapi sorcerer for thousands of years, but she dare not reveal it. However, when tribal sorcerer, Stacion Ansuni escalates the enmity between Atapi and Kumatan to an ominous level. Jai and her womb mate, Con, try to mitigate his atrocities but can two young Atapi, not even a score of years old, win against the powerful sorcerer?

THE WILD ONE

Sixteen year old Jai Cassidy thought she was finally free of her family until she is discovered by her other relatives...the ones that aren't human. Jai uses her natural perversity and cunning to escape their control, but catapults herself into the middle of a deadly feud between two alien races.

ATAPI SORCERESS

The sequel to The Wild One

Jai Cassidy is beginning her mission of reversing the decline of the non-humanoid Atapi. As a sorceress and an Atapi-Human hybrid, she is vehemently disliked by the male Atapi sorcerers and the humanoid rulers of Korvu. Her task is complicated by the treachery of a group of alien engineers, who are inciting insurrection and harsh reprisals.

THE TYMOREAN TRUST BOOK 1 - POWER RISING

The Tymorean Trust - When peace rules Tymorea - Peace reigns in the universe.

Chosen to be the Advocates of the mystical and incorporeal Guardians of Peace, twins Tymos and Kryslie must first learn to control and use the power rising in them - or it will destroy them.

On Tymorea, only the ruling Triumvirate Governors are powerful enough to guide the strong-willed alien-bred twins until they have mastered their power.

THE TYMOREAN TRUST BOOK 2 - GREAT ONES

The peace of the Guardian Planet, Tymorea, is in deadly peril. War there will create ripples of unrest and destruction throughout the settled universe.

Tymos and Kryslie, still adolescents, have barely mastered their power and Llaimos is still less than a year old, but they are the three chosen to be Advocates of the mystical Guardians of Peace, to safeguard the Tymorean Trust.

THE TYMOREAN TRUST BOOK 3 - RETURN TO EARTH
Even before the war on Tymorea, the Elders foresaw that Great Ones
Tymos and Kryslie would have an imperative mission on Earth.
But as the Tymoreans prepare to build an Earthbase to support them,
they discover that specifications for two vital protective shields are missing.
Now, nearly a century later, Tymos and Kryslie must find his work and
build the generator before the base is found.

THE TYMOREAN TRUST BOOK 4 - EARTH MISSION
Just before their graduation from the prestigious WSRA Washington
University, Tymos and Kryslie Ward deliberately disappear.
The Great Ones have foreseen the capture and death of the new Tymorean
missionaries and discovered that the leader of the Eastern Imperium
plans to undermine the United World Nations.
Tymos and Kryslie must protect their kin and prevent a potentially
devastating world war.

THE TYMOREAN TRUST BOOK 5 – ALIEN CONTACT
Tymos and Kryslie Ward, hide their Tymorean intelligence and abilities
while working as low ranked technicians at the WSRA's lunar base.
When an alien ship arrives at Lunar One, pursued by a powerful enemy
who will stop at nothing to get what he wants, only the two Tymorean
Great Ones have the knowledge and abilities to overcome him, but to do
so they must risk their sanity, and their souls.

THE TYMOREAN TRUST BOOK 6 – INVASION
Great Ones Tymos and Kryslie go to rescue the crew of Earth's first deep
space mission – and discover that Ciriot space pirates have discovered
Earth's location. When the Ciriot invade in force, the Great Ones reveal
themselves so that Earth can gain vital help. However, Kryslie becomes
the victim of Ciriot, who want to control her mind and make her betray
the people of Earth.

TRICKS
Tom and Jo Dwyer had a reputation for playing tricks – and getting
detention. They didn't seem to care about that, so long as they made their
class laugh. That was until someone began to turn their tricks against
them, and it was no longer funny.